F

An Aw

CW01590648

Brian O'Hare

Cover by
Marianna Hircakova

Edited by
Veronica Castle

Published by
Crimson Cloak Publishing

ISBN 13: 978-1-68160-065-9
ISBN 10: 1-68160-065-X

Spellings in this book are their UK version.

ACKNOWLEDGEMENTS

This book is a work of fiction. Its parishes and small towns are entirely imaginary and none of the characters, principal or minor, are based upon anyone I have known or have read about.

I have sought, however, to find authenticity in describing the nature of life lived by priests engaged in parish ministry. To achieve this I was obliged to test the good nature of some priests of my acquaintance who not only set aside time to meet with me but who answered, with an open and honest frankness, my many questions, some of which, I imagine, were rather more personal than they might have expected.

I owe a particular debt of gratitude, therefore, to Father Matthew Despard, Father Brendan Kearns, Father Andrew McMahon, and Father Niall Sheehan. If I have got anything right, it is entirely due to them. If I have got anything wrong, the fault is mine. I think that I must also add, lest there be any misunderstanding, that my clerical friends are solid and saintly men all. They possess none of the flaws of the principal characters in the book.

I owe a special word of thanks, too, to Roy McWilliams, retired gynaecologist and golfing companion, who provided me with much useful medical information, to Sr. Gertrude Stickler (Far from the Father - Marion Press) and to Henri Neuwen (The Return of the Prodigal Son – Darton, Longman and Todd) for their thoughts on the older brother of the Prodigal Son, and to Mons. Luigi Guissani (The Religious Sense – McGill/Queen's Uni. Press) for his concept of 'emotional imperturbability' which helped one of my main characters through some particularly difficult psychological traumas.

And fallen men may rise again
on wings of prayer.

Hymn

Table of Contents

PROLOGUE

2007

1

Towards the end of an afternoon lecture on Scripture, sometime during the middle of the first year of divinity studies, a senior house monitor came into the lecture theatre and whispered something to Monsignor Keenan. As he listened, the priest's eyes sought out Ray Canavan, a studious, darkly handsome youth seated in the front row. He nodded and the monitor left. The priest left the dais and approached Ray almost diffidently. "It appears that the dean wishes to speak to you, Ray," he whispered. "You are to go to his office immediately."

Ray's face registered concern. As he gathered his books, he searched his conscience but could think of no misdemeanour that would have merited a summons to the dean's office. The uneasiness had not left his face as he left, nodding briefly to the monsignor as he passed the dais. He caught a glimpse of his best friend, Dan Patterson, high in the back seats of the lecture theatre. No need to ask what Dan was thinking. His big, open face and raised eyebrows were filled with mute question. Ray lifted his shoulders to indicate his own mystification and left the room.

A few moments later he tapped on Dean Fitzgerald's door, entering when he heard the priest's somewhat peremptory, "Come!"

Ray hovered just inside the door, looking uncertainly at the dean and still wondering what this summons signified.

"Ah, Ray," Canon Fitzgerald said, half rising when he saw who it was. "Sit down, sit down," he went on, indicating a chair near his desk. His manner was almost as uncertain as Ray's, adding to the student's confusion. Ray sat down as instructed, remaining silent but still trying to read the priest's expression. Canon Fitzgerald was a tall man, early fifties, with a physique that hinted at a background of sports and fitness. Given the nature of his role as Dean of Senior House at Maynooth Seminary for Priestly Formation, he tended to remain aloof from the students. He was a fair man, even kindly, and treated the students with respect, but he was not given to displays of emotion and his dealings with his charges were invariably brisk and businesslike. This time, however, his face betrayed evidence of ... Ray wrestled for a word. Was it solicitude? The priest cleared his throat, clearly ill-at-ease now. "Ray, I'm afraid I have some bad news for you."

Ray blinked. "Bad news?"

The dean stared at the young man, pity now evident on his features. "Yes. Ray, there's no easy way to say this. I have just received a phone call from your uncle. Your parents have been involved in a car accident."

Ray flinched, registering shock. "Car accident?" He sounded almost as if he did not understand the words.

"Yes. From what I can gather, a heavy goods truck lost control on a sharp bend." The dean shook his head. "Your parents were coming around from the other side and ... there was nothing they could have done."

Ray was still trying to make sense of what he was hearing. The dean gave him time. "Were they hurt?" Even as Ray asked the question, he saw the answer on the priest's face.

"I'm sorry, Ray, truly sorry. I'm afraid they're both dead."

Ray's stricken face unmanned the priest. He seemed uncertain what to do. He simply sat and waited for Ray to assimilate the tragic news. Ray was distraught. He kept looking at the priest, his mouth trying to shape words that wouldn't come. The dean said again, "I am so sorry to be the bearer of such terrible news, Ray. Can I get you something? Water? Tea?"

Ray mechanically shook his head. "I'll have to go home," he stammered, tears beginning to form in his eyes.

"Of course. Of course. Take as long as you like. Your uncle says he'll come and collect you, if you like."

"No," Ray said quickly, almost too quickly.

The dean, slightly surprised, said, "Okay, okay. Whatever you want yourself. Would you like me to arrange for someone to take you home?"

Ray tried to think. The enormity of the news was beginning to reach him and it was crowding all other thoughts from his head. "No, Canon, no. That's not necessary. It's too far. I'll ... I'll get a bus to Dublin station and take the train from there."

The dean's businesslike façade was beginning to collapse, as he watched the boy struggling to cope with the news of his parents' deaths. "Would you like to go with me to the chapel? We could pray together for ... " his voice trailed away as Ray, tears rolling down his face, tried to control the choking heaves that were beginning to shake his body. The priest moved from behind his desk and placed a hand on Ray's shoulders as the fifth year student put his two hands over his face and gave way to convulsive, racking sobs. The priest, tears in his own eyes now, could only stand there helplessly. He said, "Let it all out, boy. Let it all out," and bowed his head in silent prayer for assistance for the young man. *Help this young man, Lord. I don't know what to do.*

He stood perfectly still, wordless, with his hand on Ray's shoulder until the student was finally able to regain a modicum of control.

"I'm ... I'm sorry, Canon," Ray said, searching for a handkerchief.

The priest quickly produced his and handed it to Ray. "Don't be silly, Ray. There's no need for apologies." He stepped back to the phone. "Look, Ray, I'm going to arrange for Dan to bring you to your room and help you to pack. And don't worry about a bus. I'll drive you to Dublin station myself."

2

The funeral was gruelling. Ray walked behind the two hearses as they drove slowly in tandem. He was flanked by his aunts, Emily and Joan, his father's two sisters. He scarcely spoke to either, lost in a lifetime of memories ... memories of his parents' obvious and constant affection for each other, of the quiet smile and amused expression that invariably wreathed his father's face every time Ray would argue passionately about some obscure issue, of his mother's singing, melodious and sweet, as she worked around the house, always happy. Tears came and went with the memories as he walked the few hundred yards to the graveyard from the church, seeing nothing, aware of no one.

The sun was shining. The grave was located at the high end of the cemetery and from this vantage a whole panorama of fields and wooded land could be seen, east and west, stretching to gentle green hills in the distance. But the beauty of the scenery was lost to Ray. Tears poured down his cheeks as he stood at the grave and watched in distress as the coffins were lowered into the ground. His insides were aching; he thought his heart would break.

"Dad ... Mum ... Dad," he called with all his mind, as if somehow he could still stop this terrible thing. "Oh Jesus, Jesus, Lord, only you can help me now. Bless daddy and mammy, Lord, bless daddy and mammy."

Somewhere in the depth of his sorrow he dimly heard the priest quote something from an old Indian poet: 'Death is not an extinguishing of the light but a turning off of the light because the dawn has come,' and for a brief moment he saw his parents smiling as they walked, hand in hand, towards a glorious morn. He found a modicum of solace in that.

Someone took his elbow and led him from the graveside. Well-wishers, one after another, came to him and uttered whispered words of condolence. Ray replied with politeness and thanks but as each left he could not have said who had just spoken to him. He did brighten briefly when a tall, distinguished man in his late forties appeared in the queue of well-wishers. Canon Tony Mulholland, once Ray's principal at St. Anselm's College, now Parish Priest of Kilnamoy parish, had been friend and mentor of Ray and his best friend Dan for several years. He shook Ray's hand warmly and placed a friendly hand on his shoulder. "I'm sorry, Ray, I really want to be with you now but I have to leave immediately. I'll definitely call and spend time with you in a few days. But in the meantime," he stepped back and stared into his young friend's eyes, "if there's anything I can do, Ray. Anything."

Ray nodded, tears in his eyes. "Thanks, Tony, but everything seems to be under control ..." He waved a vague hand at the many well-wishers and the priest clasped him once more on the shoulder as he left.

There was a small reception afterwards at his parental home for immediate family and friends. Emily and Joan had taken over the catering and had left Ray free from any anxiety about it. Ray hovered on the fringes as knots of people chatted, ate sandwiches, drank tea. Some looked his way but sensed his need to be alone. The tears had ceased. He was numb now and he no longer looked inward. Without realising it, he was watching the mourners, the various groupings, those who seemed animated and unaffected by the deaths of his parents, those who spoke quietly and carried some of his own pain, the one or two solitary souls who simply stood looking out of the windows into the garden. There were a few people in the garden as well and Ray, not quite knowing what he was intending to do, went to the French windows. A man detached himself from a group standing on the patio and came over to him. He was stout and bald, although he vainly attempted to disguise this latter condition with a streaky, futile comb-over. His face was florid, heavily jowled, and covered with a light sheen of perspiration. It was Henry, his mother's only brother. He offered Ray a hand. Ray pretended not to see it.

"How're you bearing up, Ray?" Henry asked, retrieving his hand and rubbing it on his trousers.

"Fine," Ray stated flatly, staring across the garden.

"Your aunt Bridie says you can come and stay with us for a few days, if you'd like."

Ray turned to stare briefly at his uncle, his expression registering disbelief.

"No, thanks," he replied with uncharacteristic coldness. "I'm going back to Maynooth in the morning."

He turned his gaze back to the garden and it came suddenly to rest on a tall, achingly beautiful woman of his own age. She had been studying some shrubs but looked up when she felt Ray's scrutiny. For a moment she stared solemnly back at him and then gave him a small, uncertain smile.

Ray said to his uncle, "Excuse me, there's someone here I need to talk to." He walked quickly to the girl who came to him immediately and embraced him warmly.

"Oh, Ray, I'm so sorry."

"Yeah, it's okay, Karen," Ray replied, comforted beyond measure by her sympathy and her embrace. He held her briefly, trying to prolong this little oasis of peace in which he had suddenly found himself. He stepped back to look at her. "How are you?" he exclaimed. "Gee, it's been such a long time."

"Four years, seven months and three weeks," she smiled back. "But who's counting?"

He laughed. In the midst of all this sadness, he laughed. He stood back and looked at her, unaware that the quiet smile and the amused expression that he had so loved on his father's face was now mirrored on his own. He led her to a bench where they sat down. He looked at her again. Karen. The girl next door. The friend of his childhood who, during all the years of their growing up, could rarely start a sentence without the words, "When we are married ..." It was such a joy to see her again.

"Gosh," he said, with a wide smile, "it's great to see you. When did you get here?"

"I just arrived this morning." She returned his smile. "And it's great to see you, too. Sorry it had to be under these horrible circumstances."

His smile faded. But as he looked steadily at her, the smile returned, unbidden. "Hey, you look fabulous."

She grinned back mischievously. "Are you allowed to flatter a girl like that?"

"I don't know. We haven't had that lecture yet. What have you been doing with yourself?"

"I'm working at London airport. I'm a project manager for some new developments that are going on there."

"Wow, I'm impressed." They smiled at each other again and Ray was astonished at how comfortable he felt in her company, at how her presence had brought such solace to his broken spirits. "Are you staying around?"

"No, sadly. I've got to get back tonight. I was lucky to get this one day."

Ray's heart sank. "When are you leaving?"

"In about an hour."

Neither was smiling now but their eyes never left each other. Karen tilted her head slightly and said seriously, "Are you going to finish your seminary studies?"

Ray was taken aback. He could sense that the question wasn't casual. His eyes remained locked on hers, perfect amber with tiny green flecks that seemed to glitter in the evening sun. How come he had never noticed this before? Her eyebrows moved slightly, indicating that she was waiting for an answer. He expelled a long breath and nodded confirmation. "Yes, I think so."

Karen's lips tightened almost imperceptibly but she said nothing.

Then with a small shrug and a crooked smile, Ray said, "So, doesn't look like we're going to get married after all?"

Karen let her head drop and for a moment her face was hidden by her lustrous black hair. When she looked up again, she, too, was smiling but her amber eyes hinted at tears.

After a moment, sounding innocuous, Ray asked, "You seeing anybody?"

Karen looked out over the garden, at the groups of people talking and strolling. Still staring away from him, she said, "Yes, there's someone."

Something in Ray clenched. Not jealousy, surely?

Karen kept her gaze fixed on the garden. "But it isn't really serious, at least, not for me."

Ray touched her arm. "I hope you find someone, Karen."

She turned and put a hand over his. Meeting his eyes again, she said, "You're a hard act to follow, Canavan."

Ray tried to keep his smile alive but the sadness of the past few days had left him emotionally vulnerable. Suddenly this conversation had become difficult. His eyes felt moist as he said, "I'll never forget you, Karen." Then, before the weight of sorrow could fall on him, he smiled again and said, "Boy, you were one bossy kid."

She thumped his arm, "Hey!"

They chatted for another thirty minutes, oblivious of the other guests, remembering episodes from their childhood, from their teens, even laughing aloud from time to time.

Eventually Karen looked at her watch. "I'll miss my plane if I don't go."

They both stood. Ray said quietly, "I'll see you out."

He walked her to the front gate. They stopped there for a moment, suddenly awkward. Karen said, "I'll pray for your dad and mum. I really liked them." Ray was nodding his thanks when she suddenly turned and held him in a tight embrace. "I'll miss you," she whispered and then ran quickly to her hired car.

Ray watched as she drove away. She tooted the horn and he could see that she was looking at him in her rear-view mirror. He waved and continued to watch her car until it was out of sight. Just before he turned back to the house, he raised his eyes heavenwards. "Lord, what are you at? Are things not bad enough? This is really tough! Lord, dear Lord, you're going to have to help me with this."

When he went back into the house, Emily approached him. "Was that Karen?"

"Uh-huh!"

"She's got really beautiful, hasn't she?"

Ray nodded.

"Has she left?"

Ray nodded again.

His aunt put an arm around his shoulder as they walked back into the lounge. “What are you going to do now? Do you want to stay with me?”

Emily had never married and when Ray was born she became immediately for him a second mother. His parents never had to search for a baby sitter or a nanny. She involved herself deeply in his young life and gave him an unconditional love that Ray, at the time, simply took for granted. During his childhood, it seemed to Ray that Emily had been a permanent presence in his family home yet, paradoxically, he seemed to remember spending much of his childhood at Emily's small cottage only a few hundred yards away. She never missed a Christmas, a birthday, a school play. She was a fascinated audience for all of his childhood stories and someone to run to when his mother was not there. It was perfectly natural, therefore, that she would invite him to stay with: her but Ray had other plans.

“No thanks, Emily. I’ll stay here tonight. I have an appointment with Dad’s solicitor in the morning.”

“Oh?”

“Yes, he phoned a wee while ago. Just a few forms to sign. Wants to make arrangements about selling the house.” He shrugged deprecatingly. “Apparently I have inherited close on half a million euro. I have to meet him to talk about how to invest it until I have completed my formation.” Ray looked at his aunt, tears welling in his eyes again. “Just the kind of conversation I really need right now.”

Ray’s heart flooded again with a deep sadness. Somewhere in the back of his mind there may have been the thought that he would never have any financial worries for the rest of this life. If there was, it meant nothing to him. He was conscious only of the deep ache of loss and felt that he was in a black place from which he would never find a way out.

Emily placed a gentle hand on his arm. “Why don’t you meet him some other time?”

“No, I need to go. I’ll still have to pay my way through college and so on. I’ll need some sort of income.”

“You’ll be coming back here after you’ve finished with him?” It was hardly a question.

“No. Sorry, Emily. When I’ve finished with him, I’m going to go on back to Maynooth.”

“You don’t have to go so soon, surely? They’ll give you more time than that?”

“I know, but it’s where my friends are. It’s where my life is. Hanging around here …” He looked around. “It would be too painful.”

3

Ray stayed in his old childhood room that night. Emily sent everyone home but she herself stayed on to keep him company and to be with him as he prepared for his departure the next day. His prayers that night were tear-filled, almost frantic. He sorely grieved the loss of his parents and knew that it would be a long time before those wounds would heal. But he was filled also with confusion. He wondered about his feelings for Karen. He longed to see her again. He wondered if somehow he was betraying his vocation, or whether he had a vocation at all. Watching her drive away had triggered intense feelings that he could not analyse. Loneliness? Regret? Need? He could not fathom what caused his heart to ache as it did. Was he just emotionally defenceless because of his grief or was there something else that might be a threat to his vocation? *What am I supposed to think, Lord? To feel?*

Images of Karen driving away filled his mind. Images of her lovely face before him, her deep amber eyes staring at him so intently. *Lord, this isn't right.*

Images of the coffins being lowered into the ground came too. Heartache upon heartache. It was almost too much to bear. Was meeting Karen yet another cross? he wondered miserably. Or, could it possibly have been a gift of distraction to ease the awful pain of his parents' deaths? He pressed all ten fingers into his forehead as if to rip out the tormenting thoughts. "If this is distraction, Lord, I don't think it's working." He turned an anguished face heavenwards. "I can't deal with this tonight, Lord. I don't know what's going on in my head. If it is your will, please allow me restful sleep and I promise I'll talk to Monsignor Keenan about this when I get back."

4

The sleeper's head jerks and his breathing becomes erratic.

It's dark. Someone is in the room. The blankets fall away. A small voice whimpers, "Don't ... it's cold."

"Shhhhh! I've got some sweets for you."

"Don't want sweets. It's cold."

"Shhhhh!"

A rough hand touches soft skin.

A sudden fear. Another small whimper. "What you doin'? Don't ... please ... please."

A low, deep voice. "Shhhhhh! It's all right. It's all right."

The fear grows and the little voice rises. "Don't do that. Don't do that. "

A large hand encloses the small mouth.

"Shhhhh! You mustn't wake Mummy and Daddy. They're sleeping and they're awful tired. You don't want to waken them, do you?"

The little head moves slowly from side to side. The hand withdraws and moves elsewhere.

"Gooooood boy. Goooood boy."

A small arm reaches for the teddy bear on the pillow and pulls it close. Shivering, frightened and alone, the child endures.

The visitor leaves. The child chokes back sobs, as tears run down his face. He tries to stifle the sobs with a small fist to his mouth.

"Mustn't wake Mammy and Daddy. Mustn't wake Mammy and Daddy. They're tired."

He hugs the damp teddy bear close and lies shivering.

The sleeper jerks upright in the bed, trying but failing to grasp the foggy tendrils of the disappearing dream. Gasping for breath, he slowly lowers himself back on to the pillow. He stares into the blackness and tries to empty his mind.

5

Ray returned to Maynooth that evening and, after briefly reporting his return to the dean and accepting his further expressions of sympathy, he went to his room. He was not yet ready to face the many condolences that would greet him when his friends heard of his return. His hope was that his return to these safe, much loved environs would help ease his pain but he had scarcely set his travelling bag on the floor of the room when the walls immediately began to close in on him. He found it difficult to breathe. All the sorrow and loneliness of the past few days threatened to overwhelm him. He sat on his bed and cried tears of desolation, grieving anew at the realisation that his parents were dead ... gone. He would never again see his mother's look of fond love as she brushed some imaginary speck from his clothing. He would never see again on his father's face that quiet smile that hinted at amusement, at acceptance and, somewhere behind it, love. And if he were to be ordained? Ah, dear God, his mother had so looked forward to that and now ....

Unable to remain confined in his room like this, Ray went to the hand basin, washed his face and went to seek solace in the oratory from the most profound of comforters, the Holy Spirit. Fortunately the chapel was empty. He took a seat close to the altar. His prayers were unstructured appeals to the Lord for help, for guidance, for consolation.

Images of Karen distracted him from time to time and he could not curb a guilty awareness that if he were with her now, the pain would be so much more bearable.

He knelt with his head in his hands for a long time, sometimes in prayer, sometimes lost in bitter-sweet memories. Until a large hand grasped his shoulder, he had not known that anyone had come into the oratory. It was Dan, friend of his childhood and still his best friend.

"Ray, are you okay?"

Ray turned to his friend, making no effort to hide his tear-stained face. "Ah, Dan. Hi!"

Dan was Ray's antithesis in every respect. Where Ray was trim, Dan was huge; where Ray was dark, quiet and intellectual, Dan was fair, outgoing and gregarious. But they shared the same strong faith, the same moral base, the same intense vocation. Canon Tony Mulholland, who had known them since they were eleven-year-olds at St. Anselm's, was one who experienced no surprise at the strength of their bond. But now Dan's face, filled with strongly etched freckles after a summer of sun and outdoor sports, was as sombre as his friend's. He shook his friend's hand and said, "My God, Ray, I'm really sorry about all this."

"Yeah, thanks, Dan. How did you know I was here?"

"I didn't. I just came in for a wee visit." Dan's face was filled with compassion. "How're you coping?"

Ray shrugged, struggled to say something, then lapsed into silence, looking plaintively at Dan.

"Hey, c'mon!" Dan said, exposing his white, slightly crooked teeth, in an effort to smile. "I'm meeting a couple of the lads for coffee in a few minutes at the Pugin refectory. C'mon and join us. You can't be here on your own. That's no good."

Ray started to demur. "All those people ...."

"You're going to have to face them sometime," Dan said. "And it won't be nearly as bad as you think."

Both friends left the pew, genuflected before the altar, and went out of the chapel. Dusk was gathering as they crossed the quadrangle on their way to the refectory. Dan was engaged in a diatribe on the complexities of syllogistic reasoning and thrice accursed universal negatives when he stopped suddenly in mid-flow. He had become aware that Ray was giving him no attention. Ray's eyes and attention were focused elsewhere. In the dusk he had spotted Monsignor O'Halloran, one of the Senior House lecturers. It was a cold and windy evening and the priest's head was hunched down into his chest as he crossed the quadrangle towards his room on the middle floor of the building opposite.

"What?" Dan asked, starting to grin without knowing why.

Ray wore an expression something akin to perplexity. "Dan, do you ever think just how lonely a priest's life might be?"

Dan's grin survived the question but registered surprise. "What are you going on about now?"

"Think about it. Look at Monsignor O'Halloran there, all on his own, living in confined quarters. What kind of life is that?"

Dan's eyebrows were down, the humour gone from his face. "Hey, you're not having second thoughts?"

"No, no," Ray cut in quickly, "but it does no harm to look at what's in front of your eyes. Being a priest is a lonely business."

"Ah, you'll be fine when you get out into a parish. You'll have the other priests for company."

Ray looked at him. "Have you seen the deployment in parishes lately? Most would be lucky to have three priests working in them."

"So? You bond with those guys."

"Kevin McGarrity?" Ray mentioned a fellow student whose supercilious demeanour had earned him few friends.

"Ohhhh," Dan drew the word out slowly. "Right, I see what you mean."

"There's more than a few of them about," Ray said.

"Yes, and there are many who aren't," Dan argued.

"Aren't what?"

Dan stopped, confused. "Aren't ... *about*." Then he grinned. "Will you quit messin' with my brain? Look, Ray, the whole parish will be your family. You'll have to develop a relationship with the people. You'll be devoting your life to them."

"I know, but that's hard for me. You know what I'm like. I wouldn't be good at that."

"Learn."

Ray punched Dan on the arm, smiling again. "Not to worry, it's only a side issue. Think of the benefits. What's a little loneliness?"

6

At seven o'clock precisely, on an evening about a week after his parents' funeral, Ray gave Monsignor Keenan's door a short apprehensive knock. He liked and trusted this priest and had deliberately sought him out earlier that day to ask if he could talk to him about a personal problem. He probably should have asked Father Mullan, the spiritual director who had been appointed to deal with students' spiritual lives in Senior House, but Father Mullan was shallow, lacking in any real perception, and was generally never seen except at his series of ill-prepared lectures. The spiritual director for Middle Division would have been little better. He was well into his seventies and tended to treat every request for counsel or advice as if it were an assault on his person.

The Monsignor was a larger than life figure, almost eccentric. He strode the corridors and quadrangles of the college in a long, ankle length black coat, invariably unbuttoned and flying around his lanky limbs. More often than not, he wore a black hat with a huge brim. Added to this ensemble was an impressively resonant voice, with phonetically perfect diction, that gave nothing so much as the impression of an aging thespian who had lost the ability to distinguish between the stage and normal life. The monsignor's lectures, however, were models of erudition and style and he had an intellect so sharp that it could cut steel. The students loved him. So, too, did Ray, but not simply for his academic brilliance. Ray had found in him an honest and compassionate spiritual adviser and the two had become firm friends during the student's time at Maynooth.

He had made no demur when Ray had requested the meeting and had suggested that the short break after tea, 'around seven', would be an ideal time. Ray had now arrived at his room with no firm idea of how he might broach what was worrying him.

"Oh, God, what's he going to think?" he was muttering to himself when he heard the Monsignor's booming voice inviting him to enter.

"Come in, Ray; come in. Sit down."

Monsignor Keenan's office-cum-sitting-room was lined from floor to ceiling with books. His desk was littered with journals, a couple of stacked filing trays, and bundles of students' essays. A fire was burning in the grate and two old but comfortable brown leather armchairs were placed on each side of the hearth. It was into one of these chairs that the priest directed Ray.

"How are you coping, Ray?" he asked, as they both sat down.

"I'm doing okay, Monsignor. Everybody's very kind. I'm learning to deal with it."

"I know it must be very tough. But you have all our prayers."

"Thanks, Monsignor. I appreciate that."

The priest made himself comfortable in his chair and eyed Ray calmly. "Well, Ray, you wished to talk about something?"

"Yes, Father. It's just ... I don't really know where to start."

"Ummmm!" The priest regarded him speculatively and then, in tones so familiar to Ray in the lecture theatre, he boomed, "You know, my boy, I have discovered by diligent application of metaphysics, intense syllogistic reasoning, and a dash of hard won experience that, in cases like this, the best place to start is ... at the beginning."

In spite of his nervousness, Ray grinned. "Okay, Father." He paused to collect his thoughts. "The day my parents were buried, an old friend came to offer her condolences ...." He talked for ten minutes while the priest listened in silence, calmly staring at the burning coals in the fireplace. "... and it's been bothering me ever since. I don't quite know where all of this leaves me in relation to my vocation."

"Would you say the attraction was sexual?" was the first question the priest asked when Ray fell silent.

"Oh, Heavens no, Father! No, no, nothing like that. It was just that being with her gave me such comfort. I dunno. It just broke me up when I watched her drive away."

The priest sat back, interlocked his hands behind his head, and stared at the ceiling. After a time, during which Ray was growing increasingly apprehensive, the priest said, "If I read the situation correctly, Ray, there were three things going on there. Firstly, given the grief you must have been experiencing on that day, you were emotionally very vulnerable. Any kindness from a close friend would have affected you deeply. Secondly, in the case of this girl there was already a pre-existing background of something that must have been akin to love over a long period. That would have its effect. Thirdly, you say the girl was beautiful and you, Ray, are a young man. I think I'd be very worried if you had *not* had some sort of reaction to her."

Ray, whose head was bowed, looked up, not sure if he was supposed to grin. The priest was smiling. "Ray, let me tell you now, you are going to experience this many times in your life. It's totally natural, and it's damned difficult to deal with. Do you think the rest of us are robots? We all have to go through this from time to time." The priest couldn't help laughing as Ray leaned back, his eyes widening. "Yes," he grinned, "even me."

"It's not normally something I would have a problem with," Ray said.

"Good." Monsignor Keenan smiled and sat forward in his chair again. "You know, I seem to remember that even St. Francis had a great and abiding love for St. Clare, although, as I understand it, he dealt with it by staying away from her for long periods at a time. But it happens. What you do about it is what counts."

He thought for a moment, his eyes on Ray. "I think it is clear that the problem here is your prior relationship with Karen," he said. "Adults tend to scoff at what's called 'young love' but the feelings are very powerful. Any psychologist will tell you that. You have obviously dealt appropriately with these feelings but they have remained dormant. Nothing unusual there either. Then Karen reappears in your life at a time of great emotional need. Her unanticipated presence is the catalyst that generated your present confusion. It was sudden. It was sharp. But don't be worrying about it. Her absence now is the catalyst that will help restore your equilibrium."

The priest moved forward, elbows on his knees, fingers interlocked before him. "Look, we have given our lives to God. We have undertaken to live those lives in celibacy. This, although we don't run around shouting about it, is a heroic offering. And it is heroic because the very feelings you talk about do not leave us. They are always there. The demands on us are the demands of sacrifice. It's natural for a man to seek comfort from a special woman. Male friends can only offer so much. Didn't God make Eve for Adam? It was for procreation, certainly, but there was far more to it than that. What does Genesis say? 'It is not good for man to be alone.' But the thing is, the heroism is found in our controlling those feelings, denying ourselves that special relationship and opting, instead, for a special relationship with God. Yes, we live lives that can often be lonely, often empty: except," he raised an emphatic finger, "we are not without support. God does not expect celibacy from us without giving us the wherewithal to deal with it."

Ray listened, transfixed. "And what I have been feeling?"

"Nothing to worry about, so long as you don't start obsessing about this girl. If you meet her, enjoy your time with her. But come straight back to the Lord. Don't lie in your bed thinking about her for hours like one of Shakespeare's pale lovers. It's about maintaining that little psychological gap, keeping that distance that is the mark of a priest. Friendship with a woman is possible, even a kind of love, so long as you remember that your first and real love is Jesus."

Ray straightened up, preparing to leave. "Thank you, Father. You've given me a lot to think about but you've been a great help to me."

"You'll find all sorts of little ways of protecting yourself as you grow in experience," the priest went on, as he rose to open the door for Ray, "little human moves you'll learn that will protect you."

He offered Ray his hand. Ray shook the proffered hand, smiling, a giddy relief prompting him to say with uncharacteristic boldness, “I think I see what you mean, Monsignor. Maybe I should start talking in a booming voice and get a big black hat with a wide brim. That’ll scare them all away.”

The Monsignor made a fist and held it in front of Ray’s face. “Be off with you, boy, before I say something you’ll regret!”

MINISTRY

ONE
2009

The Vatican Palace in Rome is situated on the eastern sections of Vatican Hill. Behind the Palace rises the summit of the hill with its carefully cultivated gardens into which visitors are admitted only with the special permission of the Palace's sub-prefect. At the highest points of the hills may still be seen all that remains of the Leonine Wall with its two huge towers. The Palace houses the pope's apartments but it was never built as a residence and, indeed, only a small proportion of it is used for residential purposes. There are sections set aside for scientific investigation and for administering the official business of the Church, but so massive are the wondrous collections of art that it contains that the Palace can more properly be regarded as a huge museum than as a residence.

Inside the papal palace are a large number of chapels, the most visited of which is the Sistine Chapel with its extraordinary frescoes. But not far from this is another smaller chapel in which is preserved the famous Pietà by Michelangelo, a life-sized evocation of the grief of the Madonna as she cradles across her knees the body of her dead son. From the perspective of the ordinary viewer, the figures are sculpted to scale, apparently proportional one to the other. There are many, however, who learn with amazement that the sculptor used twice as much marble for the figure of the Madonna as he used for the figure of the Christ.

This monumentally impressive sculpture is the only work ever signed by the great artist. It is said that while many of his generation admired his great masterpiece, very few appeared to know who the artist was. Angered by this lack of recognition Michelangelo decided to engrave his name on the band encircling the virgin's breast. To make doubly sure that no one would again be in any doubt as to the sculptor's identity, he also engraved his monogram 'M' in the folds of the virgin's right hand, the one more likely to be seen by the viewer.

On a day during Easter Week in 2009, three prelates stood in front of this famous masterpiece, as they had done many times before. It was, for all three of them, one of the most impressive of the Vatican's many treasures and the three, any time they found themselves together in Rome, never failed to revisit it. Like many priests who are comfortable in the Vatican's environs, the prelates were dressed casually in black soutanes. They were distinguished from their ordinary fellows, however, by the colour that bordered their soutanes, purple in one case and bright scarlet in the case of the other two. They were talking quietly, even as they admired the incredible anatomic accuracy of the musculature on the sculpted Christ.

“I wouldn't say that action is called for just yet,“ Cardinal Lorenzo Rosselli said, his English heavily accented but otherwise perfect, a result of three years served as Papal Nuncio in Dublin. “At least, nothing official.“

Cardinal Rosselli, white haired and a little stooped, was a key figure in the Vatican's Congregation for the Doctrine of the Faith. He was talking to Bishop James Flannagan from Ireland and another member of the CDF, Cardinal Frederick Stadler from Colorado in the United States. The subject of the conversation was an Irish priest, Father Arthur Owens, whose recent new book on moral theology had created a significant stir because of its liberal stance towards second marriages and homosexuality.

“We could send him a friendly letter in Christian charity,“ the burly American suggested, “wishing him well but suggesting that he exercise more caution when committing new or radical views on moral theology to print, maybe indicate one or two areas where we consider his thinking to be defective ...“

“I don't think that is necessary,“ Bishop Flannagan cut in. “By all means, send him a letter, but Canon Mulholland has well and truly taken care of the defective thinking bit.“

“Yes, James,“ Cardinal Rosselli said, “I read those articles you sent me. That young man shows a lot of promise. You'd do well to keep an eye on him.“

Cardinal Stadler looked at Bishop Flannagan with his eyebrows raised.

“A canon in my diocese,“ the bishop explained. “He challenged Father Owens in print, even appeared in a TV debate with him. Put rather a huge dent in his arguments. Nobody reading those articles or witnessing that debate will have any doubt that Owens needs to go back to the drawing board.“ The bishop wore a faint smile, recalling how the press on the day following the TV debate had dubbed Tony Mulholland the ‘smiling assassin’.

“The drawing board?“ Cardinal Rosselli, half smiling, indicated his lack of understanding.

Cardinal Stadler said, “A designer's metaphor. Some guy, architect or engineer, designs something and the builder finds a fault in the design. The designer has to start all over again. He has to ...“

“... go back to the drawing board,“ the Italian nodded. “I see. Yes, very good.“

“So who is this young feller, Jimmy?“ Cardinal Stadler asked.

“Well, maybe not entirely young, just turned fifty but a very bright spark. He's one of my parish priests. Authored a couple of important books. Organises his parish like a business corporation. Totally on the ball. I'd love to promote him again. He has so many skills I could make use of, but ...“

“On the ball?“ It was the Italian again. “Ah, yes. Football. He knows where the play is. He knows what's going on. Ummmm!“

“Heck, man! Why don't you just make him a Monsignor and get it done with?“ the American said.

Bishop Flannagan uttered a sound somewhere between a bark and a laugh. “No disrespect, Fred, but you guys in America can toss promotions around like crumbs to birds and nobody bats an eyelid. Ireland's different, very traditional, and in many ways much more subtle about these things. The priesthood remains essentially a vocation; your ordination is your big promotion. Anything after that, any advancements are ...” he searched for a word, “… burdens you undertake in the service of the Church“

Cardinal Stadler threw Bishop Flannagan a sideways look but the Irishman was staring solemnly at the Pietà, his expression that of a man who was reviewing the burdens that he had been obliged to undertake during the course of his priestly life for the good of his Church.

“You could appoint him your secretary,“ Cardinal Rosselli suggested, almost diffidently.

“Secretary? Oh, I don't know, Lorenzo,“ Bishop Flannagan said, shaking his head. “Secretary? I think he'd see that as a step down.“

The Italian hunched his shoulders in a typically expressive continental shrug and looked at his friend. “Well, there are secretaries, and then there are secretaries.“

“He's right, Jimmy,“ Cardinal Stadler grinned. “You want subtle? Man, you got subtle right there. I know secretaries back home with more power than the President.“

Shakespeare's Caesar often felt somehow diminished when Mark Anthony entered his presence. Bishop Flannagan now felt something of the same waning of his own authority as he listened to these holy but very streetwise prelates. He looked from one to the other. “I'd need to give that some thought,“ he said.

TWO

The sleeper jerks involuntarily and emits a small moan.

Mammy has put the lights out again. He had asked her not to but she told him not to be silly. 'Big boys are not afraid of the dark,' she said. He wasn't afraid of the dark, but 'He' comes when it's dark. Soft tears fall on the teddy bear clutched tightly to his small chest. The door of the room is not properly closed. He can hear noises. Daddy and mammy are going to bed. He cannot hide with them. He had tried before to go to their room but mammy always brought him back. He listens, wakeful, frightened. The sounds have stopped. The house is quiet. Mammy and daddy are in bed. Fear engulfs him. Soon 'he' will come. Have to hide. Have to hide.

The little, pyjama-clad figure, still clutching his teddy, clambers from the bed and crawls underneath it, shivering as much from fear as from cold. He waits in the darkness, hugging his toy for comfort, his ears attuned to the slightest sound. He stiffens. The door swishes on the carpet. He hears soft footsteps cross the room to his bed. Two large shadows appear some inches from his face. He hears the bedclothes being moved.

"What the fuck?"

The footsteps leave, pause at the door of the room, come back. The bed is lifted from above him and moved to one side. The little boy puts an arm over his head and cowers, foetal position, on the floor.

"You little shit," an angry whisper. "What the hell do you think you're doing?" He is roughly dragged to his feet and laid upon the bed again. "Do you not care about daddy and mammy? Do you want to wake them? Do you want me to tell them what a bad boy you are?"

"I'm not," tearfully.

"You are," his tormentor hisses violently. "You're a terrible bad boy, and I will tell, believe me. I will tell. And they won't love you any more. Is that what you want?"

Sobs.

"If you ever do that again, you wee git, I'll have your bloody life."

The child cowers, terrified by the unwonted anger, and begins to cry.

A fierce whisper. "Stop that whingin'!"

Large hands pull at his pyjamas.

The sleeper jerks upright into a sitting position, sucking in a huge, panicked breath. Wide-eyed and sweating, he gasps erratically, the gasps subsiding only slowly when he eventually becomes aware of where he is.

THREE

From behind a carefully neutral expression, Canon Tony Mulholland observed his superior. Bishop James Flannagan was a large man whose florid complexion revealed rather too much about his zest for the good things of life. He was somewhat abrupt, difficult to approach and intolerant of any challenge to his authority or beliefs. Although he performed well in the pulpit and was highly respected by his parishioners, his priests saw a rather different person, a man who had lost a level of his spirituality and fallen victim to the trappings of power. He enjoyed too much the pomp and ceremony his role permitted and, unlike many of the other Irish bishops, still favoured over-frequent use of the red biretta, the crosier and the mitre. Tony could empathise with the lure of the red but he hoped that, if he himself should ever achieve such eminence, he would be rather more discreet in its use.

Bishop Flannagan generally remained aloof from the priests of his diocese but he did tend to have one or two favourites, priests with reputations of their own, association with whom allowed the bishop a degree of reflected glory. Indeed, Tony had a feeling, one that gave him a measure of satisfaction, that he was somehow being 'groomed' for future office. To have been elevated to the status of canon before he had even reached his fifties was unusual. In

America the bishop's favour was generally enough to ensure such preferment but here in Ireland such promotions were rare and they were generally reserved for priests in their sixties. An Irish bishop, whatever his private feelings about a younger priest, would never permit himself such lack of subtlety. The new PP of Kilnamoy, Dr. Tony Mulholland, however, was a theologian of considerable renown whose reputation was enhanced by several articles in prestigious religious journals and two highly regarded books on moral theology. Writer and respected theologian, he was always going to attract the bishop’s attention.

Thus this invitation to dinner, the second since his recent elevation to parish priest, and one that came not long after the bishop’s return from Rome, came as no surprise to Tony. What might have surprised him, had he examined his conscience a little more closely, would have been the nature of his response to the invitation. His gaze turned to the room, large and, if somewhat Victorian in style, nonetheless elegant. His expression turned to approval. Familiar with it though he was, what he saw or perhaps what it represented, pleased him. Large, expensive oil paintings, clearly from another era, decorated two of the walls. Close to a huge bay window was an ornate mahogany desk, and two comfortable armchairs were placed nearby in front of a large fire.

The two men, however, were still seated at the dining table in the middle of the room as they finished a meal that had clearly delighted Tony’s bon viveur superior but which, to Tony, was just food. His appetites, if he had any, were essentially cerebral.

The bishop pushed himself from the table and padded over to a dark mahogany sideboard. He bent over one of the lower doors to reach for a wooden box filled with expensive cigars. Tony eyed his superior’s ample bulk and his smile faded momentarily. An astute observer might have noted a brief flicker of disdain. Tony was not blinded by his bishop's eminence. He had met him many times as President of St. Anselm's and had already categorised and labelled his superior, placing him in an appropriate little box.

The bishop sat down again, sucked at his newly-lit cigar and exhaled contentedly. He waved to the box on his desk. For a moment Tony resisted and then succumbed. He took a cigar, rolled it between his finger and thumb under his nose as he had seen the bishop do, and smiled. “Cuban?”

The bishop simply grinned, took the cigar from him, clipped the end of it and held a match to it until it was glowing warmly. Tony settled back comfortably in his chair and, as he exhaled the rich smoke, surveyed the room once more. *Yes*, he thought, *I do like this room*. Aloud, he said, “That was a truly enjoyable meal, Bishop, but I cannot help but feel that there is rather more to this invitation ...?”

The bishop stared at him for a moment and said without preamble, “How would you like to be my secretary?”

“Secretary?“ Tony tried to keep his tone neutral but his dismay showed.

“Don't let the title fool you, Tony,“ Bishop Flannagan said. “It's a sort of catch-all, get-out title for a very important role.“

Tony's eyebrows went up. “Catch-all? Get out?“

The bishop smiled. “I've been thinking about this for a while. You'd obviously be a secretary of sorts, organising my day, prioritising appointments, guard duty at the door of my office, metaphorically, of course. You won't be sitting outside it at a desk or anything like that. But that kind of thing. The idea of ‘secretary’ will be very necessary and will be the 'get out' for something rather more significant.“

“Significant?”

“Yes. You know what Ireland's like. I just can't turn around and give you a blatant promotion. It might look too much like favouritism and, by the way, what I'm doing here isn't favouritism. You've got skills that I need and I intend to make use of them. If I have to work a wee dodge or two to make that happen, well, that's Church politics.“

“I'm having a wee bit of trouble keeping up with you, Bishop.“

“Well, I appoint you as my secretary, right? No problem there. Lots of bishops have priests for secretaries.“

Tony nodded.

“And because you are who you are and with the reputation you have earned, nobody would blink an eye because I chose you, right?“

Tony nodded again.

“But we don't have a vicar-general in this diocese and there are lots of much older and more experienced canons than you who could do that job, and who might feel aggrieved if I were to appoint a younger man.“ Tony did not nod this time. He remained very still, scarcely daring to breathe. “So, I appoint you as my secretary but I load on a whole bunch of other important stuff and gradually people will simply come to see these things as part of your job. What do you think?“

Tony grinned. “I think it would be immodest for me to think anything, Bishop.“

“Well, there are a couple of committees that I'd want you to chair. And you'll have to stand in for me at all sorts of functions, maybe even go to Rome once in a while ...“ he looked at Tony from under raised brows. “That would hardly break your heart, would it?“

Tony's reply was a tiny, straightfaced shake of his head.

The bishop grew serious. “There's one big job I'd want you to take on. You know already, with all of these darned paedophile abuse scandals that are rocking the Church, that a number of Irish bishops are appointing special senior clerics to investigate and deal with any and all new accusations of scandals that arise. It's a very responsible job and, please God, one that you won't ever have to do in our diocese which“—he blessed himself somewhat mockingly and raised his eyes to the ceiling—“until now has been scandal free. And I hope to keep it that way. We don't need even a smidgin of that kind of publicity.“

“Will it be generally known that I'm, uh, that we have a parish investigator?“ Tony asked.

“I don't think there is any need for that at present. We'll see how the thing develops in other dioceses. Should something suddenly happen,“ he pulled a face. “Oh, God, I don't even want to think about it, but if it does, you can deal with it as my secretary. I'll not be long letting people know that you have total autonomy in the matter. I, personally, want to keep far away from that sort of stuff.“

Tony's initial dismay had turned into an intense inner excitement. This was indeed a significant promotion. Retaining a studied calm, however, he said, “What about Kilnamoy?“

“Yes, you can't stay there, that's obvious. I want you here at my house. You can have the guest suite on the third floor. You'll have an office there with your own secretary." He paused to reflect. "What do you think about Ciaran Mussen for your old job?"

"Ciaran?" Tony emitted a half laugh. "With most people, what you see is what you get. With Ciaran, what you see is only the tip of the ice-berg."

"Is that good or bad?"

"Oh, in Ciaran's case, it's good, very good."

"I always had the impression that he had become a bit of a cynic."

"That's just a pose. He didn't say anything but I rather gather that it was a reaction to ..."—Tony did not want to be seen to criticise his predecessor—"... to his earlier experiences as a curate."

The bishop let that go. "Could he do your job?"

"Absolutely."

"You seem very sure."

"He would be my ideal choice for two reasons. Ciaran is deep, deeply spiritual and very clever. He hid that from me for a while but during these past couple of years he's opened up and he's been working well with young Gerard Mulvaney and myself. He would be an inspirational mentor for young curates and has a solid spiritual base that would inform everything that he would do. That's reason enough to appoint him. But there is a second, and for me, very important reason. We have a kind of five-year rolling plan for the organisation of Kilnamoy, as you know from the reports I've been giving you, and Ciaran is now fully committed to it. He would represent a very useful continuity were I to leave. There would be no new start, no confusing of the parishioners with some entirely new plan. It would be as if I hadn't left.“

“That makes sense.“ The bishop seemed to arrive at a decision. “All right, Tony. I'll go with your judgement.“

Tony nodded and said, “They'll need another curate.“

“Yes. I was thinking about that big cheerful fella that's coming up this year, what’s his name? Patterson. He seems to have a mindset similar to your own. Might be a good addition to that team?“

“Yes, good choice, Bishop.” Tony paused, then said somewhat hastily, “What are you proposing to do with young Ray Canavan?“

“I've been thinking about him. I've something in mind for him, too.“

Tony waited a beat before saying, “Is one permitted to ask what ...?“

“Yeah, well, it's a bit delicate. Keep this under your hat. I'm going to have to separate Father Oliver McGennity from his curate down at St. Columba’s. If I leave them together much longer, one of them is almost certain to murder the other.“

Tony knew Father McGennity and considered it politic to make no comment about him. “Who's his curate now?“

“Des Lynch.“

“Oh, yes. I know him. Stocky wee man. Strong. Good priest, I always thought.“

“Yes, but he's his own man. He would never take kindly to orders that didn't make any sense, and he's got his fair share of those from McGennity. But it's now got to the stage where he won't take any orders from him at all and they're at each other's throats day and night."

"Oh dear, that's not good. You'd think two men of God would be able to work together some way or another."

The bishop looked at him from under raised eyebrows. Then he said, "Yeah, men of God. Anyway, I'm reassigning Lynch and I was thinking of putting young Canavan in there."

Tony jerked upright in his seat. "With Oliver McGennity? I don't wish to appcar disrespectful, Bishop, but do you think that's wise? Raymond Canavan is very intelligent but he's also very reserved and quiet. McGennity will eat him alive."

"Maybe not. McGennity's trouble with Father Lynch, that came because the curate has a very strong personality. Lynch does not bear fools easily, and he's forever speaking his piece. And McGennity likes to throw his weight around a bit ..." Tony was surprised at how *au fait* his bishop was with his priests' foibles. "A major clash between those two was inevitable. But young Canavan, as you say, is quiet. He'll probably just do what his parish priest tells him and there'll really be nothing for McGennity to shout about. And that young fella is also very spiritual. I think the parish could do with some of that right now. There can't be many who don't know what was going on between the other two. Canavan would be good for the parish."

Tony had grave reservations but wondered if he was being too protective of Ray. The young priest was going to have to make his own way eventually.

"You could be right, Bishop," he said. "Do you want me to talk to any of them?"

"Oh, God, no! You talk to people in advance about stuff like this and all you get is hassle. No, don't say anything to anybody. Take another month or two to ensure that everything in your parish is ship-shape for your successor. I'll let them all know by letter a day or two before they have to be in their new posts. It's better to move them quickly before they have time to think."

FOUR

1

Ray stood for a moment, staring at the front door of the parochial house. He was carrying two suitcases. He also had in his inside pocket a brief official note from his bishop, little more than three lines, telling him to present himself '... at the parochial house of St. Columba's Parish on the 10th July, 2009.' He could have done with a little more information. Exhaling a deep breath he put one bag down and rang the doorbell. After a few moments the door was opened by a plump woman, probably in her sixties, her hair tied back in a grey-streaked bun. She was wiping her hands on a kitchen drying cloth and looked quizzically at the young man on the doorstep.

"Father Canavan," Ray offered. "New curate."

She gave him a wide smile that lit up her face. "Of course you are, Father. Of course you are. Come on in. Your rooms are ready for you. I'm Mrs. Toner, the housekeeper here."

"Thank you, Mrs. Toner," Ray said and stepped into the hall.

"Down here," she said, leading him along a narrow, gloomy corridor towards the back of the house. "Your bedroom and your sitting room, or study or whatever you want to call it, are on the ground floor. Father McGennity's rooms are upstairs."

"Is the parish priest here?" Ray asked.

"No, he's out. But it shouldn't be too long before he's back."

She opened a door at the end of the corridor and stood back to let Ray enter. The bedroom was large, airy, well lit by two big windows, but it was an old-fashioned room with four straight walls and no built-in furnishings. A stand-alone wardrobe and a chest of drawers were the only pieces of furniture apart from the substantial double bed that stood in the middle of the floor. There was, however, a painting of the Madonna and Child on one of the walls. Ray put his luggage on the floor and said, "Thank you, Mrs. Toner. This is very nice."

She smiled again and pointed to another door close by. "This is your other room," she said.

Ray accepted the tacit invitation and went into his study. Again, old-fashioned in design, it nevertheless pleased him. It was large, which he liked. It had two empty bookcases, a table, two straight-backed chairs and a couple of armchairs. There was also a long flat-topped cupboard of sorts that may well have been a drinks cabinet. Ray was more interested in the flat top, a place for his beloved CD player and speakers. Although there was no television, there was a TV socket in the wall near the fireplace. Ray smiled at the housekeeper.

"Yes," he said. "With what's here, and the books and things I have in the boot of the car, I think I can make myself very comfortable." *And I can buy a small kneehole desk for my computer stuff,* he was thinking.

The housekeeper pointed at yet another door halfway back along the corridor.

"That's a bathroom, shower and toilet in there." She smiled once more and said, "Well, I'll leave you to get settled in. I'm off back to the kitchen to finish making the dinner."

Ray began the process of unloading the smaller items from the trunk of his car – books, a few framed photographs and diplomas, boxes of CDs, other knick-knacks collected over the years including some sports trophies. He was making his third foray when a car pulled into the driveway behind him. There was the sound of an aggressive hand hauling on the handbrake and a heavily built man in clerical clothes got out. His suit was rather too tight on his arms and shoulders and the sheen revealed that it had seen a year or two. His thinning grey hair was brushed straight back from a heavily jowled face. The features seemed to have settled into a permanent scowl and hinted at a life more devoted to excess than to prayer. When he saw Ray, however, he managed to muster an empty smile.

"Father Canavan?" he asked as he locked the car door.

"Yes, Father," Ray replied, suddenly nervous. He experienced a sudden and instinctive dislike for the man he saw in front of him but immediately reminded himself that this was a man of God and tried to see him as such. The parish priest came forward, put a limp, clammy hand in Ray's and left it there. Ray wasn't sure what to do with it. He gave it a brief tentative squeeze and released it as quickly as politeness would allow.

"Welcome to St. Columba's Parish," the priest said, waving the released hand at the countryside beyond the house. After a brief pause, he added, giving Ray his empty smile again, "I hope you have plenty of energy, young fella. We're a busy parish here. Plenty to keep you occupied."

"I'm looking forward to the challenge, Father," Ray replied earnestly.

The parish priest studied him for a moment and said, "Yes, well, you gettin' settled in all right?"

"Yes, Father, thank you. Just clearing the last of the odds and ends out of the car."

The parish priest went to the door. "Good," he said briskly. "We eat at six. I'll give you a bit of a run down on things then."

"Thank you, Father," Ray said to the retreating back.

2

Ray was to discover that parish business, evening visits, and Fr. McGennity's penchant for heading off to Dublin at every opportunity, were to ensure that he would not have to eat often with his brusque superior. The infrequency of their communal dining was not for Ray, however, a matter of regret. He much preferred to eat in the easy confines of the kitchen with the ever-cheerful Mrs. Toner. Occasional meals in the dining-room with Father McGennity were unavoidable, however, and a little over a week after his arrival, Ray found himself dining again with the parish priest.

The meal that evening was nicely cooked – roast chicken and roast potatoes with two vegetables, served with a French Merlot. But for all the consciousness Ray had of it, it might well have been roast wallpaper. He found himself extremely uncomfortable in the presence of the older man and was focused on not allowing his uneasiness to show. Father McGennity ate with a coarse gusto and an oafish disregard for ordinary table manners, talking all the while. His talk was not conversation, however, but a series of instructions to his new curate, given with little or no explanation or advice. He offered Ray a glass of the fast-disappearing wine at one point but Ray declined. The parish priest shrugged. "More for me," he said and poured most of what was left into his glass.

Ray interrupted at one point to ask if there were any particular methods or policies connected with some of the duties that were being thrust on him but all he received by way of reply was an oblique glance and a caustic, "Are you not just after seven years' training? You should be a lot fresher about this stuff than me."

After that Ray remained quiet, trying to eat and write rough notes on a piece of paper at the same time. It became clear that the roster of duties was heavily loaded against him but the parish priest explained that he needed the extra free time for "important administrative responsibilities".

In his room a short time later, Ray tried to expand the details of what he had written while his memory was still fresh. As well as masses and confessions, he had been asked to visit a number of sick or housebound parishioners on a regular basis. "Get the names and addresses from Mrs. Toner. She knows them all." He tried to remember and note what he had been told about the geographical areas of the parish that were specifically his to support with baptisms, marriage guidance, weddings, funerals, and anything else that would be needed. He had asked about altar servers and had been told there weren't any but that perhaps he should organise that as well. There was also a large hospital in Portbridge a few miles away. A curate from each of the various neighbouring parishes would conduct a visit there on one day per week. Ray's skin contracted with trepidation when he heard that his day for visits would be Wednesday.

He studied his growing list with concern. He wished he had been more attentive to what had been taught in the seventh year diploma. *Counselling? Home visits? Marriage guidance? What do I know about any of these things?* he thought, almost in panic. *And there's no way I can ask this guy.*

Before they left the table, the wine bottle had been emptied but Ray knew there would be further contact with Bacchus before the night was over. Two evenings before he had knocked on the door of the parish priest's room to notify him of the death of an elderly parishioner and to discuss arrangements for the funeral mass. Receiving no answer, he had tentatively opened the door with the intention of leaving a note. His superior had been slumped in an armchair, asleep, an empty glass held loosely in his lap and an empty whiskey bottle lying on the floor beside his chair. He had stirred when Ray entered and peered at the curate through half-hooded eyes. Ray, suddenly apprehensive, had stared back at the priest. Then in a rush, he explained why he had come. The priest's head was swaying slightly as he listened, trying to comprehend what he was hearing. After a moment he had waved a dismissive hand at Ray and said in slurred tones, "Sort it out yourself."

Ray was not going to risk a repetition of that particular unpleasantness. He studied his rota again. "I'll give Dan a ring," he muttered. "He'll know what to do."

Dan was to start a new job in Tony's parish of Kilnamoy in a couple of days' time but for the moment he was still at home. Ray shook his head. *Tony's parish. How does Dan always land on his feet?* There was a phone on a small occasional table just inside the front door but Ray ignored it. He had noticed a callbox at the end of the road. He'd phone from there.

"Hello?"

It was Dan who answered. After a few brief words about his new posting, Ray said, "Dan, this guy has landed me with a load of stuff and I haven't a clue ..."

"Like what?"

"Hospital visits, visiting the sick in their homes, marriage guidance, bereavement support ..."

Dan laughed. "Ray, my man, I told you back in the days that you should've joined me for work experience at the Mater Hospital. All this would be old hat to you by now"

"Dan, I didn't ring up for a lecture. I need help."

"Sorry, Ray. Look, it's all in the mind. You just have to imagine you're some priest in a film or something. Imagine the script. Play the part. Forget about Ray Canavan. And you'll find your script is very short indeed. They'll do all the talking. You only have to nod here and there, or repeat something they say to get them started again. Honestly, there's nothing to it!"

"Easy for you to say. What about marriage guidance?"

"Well, it's really not much more than spiritual guidance. Look, Ray, you're clever; you don't need me to tell you that. Once the two young things confront you, you'll see right away the kind of advice they need. And you've read all the stuff."

"Mmmmm ..."

"Hey, buddy, your problem is nothing to do with knowledge. You know that. You know far more about the theory of all these things than I do. But you're going to have to come outa that shell of yours. Smile a lot, nod plenty, and every now and again, even you will probably think of something to say."

"Gee, thanks," Ray said drily. And then, when he realised that Dan's advice was very cheering, he said with a deal more warmth, "Yeah, thanks, Dan. I'll go with the film star image. It'll do me good."

They chatted a while longer and, after wishing Dan good luck in his own new job, Ray went back to his room. The chat with his old friend had, indeed, cheered him up. Something about his parish priest unmanned him and made him nervous and apprehensive in his presence. Now he felt emotionally more stable. He could look objectively at what he was going to do and see something of a pattern in it, perhaps even a challenge.

I'll try to bring something of my own stamp to this parish, he thought, *maybe develop something that has fallen away, or doesn't exist. I'll do something to make a difference ... smarten the place up. I'll start with the altar boys, but I'll have a chance with my preaching to open a few eyes and ears as well. I'll try to engage with the people, earn their interest, not be boring or irrelevant. Effective communication, that's the key to a vibrant parish life.* He thought briefly about his parish priest and wondered just how effectively *he* had been communicating with his parishioners in recent years. Unaware, he clenched his jaws. *I don't need him. I'll keep out of his way and hope that he keeps out of mine. But he was right about one thing. I have my training. Let's see now how good it was.*

FIVE

In the dark, the door opens slowly. The little boy is awake, uncomprehending but quivering in fear, already anticipating the nocturnal visit. He pulls his teddy close and whispers tearfully, "I won't let him hurt you, Teddy. I won't let him hurt you."

A large hand caresses his hair.

An involuntary sob breaks from the trembling child. "Leave me alone. I didn't do anything. I didn't do anything."

"Shhhhh! Of course you didn't. You're a good boy."

The hand moves and the blankets are inexorably drawn down. The child huddles in a foetal position, still clutching his teddy.

He whimpers, tearfully, "Please don't ... don't ... I'm cold."

"There, there, don't cry. Come on now, you have to turn round ..."

The sleeper's eyes open wide, unable to endure the nightmare. He exhales a long breath and covers his face with his hands. He shakes his head despairingly and turns on to his back, staring into the blackness.

SIX

1

St. Columba's small parish covers eleven townlands and one small market town, Drumkillen. Built on a hill, Drumkillen allows magnificent views of the miles of rolling countryside on all sides. The boundaries for the parish were established by the Synod of Kells in 1152 when parishes in Ireland were first created, and a couple of small churches were built in the area at that time. These have long since fallen into ruin although the remains of one, with its stocky spire still standing above a couple of crumbling walls, can be seen across a hedge on one of the roads a mile or so from the town.

There is a substantial church of comparatively recent vintage in the centre of Drumkillen. It was built sometime in the early 1930s and was further modernised, with extensive renovations and an added wing, in 1973. It serves the principal needs of the parish although there is also a smaller church, still functioning, in the townland of Murnaghan's Bush, some two miles from Drumkillen. Over the past few years Father McGennity has been allowing fewer and fewer services to be held there, a source of much bitterness for the local people, especially the elderly, who resented the two mile journey into Drumkillen for mass and other devotions.

The farming community of Murnaghan's Bush wasted no time in expressing their resentment to the new curate and petitioned him to restore their dying chapel to life. Ray spoke to Father McGennity about it during his first week.

"There's hardly anybody uses that chapel any more," the parish priest said, "and there is no heating in it. Them aul' ones would freeze to death in the winter."

"Oh, I think they're a hardy enough breed," Ray replied. "Thing is, I've already offered them a couple of early masses a week, but I'm happy to do that on top of my existing schedule."

The parish priest frowned displeasure but he said, "Well, you go ahead if you want. But I tell you this. Give them an inch and they'll want a mile. You mark my words."

"Thank you, Father. And don't worry. I'll explain to them that there are limits to what we can do."

"We? We? You, sonny. You. You're taking this on, not me."

"Of course, Father. That's what I meant."

2

Mrs. Toner was a mine of information. She knew every sod in the parish from the townland of Magheraclone in the north to Tullyderg in the south, from Ballygath in the east to Legnadonnel in the west. Furthermore, she knew every one of the families who turned those sods, their antecedents, their interrelationships, and the destinations and locations of all their emigrated offspring. Mrs. Toner was extraordinary. Ray decided during his first few days in parish life that time spent with Mrs. Toner would be more valuable than anything else he could do.

Thus it was that as she did her chores, tidied the house, worked in the kitchen, Ray shadowed her mercilessly, pen and notebook never far from his hands. Although she was too loyal to say anything explicit, Ray was soon to discern from her masterly command of dark looks and expressive silences that the parish priest did not feature high on her list of favourite people. She managed also, by additional exercise of these skills, to convey the message that there were many in the parish who shared her views.

Comfortable with his new knowledge of the area, Ray finally began a series of visits, confining himself initially to the country families. He had determined to use Dan's advice and go into the houses as Ray Canavan, new curate, not as the Ray Canavan who lived in his head. It worked, too, although he very quickly discovered that the ploy was unnecessary. The welcome he received in each home was so warm, earthy, and unfussy that he was immediately made to feel at ease. Children climbed on him, dogs fawned against him seeking to be stroked, women plied him with endless cups of tea, and old farmers smoked their pipes, spat into the fireplace, and talked to him as if they had known him all of his life. It was, for him, an extraordinary experience. The naturalness of the welcome was real but Ray sensed an undercurrent, an unspoken respect, a regard that came close to admiration.

Sitting in his study that evening, Ray wondered if such adulation was a threat to his ego. He thought about Dan, immensely popular, dynamic, energetic, full of bonhomie and good cheer, and very, very positive. It was inevitable that he would win his parishioners' admiration and adulation from the very beginning of his ministry. How would he cope with the insidious ego? Ray, lying back in his armchair, gazed at the ceiling. “Not a bother,” he said aloud. “He’s spiritually sound. That’ll see him through.” Then he unconsciously shook his head as if to break free from a little niggle that had somehow got stuck among his thoughts.

He looked at his watch. Six-thirty five. He had his first christening ceremony at seven o’clock. Time to go. “Dear God, this is stressful. I can’t even remember how it goes.” He went to the bookshelves and brought down a small book on liturgical services. Ten minutes with this should refresh his memory.

SEVEN

There are two large single-sex schools on either side of Drumkillen, St. Margaret's Girls' High School and St. Colman's Boys' High School. Not far from St. Columba's Church, in the centre of the town, is St. Columba's Primary School. A recent trawl of this school had netted Ray five tiny fish, ages eight to eleven, who had volunteered to become altar servers. There were two girls and three boys and all turned up, proud in their white, floor-length soutanes, to serve Ray's first mass.

The chapel was crowded but, in his intensity of prayer and devotion, Ray scarcely noticed. The congregation, however, saw a priest who was filled with the Spirit, who prayed at the altar as if he was alone with the Lord, and who raised the host to the Father at the consecration with a profound and loving reverence. Ray did become aware of the numbers, however, when he stood to preach the homily but he felt that what he had to say was important and, ignoring his self-consciousness, he focused on the message. He felt, at the end, that he had coped adequately. He was unaware that the congregation had been deeply impressed and there were many who had listened to a homily from beginning to end for the first time in many years.

Immediately after Mass, Ray went in procession with the altar servers to the back of the chapel. The idea of waiting at the great doors to greet his parishioners as they emerged after mass placed significant demand on his psyche. It was very difficult for him. But the seminarians had been instructed in their final year at Maynooth to do all they could to get to know, and earn the respect of, their parishioners. Waiting at the church door after mass was one tactic that was particularly emphasised.

Ray sent the altar servers back to the sacristy via a side entrance and tried, in spite of his nervousness, to appear calm and welcoming. It turned out to be less difficult than he had anticipated and soon he was smiling easily, shaking hands, responding briefly to the various welcomes to the parish, or compliments on his sermon. He was conscious of other conversations swirling around him as he nodded and smiled. Two elderly women whose charity, apparently, had been shed at the back of the church, passed close by him.

"... the state of her, dressed like that in the chapel. But sure what would thon one know? More money than sense, if you ask me."

The voices faded, replaced by those of a husband and wife.

"But ..."

"No, you're coming straight home to dinner. If you go to that pub, it won't be a pint. We'll not see you for the rest of the day."

That strident voice, too, moved away and he could hear two old farmers, flat caps on their heads, arguing tongue-in-cheek about the contributions they had put on the collection plate. "That was a measly wee offerin', Jimmy. Have ye no shame?"

“Wait till I tell you, Pat. The few pounds I’ve got were hard-earned, I’ll have ye know. I ...”

“My God, d’ye hear him? Man, if I had your money, I wud burn me own.”

Raymond’s smile widened and the stout lady who was speaking to him at that moment, pressed his hand a little harder and gave him a wide smile of her own.

Eventually Ray was alone at the top of the chapel steps and he returned to the sacristy. The altar servers were gone and the sacristan was ready to lock up.

“I’m off now, Father. Don’t forget to lock the sacristy door when you leave.”

“All right, Ted. Thanks for your help.”

“’Bye, Father!”

As Ray removed his vestments and hung them in a cupboard, he thought, *So now my life has started. Parish visits, masses, I’m a priest. O God, come to my aid ...* He closed the cupboard door and stood still for a moment staring at it. Then he said aloud, “If I had your money, I’d burn me own.”

He began to laugh and was still laughing when he locked the sacristy door behind him.

EIGHT

1

"Will you stop it, the pair of ye!"

Eight o'clock in the morning and it was always the same. Had those two no concept of peace? Mrs. Amy Rafferty added fried potato bread to the plates of her teenage daughter, Maria, and her twelve-year old son, Paul.

"She started it," Paul whinged.

"I don't care who started it. I want you both to finish it. Eat your breakfast quickly now. Your father won't wait."

Both of her offspring put their heads over their plates and began to eat. Paul tried to kick his sister's ankle under the table.

"Mummy ..." Maria started.

"I don't want to know. Eat your breakfast."

Peter Rafferty emerged from his study carrying a briefcase and an armful of rolled architectural drawings. He looked harassed. Even taking work home still left him behind always impossible schedules.

"You kids ready?" he said.

"Give them another couple of minutes," his wife said. "And you didn't finish your tea. I'll pour you another cup." Her husband looked at the rolls of paper, his briefcase, and his watch. He shrugged helplessly. "Here," his wife said. "Give the drawings to me." Amy went to him and took them from under his arm. "I'll put them on the hall table. Drink your tea."

A few minutes later the two kids were in the car as Peter kissed his wife goodbye. The children waved desultorily to their mother as the car left the drive. Peter looked at his daughter in the rear-view mirror.

"Is that eye-shadow you're wearing?"

"No," Maria said, perhaps a shade defensively

"Looks like eye-shadow to me."

"I'd a lot of homework to do last night. My eyes are just a bit tired looking, that's all."

"Did you get it all done?"

"Of course."

"Okay." Maria was a studious girl. 'A' grades were her norm. Peter was proud of her although he would never mortify her with embarrassing fatherly effusions. "What about you, Paul? Were you studying last night?"

"Of course."

"Of course? When I looked into your room last night you were *working* on your play-station. In what way was that studying?"

"Hey, I was studying physics, I mean, geometry. I use play-station to help with angles and equilum ...

equilbrum ... balance and that. I get good ideas about stuff and that from it."

"Stuff?"

"Yeah, you know. Stuff."

Maria, looking out through the side window at the passing traffic, permitted herself a small smile. Family rituals. She could have written every word of this scenario before the performance began without losing one dot or comma.

St. Margaret's High School for Girls was the first stop on the morning itinerary. Her father stopped the car at the high gates that led to a long winding drive. Some cars drove on up to the wide quadrangle in front of the school building but Peter tended to be in too much of a hurry to spare the few minutes that this manoeuvre demanded. Maria stepped out of the car. Tall, elegant, she carried herself with a grace she never could have been taught. As she walked to the gate, she muttered to herself in a singsong voice, "Mind the cars on that dri ... ive, Mar ... i ... a. Will do ... oo, Dad ... dy. 'Bye ... aye."

She turned just as her father's car was starting to leave. He opened the window and leaned out, elbow first. "Mind the cars on that drive, Maria."

"Will do, Daddy," she replied, with a small wave. "'Bye!"

As she turned into the gate she heard quick footsteps behind her and a breathless greeting, "Hi, Maria."

It was her best friend.

"Hi, Tess. What's up?"

"Oh, you know. Zip, really." Tess, small, a little plump, corn-coloured hair, looked up at her friend. She never failed to see the striking beauty that Maria herself seemed utterly unaware of. "What about that awful page in Caesar's Gallic Wars. Did you get the translation done?"

"Yeah, sort of."

Tess shook her head in exasperation. "Why are they making us do that crap? What do we want Latin for?"

"You might need it if you're going to become a nun."

"Oh, yeah. Ha, ha!" And then Tess broke into a fit of giggles. "Me? A nun?"

They were still giggling when they went up the stairs and reached M4, one of the rooms on the middle floor where the fifth year matriculation students were housed.

2

Mrs. Imelda McLoughlin, Principal of St. Margaret's and local church organist, strode along the corridors of the middle floor. A strong-looking woman, stocky, conservatively dressed and with a no-nonsense hairstyle, she ruled St. Margaret's fairly but with an enviable discipline. Today, however, she was oblivious to the odd latecomer who tended to melt into the wall as she passed. She was thinking about her recent meeting with the new curate, Father Canavan, and how willingly he had listened to her ideas about a youth choir for the Saturday evening masses. She had heard him singing part of his first mass in the parish the previous Sunday and had been deeply impressed by his melodious baritone. What a wonderful support he would be, she had thought then, if only she could persuade him to help. She had broached the subject many times with Father McGennity but the old ... the old ... She tightened her lips and refused to permit expression to the derogatory appellation that threatened to sully her mind. The parish priest had never given her more than a vague, "Yes, yes. We might look into that." But, of course, nothing ever came of it.

Father Canavan, on the other hand, had been enthused and had said he would love to help her set up a young folk choir and Mrs. McLoughlin was going to lose no time in getting it started. Her immediate objective was to visit some of her classes and round up a few volunteers who could sing and others who could play a musical instrument. Already she had several conscripts from the junior classes and now she was visiting the fifth years. She knocked on a door and entered a room.

"Excuse me, Mrs Malloy, do you mind if I address the class for a moment?"

Mrs. Malloy, small, thin, somewhat timid, bounced out of her seat, almost curtseying. "Of course, Principal. Of course." She waved a hand vaguely in the direction of the seated students.

"Good morning, class."

"Good morning, Mrs. McLoughlin," came the dutiful collective response.

The principal drew herself erect and said briskly. "Girls, the new curate for our parish, Father Canavan, is very anxious to start a new youth folk-choir for the Saturday evening Masses."

There was a rustle of interest among some of the girls. A number of them had already seen the new curate. He had been the subject of more than one conversation but none wanted to appear too anxious to volunteer.

"Right. Angela, you're on the school choir and so are you, Maureen. What do you say? Are you going to do your bit for parish life?"

"Yes, Mrs. McLoughlin," came two resigned voices.

"Tess? Maria? Am I going to have to ask you?"

"No, Mrs. McLoughlin," Tess answered for both of them. "We're volunteering."

"Thank you, girls. First rehearsal is at seven-thirty on Friday evening in St. Joseph's transept in the big chapel." She nodded to Mrs. Malloy and strode from the room.

A second later she poked her head back in again. "Geraldine," she called to one of the girls.

"Yes, Miss?"

"I expect to see you there, too. Bring your violin."

"Yes, Miss."

NINE

1

Evening meals at the parochial house with Father McGennity offered little in the way of intellectual cut and thrust. They offered little, indeed, of any kind of conversation. They consisted for the most part of sucking and smacking noises, the occasional heavy grunt, and intermittent silences. Nothing about this Wednesday evening was any different. Ray ate quietly, reflecting on the nature of his life away from his priestly duties. He remembered a conversation he once had with Dan in Maynooth about the loneliness of a priest's life.

"You bond with your fellow priests," Dan had said.

Ray cast a surreptitious glance at his parish priest who was focused on gnawing the last morsel of flesh from the bones of a lamb chop. His lips tightened. *No bonding is going to happen with him*, he thought. He cleared his throat awkwardly. "I think I'll go round to the chapel and see how choir practice is going."

"Hmmmph!" Father McGennity did not lift his eyes from his plate. "As if you hadn't enough to be doin'."

2

Ray entered the chapel on the following Friday evening by the north transept. His ears were immediately assailed by unwonted noise disturbing the peace of the sanctuary. As he entered the inner door, he saw several girls of varying teen-ages running back and forth from the sacristy, carrying chairs, benches, violins, wind instruments, even a guitar. It was obvious that the girls were setting up St. Joseph's altar for the choir practice and Ray headed towards the sacristy to see what he might do to help. As he reached the door, he had to stand back to give passage to a girl struggling with a large electronic keyboard, Mrs. McLoughlin's substitute piano. Following her were two girls carrying a table, one a tall black-haired girl who was reversing out from the sacristy, her back to Ray. A smaller, plumpish blonde girl carried the other end. The table looked heavy. Ray tapped the tall girl lightly on the shoulder and said quietly, "Can I help you with that?"

The girl almost dropped the table at the sound of the male voice so close to her ear. Startled, she turned to see who had spoken. The smile on Ray's face froze. His heart constricted and he, in turn, experienced intense shock. He was looking at Karen. Except that it wasn't Karen. Karen would be almost thirty now. This girl was only seventeen, eighteen at most. But she had the same amber eyes, the same dark hair, the same lovely face. Even her smile was Karen's, a smile that was gradually fading from greeting to puzzlement to nervous embarrassment.

Embarrassment? Ray realised suddenly that he had been staring at her. He put a hand out to touch her elbow by way of apology but dropped it before it reached her. Instead he said, "Oh, I'm sorry. I was startled there for a moment. You look so like ..."

"Don't worry about it, Father," the blonde girl interrupted with a wide grin. "It happens all the time." Then looking at her friend, she added, "Although not usually with priests."

"Tess!" the dark-haired girl admonished, glaring daggers at her, but her friend simply continued to grin and shrugged her shoulders. Ray, too, grinned to cover his discomposure and said, "Why don't the two of you take the other end and I'll take this end?"

The tall girl smiled agreement and joined her friend. Ray kept looking over his shoulder now as he reversed his way to St. Joseph's altar where he could hear Mrs. McLoughlin directing operations. His mind was in turmoil. His heart was racing. He was conscious of an inner tremor that had seized his whole body. He avoided any further eye contact with the girl, totally mystified by the intensity of his reactions to this ... this teenager.

"This is insanity," he berated himself. "I've seen hundreds of teenagers over the past few years. What is this?"

They reached St. Joseph's altar and Mrs. McLoughlin approached them.

"Ah, there you are, Father. Good of you to come." She gestured to a spot in front of the serried chairs where the girl with the keyboard was standing. "Put it down here."

They set the table down and the other girl placed the keyboard on it and plugged it into an orange extension lead snaking across the floor. Mrs. McLoughlin looked at her watch. "Right, girls, get yourselves seated," she called.

"Sopranos to the front. Altos and contraltos right and left behind them, musicians at the very back."

Ray offered the two girls a quiet smile and a brief nod as they went to join the rest of the choir, the smaller girl looking sideways at her friend with that mischievous smile still on her lips. He went over to Mrs. McLoughlin. "Where do you want me to sit?" he asked.

"Oh," she pointed to a chair beside the table, "just here beside me, if you would."

Ray sat down, suddenly conscious of the appraisal of twenty-four pairs of curious eyes. He wished now he had said nothing and had simply gone to the back of the group. Fortunately, at that moment Mrs. McLoughlin addressed her group and took their attention away from him.

"Girls, I don't have to tell you that I have a voice like nails scraping on a blackboard." Everybody laughed. Ray shot a surreptitious glance at the tall girl, who was laughing along with the others.

"Gosh," he thought. "Even the same perfect teeth."

"So I have asked Father Canavan to help me with the practice." The principal smiled at the priest. "He can sing a bit." Again the group scrutiny. Ray attempted a friendly smile, trying not to look sheepish. *How the heck did I allow myself to get roped into this?* he was thinking. The teacher sat at the table and fiddled with some sheets of music. She set one in front of her.

"All right," she said. "You all know the opening hymn. It's one we sing regularly at school. So, we'll use that to loosen up our tonsils."

Ray was surprised at the quality of the singing. Obviously the hymn had been well rehearsed before and the harmonies supplied by the altos and contraltos were glorious.

"That's good, girls," the teacher said. "Now we'll take a look at the psalm. Maria, you will sing the verses and all will join in for the response." She looked at the priest. "Father, would you just run over the psalm for Maria and then we'll let her try."

Ray nodded solemnly. Inwardly he was chiding himself for feeling unaccountably nervous. *You're a priest, for God's sake. This is what you do. Relax.*

A couple of days before, he had spent an hour with Mrs. McLoughlin going over the psalm, a few responses, and the communion hymn, so he knew which psalm he had to sing. But although he knew the words by heart, he took a sheet from the table and kept his eyes fixed on it. Mrs. McLoughlin nodded at him once more and began to play the introduction. Ray sang, in his rich, musical baritone,

"Oh, sing a new song to the Lord,
Sing to the Lord, all the earth ..."

All eyes were fixed on him now, fascinated. A priest with the looks of a film star and the voice of an angel. Mrs. McLoughlin smiled quietly to herself as she studied the faces of her charges. *I don't imagine I'll have much trouble with absenteeism from this lot, she* was thinking. Ray stole another glance at the tall girl while the group sang the first response. She was watching him intently. Ray allowed his gaze to continue casually over the whole choir and finished the psalm.

"Do you want to try that now, Maria?" the teacher asked.

Ray's eyes ranged the group to see who Maria was. The tall girl was nodding shyly to the teacher. "Can I remain sitting while I'm practising, Miss?" she asked. Mrs. McLoughlin shrugged. "If it makes you feel more comfortable. Ready?"

Maria nodded. Mrs. McLoughlin played the introduction and Maria sang the first verse.

Ray watched her, trying to remain emotionally and psychologically neutral about her. But her voice, a clear, strong, ineffably sweet soprano, touched his heart. The group was watching the priest, their smiles proprietorial, waiting for his reaction. Feeling that the girls needed something from him, Ray looked overtly at Mrs. McLoughlin and nodded approval. The girls looked at each other and smiled again. Everybody loved Maria's singing.

"Excellent, Maria," the teacher said. "Now, you girls with the instruments, I hope you have been practising? Let's try that again, Maria, this time with the Philharmonic Orchestra."

There was a dutiful titter and Mrs. McLoughlin began the introduction, playing with one hand, the other in the air to conduct the musicians.

Practice continued for another hour, Ray introducing the various new pieces, the choir following him. He did everything he could not to look any more at Maria but inevitably there were times when his glance found her. Often he would find her gaze on him but she would avert her eyes immediately when he looked her way. Her friend, Tess was it? seemed to be watching both of them with an altogether-too-knowing smile.

Ray, he admonished himself for the tenth time. *Are you some sort of idiot? Be normal. Act normal. Feel normal. Quit this, now!*

When the session came to an end and the students were replacing the chairs and benches in the sacristy, Ray initially decided to slip quietly out of the chapel but he realised that that would not make sense. Any normal priest would certainly have a word of praise for the choir and especially for the lead soprano. He went over to Mrs. McLoughlin and said, “You have the makings of a great choir there, Mrs. McLoughlin. And your lead singer is terrific.”

“Thank you, Father.” She looked speculatively at him. “You’ve got a fantastic voice yourself. I don’t suppose I could persuade you to sing with us?”

Ray laughed. “Ah, I dunno. I think I’ll wait to see if you bring a few other male voices in first.”

“Well, that’s a possibility. You might be able to help us with that.”

Ray thought about that for a second. “I’ll see what I can do. Maybe there’ll be somebody interested at St. Colman’s.”

Mrs. McLoughlin arched her eyebrows at him. “Nobody rough, Father.”

Ray smiled. “I’ll be careful.”

At that point, Maria and Tess walked past, carrying chairs.

“Oh, Maria,” Ray called casually. “Lovely singing. You’re really good.”

Maria blushed. “Oh, thank you, Father,” she said, and pushed Tess, who had stopped to witness the exchange, on towards the sacristy. When they reached the door of the sacristy, Tess whispered to Maria, “I think he fancies you.”

“Tess!” Maria was scandalised. “He’s a priest.”

“Did you not see the way he looked at you?”

"Yes. It was because I reminded him of somebody. He was about to tell us who, but you had to go and open your big mouth with that stupid crack about it happening all the time."

"Well, it does," Tess said defensively.

"Don't be stupid."

They went on into the sacristy. Ray was watching them with half an eye as he finished his conversation with Mrs. McLoughlin. "Next Friday evening?" he said.

"Yes, but I'll contact you to have a wee run over the stuff before that. Maybe Wednesday?"

"Okay. See you then."

3

Ray sat on the armchair in his room that night, his breviary unopened on his lap. He blessed himself, invited the Holy Spirit into his heart, and sat for a while in contemplative silence. After a few moments he said aloud, "What was all that about, Lord? All that shock and shaking and tension?"

He let the question hang in the air. The Lord would answer in his own time and in his own way. He sat, head bowed, breviary held loosely in his hands. Eventually he spoke again. "Analyse it? You mean, examine the details?" He sat silent again, then he began to review what he thought had happened. "She turned round and I thought it was Karen. That was a shock. But goodness, I have never seen two people so alike. She's a total doppelganger, Lord." He paused. "So? So the shock had nothing to do with the girl and everything to do with Karen? The girl is irrelevant, right? So, what I have to do is work out the extent to which I still have feelings for Karen?"

He tried to remember what Monsignor Keenan had said to him about this some years earlier. 'It's going to happen. It happens to us all and we have to deal with it when it happens.' *No, that's not right. It has already happened, several years ago.* This, tonight, was not something that was happening. It was a result of something that had happened already. Then aloud, "What are you trying to say, Ray?" He compressed his lips. "I'm trying to say that Maria doesn't figure in this. I'm not bothered by her. It's memories of Karen that are bothering me."

He ran a hand through his hair and sat for a long time after that, very still, with his head bowed. When he moved again, it was to pick up his breviary. As he opened the prayer book in preparation for reading his evening Office, he said, "God, Holy Father, Holy Spirit, dear Jesus, help me. I need your grace. I have no chance on my own. Just get me through this night, please, dear Lord, and I'll be all right tomorrow."

He looked down at his breviary and began to read the first lines of the hymn for Friday, Week Two:

"Day is done, but Love unfailing
Dwells ever here;
Shadows fall, but hope, prevailing,
Calms every fear."

TEN

The little boy shivers in his bed. It is dark but he still hears night noises in the house. His parents have not yet gone to bed. He clings to his teddy bear. 'He' is in the house too. 'He' has come back again. 'He' will come. His face crumples and tears begin to roll down his cheeks, distress and powerlessness overcoming him. There is nothing the child can do. He is only little and 'he' is so big. He huddles into a ball and pulls his teddy even closer. A sob escapes his throat ... and another. He is utterly alone and wretched. He sniffles and wipes his eyes with the bear, sobbing intermittently.

Suddenly he tenses, scarce daring to breathe. He hears the sound of his bedroom door swishing on the carpet. He lies utterly still, terrified. A hand gently caresses his hair and the clothes are gently eased back from his face.

"What is it, love?" his mother's soft voice whispers. "Are you having a bad dream?"

The child turns violently in the bed and wraps his arms tightly around his mother's neck.

"I'm afraid," he sobs.

"There now," his mother smiles, "it's only a dream. What is there to be afraid of?"

The child continues to cling tightly to his mother, wanting to tell her. But 'he' will take his mummy and daddy away if he says anything. He longs to tell her but the fear is too strong. He stumbles over his answer.

"M ... m ... monster."

"Monsters?" His mother smiles. "A big boy like you must know there are no such things as monsters."

He continues to cling, resisting even as his mother tries to take his arms from her neck and ease him back under the bedclothes.

"Lie down," she says quietly, "and I'll sing you a wee song."

Unwillingly he allows her to tuck him back into bed and, while she continues to caress his head, she sings softly a song that he has loved since he was a baby. The hand on his head is comforting, his mother's sweet and lovely voice is soothing, and he lies still, the tension easing from him. He looks up at her lovely face, at the smile he sees there, at the love in her eyes, and he feels a terrible sadness. He longs to tell her but he loves her too much.

He sobs again.

"Shhhh! Sshhhh! I'll stay here till you go to sleep, my best wee boy, and all the bad dreams will go away ..."

He lies still and gives himself over to the consoling hand and the soothing lullaby and doesn't want her ever to go ... and he feels so loved ... and he feels so loved ... and ... he ... feels ... so ... loved ...

The sleeper moves slightly in the bed, exhales a long breath, and slips into a deep and dreamless sleep.

ELEVEN

Larchmount Grove is a leafy, up-market suburb about a mile from the town of Drumkillen. Only the wealthy can afford to live there and, inevitably, the area has earned for itself the soubriquet, 'Millionaire's Row'. There are fewer than a dozen houses in the area and many of the owners would have preferred separate and isolated sites for their large, elegant houses but local council regulations about greenbelt, sewage and other services, necessitated that they build in a cluster – magnificently ornate, ostentatious even, but still a cluster – within restricted limits on the edge of the town.

On an evening in early September, a large Mercedes pulled into the tree-lined drive of Number Five, Larchmount Grove and stopped outside the large pillared portico. Terence O'Hanlon and his wife, Patricia, stepped out of the car went into the house. Terence went to the drinks cabinet.

"Nightcap?" he asked his wife, holding up a wineglass.

"Nnnn ... no. I'll just have a coffee." She headed for the kitchen. "I'll make it now. Want one?"

He shook his head. "No thanks. I think I'll just have something here."

Terence was thirty-eight, a successful barrister, and a great deal wealthier than he might have been because of his involvement in a recent government corruption case that had lasted for almost two years. Patricia was beautiful, elegant and younger than her husband by two years. But she was no trophy wife. She was independently well-off, a brilliant solicitor with a large practice in Portsbridge. Their relationship blossomed when Patricia, recognising Terence's skills as a barrister, had frequently employed him to fight her firm's cases in court. A handsome, charming barrister, a beautiful solicitor—romance was inevitable. Marriage had followed some five years ago and their love for each other had remained strong. Terence carried his drink to a sofa in front of a large television. He switched it on, waited for it to warm up, then flicked desultorily through several channels before turning it off again. His wife came back into the room with her coffee and sat in an armchair nearby. Terence looked at her, tightened his lips and raised his eyebrows.

"Bit of a waste of time, that," he said.

"I dunno, Terry. He did confirm what I already knew."

"Hmmph!"

"Terry!"

After five years of marriage, one miscarriage and one premature baby still-born after a caesarean section, Patricia had discovered that she was unlikely ever to have children. Her doctor had diagnosed a placental abruption during the caesarean delivery. A few days later, in his surgery, he had explained that the placenta, which is part of the baby's life support system, had separated from the uterine lining.

"How could that have happened?" Patricia had asked, tearfully.

The doctor had looked sadly at her over the top of his spectacles. “I’m sorry, Patricia. You have been most unfortunate. It does happen but only about one percent of all pregnant women experience it.”

“How dangerous is it? I mean, was it the cause of my wee baby’s death?”

The doctor had nodded vigorously to emphasise his answer. “It’s very dangerous, Patricia, for both baby *and* mother. When such a separation occurs, it can interrupt the transportation of oxygen and nutrients to the baby. There are different degrees of such separation, of course. Sometimes only partial separation occurs but sometimes the separation can be total.”

“Can it be treated?” she asked, almost pleading for an affirmative response.

“Not really. We can treat the symptoms, if we can detect them in time. But unfortunately the condition can only really be diagnosed after the birth. We try ultra-sound, foetal monitoring and so on but there are no real guarantees with these methods. But even then, we cannot stop the placenta from detaching nor can we reattach it again.”

“Do you know why it happened to me?”

“Well, you have some abnormalities in the uterus and you are approaching thirty-five when these things are more likely to happen.”

“And if I were to get pregnant again?” she had asked hesitantly, fearing his answer.

“I’m truly sorry, Patricia. You have already had a caesarean and that increases the risk of a repeat abruption very considerably, by at least three times, I believe. The trouble is, any type of placental abruption can lead to premature birth and in severe cases something like fifteen percent will end in foetal death. In your case the abruption was severe." There was clear sympathy in his expression but he continued seriously, "And in severe cases about ten percent of the mothers can die from the haemorrhaging that can occur. It's terrible to see and I have seen it before, so," he shook his head sadly, "I would have to advise you to abandon the idea of giving birth." He put out a hand to comfort Patricia when he saw her crumpled expression. "I'm so sorry, Patricia, but I really think you would be well advised to consider some form of contraception, artificial, if you like, but preferably permanent."

Patricia put her face in her hands. Her Catholic upbringing recoiled at any mention of contraception. "I need to think about all of this, doctor," she had said, rising from her chair. "I ... I'm sorry," and she rushed from his surgery, leaving the door open behind her.

She had arrived home that evening distraught and Terence could only flutter about helplessly, trying to comfort her but not knowing what to say. The doctor's words had been too final. Patricia had talked for years about children and now, never to have any! She was inconsolable for most of that evening.

Over the next few days they had talked about the doctor's advice to use some form of contraception, Terence absolutely adamant that it was essential. Patricia, concerned about its moral import, continued to resist the idea. They argued back and forth, circling around the subject, coming back to it, but finding no point of common ground.

Eventually Terence had said, “Why don’t you go and see a priest? Surely they are bound to see that here is a sure case where contraception is necessary?”

Patricia agreed that, if she was to have any peace of mind, this was something she would have to do.

It was for that reason they had been out that evening. Terence had earlier driven Patricia to the parochial house of St. Columba’s Parish to meet with a young priest there, a Father Dan Patterson. Patricia liked the way he said Mass and his earnest yet cheerful manner of dealing with his parishioners. She had met him briefly a couple of times and felt that here was a priest she could talk to. Terence had waited for her outside the parochial house and on the way home Patricia had related to him what had been said.

“Father Dan was lovely,” she had told Terence, “very kind and sympathetic. He was very concerned about what had happened to our last child but when I told him the percentages for it happening again he got very worried.”

“Worried?”

“He wanted to help, I could see that. He wanted to help badly. But he kept saying, ‘Ten percent, Mrs. O’Hanlon, ten per cent?’ and looking really upset. I asked him what was wrong and he said that the figures meant that I had a ninety percent chance of being all right and he couldn’t see how he could allow us to use contraception in those circumstances. He said he wished he could help but that it was not up to him, that Pope John Paul II had made the situation very clear.”

“Oh, God! He’s not bringing *him* into it?”

"Terry!" she chastised him. "He's a wonderful pope."

"All right, all right. But there are millions of people dying of Aids in Africa because he's digging his heels in about contraception."

"Not him, Terry, the Church. He's simply upholding the rules."

"Hummph! The rules."

"Yes, Terry. Apparently another pope, Paul the Sixth, has made the situation very explicit in *Humanae Vitae*, an encyclical, I think."

"Yes, yes, artificial contraception is always wrong."

"That's right, and there's no room for manoeuvre."

"Crap!"

"Terry!"

"Well, there's got to be room for manoeuvre."

"Father Patterson says we have to use the natural rhythm method. Please, Terry," Patricia had reached out and touched his arm. "Please don't make this any harder for me than it is. I have to do what the Church says."

Terence compressed his lips. He could see how upset his wife was and did not want to distress her any more but secretly he was determining if he should go to the parochial house on his own and have it out with that priest. Now he tried to remain calm but was finding it difficult to do so. He sipped his drink. "What about trying another priest?" he suggested.

"What would be the point, Terry? Father Dan told me the exact truth about the Church's opposition to artificial contraception, and I knew it already, anyway."

They sat and stared at the blank television. Terence had many things he still needed to say but he knew his wife would not be able to hear them. Her religious beliefs were too strong. He finished his drink in one long swallow and said, "I think I'll go and have a bath."

Patricia caught his arm as he passed her chair. "Please, Terry," she said. "Don't be mad at me."

He put his hand over hers and bent down to kiss the top of her head. "It's all right, love. None of this is your fault. We'll be all right. We'll sort something out."

TWELVE

The following morning, Sunday, about ten o'clock, Ray entered the sacristy to prepare for the celebration of the mass at ten-thirty. On the way, he had to pass a small cloakroom where the altar-servers' soutanes were stored and where the children dressed and waited for the priest to call them. He thought he heard sniffling as he went by and he ducked his head into the cloakroom to see what was happening. There he saw Tommy, eight, sobbing in a corner and looking very frightened, and Michael, ten, awkwardly trying to comfort him.

Immediately concerned, Ray said, "What's the matter, boys?"

Both boys stood with the heads bowed and neither would speak.

"Well?" Ray persisted.

The boys' lips tightened. They refused to meet his gaze and, heads still hung, they remained silent. Ray stood looking down at them for a moment. "Okay," he said. "If that's how you want to play it." He placed himself directly in front of the children and sat cross-legged on the floor, leaving him about eye-level with them. "I am not moving from here," he said, "until you tell me what's wrong."

The boys glanced sideways at each other without lifting their heads. Eventually Tommy said, still sniffing, "The ... the parish priest ..."

Ray stiffened. "What about the parish priest?"

"He shouted at us," Michael said. "He was very angry."

"Goodness! What were you doing?"

"We came in early to get ready ..." Tommy stuttered.

"We were only laughin'," Michael said.

"That's all you were doing?" Ray said, inclining his head as if to allow room for further admissions.

Michael looked up and let his quiet brown eyes rest directly on Ray's. "Honestly, Fader. We were only laughin', and it wasn't even loud."

"We were only gigglin'," Tommy said.

Ray stared back at the earnest young eyes that were now focused on his. He reached out his hands and rested one on each boy's shoulder. "You're good lads," he said, rising from the floor. "Just go on getting ready for mass and I'll talk to the parish priest. Is he still here?"

Tommy looked terrified. "He's in the sacristy. What are you goin' to say, Fader?"

"If you shout at him, he's goin' to blame us," Michael added, his lower lip quivering.

"It's all right, boys." Ray ruffled both boys' hair and smiled with a calmness he wasn't feeling. "He won't be back. I'm only going to tell him he made a mistake."

Ray left the cloakroom and headed for the sacristy, feeling a familiar clenching in his stomach. The parish priest always said the twelve o'clock mass. What was he doing here this early? He entered to find the priest partly robed for mass, leaning over a table studying the readings for the day. He looked up and said gracelessly, "I need you to say twelve for me today, I've got to be in Dublin early."

Ray compressed his lips. "It's a bit short notice, Father. I might have had some arrangements myself."

The parish priest looked at him with an expression almost akin to contempt. "You? Sure what arrangements would you have? You never go anywhere."

Ray's lips remained tight but he felt the dark cloud of fear filling his mind. Yet he had to say something about the boys. "What did you do to the altar boys? They're scared to death in there in the cloakroom."

McGennity looked up at him. "The little bastards were kicking up a racket. No respect whatever for the Blessed Sacrament. I gave them a bit of a bollickin'."

"Do you not think you over-reacted? They're only children."

The parish priest stood up from the table and turned to face Ray. "Are you questioning my authority?' he said angrily.

"Do you expect those two wee lads to serve mass for you in that kind of mood?" Ray tried for an angry tone himself.

His superior's already ruddy complexion began to turn purple. "What's this? It's not enough I had to listen to that other wee git for four years and now you're startin' too?"

"Those little lads give up their Sunday mornings to serve mass," Ray said. "You should at least show them a bit of respect."

The parish priest went over to the sacristy door and closed it. He turned and glared at Ray. “What in blazes is the matter with you this morning?” He walked across to where Ray was standing and stood aggressively in front of him. “You don’t tell me what to do, you wee whippersnapper.” He lifted a plump finger and wagged it in Ray’s face. “I tell you.”

Ray stared calmly at the furious priest although his insides were crawling. “You’re going to drive the altar-servers away again,” he said quietly.

“Again?” Father McGennity’s voice quivered with anger. “Again? What do you mean, again?”

Ray had no stomach for this unpleasantness. In truth, he felt his resolve waver. He wanted to stand up to this aggressive priest, to show him that he would not be bullied. But the fact was that the man instilled in him a deep, unreasoning fear that he could not deal with and could not understand. He had tried to take Dan’s advice and confront him but it wasn’t working. It would never work. He was failing but he no longer cared. All he wanted was to end this. He said, trying still, however, to retain a resolute front, “Why don’t you go wherever you’re going? I’ll say both masses.”

“You’re still trying to tell me what to do, boy. I’ll ...” The parish priest continued to glare at Ray but fell silent. Ray sensed that he was torn between showing who was boss and taking the opportunity to leave early. He turned towards the wardrobe and pulled off the alb he was wearing. “It happens to be important for me to get away early, so you can say both masses,” he said, with no mollifying of tone. “But let me tell you, you want to watch your lip in the future.” He threw the alb on the deep window ledge without folding it up, picked up his breviary and stalked out of the room.

Ray leaned weakly on the divesting bench, staring unseeing at the crucifix on the wall before him. He felt utterly shattered by this experience. *What is it with this man? Has he no sense of the spirituality, or even of the dignity of his calling? How can he be filled with so much anger?* He tried to control an involuntary tremor in his hands and lifted himself wearily from the bench. He went back to the two little boys and, forcing himself to smile, he said, “It’s all right, boys. The parish priest didn’t mean what he said. He’s got stuff on his mind.” He looked kindly at them. “Okay?”

Two tiny voices replied, “Yes, Fader.”

“And you’re going to get ready to serve mass for me now?”

“Yes, Fader.”

“Good lads.”

Ray went back into the sacristy. He felt queasy and disturbed. He stared again at the crucifix on the wall. “God, is this the life you have called me to? How can I function in love, living like this? I can’t stay much longer with this man. You’re going to have to do something, Lord.”

THIRTEEN

The sleeper struggled in the darkness of the night. His limbs jerked spasmodically as he emitted soft cries and little groans. He huddled himself into a foetal position and heard a harsh, whispered command, *"Let go of that bloody teddy bear and turn around."*

The tiny child clung more tightly to his soft toy and struggled to resist the hands that were pulling at him. Each time the hands pulled a limb away from the tiny, cowering body, the child fought to retrieve it. The whisper increased in intensity and in anger.

"Right! That's enough of that. Y' know what I'm going to do? I'm going to take your daddy and mammy away. You'll never see them again."The child experienced a sudden and overwhelming terror. "No ..." he sobbed. "No ..."

"Shhhh! Shut up. Do you want me to go and get them now? Do you? Do you? Now, quit that squirming and turn around."

The child stopped struggling. His head jerked slightly as his throat, struggling to stem his sobs, emitted a tearful, glottal hiccup. Tears rolled down his face.

"You leave my daddy and mammy alone," he sobbed.

"You know what you have to do and they'll be fine," came the fierce response. "Now shut your mouth and c'mere."

The sleeper woke, tears streaming down his face. As always he had to fight to find his way back to reality but this time, even as the nightmare faded, the tears continued unabated.

FOURTEEN

The old woman, grey-haired, gaunt, heavily wrinkled, lay back on her pillow and laughed, "Ah, Lord, Father, you're a tonic."

Dan grinned back. "All this is confidential, Grace, okay? I wouldn't want it getting back to the bishop. I'd be sacked in the morning."

Old Mrs. Breen, one of the most prolific gossips in Kilnamoy, said seriously, "You know you can rely on me not to breathe a word, Father."

"Well, okay," Dan smiled. "One final wee story and then I'll have to call in on some of the other patients."

Dan was carrying out his weekly visit to a small county hospital a few miles from Kilnamoy. Despite the reputed looseness of her tongue, he liked Mrs. Breen. She was a cheerful soul who had been in hospital for a few weeks now with a wasting disease that, one of the nurses had hinted to Dan, was probably terminal. The word was that she would be moving to a hospice in Dublin soon. Dan was sorry for her because she had a ne'er-do-well son somewhere who never visited and she was always asking Dan to try to find him. At that moment, however, Mrs. Breen's nose seemed to quiver at the prospect of another morsel of juicy gossip, and wriggling a little in her bed, she said, “Well, Father. Tell me.”

Dan looked around the ward conspiratorially and then learned forward, speaking in a stage whisper, “Well, as I heard it, the bishop was visiting a junior school in one of the parishes the other day ... well, you know he’s very keen on seeing his diocese grow and he thinks that there should always be plenty of children coming along.” Dan checked again, apparently to ensure that no-one was listening and moved even closer to the bed. “Anyway, it seems that he noticed this group of young mothers waiting outside the school and he went over to them to thank them for the wonderful gift of children to the parish and he started telling them how much he hoped they would continue to add to the flock with more babies.” Grace listened round-eyed, wondering what was coming next. “Well, the head-teacher noticed this and came over and started pulling at the bishop’s arm muttering something about the bishop leaving his briefcase behind him in the office.” Dan’s grin widened and Grace grinned too, without knowing why. “But the bishop was enjoying himself,” Dan went on. “He was in full flow telling the young women that they must produce more babies, that it was good for the Church, and the head couldn’t budge him.” Dan began to chuckle but he managed to say, “The head had to grab the bishop’s arm with both hands and haul him away, nearly pulling him off his feet.”

Grace grinned widely at the picture Dan was painting. “What was going on?” she asked.

“Well, what the bishop didn’t know was that the group he was talking to was the Unmarried Mothers Club.” And Dan threw back his head and gave vent to a loud laugh. Grace put a hand before her mouth and tittered. She was trying not to laugh when she said, "Oh, God forgive you, Father, telling stories like that about the bishop."

Dan raised a finger to his lips, "Not a word to a soul, mind. All right?"

"You can rely on me, Father," Grace replied, eyeing the other beds in the ward to see who was awake.

"Right. I'll go on now," Dan said, placing a comforting hand on her shoulder. "And I'm still trying to locate Andrew. The minute I hear anything, I'll go in my own car and bring him here myself."

"Ach, thank you Father. You're a dear. And thank you for the grapes."

"Not at all, Grace. I'll be in again next week. Lie back now. I'll just give you a wee blessing before I go."

He blessed the frail old woman and, with one more pat on her shoulder, he left the ward. He walked down the corridor and took the lift to the third floor where there was a patient in Gynaecology that he had promised to visit. He emerged from the lift just as Terence and Patricia O'Hanlon came hurrying towards it. Dan smiled a greeting. "Mr. and Mrs. O'Hanlon. How are you?"

Both of them looked upset but, at the sight of Dan, Terence's face darkened. "Well, I hope you're happy now, Father," he said truculently.

Truculence never fazed Dan. Terence's unexplained truculence didn't faze him now. He looked at Patricia and said calmly, "What's wrong, Patricia?"

"She's pregnant," Terence answered for her. "That's what's wrong. And her doctor's going nuts in there in his office."

"Calm down, Terence. Tell me what's happening."

Patricia laid a restraining hand on her husband's arm and said, "Father, I'm glad we bumped into you. The pregnancy was confirmed a couple of weeks ago and Dr. Knowles has been urging me to have an abortion. I said that that was morally impossible for me and he suggested I bring my priest to see him. Terry is convinced by his arguments and I need you to hear what he has to say." She pointed to a room along the hall. "He's in his office now. Would you come back with us now and talk to him, please?"

Dan looked dubious. "It's not my role to debate medical ethics with doctors," he said. "I don't see what you expect to achieve by this."

Terence snorted. "I told you asking him would be a waste of time."

"Terry!" Patricia admonished, upset by her husband's manners. "Father, if you could just listen to what he says. He's very persuasive and I don't know what to do."

Dan held her eyes and said earnestly, "Well, I can tell you right now, Patricia, that no matter what he says, what he is suggesting is infanticide."

Terence threw his eyes to heaven and snorted to a door in the wall beside him, "I knew it. His mind's already made up. He won't consider the doctor's reasoning at all."

"Terry, please," Patricia said. She turned to Dan. "Please, Father. It'll only take a few minutes, and it would mean so much to me."

Dan studied the pleading face and said, "All right. I'll hear what he has to say."

"Oh, thank you, Father. It's this way."

She led him to an office half-way down the corridor and after a perfunctory knock on the door she rushed on into the office without waiting for an invitation. Dr. Knowles, who was writing at his desk, looked up, slightly startled.

"Ah, Patricia, Terence. Come in. Come in." He looked questioningly at Dan.

"Doctor, this is Father Patterson," Patricia said.

The doctor held out a friendly hand but his eyes were wary. "Pleased to meet you, Father." He winced a little when Dan gave his hand a hearty shake and, after quickly retrieving it, he used it to gesture them to chairs. Patricia wasted no time in broaching the reason for their visit.

"Doctor, would you please explain to Father Patterson why you think I should have an abortion."

The doctor looked at the big priest and found no encouragement in Dan's grim expression. Nonetheless, he trotted out some well-rehearsed arguments. "The simple fact is that Patricia has become pregnant against my express counsel. I understand that she tried not to, but that's another story. But the problem now is that her life, literally, is in danger." Dan simply nodded. The doctor looked at him for a moment and went on, "Patricia lost her last baby because of a placental abruption and, well, that makes it three times more likely that it will happen again." He paused, waiting for a response from Dan. Terence also was watching him very closely. Again, Dan simply nodded. He did not dispute these medical facts. The doctor joined his fingers and laid the coupled hands on the edge of his desk. "So," he went on, his lips pursed, "that puts Patricia into the 'at risk' category as defined by the U.K.Abortion Act of 1967."

He paused again, giving Dan opportunity for comment but after a moment he seemed to accept that there would be no response and he continued, spreading his hands slightly as he did so. "There are at least two categories into which Patricia falls that make an abortion in this case necessary. One is that continuing the pregnancy would be a greater risk to the woman's life than would ending the pregnancy ..." Dan shifted in his chair and the doctor paused, expecting Dan to say something but Dan said nothing. Dr. Knowles went on, "And second, there is grave risk to the child. If the placental separation is severe, the baby could suffer brain damage and it could die any time before, during or after the birth." He sat back in his chair and joined his hands in his lap. "There you have it, Father. I would strongly advise Patricia not to let this pregnancy to come to term. It's just too dangerous."

Dan nodded yet again but this time he spoke. Patricia was watching him intently.

"I'm deeply sorry that Patricia and Terence find themselves in this situation. I'm sure it's very worrying for all of you. You talk about 'three times more likely'. What exactly does that mean? Three times more than what? The average, or ...?"

Patricia sat very still in her chair, her eyes moving from one to the other as they spoke, distress visible on her face. She wanted the child, terribly, but she was frightened. She was watching Dan's reaction, however, as the doctor responded.

"Well, it just means that she's much more likely now to experience the abruption because it has happened already."

"But is it not true, Doctor, that only about one per cent of pregnant women actually experience placental abruption?" Dan had been doing some reading. "Three times that is still only three per cent."

Terence burst out angrily, "For God's sake, Father. Can you not hear what the doctor is saying? Don't be so bloody clinical. It's Patricia's life we're talking about here."

Dan turned to him. "I'm sorry, Terence, but it seems to me that the odds ..."

"No, Father," the doctor interrupted. "Your logic is spurious. Your one per cent statistic is accurate but the point is that Patricia's previous history has shown that she is already within that one per cent, and her chances of repeat abruption are now three times higher than before. That represents a very serious risk, one that, in my view, should not be taken."

Dan was disturbed by this point but, shaking his head, he said, "Leaving statistics aside, it is possible that if Patricia went to term the baby could, in fact, be safely delivered?"

"Well, of course that possibility exists but there is absolutely no way that I could guarantee it. What I can confirm is that the risks of abruption are high, and the consequences are dire. Severe haemorrhaging is a distinct possibility. There may be need for blood transfusions, intensive care, and the baby may well be born prematurely with physical or mental disabilities. Or, just as likely, it might well suffocate, literally, in its mother's blood."

Terence moved toward Patricia and put an arm around her shoulder but he remained silent.

Dan's lips tightened. "I hear what you're saying, doctor, I really do, but the problem for me is that there is one moral axiom that Catholics have to live by, that we can't ignore. We cannot do evil in order to bring about a perceived good. In this case there is a risk, I agree, but there is also the possibility of a successful birth." He turned to Patricia and Terence. "I'm sorry, Patricia, but this child, and make no mistake about it, is now a human being with human rights, and he or she is entitled to life. Abortion is murder. That's what Pope John Paul the Second said in his 1995 encyclical, Evangelium Vitae. It's murder, and you cannot condone that."

Dr, Knowles sat up in his seat, his face rigid with disapproval. "Excuse me, Father. That's just an opinion. The law says different. The U.K. Act makes it clear that some abortions are legal and necessary."

Dan regarded him calmly, "I understand that, Doctor, although I don't know why you keep quoting it. It doesn't apply here in Ireland. In any event, Patricia has asked me for moral, not legal, guidance. Our Church makes it clear that no matter how serious or tragic the reasons for an abortion are, they can never justify the deliberate and voluntary killing of an innocent human being."

Patricia turned her head into Terence's shoulder, her whole body sagging. Terence's arm tightened around her. Dan felt her fear but there was nothing he could say to soften his, and the Church's, stance. Every human being has an inalienable right to life and nobody has the right to take that gift away. Instead he said softly, and with as much compassion in his voice as he could muster, "Patricia, we cannot know what God's will is for us in matters like this. If he chooses, your child will be born healthy and you will suffer no lasting damage. We can pray for that. The doctor admits that the possibility exists. Put your trust in God's will. Whatever that is, it is ultimately what is best for us."

Terence glared at Dan over the top of Patricia's head. "I think we've heard enough from you for one day, Father." He spat out the last word like an insult. "Would you leave us to talk to the doctor, please?"

Dan rose quietly, disappointed. He said to the back of Patricia's head as he left the room, "I'm sorry, Patricia. And for you, too, Terence. I feel your suffering. I'll pray for you both, constantly."

FIFTEEN

1

October passed by with more than its share of sunshine and the land was made beautiful with gorgeous browns and yellows and reds. November passed, bleak and grey. December wasn't much better. If there were to be Christmas-card snow scenes this year, there were as yet no signs of them. The Drumkillen youth choir was practising hard for midnight mass on Christmas Eve and Mrs. McLoughlin was determined to mark the occasion with something very special. They would sing many of the usual carols but not in the usual way. Oh, no! People were going to remember her choir's singing for a long time. Ray attended many of these rehearsals and was delighted with the harmonies that were beginning to emerge. Mrs. McLoughlin tried to conscript him into a short solo performance and even talked about a possible duet with her star performer but he smilingly refused because, as he explained, he would be concelebrating the mass.

During these rehearsals he noticed Maria's eyes tended occasionally to hold his, briefly but unmistakably. Once in a while there would be the merest flicker of her lips, almost, but not quite, a smile. He fought to pretend not to notice but, in spite of his awareness of the inappropriateness of this, he could not restrain the twinges of pleasure her obvious interest gave him. He knew she was developing a crush on him, that he could never encourage it, and he tried not to show any reaction when he found her gaze on him. But something deep in his psyche was responding to Maria's regard and, try as he might, he was unable to resist the occasional glance in her direction. Almost invariably she would catch his furtive look and, although he would switch his eyes from her immediately, he knew that she was sensing, as he was, a connection.

More and more frequently, too, Maria was presenting herself in the small, informal chat-group that invariably pursued him after every rehearsal. There was a possibility, although it was not something Ray gave any voice to in his thinking, that the unhappiness of his life in the parochial house had left him vulnerable to any small signs of approval from his parishioners. He enjoyed these little get-togethers with the choir and, much as he tried to ignore it, he was always glad when Maria joined the others. There may have been little direct contact between them but her presence in the group made him much more ebullient and outgoing than he would otherwise have been.

But at night in his room he would pray, almost in tears, "Oh God, Oh God, please. It almost broke my heart leaving Karen. Please do not allow these feelings in me to grow. Please help Maria to find someone else. Lord, my vocation, my soul. Oh dear God, please, Lord."

Despite the intensity of his prayers, however, and his determination not to allow any untoward feelings to sully his priestly purity, he unconsciously looked forward to the choir rehearsals and felt a dead emptiness on the very occasional evening when Maria was unable to attend.

2

"That's an awful night for you to be in the house on your own, Father." The concern in Mrs. Toner's voice matched her words.

"Don't be worrying, Mrs. Toner," Ray smiled. "I'll be fine. I'm quite used to the parish priest staying away. I'm sure it's important, whatever it is."

Mrs. Toner's eyes looked upwards, accompanied by a slight shake of the head. Aye, she was thinking, important. Important he doesn't lose his licence if he tried to drive home. Hmmmph! They were sitting at the kitchen, finishing up the Friday evening meal she always shared with Ray. It was her custom always to leave for her own hearth immediately after dinner but more and more frequently Ray was left to spend the night in the huge rambling house on his own and she worried about him. He was barely a lad, for heaven's sake.

"Are you sure you don't want me to come back and stay with you? I can be home and make George his dinner and be back in a couple of hours."

"I wouldn't hear of it, Mrs. Toner. And besides, if you start that, it looks like you'll be living here a lot more often than you will with George. Father McGennity seems to be away a lot."

The house-keeper sniffed and her whole body bristled as she got up to clear the table. She put the dishes in the sink and said, "Don't be washin' at that stuff, now, all right? I'll clear it all away in the morning."

"Okay!" Ray smiled.

"Okay!" she echoed. "That's what you always say. But that's what I'm being paid to do. If you keep doing it," she said, smiling but brooking no refusal, "I'll just have to stay on and do it myself and my husband will have to wait until very late to get his dinner."

Ray raised his hands in surrender, laughing at her blackmail. "All right, all right. Go home and see to George. I have to go out now to choir practice, anyway. Go on, now. I'll see you in the morning."

"Okay. Goodnight, Father," she replied and went to a cupboard for her raincoat.

"You don't need a lift ...?"

"No thanks, Father. I've got the car tonight," she said as she left the room. "George is travelling with one of his mates."

3

Ray left the house a short time later to attend the usual Friday rehearsal. The weather was horrendous, strong winds and driving rain. Even though it was barely sixty or seventy yards to the church, he took his car rather than face the inclement conditions and parked in the area in front of the chapel.

Midnight mass was still a couple of weeks away but the choir was almost ready. That evening they rehearsed with gusto, singing with passion and joy. The soaring voices blended in harmonies and descants, the melodies inspired joy, and Ray, despite his natural shyness, joined in with the singing in a way he had never done before. Maria's solo, *O Holy Night*, was perfect in rhythm and pitch and during the spontaneous applause that followed her singing, she gave Ray a beatific smile to which, disarmed, he responded with a wide smile of his own. At the end of a rehearsal which had been longer than usual, Mrs. McLoughlin congratulated her singers and assured them that their contribution to the midnight mass that year would be "awe-inspiring".

There was little time for the casual chat that evening and after the usual clearing-up, the singers drifted off while Ray went into the sacristy to ensure that all was tidy and in readiness for the first mass the following morning. Some minutes later, he switched off all the lights in the church, ensured that all of the doors were locked, and let himself out by the side door. The weather had not relented and Ray, head down in the driving rain, rushed to his car at the front of the chapel. As he was about to climb in, he thought he noticed a movement in a corner of the archway that covered the main entrance. He hesitated and called aloud, "Is there someone there?"

There was a brief silence and then a soft voice replied, "It's me, Father. Maria."

He closed the door and ran to where she was standing. She was wearing only a wool sweater and jeans. She was shivering and had the sleeves of the sweater stretched down over her hands for extra warmth. Ray stood there before her, shoulders huddled against the wind. "My God, Maria, you're freezing. What are you doing standing there?"

"I usually go home with Tess and her father," the girl replied, scarcely able to pronounce the words as her lips quivered with the cold. "But Tess wasn't here tonight and because the rehearsal went on longer, I missed my nine o'clock bus."

"But what did you think you were going to do? You can't stand there all night."

"It's okay, Father," Maria said, clenching her teeth in an effort to stem the shivering. "There's another bus at ten. I just wanted to shelter in here until it comes."

"Don't be silly, Maria. You'll freeze to death there." He took his raincoat off and handed it to her. "Here, put that round you and come over into my car. I'll drive you home."

"Ah, it's all right, Father. I ... "

"It's not a bit all right. Come on now, quickly."

They both ran to the car and climbed in. Ray waited while Maria sorted his coat more comfortably around her shoulders and back. As he studied the shivering girl, the wet hair that clung to her head, the movements somehow elegant even in this confined situation, he suffered a rush of remembered emotion. It was on a night like this he had waited with Karen in a bus shelter and experienced his first kiss. Karen's hair, too, had looked like this. Ray felt an intense longing that almost overwhelmed him and, needing to break the spell, he turned and started the car. "Where to?" he said lightly, making a great fuss of turning on lights and wipers and releasing the handbrake.

"Left at the gate, Father."

He steered with studious care out of the little car park, through the gate, checked right and left with all the exaggerated caution of a learner driver and drove out on to the road.

"Where do you live, Maria?" Again, his voice was normal, almost casual, but he could scarcely breathe. Maria held her arms around herself, massaging the sides of her arms and struggling to halt her shivering. She turned to look at Ray for the first time, her eyes shaded but shining faintly in the light coming from the dashboard.

"About two miles or so along the Dublin Road, Father. It's an estate called Elmwood Grove."

"Oh yes, I know it. I'll have you home in a few minutes."

"This is very good of you, Father."

"What?" Ray laughed. "Did you expect me to leave you standing there?"

Maria smiled shyly. "I didn't know you were still there. I thought you had already gone."

Ray searched for something else to say. "How's school these days?"

There was silence and he turned to see that Maria had a genuinely amused grin on her face. "Is this you being an adult, Father?" she said.

Ray laughed. "Okay, you've found me out. I'm no good at this sort of thing."

Maria laughed, a soft, almost musical sound that caught his heart. "What sort of thing?"

"Talking to ... one-on-one conversations."

Maria was silent again. After a moment she said quietly, "Neither am I."

There was another short silence. Ray leaned forward a bit. Visibility was difficult. "Terrible night. It's hard to see." Then he said casually, "Are you an only child or are there more like you?"

"I have one brother, Paul."

"Oh? What's he like?" He could see Maria out of the corner of his eye, shaking her head and half-smiling.

"He's twelve, and he's a menace."

Ray laughed. "I've never had any brothers or sisters but from what I understand about families, it's a twelve-year-old boy's job to be a menace in his older sister's life."

Maria smiled and glanced at him. *This priest has a sense of humour*. "Well, he's good at his job," she said.

Ray laughed again and lapsed once more into silence. He had some justification for doing so. The driving rain on the windscreen was barely affected by the wipers and the headlights of two or three passing cars were making vision difficult.

Eventually Maria said, "You've got a lovely voice, Father. I wish we had been able to sing that duet Mrs. McLoughlin was talking about."

Ray laughed, embarrassed. "My goodness. Where did that come from?"

"I just love singing, Father. And I hear you joining in with us sometimes. I think our voices would blend very well together."

Ray chuckled again, unsure how to respond to this. He was thinking that girls mature very quickly these days. They seemed to have a confidence that was uncommon even ten or fifteen years before. "Well, me too, I suppose. I mean, I quite like singing," he said. "But not in front of crowds."

Maria was puzzled. "Well, where then?"

"In the shower mostly ..." Ray could have bitten off his tongue. But the sentence was out. *You idiot*, he thought. *What in the name of God is wrong with your head?*

Maria turned to look out through the windscreen.

Ray went on hurriedly, "Or in my study if the house is empty, you know, singing along with my CDs, or maybe ...

your singing tonight, *O Holy Night*, was beautiful. You never wavered on that high note. Truly great. I really enjoyed it. You'll wow them on Christmas Eve."

"Thank you, Father," Maria said.

Another period of silence ensued. Then Maria leaned back in her seat and turned towards him. "Why did you become a priest, Father?" She sounded genuinely interested.

"Ah, well, it's a vocation. Generally that doesn't give you much of a choice. It's something you feel you must do."

"Is it not a lonely job?"

Ray was unsure how to respond but he was saved from the effort when he saw the turn-off to where Maria lived. "Ah," he said cheerily. "We're here."

She directed him to an ivy-covered, two-storey house in a quiet cul-de-sac near the back of the estate. There was a porch light shining in an alcove at the front door.

"Would you like to come in, Father?" Maria said.Ray hesitated. He was finding himself in territory that was becoming increasingly difficult to navigate.

"Maybe you should come in and explain. It might look funny if you ..." Maria was hesitant, too. Her eyes, open and honest, held his. Her voice, whispering softly, was innocent of ulterior motive. Her choice of words, however, the implication they held of thoughts probably as yet unarticulated but redolent of the stuff of secret dreams, found distant echoes in Ray's psyche that left him uncertain, disturbed, afraid.

With an effort, he tore his gaze away from the girl's and focused on the house. "Yeess, I think probably you're right." He glanced back at Maria and then reached for the handle of his door. "Okay. Let's go."

They both got out of the car and ran through the rain to the porch. Maria rang the bell and they stood in an almost conspiratorial silence, neither looking at the other. Ray was unable to quell an utterly inexplicable sense of guilt. *What the heck's the matter with me?* he was thinking. *What did I do that was wrong? I couldn't have left her there in the rain and freezing cold.*

The door opened. Mrs. Rafferty stood there and, on recognising Ray, said in a surprised tone, "Hello, Father ..." She paused as she noticed her bedraggled daughter. "Maria ...?"

Ray smiled and, striving for a hearty tone, said, "Good evening, Mrs. Rafferty. I found this wet little waif on the doorstep of my church. Does anyone here recognise her?"

"Maria, what on earth ...?"

"Tess didn't come to practice tonight," Maria said in a rush. "We were finished late and I missed the nine o'clock bus and had to wait for the ten. Father Canavan found me sheltering at the chapel door and gave me a lift home."

"Come in, come in. Don't stand there freezing on the doorstep." They stood in the hall while Maria divested herself of Ray's raincoat and handed it back to him. Mrs. Rafferty continued, "Thank you, Father. That was kind of you."

"Not at all. Not at all."

"Would you like a cup of tea?"

Ray shook his head. "Ah no. No thanks. I've a sermon to write for Sunday's mass and I'm tied up all day tomorrow. So it's the midnight oil for me tonight, I'm afraid. But thanks anyway." He turned to Maria and smiled. "And if you're ever stuck like this again, please, come and tell me. The weather is too cold for hanging around outside." He looked back at her mother. “Mrs. McLoughlin would have a heart attack if anything happened to her star performer.”

Mrs. Rafferty put her hands over her mouth. “Oh, my God, Maria. The last thing you want is a cold with Christmas Eve on top of us. Into the bath with you right away and get warmed up.”

Maria turned to go on down the hallway. Then she looked back at Ray with a shy smile and said, “Thank you, Father.”

Ray smiled back. “Any time, Maria. And remember,” he offered Mrs. Rafferty an amused glance as he spoke, “no more skulking around the front of my chapel in the middle of the night.”

Mrs. Rafferty laughed and said, “Go on. Maria. Get out of those wet clothes.” She turned to Ray who was pulling on his raincoat. “And thanks again, Father. If she’d stood there for the next bus in that night, she could have caught a very nasty cold.”

Ray nodded as she pulled the door open for him and said, “It was no trouble. Goodnight Mrs. Rafferty. No doubt I’ll see you at mass on Sunday.”

“Of course, Father. Goodnight.”

He heard the door closing behind him as he ran for the car. As he was about to open the driver’s door, he glanced up at the second floor windows. His eye had caught a small movement. One of the curtains had twitched and was now held slightly open. He peered at it intently for a moment, motivated by something beyond curiosity or intellect. Suddenly he realised what he was doing and he quickly climbed into the driving seat. He sat for a moment, almost overcome by a confusion of thoughts and feelings. Taking a deep breath, he reached forward, switched on the ignition and drove off. The curtains did not fall back into place until the car was out of sight.

4

Ray did have a sermon to write. But long after he arrived home, he was still sitting in his study in front of a blank page. His brain simply would not focus on the theme of next Sunday's gospel. Scattered images behind his eyes, baffled attempts to analyse thoughts and feelings that refused to leave the hidden recesses of his mind and heart, strange feelings of guilt as he attempted to hold a conversation with the Lord about what had happened, all ensured that, whenever this sermon would be written, it would not be during the aftermath of his encounter with Maria. At times he sat at his desk, head bowed, his hands clasped so tightly in front of him that his fingers were white.

Pleading with the Lord for help, he said aloud, "Lord, what is going on here? Is this some kind of test, Lord? Something in me is drawn to that young girl, and I need to fight it. Lord, please, help me. I cannot understand these intense feelings, yet I do not believe I am allowing myself any feelings. I am trying with all my heart, Lord, to treat Maria like all of the others. I like her, of course, but I like many of the others too ..." His mind interrupted the prayer, unbidden, 'So why don't you feel the same disappointment when they miss practice as you do when Maria is absent?' With a despairing expression he answered as if it had been the Lord who spoke, "I don't know, Lord. I don't know. Oh God, please, please help me out of this." Mentally exhausted, he sat silently, thinking about Maria, her wet hair as she stood at the church door, the strange look she had given him in the car outside her home as if they shared some unknown secret, her shy smile as she bade him goodbye, and he prayed again, "And help Maria, too, Lord. I don't want her to be hurt in any way by this."

By what? His mind was racing again. 'You gave her a lift home. And you only said ... What did you say? "It was a horrible night. How was school. Ah, here we are." What are you getting so uptight about? What was there in any of that that should generate this guilt-ridden angst? Oh yes, there was that crack about the shower.' *Ah, come on! That was totally unintentional.* 'Maybe so. Maybe so. But something's up with you, boy, and you need to get your head sorted.' He leaned forward, elbows on the table, his head in his hands. *Is it because she's like Karen?* He forced himself to remember his childhood love. He could see her running to her car on the day of his parents' funeral. That had been a moment of intense pain for him. Did he feel the same pain now? He watched the memory playing on a screen in his mind and felt somehow removed from it. He tried to recall the emotions of the time but he couldn't. The pain was gone. How could that be? He rubbed his face with his hands. "Lord, Lord, please. What does that mean?"

Midnight came and went, and the anguished young priest still sat in his study, alternating between prayer and guilt and confused introspection as he sought the ease of conscience that would allow him to go to bed. His prayers, his pleadings, his distress about what was happening to him, exuded genuine mystification. He was unable to discern that something in his deepest heart of heart had control of his emotions, perhaps even part of his will, that his wretchedness was a surface response to a vexation of spirit that lay far beyond his conscious reach.

SIXTEEN

The nightmares have returned with a vengeance. During the previous few weeks he had found a modicum of peace. Bedtime had no longer brought the terrible tension that made sleep so elusive and so little desired. Sleep had, for a time, become uneventful, restful, leading him to believe that he was finally rid of the dreams. But now, every night, the horrors are more vivid than ever ...

In his sleep-state he experiences the same awful sick anticipation, the helpless fear. The physical sensations are equally overpowering, futile struggles against powerful arms, anguished pleas stifled by a rough hand, grating bristle against soft flesh, pain ... ... the sweating hyperventilation as he bursts into despairing wakefulness. But he is not awake. He moans but his body remains still, revealing nothing of the panic and futile struggle in his nightmare as ... *the child tries to fend off the powerful hands that pull him, inexorably, out of the foetal position that is his only feeble defence. Confusion intrudes as two leering faces hover in the darkness above him, merging and separating, both the same and yet, not the same. The faces share the same intent and cruel expressions, the same beady eyes, the same wet lips, but one is different, one is new. The child's hands beat helplessly against powerful arms and he whimpers in fear as his mind unconsciously tries to comprehend the additional presence that should not be there yet does not seem strange. He pleads in vain for the succour that will never come as the faces swim in and out of the blackness like two ghostly apparitions.*

Grunting and heavy breathing, and the movements that accompany them, are shrouded in the darkness but it is a darkness that offers no alleviation of the familiar but vile abuse that tortures his small body. A thick hand covers his mouth as he tries, first, to restrain his involuntary squeal as the pain sears him and then simply to breathe as the hand squeezes ever more tightly against his lips. The faces swim above, discernible even in the darkness, one silent in lustful intensity, one shouting, spitting, threatening. The child, in utter dread, no longer able to endure, shakes loose from the restraining hand and screams ... and screams ... and screams ... And the sleeper jolts into wakefulness, the echo of the screams ringing in his ears as he stares wide-eyed into the darkness of the night wondering where he is.

SEVENTEEN

1

Dan looked into the puzzled eyes of the young couple before him. He knew that they had expected something rather different from him, the young, popular and modern new priest who was such a breath of fresh air in the community. It was almost Christmas now and Dan had already made a considerable mark on the parish. He had fought tirelessly to achieve more laity involvement in the running of the parish. He had sought to do this firstly through attending meetings of the various parish and local societies, initially to get to know his parishioners and latterly by persuading the more resourceful and forward-looking to form the new parish 'core group' that Tony had mooted but had not quite managed to bring into being. That the group now existed was largely Dan's doing. Virtually every night of his week was taken up with attendance at meetings. He had meetings with the 'core group', of course, as well as meetings with the local Gaelic Athletic Association club as he sought simply to be a spiritual presence in this deeply Irish organisation. He met with kids in a small Youth Club in order to help them make sensible use of their evenings. He was working with his colleague, Father Gerard Mulvaney, in trying to find more meaningful ways of involving parents of children in the primary school in the preparations for the sacraments of Eucharist and Confirmation. He was trying, too, to make himself available to young couples preparing for marriage, offering, what he described in the Parish Bulletin as, 'a pre-marriage counselling service'.

It was in his capacity as 'pre-marriage counsellor' that he was now meeting with this young couple. The meeting had barely started but already there was evidence that it was going to be difficult. Dan was uncomfortably aware that priests abroad, in Europe, in America, and, indeed, not too far from his own parish, were tending to pass over in silence the issue of pre-marital cohabitation. Nothing in Dan's spiritual make-up could allow him to follow that lead. Cohabitation was wrong; it was sinful. How could he condone celebrating the sacrament of marriage and, indeed, the receiving of the Eucharist at the marriage mass, when the couple were clearly not in a state of grace? Yet he had already lost one couple who had stormed out of his room when he tried to explain the truth to them. Now here was another couple, two very pleasant and mannerly young people, who had quite happily admitted to him that they had been living together for over a year and had decided to solidify their relationship by getting married.

Eamon Donovan, tall, well-built, dark-haired, was still grinning, but his eyebrows were down, as he said, "Excuse me, Father. I don't understand. What do you mean, you can't marry us?"

Dan tried to refrain from an immediate response. He would lose this couple, too, if he started haranguing them like some sort of fundamentalist. But the commandments were there and they had to be obeyed. He offered them both his friendliest smile. "No, Eamon. I didn't say *I* couldn't marry you, but I am trying to say that the *Church* can't marry you if you are living together. You need to be in a state of grace to receive the sacrament of Matrimony."

Helen Murphy, a lovely girl with the same dark Irish looks as her boyfriend, said seriously but almost in disbelief, "You're telling us we're living in sin?"

Dan shrugged his shoulders. "I don't want to be that blunt about it, Helen, but how else would you describe it?"

"But we love each other; we're totally faithful to each other. We live honestly and work hard. We even go to Mass. We ..." She looked helplessly at Eamon for support.

Dan had gone to Ciaran, his parish priest, for advice after his previous debacle with a young cohabiting couple. He knew that he had perhaps been too direct, too forceful in explaining to the young pair the error of their ways. He had focused too heavily on the aspect of sin and had antagonised them almost from the start of the meeting. Now he looked in danger of doing the same thing again. Ciaran had offered some useful advice and Dan was too intelligent not to see the value of it.

"Don't start making them uncomfortable and putting them on the defensive. That just won't work. Work with them."

"But Ciaran, they must be given the truth of the gospel. I can't just ignore ..."

"No one expects you to, Dan. It's your approach I'm talking about. Speak the truth, of course, but speak the truth in love. Don't be accusatory. Show them that you understand," Ciaran had grinned, "even if you don't."

"But how do I get around the cohabiting?"

"You don't. You're going to have to try to get them to understand that they have an obligation to live separate, chaste lives in the run-up to the wedding. But do it in gentleness, Dan. Don't bellow at them."

Dan had answered, affecting injured innocence, "I don't bellow."

Ciaran had grinned again. "Maybe not with your voice, Dan, but even your quietest words often contain a distinct element of bellow".

Dan had been quiet for a moment, then said, thoughtfully, "You're not the first to say something like that to me. I had a couple of friends at Maynooth who were always on at me about it. But, Ciaran, right is right. People need to know that."

"I agree, Dan. I agree. But gently. Think about their feelings. Yes, I fully agree that you have to make your point, and the Church's point. Absolutely. But ease your way into the point you need to make. Okay?"

Dan now looked gently at Helen and felt her hurt. "Look, Helen, Eamon. First off, I am not blind to the fact that couples are living together all over the place without being married, in the cities, in the towns, in the country, in America, in England, in Ireland and even here at Kilnamoy. Television and films have made it such an ordinary thing that it seems to occur to almost no-one to question the morality of it any more. So, I can see why you're surprised at what I'm saying. But ..." he paused for a moment unsure about where to take this. "As Catholics, we, all of us, in the way we live our lives, are expected to give witness to the truth of our faith. We all do this in various ways and I would say that engaged couples are asked for the courageous testimony of chastity as a visible sign of their belonging to Christ." He stared for a moment at the silent couple.

Eamon was scratching his head. "I'm a bit lost here, Father."

"Well, to put it simply, Eamon, I suppose I'm talking about the Ten Commandments and in particular, the sixth, which deals with issues of sexual morality."

"But surely things have moved on, Father? I mean, we're living in the twenty-first century now. Times have changed; moral attitudes have changed."

Dan was shaking his head gently as Eamon spoke. "That's what I was saying earlier, Eamon. Society today has fallen victim to a spiritual malaise fed by TV, the Mass media, the crazy lives of so-called celebrities. Attitudes may have changed, but morality hasn't changed. Morality doesn't change. And deep down in people, if they stop to truly examine their attitudes, they will find a God-given awareness lurking there about what is right or wrong."

Helen was listening intently, her expression deeply serious. "If I hear you correctly, Father, you're telling us to live in separate houses or something or the Church won't marry us?"

"It's not just that. You have to ..." Dan began but caught himself and said. "I can't tell you to do anything, Helen, I don't have that authority. And it is not a case that the Church won't marry you. The Church can't marry you unless the ceremony is free of any what are called 'contradictory signs'. I'm sorry. I don't mean to sound rigid but ..."

The young couple looked at each other, communicating almost telepathically. It was not difficult, however, for Dan to read their thoughts. Helen put them into words. "But you can't expect us to separate now, Father? It's Christmas."

Dan almost had to bite his tongue to prevent his immediate response. It had been on the tip of his tongue to ask Helen if there was a better time than Christmas to look at their lives and get them in order. Instead, remembering Ciaran's injunction not to accuse, he tried to smile his gentlest smile. He could not have known that Eamon found his expression patronising.

"Well, Advent is a time of waiting, isn't it? Would it not be a good time, in the few months before your planned wedding to aim at deepening your love by living chaste and separate lives? This waiting period will also give you time to reflect on your decision to marry and perhaps we could meet a few times to talk about Catholic teaching on marriage and sexuality."

"Father," Eamon interrupted, "we're perfectly happy with our decision to marry. We didn't walk into it lightly."

"Of course you didn't," Dan responded quickly, "but, truly, a chaste separation before the wedding is the best way to prepare for your marriage."

"All right, Father. You've given us a lot to think about." Eamon stood up and moved aside slightly to allow Helen to do the same. "We'll have to go home now and discuss it." Helen, still seated, stared at her boyfriend, uncertain, perhaps wondering if she should persuade him to stay longer. But Eamon was adamant. "C'mon, Helen. We'll talk about this at home."

Rising from her seat, Helen looked helplessly at Dan and then followed Eamon who was already walking to the door. Dan, feeling deflated, thought, I've blown it again. Trying to retrieve the situation, he called after them with as much warmth as he could muster, "If you feel that you need to talk some more about this, my door is always open."

"That'll be fine, thank you, Father," Eamon said neutrally, holding the door open for Helen. "That'll be fine." And at that, they both left.

Dan groaned, staring at the door that Eamon had closed carefully behind him. *What do they expect from me? Surely there is still enough of an understanding of their faith in them to make them see that I could not have said anything else?* But, despite his conviction that he had spoken the truth with love and concern, he could not help feeling that he had failed again in his pastoral duty, that he should have handled the interview differently and found a way to assist the young pair along a path towards conversion.

2

"Och, Dan! Not again?" Ciaran's face was a mix of exasperation, amusement and sympathy.

"Ciaran, I did everything you told me. They just weren't prepared to listen. I mean, what else am I supposed to do?"

"Ah, what was it you think I told you?"

"To inform them with love, to be gentle, not to be judgemental." Dan held up his hands, looking questioningly at his parish priest.

"Mmmm! Did you mention living in sin, adultery, the sixth commandment, chastity.?"

"Yes, of course. How could I avoid that?"

"How many meetings have you had with this couple?"

"Ah, one."

"And how long were you into this meeting before you brought those things up?"

"Quite a while. Maybe half an hour."

"Dan, Dan. Can you not see? It's an issue of patience. I suppose you wanted their assent to chaste separation signed, sealed, and delivered before you would even discuss anything else?"

"Gee, I wasn't that bad ..." Dan started and then, ruefully, "Well, maybe it was a wee bit like that."

"Don't get me wrong, Dan. I understand exactly where you're coming from, and I agree with you. There's an indifference, even an apathy, among Catholics nowadays to their faith, our faith, and that poses a great threat and a great challenge to all of us, one we need to meet head on. But we don't meet individual people head-on. That's the time for circumspection and kid-gloves. Too aggressive an approach will simply drive them away."

"But, Ciaran, there's so much going on, so much to fight. I mean, we're trying to save the very sanctity of marriage here."

Ciaran nodded and was silent for a moment. Then he said, "Nobody ever said it was going to be easy, Dan. And the couple walked out on you. That was their choice. You were very unfortunate, this last wee while, to meet two couples who were so intransigent. They've clearly been having problems with their faith even before they met you. And I think it's going to get worse, for all of us. It's really tough on young people nowadays. The TV and the cinema and the aggressive secularism in the media ... the devil really is having a field day with those."

Dan's expression expressed puzzlement. "So, what are you telling me?"

Ciaran shrugged. "It's not all your fault, Dan. Maybe you have a bit to learn about how you approach these things, but I wouldn't want your heart anywhere other than where it is."

EIGHTEEN

1

Ray's alarm rang. It was five-forty five a.m., three days before Christmas. Every morning at this time it was his habit to slip out of bed, don a fleece-lined tracksuit and a woolly hat, and go for a five mile jog. His parish priest had scoffed scathingly when he learned of this.

"Keeping fit? Waste of time. No matter what you do, you'll be exactly like me when you're my age."

Ray had unavoidably been drawn to scrutinise his paunchy superior, the hunched shoulders, the jowly cheeks, the red-veined face, the heavy bags under the eyes, and fought to conceal any indication of the contempt he was feeling. *I won't ever allow myself to disintegrate like that.* "Well, you know, Father," he said, "fresh air, physical well-being, endorphins, help you deal with the pressures of life."

His superior had simply turned away with a grunt. "Hummmph! Endorphins."

Ray put out an arm to switch off the alarm and felt a sudden sharp pain in his left shoulder. He massaged it for a moment, wondering what might have caused it and climbed out of bed. He was feeling mentally weary, depressed even. Since he had arrived at Drumkillen, he had always enjoyed pounding the early morning pavements around the little town, hearing the rhythm of his powerful strides as his trainers hit the ground, watching his breath stream behind him in the cold air. It was physically demanding, especially during the cold mornings of winter, but more and more it had become a necessary antidote against the unease of spirit with which he found himself starting each day and against the sleepless nights that were becoming a feature of his life.

Now, however, he was beginning to experience a peculiar fatigue that sapped the joy out the morning run and he frequently arrived back at the parochial house exhausted and depressed. He dragged himself from his bed with a whispered "Good morning," to his maker and to his guardian angel and began to dress. He missed the customary anticipation with which he had started his runs in the past. This morning felt no different from the mornings of the past week or so. He rubbed his shoulder again and tried to ease the irritation with some wide circular arm movements. Then, pulling his woolly hat down over his ears he let himself quietly out of the house.

He had difficulty getting into his stride. Somehow the energy, the spring in his step, wasn't there. He ran to the edge of the town and along the main road into the countryside. It was still dark but there was more than enough light from a line of sodium lights that stretched for some miles along this road. They were there to light up the town's environs but they also serviced the three small housing estates that had materialised in recent years on the outskirts of the town.

Ray was breathing heavily but forced himself to keep running, hoping soon to find his second wind. His feet were hitting the ground like blocks of wood. He was dragging them rather than springing from one long pace to the next. A couple of miles passed like this but there was no lessening in the effort the exercise was demanding from him. He was considering slowing down to a walk when he discovered that he had come to the entrance of Elmwood Grove. He ran on, past the older houses at the front and into the estate. He found himself at Maria's house and for a moment he stopped, staring up at the second-floor windows, made visible by a streetlamp nearby. All of the curtains were drawn and there was no movement at any of them. He continued to stare, feeling nothing, scarcely aware of where he was. Then, with a start, he realised how utterly foolish this was and he began to run back the way he had come.

For some moments his weariness left him and he ran with something of his old vigour. But he was unaware of that as he began to question himself about the sheer idiocy of what he had just done. *What on earth took you there?* he admonished himself. *What if you had been seen? What if Maria had seen you?* He shook his head as he ran, mystified and deeply concerned. Something was happening to him. He was acting totally out of character and seemed powerless to stop himself.

He was sweating profusely, despite the morning cold, when he eventually let himself into the parochial house. He headed for the shower and, as he stood there with the water beating down on him as hot as he could bear it to ease his aching shoulder, he raised his eyes to heaven and in deep distress, cried, "What is wrong with me, Lord? Lord, I need your grace. Lord, why don't I feel your presence? Why have you forsaken me?"

2

Mass that morning was difficult for Ray. He struggled to maintain his focus on the Spirit and on the prayers. His shoulder hurt every time he held up his hands in blessing. He stumbled over the prayer of the Preface, losing concentration in the middle of it. It was holiday time and he found himself searching the congregation to see if by some chance Maria had come to the morning mass. He did not see her and felt a stab of disappointment. When it came time to pray over the bread and wine during the Offertory, he was overcome with a sense of guilt and, after bowing over the wafer for several long moments that had some members of the congregation staring questioningly at each other, it was only with an effort of will that he was able to pronounce the words of transubstantiation, "This is my body!"

As he held the host up for the congregation's adoration, he ignored the pain he was experiencing and prayed almost frantically, "Oh, Lord, forgive me. Oh, Lord, send me your help. Oh Lord, forgive me."

After mass he came out from the sacristy and knelt in one of the front pews, his head in his hands. He tried desperately to pray but something dark was imprisoning his spirit. He knelt for a long time but could only look into the blackness created by the hands that covered his eyes. He seemed incapable of conscious thought. There were several murmured 'Oh, Gods' but no coherent prayer found its way into his thoughts. At one point he found himself saying something to the Lord about being afflicted by a dark night of the spirit and pleaded that such a test was beyond his capacity to endure, that he could not cope without a real sense of the Lord's grace and his comforting presence. As he continued to kneel, he dropped his left hand to his side and, eyes closed and intent, he began unconsciously to massage his shoulder with his right hand. He became aware of the pain and, asking God once more for the grace he needed to get through the day, he rose from the pew, genuflected and left the chapel, deeply afflicted in heart and spirit.

3

Ray found himself becoming increasingly victim to an unrelenting lethargy that sapped his energy and made his ordinary day-to-day parish work seem interminable and exhausting. The nagging pain in his shoulder had now moved to his neck as well, making normal head movement difficult. He no longer went jogging in the mornings, scarcely able, indeed, to rise in time for morning mass, especially the early masses at Murnaghan's Bush. He now found himself regretting his impulse to offer these masses, particularly since the congregation rarely exceeded a dozen people. If his state were to get any worse, he would have to consider cancelling these masses and asking the parishioners to attend the later mass at Drumkillen. And what a perverse delight that would give McGennity.

But worst of all was the depression he was suffering, a black despair that almost overwhelmed him as he woke each morning. He was no longer able to turn to the Father and ask for help to live the day. He no longer had the spiritual energy to offer his usual morning greeting to his Guardian Angel. His waking moments were plagued instead with a desire to fade into nothingness, to lie still and unmoving, to escape a life that seemed to have less and less meaning. Only a strong sense of duty, which somehow seemed to survive in the dark melancholia that characterised his waking moments, enabled him to drag himself from his bed into another empty day.

The only consolation each day was his morning mass. Somehow, through the grace of the liturgy and the proximity of the living host, his spirit was able to absorb sufficient vitality to help him through the day. But it was a limited energy. He could give the day only minimal effort. His prayer-time suffered as did his ability to pray. Parish visits, except the most essential, were abandoned. He was spending more and more time sitting in his study, doing nothing, thinking nothing.

This change did not go unnoticed by Mrs. Toner who found herself becoming increasingly worried by the young priest's behaviour. She tried to ensure that nothing of the change came to the parish priest's attention but there were one or two of her friends who had remarked that Father Ray was, "... lookin' pale and tired these days. Is the oul' so-and-so overworkin' him, d'ye think?"

The housekeeper suffered no compunction in allowing that analysis some credence but she knew there was some deeper malaise troubling the curate. She tackled him about it in the kitchen one evening a couple of days before Christmas.

Ray's response to her concerned enquiry was the same as always. "I'm fine, Mrs. Toner. Don't be worrying yourself about me."

"Y'er not a bit fine, Father," she persisted, arms folded as she stood with her back to the cooker staring at him. "Y'er not yourself at all these days. Are you sick?"

Ray, who had been toying with the food on his dinner plate, pushed it quietly away from him. He looked at the housekeeper and tried to smile. "Of course I'm not sick. What gave you that idea?"

"Y'er not eatin'. Y'er spendin' far too much time by yerself in that study. Y'er not yer usual cheery self at all. Now, I'm not leavin' here till ye tell me."

Ray sighed. “It’s this awful pain in my shoulder. I told you already. It’s just that it’s in my neck as well. It’s wearing me down and I’m feeling tired all the time. That’s all. It’s probably the winter. I’ll be fine when the sun gets at it.”

“Y’er very young to be getting’ them kinda aches,” Mrs. Toner said and crossed the kitchen to a cupboard in the corner where she kept her handbag. “But I’ve brought you a tube of the stuff George gets from the doctor for his back. Rub that on ye after a hot bath. But ye should really go to a doctor and get him to look at ye.”

Ray accepted the tube of ointment she handed to him and said with a small smile, “Thanks, Mrs. Toner. I’ll rub it on tonight, I promise.”

Mrs. Toner sniffed and went out into the hall to get her overcoat. “Mind ye do. Why don’t ye go and have a bath now and get to bed early. A good night’s sleep would do ye the world o’ good.”

“Indeed, it would, Mrs. Toner,” Ray replied with feeling. “Indeed, it would.” He watched her as she fussily buttoned her coat. “Aye, maybe you’re right. I think I’ll try for an early night and see what happens.”

“All right, Father,” the housekeeper said, pulling on a pair of gloves. “I’m away now. Don’t forget to rub that on ye. And if it doesn’t help, y’er goin’ to the doctor, right?”

“Okay, Mrs. Toner,” Ray said, with a resigned nod.

“Aye, okay, Mrs. Toner,” she mimicked. “If y’er no better tomorrow, Father,” she said, wagging an admonishing finger at him, “y’er goin’ to the doctor, even if I have to drag ye round there myself.”

"All right, Mrs. Toner, all right." Ray found a small chuckle somewhere. "I will. I will."

She sniffed again and, gathering up her handbag, headed for the door. "Goodnight, Father. I'll see you tomorrow."

"Goodnight, Mrs. Toner," Ray called after her. "And thanks for the ointment."

4

The ointment, a strong embrocation that smelt foul, did offer Ray a modicum of relief from pain that night but its effects did not persist into the following morning. He woke, scarcely able to move his neck and still feeling exhausted. He experienced a vague disappointment that Mrs. Toner's magic elixir had done nothing to alleviate the bleak depression that shrouded him. Maybe she's right, he thought. I'm going to have to see the doctor. The very thought exhausted him but he knew that he would have to make the effort. He sighed wearily. I might get a chance to nip round after mass.

As he was putting on his overcoat to leave the house, he heard the post drop into the hall. He went to lift the letters and put them on the small table near the door. Before leaving them down he riffled through them, letters, bills, Christmas cards, not really caring whether or not there were any for him. There were four cards for him which he took to his room and threw on the table. He was about to leave when it occurred to him that he could well bump into one or two of the people who sent the cards. "Better know who they are," he muttered to himself. "They'll be expecting a 'thank you'."

Two of the cards were from parishioners whose names he vaguely recognised. The third was from a friend at Maynooth who was to be ordained sometime during the following spring. Ray's heart lifted at that. "I must write to him soon," he was mumbling to himself while he opened the fourth card. It was from Maria. He stood staring at the brief message. *Happy Christmas, Father Ray, from Maria.* He studied the words, whispered them aloud, touched them with his fingers, trying to squeeze more meaning out of them than was there, trying to see whether, in these simple words, there might be a deeper meaning.

He reached for the envelope. It was addressed to Father Ray Canavan. Father Ray? Was there a special significance in her use of his Christian name? And why not Father Raymond? *Don't be daft. Everybody calls you Father Ray.* He set the card upright on the mantelpiece and looked at it again. It was a Nativity scene. Well, you can't really try to make something out of that, he thought. Then he shook his head and upbraided himself, "It's only a Christmas card, you idiot. Get a grip." Nonetheless, despite his earlier depression and unknown to him, there was a quiet smile playing on his lips when he left the house.

Some time later, Ray was standing shirtless in Doctor Sean Hollywood's surgery. The doctor was standing behind him, probing his shoulders and neck. Sean, a hefty, red-faced man nearing retirement, was looking at Ray's back over a pair of half-moon glasses. His fingers pressed firmly here and there as he tested for muscle bunching or any signs of dislocation. His gaze was intent but he looked puzzled.

"Where exactly is the pain coming from, Father?" he asked, moving Ray's left arm up and down.

Ray hunched his shoulders a bit and said, “I don’t know. There doesn’t seem to be any obvious source. It’s just sore all over. Sometimes I think it’s coming from the back of my neck but the shoulder was sore before that.”

“Hmmmm! Okay, put your shirt back on.”

Ray dressed while the doctor wrote something at his desk. He put down his pen and looked at Ray, puzzlement evident on his features. “I can’t find a thing wrong with you, Father,” he said. “I mean, I know your shoulder and neck are paining you, but there’s no reason for it that I can see. It must just be the result of a draught. Maybe you pulled a muscle sometime recently but,” He shook his head in mystification. “I just can’t find anything. Give it a week or two and if the symptoms persist, get back to me. I’ll give you a rub in the meantime and some painkillers. Take them as you need them.” He handed Ray the prescription he had been writing. “That fatigue and the depression bother me a bit,” he went on. “But maybe they’re a reaction to the pain in your shoulder. I think I’ll leave that sit for a wee while as well. I don’t want to start you on Prozac or anything like that unless it’s really necessary. Your history doesn’t seem to warrant that at the moment.”

“Okay, Sean. Thank you.” Ray said, feeling disappointment. He had hoped for something more.

“Come back and see me in a couple of weeks,” the doctor said as he held open the door of his surgery. “If things haven’t improved, I can arrange for some more specific tests.”

“Thanks, Sean.” Ray nodded to him as he left the surgery. “Goodbye.”

“Goodbye, Father.”

NINETEEN

1

Drumkillen chapel was packed for 'Midnight Mass' on Christmas Eve, in the year 2003. In recent years the Mass tended to be scheduled for nine o'clock in the evening but, while one or two might have referred to it as the 'Christmas Vigil', no one ever considered referring to it as 'evening mass'. It was traditionally called 'midnight mass' and it is doubtful if that will ever change. The parish priest came up through the body of the chapel and into the sacristy to get vested for the Mass. He said to Ray who was already pulling on his alb, "Heck of a crowd here tonight."

"It's the new choir," Ray said. "You've got family members, relatives, school chums. The word's got around."

"Humph! I hope they're not going to be disappointed."

Ray, who was to concelebrate the mass, adjusted the cincture around his waist and said quietly, "I think you might be pleasantly surprised, Father."

Even as he spoke, the opening bars of The First Noel came to them from the altar. Father McGennity listened for a moment and then said grudgingly, "Not bad. I like the idea of the harmonies. Adds something to it."

Ray smiled quietly and pulled on his chasuble. "I'll go and check on the altar servers," he said.

Five minutes later the procession of four altar servers and two priests emerged from the sacristy and on to the high altar. The choir were ensconced on the altar, to the right and back towards the tabernacle. As the two priests climbed the steps, Ray glanced at the choir and gave them a smile of encouragement. He could not avoid Maria's intent gaze which held his for an instant before he turned his back on them to kiss the altar table in unison with Father McGennity. Perhaps it was the atmosphere in the church, perhaps it was the fact that Maria was seated only a few feet from him but, whatever it was, Ray found himself experiencing an ease of heart and a sense of anticipation that lifted him out of his depression for the first time in days.

The singing was marvellous. Moved by the importance and the solemnity of the occasion, the choir sang like angels and Ray found himself enjoying every moment of it. Father McGennity preached a predictable, if somewhat dull, homily about the real message of Christmas, urging his parishioners not to be too caught up in the tinsel and the glitter of festivity. Ray was seated facing the audience during the homily and he knew that many eyes were focused on him. He fought strenuously, therefore, to remain impassive and expressionless as the parish priest went on to exhort his listeners to avoid an excess of eating and drinking during this holy season.

The choir sang again during the Offertory, sang a softly harmonious version of *Ubi Caritas* during communion, and when the Eucharistic ministers were returning their chalices to the tabernacle, Maria stood to sing *O Holy Night.* The congregation was transfixed. As Maria's soaring soprano filled the church, Ray felt tears prickle the back of his eyes and he had to focus rigidly, head bowed, on the joined hands in his lap lest he betray himself. When the last strains of Maria's glorious singing faded into echo, there was a bustle of approval from the congregation as they breathed again, nodding and smiling at each other, deeply moved by the lovely hymn and the sweetness of the singing. After the final blessing the choir sang *Silent Night* and the priests and the servers left the altar.

For once, however, the usual scramble for the exits did not occur. No one wanted to leave until the last notes of the carol were sung. Mrs. McLoughlin was playing the piano with one hand, conducting wildly with the other, and smiling with delight. The choir had surprised even her. When the singing was over, the congregation burst into long and sustained applause and Mrs. McLoughlin rose from her seat, clapping as loudly as any of them. The choir-girls stood smiling sheepishly at each other, uncertain whether to bow or nod. Eventually the congregation began to file out of the church and some of the girls started gathering up song sheets and music stands while others began to carry chairs and benches into the sacristy.

Father McGennity emerged from the sacristy and, as he headed for the side exit, he took time to say to the girls in a show of unwonted expansiveness, "Well done, girls. That was beautiful singing. Well done. And thank you again, Mrs. McLoughlin, for your hard work in training these girls."

"Thank you, Father. Happy Christmas!" she said and, as the parish priest left she turned to the girls, making shushing noises. "Work quietly now, girls. Remember where you are."

Ray stayed in the sacristy stacking the chairs as they came in and, after some moments, he found himself suddenly alone. He was standing there, somewhat mystified, when one of the girls came in and said, with an odd smile on her face,

"Father, Mrs. McLoughlin wants to see you a minute."

Ray nodded. "I'll be right there." He adjusted some stacked chairs that were precariously balanced and went, unsuspecting, out to the altar. The choir were gathered there in a group, with Mrs McLoughlin standing in front of them. All were looking at him and smiling widely.

Ray's eyebrows went down. "What's going on?"

Mrs. McLoughlin smiled at him and looked at the choir. "Maria," she called.

Maria came out from the group and produced from behind her back a small package wrapped in Christmas paper. She came over to Ray, smiling shyly, and said, speaking as if she had learned it by rote, "On behalf of Mrs. McLoughlin and the choir, I have been asked to present to you this small Christmas present in thanks for your help and encouragement of us during all of the practices."

Ray was taken aback. He smiled at Maria and then turned to the choir. "Girls, you didn't need to do this. I enjoyed every minute of the rehearsals. Being there was no hardship for me. But thank you all very much. And your singing was wonderful tonight." And he smiled at them again.

Immediately all of them began to clap and sing, *"For he's a jolly good fellow ..."*

Ray could only stand there smiling, careful not to let his gaze linger on Maria. Some of the parents were still sitting in the pews waiting for their daughters and they, too, began to clap. Ray held up his hands, palms outwards. "All right, all right. Enough already. Thank you. Thank you. That'll do now, that'll do."

The applause and the singing degenerated into laughter and with a chorus of "Good night, Father" the choir began to disperse. Mrs. McLoughlin went to the foot of the altar to speak to one of the parents. Ray glanced around and saw that no one appeared to be paying any further attention to him. He turned to Maria who was still standing beside him and said, "Thank you, Maria." He held up the small packet. "Did you have anything to do with organising this?"

Maria smiled, slightly embarrassed. "We all collected for it," she said. "It's a gold ball-point pen." She hesitated and then said shyly, "But it was me who took it to the jewellers to get your name engraved on it."

They stood looking at each other. Then Ray said, smiling. "Oh, by the way, I got your card. Thank you. It was nice of you to remember me."

Maria's smile was wide. "Oh, that's all right, Father. I wanted you to know ... I just wanted to ..."

"I'm sorry, I didn't send you one."

"Oh, no worries, Father. You couldn't just send m... m ... .I mean, you couldn't be expected to send cards to everybody in the parish."

Ray smiled. "Yes, that's true but ..." He stalled, and then, in a rush, "Yes, yes, you're quite right."

"And I'm sure we'll all be sending cards."

Ray nodded and repeated, "Well, it was nice of you." Conversation stalled again. Ray stared into the chapel. "Are your parents taking you home?"

Maria pointed to a group near the exit. “Yes, they’re over there waiting for me.” She stared at him, her smile fading, “I ... just wanted to wish you a happy Christmas.”

“Thank you, Maria. I hope you have a happy Christmas, too.”

“Are you going home to your parents or ...?”

“No, I’ll be staying here. My parents are dead. I have no brothers or sisters so I’ll just hang around Drumkillen. Well, I do have an aunt. I’ll probably drive over to her for New Year’s Day.”

Maria’s expression became downcast. “Mrs. McLoughlin says there’ll be no more practices for a month or so.”

Ray smiled, trying to pretend he did not fully understand what Maria was saying. “Oh, that’ll be a nice break for you.” he said.

Maria stared at him and said seriously, “I’d rather have rehearsals.”

“Oh? You really do love singing, don’t you?”

Maria looked at him again, a hint of frustration in her eyes. “It’s not just that, Father. It’s ...”

Ray noticed Mrs. Rafferty approaching them. “Ah, here’s your mum.” And then, unwittingly, without thought, he whispered quickly, “I know what you’re saying, Maria.” Then he turned to her mother and said, “Hello, Mrs.Rafferty. And what did you think of Maria’s performance tonight?”

Mrs. Rafferty smiled. “Oh, we’re very proud of her. Wasn’t she marvellous?”

"She was indeed. They were all great. Drumkillen now has a very fine choir."

Mr. Rafferty appeared behind his wife. "Good evening, Father," he said. "Lovely ceremony." He looked cheerily at his wife and daughter. "Well, are we going home tonight or what?"

Maria walked down the steps towards him and turned once more to Ray, trying to hold his eyes. "Goodnight, Father. Happy Christmas!"

"Good night, Maria. Goodnight Mr. and Mrs. Rafferty. A happy Christmas to you all." He smiled at them and, with the briefest of glances at Maria, he went to join Mrs. McLoughlin.

2

When Ray finally settled in his study that evening to say his night prayers, his mind was in turmoil. He knew that the feelings he was experiencing for Maria were damaging to his priesthood and to his relationship with God.

"Lord," he said aloud, as he opened his breviary, "I didn't ask for this. I don't want this. Please help me." He waited, seeking some sense of the Lord's presence, of his listening. But tonight there was only darkness. He strained into the darkness, eyes shut, to find some connection with Jesus. "Are you there, Lord? Why can't I ...?" He sat totally still, seeking that comfortable togetherness with God that was always so much a part of his prayers. But tonight there was nothing. "Oh, God, I ... I can't pray like this."

He turned the pages of his breviary to the evening prayer hoping to find a way to pray through the printed words. He read the first few lines of the opening psalm with attention but somehow the words did not ring true for him.

'I will praise you, Lord, you have rescued me
And have not let my enemies rejoice over me.
O Lord, I cried to you for help
And you, my God, have healed me.'

The lines were as familiar to him as much-loved poetry but this night, as he spoke the words quietly, he felt somehow betrayed. His mouth continued to articulate the prayer, "O Lord, you have raised my soul from the dead," but in his sense of their inappropriateness to his situation, his mind wandered.

The murmured office continued unabated but Ray had no consciousness that his focus was now on the reason for his cry for help. He was replaying in his memory the scene at the altar after midnight mass. He was seeing Maria's beautiful hazel eyes, with their flecks of green, as he remembered her soft voice earnestly informing him that it was she who had arranged the engraving on his new pen. He was recalling the frustration in those same eyes when he resolutely refused to respond to her implicit plea for some tangible connection with him. With a start, he realised that it was the same plea he was making to his Lord and that his attention had wandered from his prayer. "Lord, I'm sorry," he breathed and returned his focus to the words before him.

"His anger lasts a moment; his favour all through life.
At night there are tears, but joy comes with dawn."

He shook his head. "No Lord, depression and pain and utter exhaustion come with dawn."

Yet tonight he had felt something akin to joy. He heard again Maria's voice soaring like an angel's into that gloriously moving high point of her solo. He heard again the swelling climax to the hymn,

'... down on your knees, O hear the angel voices
O night divine, O night when Christ was born,
O night di ... vi ... i ... i ... ne ...'

The towering, beautifully sustained cadenza echoed over and over in his mind, transporting him back to the moment of the singing, to the subsequent hush in the chapel of utter appreciation, to the face of the singer, to his own unforgivable lapse, *"I know what you're saying, Maria."* He never should have said that. His office forgotten, he closed his eyes and raised his head, "Oh God, what have I done? What have I done? Why did I say that?"

He rocked in his chair, distressed, confused, fearful. He could not know that something dark and threatening buried in his psyche was forcing its way to the surface, was taking hold of his mind, of his heart, of his emotions. He could not see that in unconscious effort to escape the increasing grip of this dark horror, his mind and his heart sought solace in light, any light, Maria's light, that would ease the depth of the depression that was threatening to overwhelm him. He could not know that his very soul was beaten almost into subjection, that his prayer now needed a force of will that his dull listlessness was less and less capable of supplying.

His dreams that night were a confused kaleidoscope of senseless images but one sequence played over and over in his mind during the night, leaving him with the full memory of it in the morning, causing him to wake exhausted and victim more than ever to his now constant depression. In the dream he had found himself standing in a huge vista of crumbling walls, heaps of rubble and stones, ruined buildings as far as his eye could see. It was as if a huge bomb had utterly demolished some war-torn town, he did not know where. All he knew was that here was a landscape that was alien and dead. Suddenly, some distance away, he caught a glimpse of Maria, a single flash of colour in the grey desolation, climbing over a broken wall. He shouted and tried to run after her but his movements were sluggish. Try as he might to catch her, he felt as if he were running through glue. His limbs were almost incapable of movement. He forced his way forward to where he had seen her and once again caught a glimpse of her, several yards ahead, disappearing behind a huge pile of rubble. “Maria!” he shouted. “Maria!”

If she heard him, she gave no sign. When he got to where he had last seen her, she was gone again. For what seemed like hours he searched in desperation, forcing himself to climb crumbling walls, to clamber across heaps of debris, to rush to the point of exhaustion around grey featureless corners, but his dream afforded him no further glimpse of ... of *She, most beautiful woman, lovely as Tirzah ...*

And a chorus from the Song of Songs tortured the rest of his sleep:

‘I beg you ...
by the gazelles and hinds of the field,
not to arouse or stir up love
before her time has come.’

TWENTY

1

Christmas dinner at the parochial house was a cheerless affair. Mrs. Toner was in and out of the dining-room, passing the odd comment about this parishioner or that but otherwise conversation was desultory and sporadic. Towards the end of the meal, after Mrs. Toner had left to join George at her daughter's, Fr. McGennity rose from the table and carefully folded his napkin.

"I have to go to Dublin for a couple of days. I promised some friends I'd call. You'll be able to hold the fort here, won't you?"

"Of course, Father. No problem. It'll be quiet for a day or two," Ray replied.

The parish priest nodded brusquely and made for the door. He stopped and looked back. "There's not much point in my hanging around. I'll probably go on in an hour or so."

"By all means, Father," Ray said. "You don't want to be driving in the dark. And don't worry," he added, a touch pointedly, "I'll clear up here." But the barb, in truth, was half-hearted. He much preferred to have the house to himself.

"Yes indeed. Right. Okay, then. Ah, happy Christmas!"

"Happy Christmas to you, too, Father."

2

Despite his preference for being alone in the house, Ray found this Christmas Day long and anything but happy. He struggled with some pointless television pap for a while, gave up on it and tried to read. He couldn't focus on the words. His mind raced back and forth from the midnight mass to the strangely coherent dream, from Maria's pleading face to the twitching curtain on the second floor of her house. He threw the book aside and paced the room, stopping to stare dejectedly out of the window in the direction of the Elmwood Grove estate. *Lord, God, what is wrong with me?* He shook his head and headed purposefully for the dining room. "Right," he muttered. "I'll clear this mess up and leave the kitchen spotless for Mrs. Toner in the morning."

A couple of hours later he was back in his study again. He had found a passably interesting movie on television that he felt he could watch. He settled himself in his armchair and tried to lose himself in the interaction between the characters. Towards the end of the film, the phone rang. He dragged himself from the armchair and went out into the hall. He lifted the receiver and said, "Parochial House. Father Canavan speaking." There was no response. Ray tried again. "Hello? Is there someone there?" The line remained silent but Ray could sense a presence at the other end. His priestly instinct led him to further enquire, "Hello, hello, are you troubled ... in any kind of need? Do you need my help?"

At that point, there was a sudden click at the other end as the caller hung up. Ray replaced the receiver, his expression puzzled. He went back to the study, noticing that dusk was already turning the window black. *I wonder if that was someone with a problem,* he mused. *Or a prank caller?* Or, he could scarcely allow himself to consider the possibility, Maria? *Don't be daft. Why would she call and not say anything?* He sat down in front of the television again but the call had generated a restlessness in him that caused him to lose all interest in the flickering shadows on the screen in front of him. His thoughts fluttered, unsettled, like a small agitated bird in a cage. It couldn't possibly have been Maria, could it? He went back into the hall and opened the front door of the house. He stood there peering into the drab emptiness of the front garden and the road beyond. Nothing moved in the still evening, not even the last remaining leaves on the occasional bare tree.

It was not raining but the evening was dank. The beginning of a heavy December fog hung in the air, becoming increasingly impenetrable in the growing dusk. It was cold and uninviting but Ray, without conscious decision, almost without volition, went back into the house and pulled on a heavy overcoat, gloves and his woolly hat. As he pulled the front door shut behind him, he thought dejectedly how much he would have preferred to jog but he simply did not have the energy. He would have to settle for a walk.

Ray knew that there was something wrong with him. He did not know what. He did not know that he was gradually losing touch with himself. Something in his psyche was succumbing to a dark desolation, beginning to move him in ways and attitudes and feelings that were not his. And in that darkness, something was trying to hack and claw its way to a point of ease and solace that somehow signalled danger as much as it signalled peace. Yet something else in him did not want to recognise this fact. To acknowledge it would demand that he arrest any movement towards the only light that seemed to be shining on his emotive horizon. His intellect disengaged from his emotions and found itself toying with a line from Thomas Merton. It was something like, '... frequent darkness and increasing contradictions.' When Ray had read that line some months before, he could not grasp what Merton meant. Now he wondered. But then he shook his head dismissively. Whatever the lines meant, they had nothing to do with this.

Something of a fugue state was beginning to inhabit his consciousness as he made his way on to the main road and towards Elmwood Grove. He walked steadily into the growing night, his face impassive, feeling nothing, thinking nothing, seeing nothing. He simply walked, drawn by instinct or need or ... he did not know. He was not even sufficiently aware to ask himself the question. He could not know that a battle had begun in his subconscious, that some part of his mind was rejecting any impulse to analyse and explain what he was doing, and that another part, weak, feeble, failing, was trying desperately to draw the attention of his heart's core to the truth of what was happening.

He arrived at the entrance to Elmwood Grove without surprise or elation. He simply checked to ensure that the estate was empty of passers-by and, keeping to the shadows provided by various trees and hedges, he walked on towards Maria's house. Sheltering safely in the dark lee of a huge hedge of leylandii that should have long before been cut down, he studied the windows of Maria's house. Some of the tension drained from him as he stared at the house, one or two windows showing chinks of light behind the heavy drapes that covered them. Feelings and thought began to return. *My God! What am I doing here?* He made to walk away but found his eyes drawn back again to the chinks of light. He walked backwards for a few feet, not wanting to leave but aware now of the utter futility of what he was doing.

His heart was heavy as he emerged from the estate on to the main road. *So what do you think you achieved by that nonsense,* he chided himself, *apart from making yourself feel twenty times worse?* He walked home, aware again of the wearying lassitude that slowed his pace, of the pains in his neck and shoulder, of the priestly conscience that was shrieking at him now to stop this nonsense and get his life, and his spirit, back on track.

TWENTY-ONE

1

Ray was sitting on the three-legged stool in the corner of the boxing ring, bruised, bleeding and exhausted. One of his seconds was throwing water over his head and sponging blood from his eyes. He could hear the bell ringing insistently, demanding that he return to the fray. He pushed a tired fist out in front of him as if to ward off the bell, his opponent, his seconds, anyone or anything that demanded movement. "I'm too tired," he groaned.

"You have to get up," his trainer was urging him. "There's the bell. Get up! Get up!"

Ray was too exhausted to move but the bell wouldn't stop. Its clangour filled his head, demanding response. Then suddenly he sat upright in his bed, lifting his hands to his head. "What ...?"

But the bell kept ringing and suddenly he realised that someone was at the front door. He reached for his track-suit which was on a nearby chair, glancing at the luminous dial of his bedside clock as he did so. Twenty to three. Who could be calling at this hour of the night? He pulled on his clothes and a pair of slippers and hurried through the darkness of the narrow corridor. The bell stopped ringing before he reached the door but he struggled with the heavy mortise lock, muttering to himself, “Hold on a minute, I’m coming.”

He dragged the door open and Maria, who had apparently given up hope of an answer, had already reached the front gate. She had turned, however, when she heard the key in the lock and was walking back towards him. She was wearing a duffle coat and jeans but he could see that she was freezing in the cold night air.

“Maria!” he exclaimed, amazed. “What on earth ...?”

She huddled in the coat, arms clasped around herself. She was shivering violently as she tried to say, “I ... I waited over there for ... for an hour or so to make sure that Father McGennity w ... w ... wouldn’t be back. I ... I ...”

“Come in a minute,” Ray said, “before you catch your death of cold out there.”

He stood aside as she went past him into the hall. “What are you doing standing out there in the middle of the night?” But, without waiting for an answer, he went on, “Come on down to the study. There’s a bit of a fire left. I’ll stoke it up.” He looked at her as he turned on the light. “My goodness, you’re blue with cold. What are you ... What ...?” He couldn’t frame a coherent question. He waved her to an armchair. “Sit down. Sit down. I’ll try to get this fire going.”

Maria sat on the edge of the chair, her shivering continuing unabated. Ray did what he could with the fire, putting on a few small sticks to speed up the blaze. But it was going to take a few minutes. He looked at the frozen girl, her lips quivering, her breaths coming in ragged gasps. He moved towards her, one hand stretched out. “Come here,” he said. “Come here. Stand up. I’ll put my arms around you for a few minutes to try to get some heat into you." Maria hesitated, still huddled on the chair, staring at him with wide eyes. "It's all right," he said, looking at her seriously. "It's going to take that fire a few more minutes and you'll have frozen to death by then."

Maria responded with a brief, shy smile and got up to meet him, her arms still huddled around her. Ray pulled her close, rubbing her back and the sides of her arms with, what he hoped was, clinical detachment. They stood like that for a few moments, Maria with her head down against his shoulder, her hands under her arms, and Ray, standing upright like a soldier on guard duty, massaging her back and arms. Suddenly Maria put her arms around Ray's chest and clung to him. Ray, startled into stillness for a moment, stood with his arms apart looking down at the top of her head. But Maria was still shivering, so he finally put both arms around her and they remained like that, wordless, until the girl's shivering finally began to subside.

Ray's mind was whirling. He was utterly confused. He had many questions to ask her but he found that when he wanted to speak he could think of nothing to say. Her closeness was beginning to affect him. He remained very still but he wanted to stroke her hair, touch her face, look into her eyes ... mad things. He stepped back, disengaging himself from Maria's arms, and said quietly, "Okay. Let's sit and talk. But first, would you like a cup of hot tea, hot chocolate, coffee?"

Maria perched again on the edge of the armchair. Her eyes were still wide, almost fearful, when she looked up at him and her voice was so low that he could scarcely hear her. "Coffee, please."

"All right," he said, poking the fire into life, "I'll just be a minute." He smiled encouragingly at her. "Warm yourself there till I get back."

A few minutes later he was back with a small tray containing two cups of coffee, a small milk jug and a plate of chocolate biscuits. Maria was still sitting as she was when he left her.

To ease the tension he said, "I need help to get rid of these chocolate biscuits or I'll blow up like a balloon."

Maria smiled, a nervous tight-lipped little smile, accepted a coffee and balanced a biscuit on her knee as she poured some milk into her cup. Ray took the jug from her and put it on the tray which he placed on the table. He sat on the chair opposite Maria and looked at her over the rim of his cup as he sipped his coffee. Maria glanced at him and then at the fire as she nibbled her biscuit. Ray wondered how he could ask her what she was doing here without sounding like a schoolteacher. When she glanced his way again, he raised his eyebrows and smiled enquiringly, hoping that she would be the first to break the ice.

Maria finished her biscuit and looked at Ray, this time holding his gaze. "I'm sorry, Father," she whispered.

"For what?"

"Disturbing you in the middle of the night, getting you out of bed."

"That's not a problem, Maria. But why ...?"

"I just kept thinking about you here on your own on Christmas Day. I was out for a walk ..."

"At a quarter to three in the morning?"

Maria shrugged slightly and went on, "… and I noticed that Father McGennity's car was away. I know he stays away overnight quite a lot."

"Oh? How did you know that?"

"Everybody knows. But I saw your car was here."

Ray, guiltily thinking about his own walk, did not ask why she had been outside the parochial house. Instead he said, "And how did you get here? And when? Do your parents know you're out?"

Maria shook her head. "No. I waited until everyone was asleep; then I slipped out."

"What time was that?"

"Shortly after one."

"Goodness! And you walked here? What time did you get here?"

"I'm not sure. About twenty to two, I think."

Ray sucked in a breath through his teeth. "Heavens! You've been standing outside for over an hour, in that weather?"

"I wasn't sure if Father McGennity would be coming back. I wanted to be sure."

"Sure? Ah, sure of what?"

Maria flushed but she said, pleading with her eyes for him to understand. "I wanted to wish you a happy Christmas, maybe stay a wee while with you for company. I didn't want the parish priest suddenly appearing ..."

Ray looked at the girl, his heart deeply moved by her naïve innocence. He wanted her to stay and, realising that, he was filled with guilt. "Maria, that was a lovely idea, but you can't stay here in the middle of the night. I'll have to drive you home."

Tears started into Maria's eyes. "Please, Father, this was so hard for me. Please, let me stay a little while. We never talk. I'll go in a little while."

Ray stared into the hazel eyes, at the green flecks emphasised by the glistening tears, and he felt his heart melt. He knew he should take her home immediately. He knew that he should not encourage her obvious crush on him. But he also knew that his depression had utterly lifted. Despite the tension he was under, he felt suddenly alive again, excited, sensing a joy in this meeting that was in utter opposition to everything he had been experiencing for the previous couple of weeks. And he thought, "She's here now anyway. What harm would another hour do? Maybe we can talk some sense into each other."

2

Traffic into Drumkillen on St. Stephen's Day was not normally heavy at the best of times and at five o'clock in the morning the main road was empty of cars. About fifty yards from the entrance to Elmwood Grove Maria said, "Maybe you should drop me here, Father. I can slip quietly into the estate without anybody noticing."

Ray was doubtful. "If I stop here at five in the morning and someone happens to drive by, it might look at bit peculiar. My car is fairly well known." He looked at the solemn face beside him. "I'll drive half-way into the estate. I won't go as far as your house. If anyone sees my car coming out they'll just think I was visiting somebody there."

Maria nodded seriously. "Okay, Father."

Ray turned into the entrance and drove the car quietly to a shadowed spot between two streetlamps. He turned the car-lights off but left the engine running. He looked again at Maria who was half-turned towards him.

"Thank you for being so kind, Father," she said, "I ... I really enjoyed my visit with you"

Ray's expression was gentle and he gave the girl a slow, quiet smile. But his mind was racing. His heart was full. There was much he could have said, none of it appropriate. He simply said, "It was nice of you to come to see me, Maria, even if it was at an hour that could hardly be considered normal." Maria's shy smile tore at his heart. He was less and less able to see past her loveliness. With an effort he said, "You'd better go."

Maria nodded but seemed reluctant to move. It was as if she had something yet to say. Then in a rush she said apologetically, "That was me on the phone tonight, Father." She stared at him, begging understanding. "I just wanted to hear your voice. I couldn't speak because I didn't want Dad or Mum to hear me on the phone. I'm sorry for hanging up like that."

Then before Ray could respond, she leaned suddenly forward and kissed him gently on the cheek. Her eyes were glistening with new tears as she pulled quickly away and opened the door. Just before she stepped out, she turned to him again and whispered, "I'll miss you during the holidays, Father." She got out quickly, closed the door gently, and ran soundlessly to the far side of the street.

Ray stared after her for a brief moment and then reversed the car into a nearby drive before turning back on to the main road.

"Oh God! Oh God! Oh God!" he muttered, as he drove back towards the parochial house. "What am I doing? What have I done?" He was assailed by feelings of guilt yet stared at the dark road before him trying to identify specific fault. Maria had come to *him*. To send her away, almost freezing to death, would have been unconscionable. He had been circumspect in what he had allowed himself to say but ... his mind replayed the couple of hours they had spent together in his study. Perhaps he had been too willing to let her stay. Thirty minutes would have been sufficient to restore her body heat. Then he should have driven her home. But she was so alive, so vibrant.

They had talked easily about ordinary things. She had risen from her chair at one point and had walked around the room, looking at his sports trophies, reading the details on his framed diplomas, shyly admiring the photographs of his first graduation and his ordination. She had examined his CD collection, nodding in recognition at the various classical labels and suddenly exclaiming in delight, "Eva Cassidy. I love her. She's brilliant."

"I know," he had replied. "According to the Guardian she was one of the greatest voices of her generation."

She had been studying the list of songs at the back of the box and then looked up shyly. "This one is beautiful," she had said and inserted the CD into the machine. She selected a track and stood by the machine during the slow melodious opening. Ray had listened with her, his heart already caught by the plaintive, achingly sweet violin. Then Maria sang too, her pure voice soft but effortless, telling of lovers before a winter fire in the darkness of night, of colours from the flickering embers painting their faces, now orange, now gold.

Ray had not been able to take his eyes from her. He may or may not have been familiar with Noel Coward's comment about the potency of popular music but he was now experiencing its power in its full force. He had sat, entranced, unaware that he was smiling. Maria had continued to sing, leaning slightly towards him, her voice slightly less muted but remaining ineffably sweet. It was clear from her expression and her own soft answering smile that she was pouring her heart into the words, words of love, words to say that even now she was beginning to know his heart, words to say that his smile, his sweet face, would remain forever engraved in her memory. "That was beautiful, Maria," Ray had breathed when the song ended, "absolutely beautiful. You really have a wonderful future as a singer."

Maria had flushed, clearly pleased by his praise, but as she sat down on the armchair again she shrugged her shoulders and said, "Oh, I don't know. I'm really hoping to study medicine."

Ray had nodded. "A noble calling," he had said, immediately chiding himself inwardly for sounding like a stuffy college professor.

"What is university life like?" Maria had then asked.

Ray had been stunned by the strength of his reaction to that question, a sudden stab of jealously followed by an equally debilitating stab of regret that she would experience college life far from him. But he had tried to answer her question and she had sat enthralled by tales of his days in Maynooth. Ray had seldom in his life talked so much about himself, or for so long, but Maria's ingenuous responses, her intense interest in everything he had to say about himself, had allowed him to escape from the depression and the pains that for weeks now had been constant companions into a world of youthful laughter and easeful friendship.

As the road continued to fall away on either side of him, he drove mechanically, scarcely registering his surroundings. He was looking back at himself, sitting comfortably in his armchair, talking quietly but with a deal more animation than was his wont, smiling at the lovely girl sitting across from him. At one point she had risen from the chair, removed the duffle-coat she had been wearing and threw it over the back of her chair. Ray had experienced a moment of unease at that point, fearful of the feelings he was experiencing but he forced himself to continue talking quietly. Maria had sat down again, her legs curled under herself, one elbow on the arm of her chair, her hand supporting her chin as she leaned towards him, her gaze fixed on his as he talked. Oh God! What was so wrong about that? And a voice, sharp and impatient, sounded loudly in his head. *Raymond, you were loving her. And she was loving you. That's what was wrong. You're a priest, man. Where's your reason?*

When he had eventually forced himself to declare that it was time to take her home, he had risen and held her coat for her while she put her arms into the sleeves. Did he brush against her at all? Even slightly? "Oh, God," he whispered aloud in anguished guilt, *I don't know. I don't know*. But she had turned to him at that point, not six inches from him, and stared solemnly into his eyes for a long moment. And all he could do was stand there and stare back, making no effort to break the spell. *Well, you did step back and indicate the door. Oh yes, very laudable. But not before you had a very intense conversation with the girl. No, no, you didn't use words, my friend, that's true, and neither did she, but you both spoke volumes to each other, volumes.*

Ray slowed to drive his car back into the parking place in front of the parochial house. When he attempted to get out of the car, the dreadful lassitude that had afflicted him over the past weeks was back. So, too, was the depression. He had to haul himself out by pulling on the steering wheel with one hand and pushing against the seat with the other. He felt like a tired, old man. He locked the car and let himself back into the house, overcome with weariness and mental exhaustion. Even the pains were back and he was almost hunched as he made his way along the corridor to his bedroom.

As he flopped into bed he raised a tortured face to the ceiling. "Lord," he cried aloud, "this is way beyond my strength. When I am with her she is my solace. There are no pains, no weariness, no depression. I live when she is near; I disintegrate when she is not. Why are you allowing this to happen?" He lay awake, staring at the ceiling, his mind alternating crazily between visions of Maria and lines from Psalm 41,

'My soul is cast down within me ...
Why have you forgotten me?
Why do I go mourning,
oppressed by the foe?'

When eventually something resembling sleep did come, it was filled again with tortured dreams of frantic chase through the ruins of the bomb-blasted town, searching, searching, for Maria, until prodded again into wakefulness by the exhaustion of frustration and the heartbreak of failure.

TWENTY-TWO

1

"Myocardial infarction?" Tony's voice registered puzzlement.

"Yes, a heart attack, I suppose you might say, although that descriptor is altogether too vague."

Tony was standing in a corridor of Dublin's Mater Hospital, speaking with one of the attending physicians. Bishop Flannagan had been admitted the previous night, having collapsed at a friend's house during some post-New Year celebrations.

"It sounds a bit like angina." Tony's own father had suffered from angina and the report he had heard of the bishop's symptoms seemed similar.

"No." The consultant shook his head and reeled off a jargonistic explanation with no consciousness that his language was in any way impenetrable. "We're pretty good now at detecting small infarcts and distinguishing them from unstable angina. We now have some highly sensitive and specific markers of cardiac muscle necrosis which, even in the absence of electrocardiographic changes, are capable of detecting infarction. In your friend's case, blood supply to one of the main cardiac arteries is blocked. We have tests still to do, of course, but you could be looking at by-pass surgery."

Tony pondered this. "And if surgery can be avoided ...?"

"Well, we'll need to get the blood flowing again. The patient is going to have to quit smoking, cut well back on alcohol, and do some exercise to lose weight."

Tony winced. He had a sudden vision of the bishop in jogging gear and shook his head as if to clear the image. *I don't think so,* he thought. Aloud he said, "Thank you for that, doctor. I'll pop in and see him for a few minutes."

The doctor nodded and walked off down the corridor. Tony went to the door of the bishop's small private ward, knocked, and poked his head in. The bishop was lying on his back, slightly raised on to a couple of pillows. There were wires and tubes linked to an ECG machine and a drip on a tall stand but the bishop was awake and seemed otherwise comfortable.

Tony went on into the room and pulled a nearby chair to the side of the bed. "Well, Bishop," he said. "You gave us all quite a scare."

The bishop snorted dismissively. "A lot of fuss and bother over nothing. I should be out of here already but they insist on doing all these bloody tests."

Tony laughed and said, "Ah now, you'll have to take it a bit easy for a while. The doctor is talking about cardiac problems."

"Hmmph! Might be that, might only be indigestion." He paused and then looked resigned. "But I suppose I'd best let them get on with it."

"Yes, I think that might be wise," Tony said.

There was a slight pause and then the bishop said, "I'm glad you came to see me. It might be that I will be off work for a while. You're going to have to hold the fort."

Tony's face remained expressionless but he was experiencing a small tremor of inner excitement. "Yes, well, with you in the background offering advice and keeping an eye on me, I suppose I could handle it," he said carefully.

"Of course you can. You can check my diary and fill in for me as much as possible over the next few weeks. Not that there's an awful lot. Oh yes, I'm scheduled to go to Rome the second week in February. Maybe you'll stand in for me there. I like to keep abreast of what's going on."

"That won't be a problem, Bishop," Tony replied neutrally. "I think I can manage that. I'll clear my own diary for that week."

A nurse came in carrying a tray with syringes and some phials and small dishes. "Hi there!" she said breezily. "I've come to collect some blood."

Tony rose from his chair. "I think that's my cue to go."

"Oh, you don't need to go on my account," the nurse said. "I only need three or four small phials. You can stay and watch if you like."

Tony said seriously, "I think I'll forgo that pleasure, thank you." He turned to the bishop. "Don't worry about a thing. I'll take good care of everything."

"See that you do," the bishop said and then added with a grin, "And Tony, you will be held to account for all and any scandals that occur while you are in charge."

"Don't worry, Bishop," Tony grinned back. "If anything was brewing, I'd know about it already."

"Good man."

Tony nodded. "Take it easy while you're here, Bishop. Rest and enjoy yourself. I'll be back to see you in a couple of days."

2

The phone rang while Ray and Father McGennity were finishing their evening meal. Father McGennity was sitting back on his chair holding the day's newspaper open in front of him. Ray was staring bleakly into his coffee cup.

"Get that, will you," the parish priest muttered from behind his paper.

Ray rose sluggishly from the table and went into the hall. He lifted the receiver. "Parochial house. Father Canavan speaking."

"Hello, Ray. How are you? Happy New Year!" It was Tony's voice.

Ray perked up immediately. "Hi, Tony. Good to hear your voice. Happy New Year to you, too."

"Thanks. Well, how're things?"

"Oh, you know. Doing a bit here and there."

"Look, are you about tomorrow evening?"

"Thursday? Yeah, I've nothing on, as far as I know."

"Good, I'd like to come and see you. Have a wee chat."

Ray's blood froze. Surely he couldn't have heard about Maria? Oh God! Had someone seen them slipping out of the parochial house at five in the morning? Ray fought a rising panic and tried to sound natural as he said, "Yes, that'd be great. I look forward to that, Tony."

"Good. You'd better let Father McGennity know. Tell him the visit is unofficial. I'm only visiting a friend. We don't want him getting paranoid about it."

Ray forced a laugh. "Okay, I'll let him know."

"I'll drop in after your evening meal. Half six? Seven?"

"Either's good," Ray said.

"See you then. 'Bye!"

There was a click on the other end as Tony disconnected. Ray replaced his own phone slowly. So, it was just a private chat? *Still, that doesn't mean he's not coming to talk about Maria. Dear God! How could he have heard? Well, no point in worrying until he gets here.* Ray tried to quell his growing anxiety and went back to the dining room to tell the parish priest about the canon's impending visit.

Ray was on tenterhooks all of the following day. He rehearsed a half a dozen possible explanations for Maria's presence in the parochial house in the small hours of the morning but none of them sounded remotely convincing. He tried to lose himself in his work, carried out a couple of long-neglected sick visits, called into the school to see Mrs. McLoughlin about her pastoral plans for the next term, all of which demanded his attention but did little to quell the nagging anxiety that followed him around during the day.

At seven the doorbell rang. The parish priest got there before Tony, greeted the canon cordially and spent a few minutes with him in general conversation. Ray hovered in the hall until the exchange was over and greeted Tony with a warm handshake. "Great to see you, Tony. Come on down to my study. There's a good fire lit."

"Thank God for that," Tony smiled. "That's some night. I hate the rain on my windscreen at night. All those flamin' on-coming headlights; half the time I can't see where I'm going." He pulled off his overcoat and gloves as they entered the study and handed them to Ray who threw them on a table. As Ray turned back to invite Tony to sit, he saw a sudden startled expression creep on to the canon's face. "My God, Ray!" Tony exclaimed. "What on earth have you been doing to yourself?"

Ray gestured to an armchair, inviting Tony to sit. "Uh ... what do you mean?"

"Look at you! You've lost weight; you're deathly pale; your cheeks are all hollow. What ...?"

Ray smiled. "Oh, that? It's just something ..." He raised his hands. "A few weeks ago I started to get this pain in my neck. It's gone into my shoulders as well. It's very wearing. It's giving me a bit of bother and it doesn't seem to be going away. That's really all ..." he trailed off.

Tony was filled with concern. "I have to be honest, Ray. I don't like the look of you at all. Have you been to see a doctor?"

"Yeeess, but he didn't really seem to know much about what the problem is. He gave me some painkillers."

"Aye, painkillers. The general practitioners' fallback when they haven't a clue." He stared at Ray. "I'm sorry to be going on, Ray, but you really do look terrible. It's hard to believe a pain in the neck could do that to you."

"Well, I've also been troubled with a pretty severe depression, especially in the mornings, and I seem to be exhausted all the time."

"Mmmm! That makes more sense. I mean, it explains your appearance. But what have you to be depressed about?"

"I've no idea. It's just there. No reason for it that I can see."

Tony stared into the fire, clearly searching for a suggestion that might be useful. After a few moments, he turned to Ray again and said, "I'll tell you what. I have a good friend in Dublin, Tim Bathgate. He's a specialist who has his own practice. He has a great reputation as a diagnostician. I'm going to make an appointment for you with him. He's very busy so I don't imagine he'll be able to see you right away. But I'll push him a bit. Maybe two or three weeks, okay?"

"Yes, Tony. That's kind of you. This thing is beginning to get me down. I'd be glad to have it diagnosed and sorted."

"Good."

They sat in silence for a while and then Ray said, "Can I get you something, tea, coffee, something stronger?"

Tony smiled. "Night like that, I wouldn't mind a wee hot toddy."

"I think you're in luck. There's some whiskey in the kitchen, and I know where Mrs. Toner keeps the cloves. I'll go and boil the kettle."

When Tony was comfortably sipping his drink, he told Ray about the bishop's illness and his new role as 'stand-in bishop'. He chatted a while about his impending visit to Rome and some minor changes he might make in the diocese now that he had control. Ray had listened quietly but during a pause in the canon's complacent musings, unable any longer to endure the suspense, he said, "What did you want to see me about, Tony?"

"See you about? I can't come and sit with a friend to see how he's getting on?"

Relief flooded through Ray and expressed itself too strongly in his response. "Oh, you're just visiting?"

Tony looked at him quizzically. "Yes, that's all! What did you think I wanted to see you about?"

"I didn't know. I was just trying to puzzle it out and couldn't think of anything. I thought it might have been parish business."

"Yes, well," Tony stared intently at Ray, taking in yet again his gaunt pallor, "you may just forget about parish business for the time being. You're in no state to be carrying out a full schedule of duties. Let's get you well again first."

"Thanks, Tony. That's kind of you."

"Not at all, Ray. Your health is the important thing." He held up the hot whiskey and smiled at Ray. "Happy New Year again and let's hope Dr. Bathgate can sort out your problem."

TWENTY-THREE

1

It was a Friday night, or perhaps Saturday morning, in the middle of January. Ray was in bed. He was not asleep, however. He had given up trying. The tossing and the turning and the attempting to relax generated more tension than rest, so he had switched on the light and was attempting to read. He found this, however, almost as difficult to do as to sleep. The words swam before his eyes as his mind kept darting back, again and again, to Christmas Night, now three weeks past, when Maria had come to visit him. Tonight Father McGennity had again gone off to Dublin for the weekend and Ray wondered if perhaps his being alone in the house again was generating his restlessness.

Or was it that something dark, something that for years had lurked, unconsciously subjugated, deep in his psyche, was beginning to thrust itself upwards, affecting his spirit, clouding his judgement? During the previous three weeks his behaviour had begun to border on the obsessive. Despite his every effort of will, he would find his eyes constantly ranging the chapel during morning masses, hoping to see Maria in the congregation. There were odd times when he bizarrely found himself driving or walking past her house late at night, just to be where she lived, perhaps even hoping for a glimpse of her. And all the while he endured tortured inner argument about the nature of his behaviours and the demands of conscience. He knew that his actions and his thoughts were irrational. But equally he knew that something inside of him was changing. In the almost overpowering depression, in the deadening lethargy that sapped his will as much as his strength, he could sense that he was losing control of his emotions and he spent endless agonised hours futilely trying to find some explanation for what was happening to him.

He did struggle with some success, however, not to contact Maria or to let her know about his feelings. She was young, innocent, probably in love with him, but if word ever got out about their relationship, no matter how tenuous it had been, she would suffer horrendously from the rumour-mongering of vicious tongues. He had bumped into her briefly in town a few days ago and, despite the pain it gave him, despite the obvious joy she had expressed at the accidental meeting, he had tried to impress upon her, as gently as he could, that they could never do that 'middle-of-the-night thing' again. He knew that in doing so he had acted properly and in accordance with his conscience but now, in the deep and lonely middle of the night, something in his heart wished that he had not been so final. Now she would never come again. But that was as it should be, wasn't it? *Yes, dear Lord, yes, but what is it that lurks in me, twisting in pain, railing at that decision, demanding to know the sense of it?*

Deep in despair, aching in every muscle and so lethargic that prayer was an impossible duty, he longed for the emotional, physical and mental peace that her presence had brought him. He turned to his book again, the same paragraph that he had already read about five times without assimilating one iota of its meaning. And the doorbell rang. Ray was momentarily startled and then, as he struggled out of bed, he exclaimed aloud, "Oh God, I hope that's not Maria."

But the sudden thudding of his heart, the tightening in his chest, the electric tingle that surged through his entire body, gave the lie to his words. He dressed quickly and went to answer the door. In the wash of light that fell out from the hall behind him, there stood Maria. She was dressed in a long dark coat and had a tight, woollen, multi-coloured cap (what some of the girls called a 'beanie') pulled down on her head. It did not, however, conceal all of her shining black hair, some of which still framed her face. She also wore a matching scarf around her neck. She stood in front of the door, her hands in the pockets of the coat, her shoulders hunched against the raw January wind. She did not speak but simply stared at Ray, her expression pleading and somehow anxious. It was as if she was presenting herself to him and was fearful of his response.

"Maria?" Ray said.

And then he stood, equally silent, holding the door half open as he stared back at the girl. He stood in the wonder of her presence, unable to suppress the thought that never had he seen anything so lovely. But with the thought came the realisation that Maria's brow had furrowed and that her anxiety was increasing. Contrite at his lack of response, he quickly pulled the door fully open and whispered, "Come in, come in!"

Maria walked past him and on down the hall to his study. He followed her and as she stood in the middle of the room, her hands still in her pockets, her shoulders still hunched, he moved to the fireplace and stoked the fire into life. It was not difficult to do since he had left it fully banked with a couple of shovels of slow-burning coal before going to bed. Now he was wondering why he had done that. Had he subconsciously anticipated her visit and left the fire burning in readiness? He turned to Maria. She still radiated tension, even guilt, as she searched his face for some indication of welcome.

Ray smiled and waved her to a chair. “Sit down, Maria,” he said gently. “Sit down. I’m glad to see you.”

Maria’s face broke into a huge smile and she almost sagged with relief as she exclaimed, “Oh God, Father Ray, I’m so glad. I was sure you’d chase me away. But I just had to see you.” The smile died and her eyes misted. “I’ve missed you so much.”

She began to struggle out of her coat and Ray moved to take it from her. As she sat down in front of the fire, he laid her coat on his desk and came back to join her. His mind was churning as he wondered how he should deal with the situation but he could not restrain the delight and the joy he was feeling.

Maria was looking at him, a hint of concern in her eyes. “You look a bit pale, Father. And the other day, you could hardly turn your neck when I was talking to you. Are you all right?”

Ray smiled and said, “Are you deliberately trying to avoid talking about why you’re here when you’re supposed to be at home tucked up in bed?”

Maria’s answering smile was shy but there was something impish in it. She simply nodded her head and said, “Yes.”

Ray couldn’t restrain a laugh. Then he shook his head again and said, “Now I know what that nun was going on about when she started singing, *How do you solve a problem like Maria?"*

"Oh, I loved that film," Maria said, laughing.

"I'm sure you did. And you'll talk about anything rather than why you're here." Ray's indulgent expression, however, removed all sting from the words.

Maria said, serious again, "I will talk about that, Father Ray, honestly, but, really, are you all right? What's wrong with your neck?"

Ray shrugged. "Ohhh, it's been like that for a few weeks. And my shoulders, too. The doctor can't figure out what it is. The bishop's secretary, Canon Mulholland, is a friend of mine. He's arranging for me to see a specialist."

Maria's concern deepened. "Is it serious?"

"I don't really know. It came on me suddenly and it just won't go away." He shook his head dismissively. "But it should be all right. Might be a bit of arthritis or something."

Maria started to speak, then checked herself, seemingly unsure about what she wanted to say.

"It's all right, Maria," Ray said. "You don't have to worry about what you say to me. Just be yourself."

Maria fiddled nervously with her hands. "It's just that when Dad gets a sore neck, Mum always massages it for him and he says it does him the world of good. I sometimes do it, too. I could try to ease your pain a bit, if you'd like."

Ray raised his eyebrows. "Hidden talents? Well, all right. I must say that it would be nice if I could get a break from the pain for a while."

Maria got up, smiling nervously, and moved behind his chair. She placed her hands on his shoulders. “Where is it sore?”

Ray told her and gave himself over to the relief he was experiencing from her probing fingers as she pressed and massaged his aching muscles. He was amazed to find how easily the pain was lifting. After a moment he said, surprised, “That’s great, Maria, thank you. The pain’s all gone. You must have your mother’s healing touch.” Maria remained standing behind him, smiling, her hands still on his shoulders. He took one of her hands and pulled her round towards the other armchair. “Sit down now and tell me why you’re here.”

She sat, and again that wide-eyed look caught his heart. It was a look of questioning innocence, of insecurity, of anxiety. She was trying to frame words that would answer his question but she was having difficulty. She raised her eyes to him, almost pleading with him not to force the issue. He didn’t want her to feel pressurised by his question which, in truth was asked simply to hide his own nervousness. He already knew why she was there.

“It’s okay, Maria. It’s okay. Silly question.” He saw the tremor in her hands and knew that it was not because she was still cold. He smiled to cover the discomfort of the moment and went over to the CD player. “I’ll just put on some quiet music.”

Maria nodded, smiling more naturally now. While Ray was inserting a CD into the machine and selecting a track, Maria came over to the desk and started to look through some of the other CDs. She stopped at one, her face wreathed in a smile of pleasure. “Every time I see an Eva Cassidy CD, I just can’t pass it.”

He returned her smile. “I know. You couldn’t stop talking about her the last time you were here.”

“Well, I just love her singing. And *Fields of Gold* is on here. Can we play that? It’s one of my favourites. I got to sing that at the last school dance.”

“Oh?”

“Yes, some of the girls told the band that I could sing a bit and they made me come up. That’s what I sang.”

Ray smiled. “And I’m sure you made a wonderful job of it.”

Maria nodded but she seemed tense. She was studying Ray and her hands, which were holding one of his CDs, were shaking again, almost as if she had something to say but was overcome with nerves. Ray selected the track she asked for, and looked at her with his head to one side.

“Well?”

“The school dance ... I was just wondering, Father Ray, do you ever dance?”

Ray uttered a surprised bark. “Dance?” He chuckled at the incongruity of the question. “No,” he said. “I don’t dance. I don’t know how to.”

Eva Cassidy continued to sing, filling the electric silence that had fallen between them. Maria held out a tentative hand and, her voice low, quivering with nervousness, she said, “If you like, I could show you.”

Ray demurred, wrestling with his conscience. He was grinning but shaking his head. He could see, however, that Maria was no longer smiling. *Could she have been harbouring secret dreams of something like this?* Maria’s eyes begged him to take the proffered hand but already it was dropping to her side and an embarrassed flush was beginning to appear on her face. Ray stood tense, reluctant, but he couldn't bear to cause her discomfort. Quickly he took the falling hand and smiled. "Okay, it might be fun. What do I do?"

Maria's look of gratitude speared his heart. She needs so little from me, he mused, as she took his hands and placed one on each of her hips. Then she placed her own hands, loosely joined, around his neck. "This is the way we do it these days," she said.

She took a short step backwards and then another, both in time with the music. With her hands locked behind his neck, Ray had little option but to follow. Maria was swaying slightly from one foot to the other and Ray found that, listening to the music, he was doing the same. He grinned sheepishly and, looking down at Maria, he said, "Well, what do you know? I'm dancing," and followed her as she moved gently around the room while Eva Cassidy sang of quiet strolls in golden fields, cascading golden hair, and the look of love that gives everything its magic.

Maria was staring intently into Ray's eyes, no longer smiling. They were barely moving now, swaying more or less on the one spot. But he could sense a tension in her, and there was a slight tremor in her body. She was still very nervous, he realised, so he said, "Sing for me."

Her eyes widened, momentarily startled, but after a moment she began to sing with Eva. Her voice, low and plaintive, transcended the song and as she sang, her eyes pleaded, and her heart pleaded, for him to love her, to be with her, to walk with her in golden fields.

Ray could scarce breathe. He was utterly afraid to make a wrong move, say the wrong thing, lest he spoil the enchantment of the moment. Maria stopped singing, stopped dancing and, raising her face to his, kissed him, a very gentle kiss, little more than a soft touching of the lips. She leaned back with a little jerk to look at him again, warily watching his eyes, his face.

Ray was transported to a world he did not know. The intensity of his feelings no longer frightened him. He was beyond thought. He was beyond reason. All he could see was the beautiful face before him, radiating love, love for him. He put his arms around her and, bending his head, kissed her. And with that simple act, he opened the door to horrors in his life beyond anything he could have imagined.

TWENTY-FOUR

After dinner the following evening, Ray found himself standing nervously outside the door of the parish priest's room. He raised his hand to knock, then dropped it again. He needed to confess his sins but he wondered if this man was the right priest for him. Yet he couldn't go to Tony or Dan with the burden he was carrying. At least he did not care what this man thought of him so with him it would be easier to confess. But was that what the sacrament was really about? His whole body sagged and his face was a mask of anguish. "Oh God, Ray," he muttered. "Go on! Knock and get it over with." He straightened and without further thought rapped on the door.

"Come!" Father McGennity's voice was peremptory. Ray opened the door quietly and peered into the room without moving from the hall. "Well, what is it?"

"I was wondering, Father, if ... if you would hear my confession."

The parish priest showed his surprise but he quickly recovered. "Oh, right. Of course. Do you want to do it here?"

"Yes, Father. I can kneel there beside your chair, if you don't mind."

"Okay", the priest said, rising. "I'll just get my stole." He went to his desk and removed a thin purple stole from a drawer. He placed it around his neck as he sat down again, gave Ray a perfunctory blessing, and said, "Okay, son, off you go."

Ray knelt beside the arm of the priest's chair and blessed himself. "Bless me, Father, for I have sinned. It is some weeks since my last confession." He glanced at Father McGennity who was staring impassively at the floor. "I'm having trouble saying my office, and my prayers ...." He paused. Father McGennity just nodded. "I have terrible distractions when I'm saying mass ...." He paused again, trying vainly to think of more venial sins he could confess before he broached his real reason for being there. Then he said in a rush, "Father, I have had sex with a girl."

Father McGennity didn't lift his head but he said, "Well, I could tell something was botherin' you. You've been looking pretty cut up lately. But don't be beatin' yourself up about it. You're doin' nothin' dozens of priests haven't been doin' before you. Heck, I could give you a long list of sexually active popes ..."

"That's ... that's all right, Father. No need."

"Well, you'll know then that it's natural, almost impossible to avoid. You took a vow of celibacy, son, not a vow of chastity. You're goin' to trip up once in a while, but say your prayers and do the best you can. Is the girl local?"

Ray, rigid with shock at his superior's attitude, could only gasp, "Yes."

"What age of a girl is she?"

"I'm not sure. It never came up. I would guess about seventeen or eighteen."

The priest sucked a hissing breath through his teeth. He was silent for a moment. Ray said nothing.

"I have to tell ye, boy, you're ridin' close to the wind there. You'd better be sure she's eighteen. Any younger and you're in real trouble."

Ray remained silent. This conversation had taken a turn that left him wordless. What did all of this have to do with repentance and forgiveness?

Then the parish priest said, "All right, is that all?"

"All?"

"Yes. D'ye have any other sins?"

"Oh, no, Father."

"Right. Are you sorry for these sins and all the sins of your past life?"

Ray was nowhere nearly ready for this point of the confession. He wanted to hear that he was saved by God's mercy, that it was for sinners like him that Jesus died on the cross, that he was justified by the gift of God's grace, given to him by the redemption of Jesus. He wanted to hear about God's love for him, about hope, about salvation, about simple repentance. But in his distress, he was rendered incapable of any other response than, "Yes, Father."

"For your penance say one Our Father and three Hail Marys. Say your Act of Contrition now while I give you absolution."

Ray said the prayer of contrition, scarcely aware of the words. He was stunned and shocked by the parish priest's attitude. The cynical indifference to his sin, the unfeeling wisdom of the world that substituted for spiritual comfort, was not how he had hoped to be absolved. The priest concluded the prayer of absolution, saying, "... through the ministry of the Church, may God give you pardon and peace, and I absolve you from your sins in the name of the Father, and of the Son and of the Holy Spirit. Go in peace, my son, and try not to sin again."

Ray rose mechanically as the priest removed the stole and began to roll it up.

As Ray walked to the door, Father McGennity looked after him and said, oddly lacking his customary aggressiveness. "There's enough scandal among the Irish clergy already without you addin' to it. If you have to be at this sorta thing, do it well away from here." Ray's head was down. He did not speak. Father McGennity continued, oblivious to Ray's revulsion. "One piece of advice I can give you, son, is to make damn' sure you don't get caught." He stared at the younger priest and something shifted in his eyes. It was as if a memory had flitted through them. "Look, you're young," The parish priest sounded almost compassionate. His curate was revealed as a sinner like himself. He could afford to be magnanimous now. "The time'll come when you'll realise that this is no big thing. So don't take on the way you're goin' or you'll worry yourself into an early grave."

Ray managed a "Thank you, Father," before he closed the door behind him. He had to lean on the other side of it as soon as he left the room. Never could he have imagined a confession so devoid of grace or a confessor so venal.

"Oh God," he groaned. "Have I confessed my sin or have I not? I know, Lord, that Father McGennity, regardless of his attitudes, is your personal representative in the sacrament but, dear God, he did not speak your words. How could he have been so cavalier? The sin I have committed is mortal."

And he hung his head as a sharp memory stabbed him. When he had left Maria home the previous night she had clung to his arm in the car, her head on his shoulder, content to remain silent. Ray had been silent too but his was the silence of mounting guilt and confusion. When Maria had been about to get out of the car, he had said, "Maria, we can't do this again. It's ... it's wrong."

Her eyes had filled immediately with tears of shock. "But why, Ray?" The 'Father' had been disregarded sometime during the night. Her voice was filled with hurt and betrayal. "How can anything so beautiful, so full of love, be wrong?"

Ray had been able immediately to think of a dozen reasons, theological, spiritual, social; but none, he knew, that would satisfy Maria. He shook his head in sadness, begging her to understand. "I don't know," he had replied. "I only know it's wrong. It's a mortal sin. We must not do this again."

Maria had turned away with a low keening wail and had run off, leaving the door of the car still open. Ray had debated briefly with himself about whether he should follow her but he had no comfort to offer. He closed the car door and left. The memory of the pain of that moment now flooded his being and he pushed himself from the parish priest's door and staggered to his own room, racked with spiritual and emotional misery.

RETRIBUTION

TWENTY-FIVE

1

"She's what?" Father McGennity shot back in his chair as he glared at Ray. Then he put his hands on his head and rocked forward. "Oh, my God!" The words were filled with a mix of horror and alarm. He glared at Ray again. "What have you done, you stupid gabshite? How could you have let this happen?"

He rose from the chair, shaking with anger, and paced to the window. He stood looking through it for a few moments, every sinew tense, lost for words. Ray stood silently before the desk, feeling again the deep-seated fear that always overcame him in the face of the parish priest's outbursts. Father McGennity came back to his desk and stood close to Ray with his hands on his hips, his eyes bulging.

"You stupid, stupid alex!" He was shouting in frustration now. "Have you any idea of the trouble this will cause?"

Despite himself, Ray backed away. "I don't know how it happened," he stuttered. "It ... it was only the one time."

"Did you not think to protect yourself, you thick amadan?"

"No, no," Ray said defensively. "I never planned for it. I never wanted it to happen ..." His voice trailed away.

"Oh, aye! You say that now. You never wanted it. Gimme a break." He raised his face to the ceiling and paced away again. "Oh God," he groaned. "What the feck are we goin' to do? If this gets out ... bloody hell!" He turned to Ray again, veins now standing out on his neck, almost spitting. "I can't believe that you could have been ..."

"It was totally accidental," Ray tried to explain. "It ..."

Father McGennity silenced him with a violently dismissive wave of his arm and grunted, "Arrgh! I don't want to hear it." He sat down behind his desk again and put his head in his hands. Again Ray tried to explain but the angry priest, without even looking up, shouted, "Get outa my sight before I do something I'll regret."

Ray turned to leave. He had taken only a step when the priest snarled after him, "Where the hell do you think you're goin'?"

Ray said uncertainly, "You told me to leave."

The parish priest stabbed a finger at a chair in front of his desk. "Sit you the fuck down!" he rasped. "You're goin' nowhere till we sort this out." He got up and went to the window again. He stood looking out with his back to Ray and after a moment inhaled a deep breath. He expelled it slowly and his tension seemed to ease as he arrived at a conclusion.

"Right!" he said. "This thing'll have to be aborted and that girl will have to be silenced."

Ray was appalled. "Aborted?" he gasped. "Silenced?"

The older man turned to face him. "What are you, a feckin' parrot now? Yes, aborted. Yes, silenced."

Ray could scarcely breathe. “But Father, it’s an excommunicable offence to procure or assist in an abortion.”

“Ach, that’s very questionable. Is murder excommunicable? And that’s far worse.”

“But abortion is illegal here.”

“Don’t be worrying about that, there’s ways round it. She’s legally entitled to counselling, information about her options. If an abortion is felt to be needed, she has the legal right to seek one outside of the country.”

“Go to England?” Ray was aghast. Ray had heard sad stories of many dead-faced young Irish girls who had to travel to England for ‘the operation’.

“Nooo, nearer than that. The important thing is that if this gets out, it’ll wreck the parish. It’ll wreck the bloody diocese. How far gone is she?”

Ray, stunned out of thought, replied mechanically, “I think about nine weeks.”

“Nine weeks. Hmmph! Well, that gives us some sort of room for manoeuvre. Somethin’ as early as that can be dealt with quietly. The parents won’t need to know.”

“What are you saying, Father?” Ray was aghast. “We can’t do that.”

“No? You’d rather see the diocese, the whole Church in Ireland, up to its eyes in shite again, would you?” His eyes narrowed and bored into the intimidated young priest. “Get this, son. You’ve screwed up, big time. I’m your boss and I’m goin’ to do my damnedest to sort this. And you’ll bloody well go along with me. And I am goin’ to have to report this to the bishop but he’ll go along with me too, don’t worry.”

Ray paled. “But I told you this in confession.”

“You’re only just now telling me about the pregnancy.”

“But ...”

“I’ll tell you what,” the parish priest sneered. “I’ll tell the bishop you made her pregnant, but I won’t tell him how you did it. Will that cover your seal of confession?” He looked at his watch. “I want you and that girl here in my office at four o’clock today. I want this over and done with.”

Ray sagged in his chair. He had no fight left in him but he was worried about Maria. “How am I going to do that? If I’m seen talking to her ...”

“You had no problem figurin’ out how to get her pregnant; you should have no bother figurin’ this out. Get her in here.”

Concern for Maria gave Ray a modicum of courage. “Father,” he said, “I can’t bring that innocent girl here for you to rip her to pieces.”

Father McGennity snorted loudly. “What the hell do you take me for? I know how to talk to her. None of this is her fault. It’s you who caused all this bloody trouble. Now, get out of here and gimme time to think.”

Ray staggered to his study feeling sick and drained. He could not think. He was still horrified by what the parish priest was suggesting but the intimidation remained strong and the only fixed thought in his head was that he would somehow have to get Maria to the parochial house for four o’clock. He could not go to St. Margaret’s himself. If they were seen leaving together it would excite all sorts of gossip. He sat in a chair, shaking, shattered, helpless. He looked at his watch. Twelve-forty. Maria would probably be on her lunch break. Almost without thought, he got up and went to the phone in the hall. Although he never called her, he had the number of the new mobile Maria's parents had given her for Christmas burned into his memory. He dialled the number, shaking, not even sure what he was going to say. After a few rings, Maria's voice sounded in his ear.

"Hello!"

"Maria, it's Ray. Can you talk?"

There was a moment's silence and then a surprised voice, "Yes, hold on a wee minute." There was some rustling, another silence, and then, "It's okay. I'm on my own now."

"Where are you?"

"I'm in the corridor outside the refectory." Another brief silence and then her voice again, hesitant, unsure. "Is everything all right?"

Ray was about to tell her that the parish priest wanted to see her at four o'clock but he suddenly realised that she would probably panic. Instead he whispered, "I'm phoning from the hall in the parochial house, so I can't really talk. Could you come and see me in the parochial house at four o'clock?"

Again a silence. Then a quiet, timid voice. "Have you thought of something?"

Ray held the receiver to his chest for a moment and raised his eyes to heaven for forgiveness. Then he whispered once more into the mouthpiece, "Yes, Maria."

"Okay." Her voice sounded lighter as she whispered back. "I'll be there."

Ray replaced the receiver. He was overcome with the weight of his deceit and had to stretch out an arm against the wall to support himself while he covered his face with the other hand. He was near to tears and he hung over the phone for a few minutes trying to collect himself. *Oh God,* he was thinking, *she'll die. She'll die when she finds out why I brought her here. But I couldn't tell her the truth. She'd have been in a total panic all afternoon.* A wave of despair washed over him. *What am I going to do?*

2

Ray went back to his study and sagged into an armchair. The pain in his neck and back were excruciating now. He was exhausted, mentally and emotionally, but the dread of the impending interview with Maria and Father McGennity still filled his mind. He moved his head around, seeking to find a comfortable position against the back of the armchair, and tried to relax, perhaps even steal a few minutes' sleep. There was a quiet knock on the door. He raised his head wearily and called, "Yes?"

The door opened slowly and Mrs. Toner poked her head in. "Are you all right, Father?" she asked tentatively. "I heard a lot of shouting coming from the parish priest's office."

"Yes, I'm fine," Ray replied brusquely. He didn't need this. "Please don't concern yourself about it, Mrs. Toner," he continued stiffly. "It's confidential parish business."

Mrs. Toner looked at him for a moment, hurt. Then her lips tightened and she quietly withdrew, closing his door with exaggerated care. Ray turned his head away, annoyed at his uncharacteristic abruptness. "Oh, hell," he muttered. "Now I've gone and offended her as well." But the depth of the trouble he was in surged over him again and he groaned, "Oh Lord, Lord! If only that was all I had to worry about."

He laid his head back on the chair again. The past few weeks had been wretched, filled with loneliness and a corrosive guilt that would not leave him. And the memories that tortured him during his waking hours and during his sleeping hours tortured him yet again. He had heard nothing from Maria for a more than a week after that night she had fled in tears from his car. Those had been difficult days for him, strange days. His moods had fluctuated wildly. There were times he was in a deep depression that left him incapable of thought. There were times when his heart ached for word from Maria, for opportunity to offer her some comfort. There were times when physical pain and a desperate fatigue almost overcame him. And there were times, odd occasional times, when a strange coldness came over him, a coldness that allowed him to stare out at the world with dead, emotionless eyes, to function mechanically, without feeling. Paradoxically, although it was in this condition that he suffered least, it was the state that he dreaded most. It was in this bleak landscape that he was most lost. Prayer meant nothing to him here. Neither did his relationship with God, his priestly role, nor his love for Maria. For this reason he fought against its lure and tried to remain in his suffering.

During these days, too, he had attended two appointments with Doctor Bathgate, with a disappointing outcome. He had been subjected to an intensive examination on the first occasion in the doctor's own surgery. After much probing and poking, a seemingly interminable series of questions, and a deal of head-scratching, Dr. Bathgate, a slight, balding, but very energetic man, had professed himself puzzled. He sat down at his desk and began to write something.

"I'm going to have to see you at my hospital clinic the week after next," he said, "but I'll need x-rays, an EMI scan, bloods, and one or two other tests. I'll organise appointments for you within the next couple of days." He had looked up and smiled at Ray then. “You must be somebody special. Canon Mulholland was very insistent that you be treated as a top priority.”

Apart from a thin smile, Ray offered no response to this.

He had to go to the hospital for the tests a few days later and then, a week after that, he had turned up for the clinic appointment as requested. Dr. Bathgate had enlisted the aid of another consultant and they had stood looking at x-rays and other results talking earnestly to each other all the while as if Ray were not present.

Eventually they turned to Ray and Dr. Bathgate said, “This is all a bit baffling, Father. We’ve managed to rule out brucellosis, thyroid imbalance, and possible diabetic tendencies. Mr. Gavigan here wonders if your problem might be an onset of polymyalgia rheumatica and, although I can find no evidence of it, I have to admit it is a possibility. It would explain the pains and, to a degree, the fatigue.” He shook his head with pursed lips and went on, “But I’m worried about the depression. I don’t know if it is directly connected to your physical ailments, but if it is ...” He raised his shoulders and turned sideways to look questioningly at Mr. Gavigan.

The consultant, hefty, with a substantial mane of greying hair, spoke sonorously in a deep, upper-class accent. “There might be a possibility, just a possibility, Father, I can’t be definitive, that your physical problems and your depression are psychosomatically linked. But neither of us is qualified to affirm that.” He paused, looking intently at Ray, almost as if he was searching for something in Ray’s eyes that might have been missed in the earlier examinations. “The thing is, I had a lady in here a couple of years ago with symptoms very similar to your own and the physical pains were later diagnosed by a psychotherapist friend of mind to be a direct result of some deep-seated childhood trauma that had been repressed for years." He spread his hands. "If you would like, Father, I could arrange an appointment for you ..."

Ray was troubled by this. Something dark had passed behind his eyes as the doctor was speaking but he said, "I have no consciousness of any repressed memories."

Mr. Gavigan smiled. "I don't doubt that, Father. Repressed memories would be, well, repressed. You would not be aware of them. But I'm only talking hypothetically here. We're not usually this stumped looking for a diagnosis and I wouldn't mind checking out the psychosomatic possibility, if only to rule it out."

Ray had no fight in him. He was too tired. "All right," he had replied wearily. "Set it up and I'll go and see Mr ..."

"Mrs. Mrs. Barbara Whitfield".

And that was how that visit had ended. Ray was still waiting to hear from Mrs. Whitfield. She did not, however, feature prominently in his thoughts. Other concerns had priority.

His nights were worse than the days. Sleep was elusive and the hours of darkness were punctuated with bouts of heartache followed by guilt-ridden introspection. He frequently found himself wandering to the kitchen in the small hours, seeking feeble respite in a cup of tea as he stared blankly at the table in front of him. His occasional, if rare, moments of sleep were constantly disturbed by the recurring dream of the devastated landscape where he continued to search, frantically but in vain, for Maria. In more recent versions of the dream he had become conscious that he was being watched. He had become aware of a dark menacing figure, no more than a shadow on the edge of his vision, that hovered at the corners of broken walls or on the perimeter of mounds of shattered masonry. There were times when the dread was so powerful that he was convinced the presence loomed directly behind him, but no matter how quickly he turned to identify it, it would disappear. These dreams left him fearful and confused when he awoke from them, his spirit still fogged by tendrils of misery at his inability to find Maria and his nerves jangling in trepidation as he tried to fathom the significance of the threatening spectre that haunted him.

But life had to go on and, despite an increasing desire simply to lie in his bed and ignore everything, he still struggled to push himself each day into his priestly function. One Saturday morning, towards the end of January, he had been sitting in the confessional. It was a wet and windy morning and not many had turned up. During a lull he was struggling to read a part of his office when he heard a gentle tap on the little door in front of the grille. He pulled it back and waited for the inevitable, "Bless me, Father, for I have sinned ..."

This time, however, there was silence. He could see the vague form of the penitent kneeling on the other side, however, and he said gently, "Yes? Would you like to make your confession?"

There was another moment of silence and then a soft voice whispered, "Father Ray, it's me, Maria."

"Maria?" He had fought to control the host of emotions that seized him and he, in his turn, was rendered silent. Maria waited a few seconds and then, nervously, said, "Father Ray?"

He strove to speak. “Yes, yes, Maria. You ... caught me by surprise.”

Maria waited a beat and then, clearly not far from tears, she whispered, “I’m sorry I ran away.”

“Maria, please, you’ve nothing to be sorry for. It is I who owes you an apology.” He could see Maria’s head go down and he sensed rather than heard her quiet sobs. “Oh, please, Maria, don’t cry, don’t cry.”

Through her tears, Maria whispered, “Can we talk sometime?”

“Yes, Maria, we’ll talk, but not here.” He paused, uncertain how to proceed. Then he simply said, “Do you want to make your confession?”

“Oh yes, Father,” she said breathily, “I’ve been scared to death having a mortal sin on my soul.”

Ray’s heart lurched. Oh God, what have I done to this poor girl? He said quickly, “Maria, don’t think like that. I should never have said that to you. God has nothing but love for you. The sin was mine. I am a priest. I should have known ...” Then, realising that this was not the place for such confidences, he said, “We’ll talk about this later. I’ll hear your confession.”

Maria repeated the ritualistic opening formula and then stalled.

Ray helped her. “It’s okay, Maria. Take your time. Just give me a hint and that’ll do.”

“Father, I ... I made love.”

“Okay, and are you sorry for this sin?”

“Oh, Father, I want to be, if it’s a mortal sin.” And then she said in a rush, “But I can’t feel that it was. I ...”

“Hold on, Maria. It’s enough that you want to be sorry. And mortal sin, I don’t believe you committed a mortal sin, so don’t be worrying about that.”

“But you said ...”

“I know, I know. But listen to me, now. Mortal sin requires grave matter, full knowledge and full consent. I’m sure you weren’t thinking about stuff like that when ...”

He paused and then Maria said hesitantly, “Oh, no, Father, I wasn’t thinking about anything like that.”

“Maria, God loves you so much. You can’t imagine how much he loves you. Don’t be upsetting yourself about the mortal sin thing. Just thank God for his love and know with all your heart that he forgives you.”

“All right, Father.”

“And are you sorry for all your other sins?”

“Yes, Father.”

“Okay, you’ve made a very good confession, Maria, and you don’t have to worry about the sin any more.”

“But, Father, I still love you ...” There was a catch in Maria’s voice and she fell silent.

Ray hands were clenched so tightly before him that he was in danger of breaking a bone. Striving to remain calm, he said, “There’s no sin in love, Maria. Don’t worry about that. We’ll talk about that some other time, all right?”

“Promise, Father?”

“I promise. Now, say your Act of Contrition and I’ll give you absolution.”

Maria hesitated and said, “Father, you didn’t give me any penance.”

Tears leapt into Ray's eyes. He couldn't speak.

"Father ...?"

Ray struggled to keep the emotion from his voice. "You've suffered more than enough, Maria. Offer all your heartache to God and you couldn't do a better penance. Now, say your Act of Contrition."

He heard the door on the other side of the confessional opening and closing. He said the prayer of absolution over Maria and when he was finished he said, "You've now been forgiven for all your sins. Go in peace. And Maria, don't be unhappy, please. I'll try to get in touch. There's somebody on the other side. I'll have to go." He had sensed Maria's reluctance to leave but, obligated to hear the other penitent, he pulled the grille door closed and turned to the other side.

Now in his study, remembering that confession, he remembered as well the mock confession scenarios that had been played out during his formation years. The tutor had come up with some extremely weird situations but ... Ray shook his head, tight-lipped. Nothing could have prepared him for this. And he had meant it when he promised Maria they would talk. He owed her that much. But over the next few days he seemed unable to find a way to contact her. He could not phone her at home, and phoning her at school was equally out of the question. He had hoped to bump into her in town but that didn't happen. Eventually Maria herself had phoned him one evening at the parochial house. Fortunately Father McGennity was out and Mrs. Toner had gone home. She had sounded hurt and tearful when she spoke, "I thought you'd promised we would talk?"

"I did, Maria," he'd said, "and I meant it. But I couldn't find a way to contact you and you never seemed to be in town. So I was waiting for the choir practice next Friday night."

There was silence on the line.

"Where are you now?" Ray had asked.

"I'm at home. Dad and Mum have gone to a parents' night with Paul. I'm on my own for a couple of hours." She paused and then, pleadingly, "Can I come and see you?"

"Oh, Lord, no, Maria. That would be far too risky. Your dad and mum could land home any time. We'll talk for a wee while now and maybe arrange something." But what? He had been puzzling over that for days and had come up with nothing. All he knew was that they could never be alone again.

Maria had broken the silence. In a small voice, tense with worry, she had asked, "Father, do you not want to see me any more?"

"Oh, Maria. If only it were that simple. You're still at school. I'm a priest. Can you imagine the scandal there would be if we were caught together?"

"We could go away ..."

"Go away? Maria, you have your whole life still ahead of you, university, medical training. You can't throw that away."

"I don't care about any of that. I miss you so much."

"Maria, please. Stop and think ..."

"No," she had cried, her voice tearful and filled again with hurt, "you don't love me. If you loved me, you couldn't talk like that," and he had heard her sobbing.

Ray had been suffering his own distress. He had wanted to ease her pain but if he talked to her about love, he would fuel her fantasies. He could tell her he loved her, that he too suffered a terrible loneliness, but would she be mature enough to understand that there could be nothing else, ever? Regardless of his own feelings he'd have to make her see the truth. To do otherwise would be ... ah dear God! The enormity of what he had allowed to happen was tearing at his conscience.

"Maria, please, understand that I am a priest, a priest forever. I can't give that up. I should never have allowed things to get as far as they did. That was unpardonable."

"Ray, Ray, what are you saying? Please, Ray ..." Maria had sounded distraught.

"I'm saying you'll have to forget about me, Maria. I have done you a terrible wrong and I'm so, so sorry. But you're young. You'll ..."

"Don't tell me I'll get over it, please," Maria had cut in, crying "I thought you at least would have understood."

Ray shifted in his armchair and covered his face in his hands as the pain of that moment overwhelmed him again. It had only been in this experience of her pain that the full realisation of what he had done to this innocent young girl had finally penetrated his consciousness. The phone call had ended badly. The more he had tried to force her to accept the truth, the more she had doubted his love. In the end she had hung up on him, vowing never to speak to him again. And, for a few weeks, she didn't. She didn't turn up on Friday's for choir practice. To keep up appearances he had asked Mrs. McLoughlin what had happened to Maria and was told that she was worried about her studies and wanted to take a few weeks off. He had seen her at mass with her parents a couple of times since and she had looked at him with such ineffable sadness, a sadness that tore so violently at his heart, that he had almost slumped on the altar.

After that he had spent tortured hours wondering if there was anything he could do or whether he could have handled the situation differently. And then there came that fateful evening when she appeared again at the parochial house door. Her voice was terrified when she whispered, “I’m pregnant.”

His own blood had run cold and, stiff with shock, he said, “Pregnant? Are you sure?”

“I’ve done two home tests. Yes, I’m sure. Oh, Father Ray. What am I going to do?”

Her face had crumpled into tears as she looked at him, beseeching him to make it right. He took her into his study and allowed her to cry in his arms while he himself stood holding her, his mind and spirit in turmoil. He rested his cheek on her head as he held her and began to say, over and over, “Don’t cry, Maria. It’ll be all right. It’ll be all right.”

When her sobbing had subsided, he released her and said seriously, “Look, Maria, give me a couple of days to think about this. I need time to think, and then we’ll see.”

Ray remembered guiltily the look of utter trust which she gave him at that point. He had told her to dry her eyes and had smiled reassuringly at her as he spoke. “Father McGennity is out on a sick call,” he had told her, “but he’ll be back soon, so perhaps you should go on home. I’ll give you a lift part of the way. But please remember, Maria, you’re not alone in this. I’ll think of something.”

She had thrown her arms around him again at that point and held him. “I feel so safe when your arms are around me, Ray.”

But he had not the smallest inkling of what he might do and now Father McGennity was demanding that the child be aborted. He must know the Church's stance on that, and yet Ray had the clear impression that this was not the first time his parish priest had been involved in procuring an abortion. Had he subconsciously, even in his panic, chosen to seek advice from this worldly priest, with some vague awareness that an abortion might be the outcome? His blood froze at the thought. "Dear God! Am I that far gone?" he moaned, twisting in his armchair in restless despair.

He remained in the chair, tormented with guilt and stricken with the realisation that no matter what choices he was to make now, his life was destroyed. In his anguish he scarcely noticed the passage of time until the heard the doorbell. He looked at his watch. Four o'clock. Maria! He rushed to the door to find Mrs. Toner emerging from the kitchen, wiping her hands in a towel.

"It's all right, Mrs. Toner," he said as calmly as he could. "I'll get this. It's one of the choir girls. We're going to have a short discussion with Father McGennity."

Her brows went down and she made no attempt to conceal her puzzlement. She turned and went back into the kitchen.

3

Ray opened the door for Maria. She stood nervously on the doorstep, peering into the hall.

"Are you alone?" she asked.

"No," Ray was almost whispering. "Mrs. Toner's here."

Maria's eyebrows went down. "Then why ...?"

Ray put a finger to his lips. "Shhhh! Come with me. I've spoken to Father McGennity. He's got some ..."

Maria pulled back in panic. "Oh, no, Ray, no! I can't go in there." And she turned to run away.

Ray took hold of her wrist and pleaded, "Please, Maria, he's cool about it. He only wants to help." She continued to try to pull her arm loose from his grip, making terrified little moaning sounds. "Please, Maria. I'll be with you, please, trust me."

"You betrayed me," she cried, still struggling. "You shouldn't have told him."

"Maria, please. We need his help. He knows about these things."

Maria's struggles eased and she stared at him. Her face crumpled and she started to cry. Ray was in a panic. He pulled her into the hall and closed the front door. He gave her his handkerchief and said, "Maria, I'm here with you and will be with you until all of this is over. Please wipe your eyes. We'll go on in now. It'll be all right, honestly."

Maria seemed suddenly bereft of strength. Her shoulders slumped and she gave him a look filled with hurt. Ray felt her hurt keenly but his inexplicable fear of the parish priest was still driving him. He gestured to the office door and said, "Come on in with me now. I'll be with you he whole time."

He knocked on the door quietly and opened it when the parish priest shouted, "Come!" He led Maria in, holding her arm behind the elbow. She was trembling, clearly terrified. Father McGennity was seated behind his desk. Two chairs had been placed directly before it. He stood up as they entered.

"Father, this is Maria," Ray said.

The parish priest recognised her. "Oh," he said, with surprising civility, "you're the girl who sang that lovely hymn at Christmas." Maria had her head down, too frightened to look at him. She said nothing. "Sit down," the parish priest went on, "both of you." His voice remained relatively calm. Ray could only guess at the internal effort his boss was making to maintain this kind of control. "Now, Maria," the parish priest said. "I know the situation, so I'm not going to be asking you all sorts of horrible questions, so don't be worrying about that, all right, child?"

Maria glanced up at him without lifting her head and nodded.

"All I want to do is to try to decide what is best for you," the priest said. "You're one of my parishioners and I want to save you from scandal, if I can."

This time Maria looked up. "Thank you, Father," she whispered.

"That's all right, child. It's my job. And talking about scandal, do you know what the seal of confession is?"

Maria looked puzzled at the question but answered, "Is it that priests can't tell anybody's sins outside confession?"

"That's right!" he said. "But there's more to it. Neither can you," he said with a great show of certainty. "It cuts both ways. Now," he opened a drawer in his desk and took out his stole. "I'm going to put this around my neck, okay? It means that everything we say here is between the three of us and no one of us is allowed to breathe a word of it outside this room."

Ray couldn't believe what he was hearing. He tried to interject. "Father ..."

The parish priest silenced him with a glare. "We don't need any interruptions from you, Father. You've caused enough trouble already."

Ray subsided and Maria looked wide-eyed from one to the other, amazed by the disrespect with which the parish priest had treated Ray and amazed, too, at Ray's weak submissiveness. The parish priest turned again to the girl. "Well, do you understand what I'm saying?"

Maria, head down, whispered, "Yes, Father."

Father McGennity wasn't satisfied. "I'm not sure that you do. You talk about this to anyone else now and it would be a very grave sin indeed. It would put your immortal soul in eternal danger. Now do you understand?"

Maria stared at him, her terror welling up again. "Yes, Father." The 'yes' might have been more positive but her voice was quavering.

"Good." The parish priest adjusted the stole on his neck and tried for a gentler tone. "How old are you, dear?"

"Sixteen."

Father McGennity's eyes bored into Ray's. He fought to control the rage that suddenly burned there. Ray's shocked expression didn't mollify him. He took a deep breath and forced himself to continue in the same saccharine-sweet voice, "In Ireland that's under the legal age of consent, Maria. Do you know what that means?"

"I ... I think so, Father."

"I'll tell you what it means." The priest's voice was suddenly gruff. "It means that Father Canavan will be sent to prison if word of this ever gets out." Maria looked at Ray, horrified. Father McGennity continued brusquely, "It's no use looking at him now. I'm the one that'll have to figure this out for you."

Maria's terror returned and she trembled in her chair. Ray longed to hold her hand, to offer her some support but his own fear was as acute as the girl's. Her true age had come as a total shock to him and the parish priest's brutal warning had hit him as hard as it had hit Maria.

The older priest had been staring at them in silence. Eventually he said, "I've thought long and hard about this, child. I have had to consider your future, I have had to consider Father Canavan's future, and I have had to consider the reputation of the Church in Ireland. The only thing I can see that answers all three problems is for you to have an abortion."

Maria's head shot up. "An abortion? Oh no, Father." She almost wailed in terror, "I'd be ..."

"Are you a Christian girl or what?" Father McGennity snapped

"Yes, but ..."

"Yes but nothing. What kind of Christian are you, trying to put your own selfishness ahead of the Church and your parish?"

Maria looked at Ray, her eyes stark with fear. Ray hung his head. He had no more control of the situation now than had Maria. Father McGennity spoke again, trying for a more persuasive tone. "Look, it'll be all right. If you are only a couple of months pregnant, the process takes only a few minutes." He paused and tried to catch the girl's gaze. "You're not the first girl to be in this kind of trouble. We know about these things. It would be far worse if your mother and father found out, and all your friends at school. What do you think they'd be saying if you were the cause of Father Canavan going to jail?"

Maria recoiled, looking confused and dismayed. She looked again to Ray in mute appeal.

"You don't have to do anything on your own" Ray said gently, holding her gaze with his. "I'll always be with you to support you."

"How ...?" Maria was unable to frame the question.

"Well, the thing is," Father McGennity said, "you need a doctor to refer you to a local hospital. But we can't have that kind of stuff being bandied about around here. I have a doctor friend who knows the ropes. He owns a private clinic near Castlemore up north. Ostensibly its purpose is to cater for rich people who find themselves with STDs ..."

Maria looked mystification at Ray.

"Sexually transmitted diseases," he informed her, tight-lipped.

Maria's head went down. McGennity ignored the interruption and went on, "But, in certain circumstances, he can perform other services. He's very discreet but he's also pretty damned expensive."

"Expense isn't an issue," Ray responded mechanically.

"Okay, then. An appointment has already been made for you. If you turn up at ten o'clock next Tuesday morning, you'll be sorted in a few minutes flat. They'll give you a cup of tea and a wee rest afterwards to make sure you're all right and you'll be on your way again in an hour."

Ray was shocked by the suddenness of these arrangements but ever mindful of Maria's feelings, he managed to hide his own. He said, and a terrible darkness filled his mind as he spoke, "I'll take you in my car, Maria. We should be able to work this around school times so that your parents don't find out."

Father McGennity stood up and made a show of removing and rolling up his stole. "Right," he said, "So that's settled." He looked down at Maria. "You'll be right as rain the next day and you'll have forgotten all about it by next week." He bent to put the stole back in the drawer but stopped and held it out for Maria to see. His expression hardened. "And don't forget that you're bound by the seal of confession."

TWENTY-SIX

1

Ray drove in silence, mechanically, scarcely aware of what his hands and feet were doing. As he stared though the windscreen, he was acutely conscious of the frightened girl beside him, huddled in the corner of the front passenger seat. She was unresponsive to his attempts to comfort her, recoiling from his gentle touch, panicking, uncommunicative. But he could not blame her. His own spirit, too, was in turmoil. Everything about what he was doing was wrong. He had gone back to the parish priest to try to discuss the issue, to find some other solution, and Father McGennity's voice still roared in his head: "That young girl has a bright future. Do you want to destroy her life because yer moral abstractions get in the way? Time you took a look at real life, boy, and examined the true morality of the situation. Makin' an under-age schoolgirl pregnant? Disgraced forever is what you'll be. Is that what you want? But never mind that, you'll go to jail. Don't doubt that. And how will that serve anythin'? If you have any respect at all for this parish, for the priesthood, for the Church in Ireland, you'll sort this out, right now. That's where yer moral duty lies. Look at the damage other paedophiles have done to the Church."

"Paedophiles?" Ray had been aghast.

"Wasn't she under age? What do you think people are goin' to say about you? You can't let this happen, boy. There's far more at stake than your reputation or your petty moral misgivin's. The only way to sort this is an abortion."

Ray tried to still the noise in his head and looked at Maria. He tried again to talk to her. "Please don't be scared, Maria. It won't be so bad. By tonight all this will have gone away." Maria tucked her legs a little more tightly under her and shrank even further into her seat but she made no response. "Look, I phoned the doctor, Maria, and asked him exactly what he was going to do. It won't be so bad, honestly." He left that hanging in the air.

After a few moments Maria said, her voice scarcely audible, "What's he going to do?"

Ray had to fight a wave of nausea as he attempted to answer her question. What he was about to say was so antipathetic to his conscience and to his moral sense that he wanted to vomit the words out of the window. But somehow, McGennity's influence over him remained so powerful that he was unable to turn away from where it was leading him. "The doctor says that there are many girls your age who come to him with the same problem. He has the greatest sympathy for your plight and is very anxious to help."

"But what about the risks?"

"That's exactly what I said and he said, 'What risks? There is far greater risk in letting the pregnancy go to term than there is in an abortion during early stages'."

"But I was told about long needles and terrible bleeding and ..." Maria's voice tailed away in a tremor.

"Ah, dear God, no. It's nothing like that, Maria. Nothing like that."

"Do you know what ...?"

Ray had wanted to avoid the stark details but her imaginings were terrifying her. "Look, the procedure is a simple one. The doctor called it 'vacuum aspiration'. You get a small local anaesthetic and a tube is passed into the womb. It only takes a minute. The pregnancy is ended by suction. No needles. That's old backstreet stuff. And then it's all over. You are asked to rest in the recovery room for a wee while and then you go home. That's it. Nothing more frightening than that."

Although Ray had tried to sound comforting, bile so sour rose in his throat that he had to stop speaking. But Maria unwound her legs and relaxed a little more in her seat. She still looked pale and apprehensive but the terrible fear had left her.

2

The clinic stood, secluded, in several acres of wooded grounds and could only be approached via a long, winding driveway. The drive opened out on to a large gravelled expanse that seemed to surround the tall, two-storey building that confronted them, an architecturally unspectacular edifice, with flat grey walls largely covered in ivy. There were no obvious markings for parking and the three cars that were there seemed simply to have been abandoned. Ray stopped his car close to the front entrance of the house and accompanied a trembling Maria to the door. A housemaid answered their ring and directed them to Dr. Byrne's clinic on the first floor.

Ray opened the clinic's door and stood back to allow Maria to enter before him into the reception area. She was wearing her long coat and jeans. Ray, too, was wearing jeans and a grey sweater over a red checked shirt. He did not have to try to give the impression that he was simply a worried boyfriend. It was written all over his face.

The reception area was spacious but its décor was strangely joyless, even depressing. Everything, the high reception desk against the far wall, the small occasional table, the few chairs, the walls, even the tiled floor, was a uniform off-white. It was a place that encouraged reticence and whispering. Ray spoke briefly to the female receptionist seated behind the desk. She pointed to a corridor leading off from the wall behind her and told them that Doctor Byrne's office was the second door on the right. They knocked and a voice invited them in. The doctor wore a white coat and black horn-rimmed glasses. When he stepped out from behind his desk they could see that he was tall, almost gaunt. He smiled a warm welcome, however, shook hands with them both and asked them to sit down. He, too, went back behind his desk and sat down.

"I just wanted a few words with you both before we proceed." He did not seem to know that Ray was a priest. The parish priest had obviously chosen to keep matters as discreet as possible. "This procedure ... Maria, isn't it?" Maria nodded solemnly. "It's perfectly safe." He hesitated. "I take it you would prefer to keep your parents out of the loop?"

Maria looked at Ray and then nodded again.

"Well, as I say, it's perfectly safe but," He looked out over his glasses at Maria. "I have to advise you that it is much better to take precautions than to have to go through this. You will be careful in future, I trust?"

Maria blushed and put her head down. The doctor stared at her for a moment, and then went on, "Did someone tell you what's involved?"

"Yes," Maria whispered.

"You know then that, since you are in the very early stages of pregnancy, this is a pretty simple procedure?"

Again Maria whispered, "Yes."

"And have you any questions about it?"

"I've heard that abortion can lead to terrible depression ...?"

The doctor made a face. "The things people say. No, no, Maria, no. There'll be nothing like that. Most girls, and women too, feel relieved once it's over." His mouth went down a bit. "There are those, of course, especially the older women, who might feel that having to have an abortion is regrettable but, if the procedure is necessary, the vast majority have no emotional problems after it."

"The vast majority? Does that mean some people do ...?"

"Yes, but," the doctor cut in quickly, holding up a finger, "you will find that those who suffer subsequent psychological problems already had many other such problems to begin with and that their unwanted pregnancy was only one of those problems."

He sat back, waiting for the next question. Maria looked at Ray again and then at the doctor. She began to nod and then said hesitantly, “Well, all right, then. I will go ahead.”

The doctor joined his hands, rubbed them together briefly, then stood up again. “I’ll just get nurse to take you into the surgery, and ...” He looked at Ray.

“Tim,” Ray said.

The doctor nodded. “Tim. Fine. And are you ...?”

“I’m a friend,” Ray said.

“Ah, yes, of course you are. Well, you will wait in the waiting room, Tim.”

Ray’s stomach lurched. The moment had come. He fought another wave of nausea and stood up. He placed a comforting hand on Maria’s shoulder and struggled to sound calm. “I’ll be right out here if you need me. I won’t move.”

Maria gave him a wide-eyed look but, apart from a scared nod, made no other response. They went back to the waiting room where the nurse was already waiting to take Maria to the surgery. A hefty young man in a white hospital jacket now sat behind the reception desk, studying some typed pages. He glanced briefly at Ray as he sat down in one of the chairs but there was no other indication that he was aware of Ray’s presence.

Ray sat down and picked up a magazine from the small table in the middle of the room. He flicked though the pages but saw nothing of them. During the days of waiting for this appointment, he had found himself again in that cold place where his feelings left him. He had little awareness that during the recent months his psyche had suffered significant trauma but he did know that his physical pains, his emotional stress, the depression that wearied his heart and mind and soul, had sapped his will to the extent that he was virtually incapable of acting autonomously. This had led him to wonder if he had suffered some kind of emotional overload that had drained him of his spirit, of his heart, and even of his conscience. Somehow his condition and his strange fear of the parish priest had rendered him putty in the older man's hands but how could he ever have agreed to assist in the procurement of an abortion? That was a terrible sin. He closed his eyes in inner agony and tried to fathom what it was that had brought him to this waiting room, to this abortion clinic.

And it was here in these cold, clinical and colourless surroundings that so mirrored his own psychological landscape that his moral sensibilities, his repugnance at the terrible wrong that was about to be done, flooded his heart and mind with a terrible suddenness. *I have to stop this. I have to stop this.* Instinctively he leapt to his feet and, rushing around the little table, he began to run to the corridor that led to the surgery. The burly young man behind his desk was on his feet in an instant, almost as if he had been expecting this. He immediately barred Ray's entry to the corridor and Ray began to shout the words that were drumming in his head, "I have to stop this. I have to stop this."

The attendant held Ray firmly back by holding his two shoulders. He was immensely strong but his voice was calm. "It's okay, pal," he said. "I know where you're coming from." He began to push Ray away from the corridor entrance. "If I had a pound for every time I had to deal with something like this, I could be retired by now." He kept pushing Ray, without any violence but with quiet determination, backwards to his seat. "What you're feeling is very common, but you'll be glad in a week or two that I stopped you." He kept talking quietly, still trying to force Ray to sit. "You've no idea of the number of times that young fellows like yourself come over to thank me when they come back with their girls for the post-abortion check."

Ray's face crumbled and he sagged into the man's arms. The man helped him into his seat. "You're probably too late to do anything about it now, anyway. My guess is that your girlfriend is already in the recovery room." He patted Ray's shoulder sympathetically, still talking to calm his panic. "You wouldn't be here, man, if there were not a whole pile of problems attached to this pregnancy. Believe me, when you've had a while to think about this and you realise that your problems are all gone, you'll feel nothing but relief."

Ray sat in his chair, elbows on his knees and his head in his hands. He tried to pray but no prayer would come. All he could feel was the onset of that terrible deadness again, a closing down that started as a physical clenching of the stomach, that worked its way up through his throat and into his head, that blanketed his brain and his feelings, that left him in a state of total aridity, a cold and uninvolved detachment. He did not move but the panic had left him, feeling had left him. He waited in a mental vacuum where, if there was even thought, he was unaware of it.

The attendant went back to his desk and began to read his papers again, glancing with some curiosity now and then at the suddenly quiescent visitor. They remained like that, almost a tableau, for another half hour. At one point a well-dressed woman in her thirties entered the clinic, noticed Ray and hesitated. But seeing that he was oblivious to her presence, she tightened her lips and almost tiptoed to the attendant. They had a whispered conversation for a few moments and the attendant then gestured to one of the chairs. She paused briefly to pick up a magazine from the table and, with one more surreptitious glance at Ray, sat down and immersed herself in the magazine's pages.

A few moments later a door opened and footsteps could be heard in the corridor. Maria came out, looking wan and downcast. She was followed by the doctor who went immediately to Ray. "Everything went fine," he said quietly. "There'll be no problems but maybe could come back in a couple of weeks for a wee check-up?"

Ray rose from his seat. His voice betrayed none of the chaos that was churning his insides. "That's okay, doctor. I'll bring her here." He looked at Maria. She seemed somehow smaller, lifeless, drained of the vibrancy that was so much a part of her. He held out a hand and she took it, almost childlike. He nodded to the doctor and to the attendant and led Maria out.

They were still holding hands when they reached the car. Ray turned to her and said, "How are you feeling?"

Maria stared at him, her face pale and sad and then she began to sob. She kept staring at him through the flood of tears that began to stream from her eyes. Her sobs became stronger, seizing her whole body. She fell into Ray's arms and they stood there at the side of the car, both lost in their own agony. After some moments she lifted her head from Ray's shoulder and, her face wet with tears, she held his gaze and whimpered, "This was our baby, Ray, yours and mine, and we've murdered it. We've murdered our child, Ray."

TWENTY-SEVEN

1

For those who choose to ignore the demands of religion, or remain oblivious to the prompting of the spirit, the only logical option is cynicism. Some, perhaps those who are susceptible to questions about the nature of life and of being but who cannot believe in a future eternity, may go further. They may seek to anaesthetise themselves with the stoic ideal of inner control, with a calm detachment from emotion or from any kind of moral sensibility. They will try to live lives wrapped in a veneer of normality but they are obliged, by the very necessity of this conception of existence, to ignore their humanness and their humanity. In essence they become shells, bodies without spirit.

Ray had never given such psychological complexities any thought but during the days following the abortion of his child, he found himself living in an implacably emotionless place. It was not that he had deliberately sought to exercise this cold and selfish impassivity. He would not have known how. Indeed, although he had some awareness of it, he had no knowledge of its source. Perhaps it was a subconscious defence-mechanism, something in his psyche that may have sensed that his entire mental and emotional equilibrium was in danger of disintegration and had closed down his emotions. Perhaps something in his soul could not cope with his sin and had repressed all feeling. Or perhaps he was running from a human hurt so deep that the facing of it was beyond endurance.

Whatever the reason, Ray passed his days in relentless and unassailable frigidity of mind and heart. Father McGennity had once or twice tried to converse with him but found himself silenced and edgy at the cold stare that was Ray's only response. Ray had not seen Maria since that day at the clinic and, while he had some intellectual consciousness that she must be suffering, he was incapable of empathising with it or of making any effort to contact her. The day of her follow-up appointment had come and gone but she had made no attempt to contact him. From this he deduced that she was sufficiently recovered from her ordeal to need no further support.

Mrs. Toner had been something of a thorn in his side during this time. She could see how pale and uncommunicative he had become and was desperately worried about his health. She fussed around him, constantly knocking on his study door with soup or enquiries about anything he might need. These frequent invasions were kindly meant but they were distractions he did not need and caused him a deal of unintended stress. He dismissed her ministrations with an offhand civility that hurt her feelings but did little to dampen her concern or the ardour with which she continued to mother him.

The one place where his wall of stoicism was fragile and prone to collapse was on the altar where he said his daily mass. He had deliberately feigned sickness for a couple of days after the abortion, desperately unwilling to compound his sacrilege by a hypocritical sacrifice and a mortal disrespect for Christ's body. There was, too, the issue of excommunication. Ray's mind continued to veer from the awful thought, refusing even to contemplate it. But he could not help wondering if he was now even a member of the Catholic Church much less one of its serving priests? He forced the thought resolutely from his mind. He was still working in the parish and he knew that he would eventually have to return to the altar. Was there some way he could continue to say mass and minimise his sinfulness? This was the thinking of a distressed and panicked mind. The young priest was now incapable of thinking rationally. He toyed with the idea of invalidating the Consecration by not mingling the wine and water or, perhaps, by pretending to offer the gifts in silence while actually refraining from uttering the words of transubstantiation.

He had once talked to Monsignor Keenan about priests who have to say mass while in sin. The monsignor had referred to a perception in the Catholic consciousness that fostered what he termed 'the myth of clerical sinlessness.' "Priests do sin, of course," he had said, "but most understand the nature of sin and the need for repentance and forgiveness, much as their lay parishioners do. But sadly it seems that, for an awful lot of people, if a priest sins, especially if it is a sexual indiscretion, there is no redemption for him. People come baying for his blood like a pack of ravening wolves." He shook his head, almost in disbelief. "God gives us umpteen chances for new beginnings, every day, and priests are included in that deal. Wouldn't you think the people would understand that?" He had stared at Ray in silence but his eyes were not seeing him. They seemed to be looking back into the past. Suddenly aware again, he had focused on Ray and said, with a mix of sympathy and sadness, "But the pity is that some priests tend to think like that, too, particularly when it concerns themselves. They fall apart under the pressure of their guilt. They tend almost to despair in the same way Judas did and sometimes lose their faith altogether."

"But how do they say mass?" Ray had asked earnestly. "How can they allow themselves to say the words of the consecration, to hold the host with sinful hands, to receive sacrilegiously the body of Our Lord?"

"May it please the Lord that you never have to face this, Ray," Monsignor Keenan had replied, "but some priests in such state tend to function institutionally, meeting the demands of the institution without allowing themselves to interiorise the conscientious dilemmas that might arise. They simply go through the motions. They just do their job."

In the end, when he did return to his priestly duties, Ray decided that such an approach would be the best way to resolve his dilemma and in his masses of recent days he persuaded himself that he was simply 'doing his job', going through the prescribed words and rituals with clinical detachment. There might have been one or two intuitive souls in the congregation who wondered why they could no longer sense the intense devotedness they had come to expect from the young priest but, if there were, they made no mention of their concerns.

Despite his dispassionate ritualism, however, the consecration remained for Ray a period of acute spiritual and emotional anxiety. His numb indifference could not quell something in him that still responded to the supreme sanctity of that moment and each time he prayed over the host, "This is my body", his hands trembled with guilt and his mind was filled with the echo of Maria's stricken lament, *"This was our baby."*

After two weeks of this, Ray knew that he could no longer function as a priest. He was going to have to meet with Tony and ask to be removed from his ministry. On the very day that he made this decision, he received a phone call from Barbara Whitfield. There had been a cancellation and she could give him a couple of hours the following afternoon. Ray's first reaction had been to tell her that he no longer needed her help but some instinct over-rode his apathy and, after a moment's indecision, he told the psychotherapist that he would see her then.

2

Mrs. Whitfield was something of a surprise to Ray. He had given no thought to what the psychotherapist might look like but he may well have been expecting to meet someone thin, dark and intense. Mrs. Whitfield was nothing like that. She was short, almost dumpy, and had silvery white hair. She wore a beige cardigan over a coffee coloured blouse and a pair of dark brown trousers. She had a kindly smile and when she shook his hand and led him into her 'inner sanctum' as she called it, she was, he could not refrain from thinking, 'motherly'. The room was book-lined, carpeted and, not surprisingly, had a substantial desk. But there were also two comfortable armchairs in front of a fireplace in which a cheerful turf fire sparked and spat.

"Sit down, please. Sit down and warm yourself," she said, taking Ray's overcoat and hanging it on a hook behind the door. "That's a very cold day. Would you like some tea, coffee?"

"Coffee would be nice," Ray replied, ill-at-ease.

She lifted a phone on the desk and spoke quietly into it. She came back to the chair opposite Ray and sat down. “Coffee’ll be here in a minute,” she smiled. She kept smiling as she studied the nervous young priest. “Why don’t you relax? I’m not going to eat you.”

Ray grinned and was able to lose some of his stiffness. “Okay,” he said.

She got up from her seat and came back with a thin folder. She sat down again and waved it at Ray. “I got a few details from Declan Gavigan but ...” She looked quizzically at Ray. “Do you have any idea what we do here?”

Ray shook his head. “No,” he said.

She smiled again. “We talk.” She spread her hands. “That’s all.”

There was a knock on the door.

“Ah, that’ll be Yvonne. Come in, dear” she called. A young woman, obviously a secretary, came in with a small tray containing two cups of coffee, a jug, and some biscuits. Mrs. Whitfield rose and took the tray. “Thank you, Yvonne.” The secretary smiled and left. Mrs. Whitfield set the tray on her desk. She turned to Ray. “Milk?”

“No, black’s fine, thanks.”

She handed him one of the cups, offered him a biscuit and, taking a cup for herself, returned to her seat.

Ray raised his eyebrows. “Talk?”

“Uh huh!”

“Well, I have to be honest with you, Mrs. Whitfield ...”

“Why don’t you call me Barbara?”

"Okay, I have to be honest with you, Barbara. 'Talk' is a very vague word for me. I truly believe I would understand better what you do if you gave me some of the jargon."

Barbara smiled. "All right. There are many kinds of psychotherapy. There are psychodynamic, behavioural, cognitive behavioural, regression, diagnostic regression, past-life regression ..."

"Past-life regression?" Ray looked sceptical.

"Yes, like the time you were a Roundhead or something in the sixteen-forties." She pulled a face. "I hold no truck at all with that notion of reincarnation. I believe that the past-life scenarios are books people might have read or films they saw as a child. But all of these therapies have in common the fact that they are 'talking therapies' with different focuses and, believe me, they are very useful in helping people to overcome stress or emotional problems, and sometimes, as in your own case, at least as I understand it, psychosomatic problems."

"I'm not so sure about that," Ray said defensively. "How long does it take to ...?"

"Well, diagnosis is the first essential step. After that, there's therapy which usually requires a series of weekly one hour meetings. The number of weeks would depend on the extent of the psychological damage, if any," she added hastily as Ray made to speak. "But as you say, Declan was only guessing that you might have a problem that requires psychotherapy. Meetings usually last an hour but, just in case Declan is right, I have decided that we'll go on for two hours today, if necessary, to try to get to the bottom of what's troubling you."

"How do you propose to go about the ... diagnosis?"

"Well, from what little Declan told me, I have to think I might go the regression route."

Ray's eyebrows went down. "What does that involve?"

Barbara sensed his concern. She said, "Look, Father," she paused to give him a questioning gaze: "You are a priest, aren't you?"

Ray said, "Yes, but please call me Ray."

"All right. Ray. It will involve total and complete honesty on your part. You can't hold anything back. Everything is confidential. It's like the confessional. There is no judgementalism here, simply a quest for truth and healing. Are you okay with that?" Ray nodded. "Good. Diagnostic regression is used when a person is uncertain of the true origin of an emotional or psychosomatic physical condition."

Ray sat back in his seat and threw up his hands. "I'm quite sure there's nothing. I would remember."

"Okay, then. That's how we'll start."

"What do you mean?"

"We'll see what you remember about your life and how far back your memories go. I don't want to make any assumptions but if there is a past hidden traumatic memory, perhaps domestic violence or abuse ..."

"My dad and mum?" Ray exploded, half laughing at the preposterous notion. "Absolutely no way. I can tell you that right now without any regression."

"All right," Barbara said calmly. "I believe you. But I'll take you back through the years to see if we can find anything that might have contributed to your current problem."

Ray nodded acquiescence.

For the next fifty minutes Barbara pressed Ray to remember aspects of his formation and training at Maynooth, his years at St. Anselm's, his primary school days. The clearer Ray was about specific times, the more quickly Barbara would move to another period of his life. When they got to his childhood years, Ray's memories were scarce indeed.

"Do you remember any early Christmases?"

Ray shook his head.

"Childhood birthdays? Special occasions? A significant individual moment with one or other of your parents?"

Again Ray had to shake his head slowly as he tried to recall something, anything, that would help Barbara. "No," he said. "It's just too far back."

Barbara bit her lower lip. "Mmmm! That's a bit odd. Most people have little scattered childhood memories, but all right, I'll take you on to something else." She wrote for a few minutes on a page in the folder and looked up. "Do you have any recurring dreams or nightmares that you can recall?"

A cold hand grabbed Ray's heart. Barbara noticed his reaction.

"There is something, isn't there?"

"Well, yes and no," Ray replied.

"Tell me."

Ray sat back in his chair, folded his hands in his lap and stared into the fire, trying to find the words he needed. "I do know that I have had nightmares over the years. I often woke up in a cold sweat. But no matter how hard I tried, I could never remember what they were about. But all my friends have had nightmares. I mean, what's so significant about that?"

Barbara just said, "Do you have any such nightmares now?"

Ray stared into the fire again. "I think so, yes, on and off. But, well, there's this dream I keep having. I'm in this blasted landscape, I mean, like it was blasted to pieces by a bomb or something, broken walls, demolished buildings, stones and rubble everywhere. It's a bleak and terrible place and I am all alone. But then there appears in the distance a girl. I know who she is. She's one of the girls in the choir."

"Is she a girl you like?" Barbara asked neutrally.

Ray nodded. "Yes, but in the dream she's some distance away and I try to run to her, but she disappears around corners and I chase after her. But I never find her. That goes on for ages and then the dream ends."

"Ummm! That might explain something about your present life but it doesn't really ..."

"There's something else," Ray interrupted.

"Oh?"

"Yes, lately in this dream I see, well, I don't actually see, but I am aware of a dark, menacing figure in the dreamscape watching me. He's sometimes just behind a wall or hovering near a corner."

"He? How do you know it's a he?"

Ray looked surprised. "Well, I don't. I just assumed it was."

"Menacing? Does the figure frighten you?"

"Yes."

Barbara wrote again in her notes. When she looked up she said, "I think that is very significant."

Ray stared at her. "What does it signify?"

"Oh, I couldn't say yet. I just know it is significant."

"Can you make any sort of a stab at what it might mean?"

Barbara hesitated. "I'd only be guessing, Ray. But it seems to me that there are two separate things going on here. I have the sense that the girl you refer to means more to you than you have implied and in the dream you can't catch her. You're a priest, she's unattainable. That's why you can't catch her. But if you were to let yourself go to her in real life, then the broken and desolate landscape is your life or an image of what you believe your life might become. Everything in your life would be ruined."

Ray continued to stare, stone-faced, into the fire.

"But the shadowy figure is something else. It doesn't fit that pattern." Barbara, too, stared into the fire. "I think, if I put this together with the information I received from Declan, the pains, the depression, the terrible lethargy, and now this looming presence in your dream ... " She paused to look directly at him. "What seems to be happening here is that some trauma did occur in your childhood and it is starting to work its way up through your subconscious into your memory. Your body is the first to react to that sort of thing. The pains could be resulting from repressed anger or some other strong emotion. And now this figure in your dream, it could be a representation of the cause, or the causer, of the trauma." She turned earnestly to Ray. "You do have a blank spot in your childhood years, Ray. We're going to have to find a way into that."

Ray said helplessly, “But I just can’t remember.”

Barbara joined the tips of her fingers together and said quietly, “Would you have any objection if I were to try hypnotherapy?”

“Hypnotherapy?”

“Yes. It’s very straightforward. I just put you into a light trance state. You will be very relaxed, and I take you slowly back in time to your childhood years. Sometimes the repression can be very severe and hard to break through but it seems to me that the memory is already trying to assert itself. I think we should be able to get to the bottom of this today.”

“Are there any side effects?”

“Not from the process itself, but I was going to warn you that if the memory is very traumatic, if something so terrible happened that you have had to repress it, then the recovery of the memory can lead to anger and distress, maybe a terrible frustration or perhaps a deep shame. These can be difficult to deal with and are why follow-up therapy is needed.” She looked solemnly at Ray. “You may also experience some blinding headaches as different memories return. Do you still want to try?”

Ray expelled a heavy breath. “If there’s anything there,” he said, “I suppose we should try to find it.”

Barbara got up from her chair and went to her desk and pressed a switch. Soothing music, low and very relaxing, filled the room. She stood behind Ray and touched his forehead with the tips of her fingers. “I just want you to relax. Don’t be worrying about anything. Listen to the music but really hear only the sound of my voice ... just my voice. Do you hear me, Ray?”

"Yes."

"When I tell you to, I want you to count slowly backwards from ten, and when you get to one, you will fall into a relaxed sleep. Are you listening, Ray?"

"Yes."

"All right. I want you to count slowly backwards from ten. Start now."

Ray counted slowly, his voice weakening as he progressed through the numbers and ceasing altogether when he got to one.

"Can you hear me, Ray?"

"Yes."

"It's your first day at primary school. How old are you?"

Ray's voice acquired a childlike lisp. "Five."

"Did you have a birthday that year?"

There was silence and then, in a happy voice, "Yes, Tommy and Stephen and Karen and Olivia are at my party. They have brought presents."

"That's nice. Can you go back two years to your third birthday?"

There was silence.

"Ray?"

Ray's voice was a frightened whisper. "He's here ..."

Barbara tensed. "Who is here, Ray?"

"Him." This with a frightened whimper.

"Why is he at your party, Ray?"

"He's my uncle Henry. Sometimes he lives here with us."

"Why are you afraid of him?"

"He does things to me in bed ... horrible sore things." Ray was panting, each word filled with fear. He was becoming increasingly agitated, moving around in his chair as if seeking escape. "Please, please, don't let him touch me." Ray began to curl up in the armchair into a foetal position.

Barbara had heard enough. "Ray," she called gently, trying to break through his terror. "Ray, I want you to count slowly up to ten. Count with me now. One ... two ..."

Ray began to count and as he did so his struggles ceased.

When he reached ten Barbara said, "You can wake up now, Ray. You do not have to be afraid any more."

Ray opened his eyes and looked down at his posture in mystification. He unfolded himself and sat back properly, looking questioningly at Barbara. "How the heck did I get like that?"

"I'll explain in a minute. Do you have an Uncle Henry?"

"Yes, my mother's brother. Why?"

"How do you feel about him?"

"Ambivalent, well, to be honest, I just can't like him. Even the very look of him, God forgive me! He's got that red, bleary, debauched sort of a look, just like my parish ..." Ray's voice trailed away in mystification as if some thought just beyond his reach was trying to manifest itself. After a moment, he repeated, " ... just like my parish priest. But I never see him now."

"Did he ever live at your house?"

Ray rubbed his eyes with his hands, struggling to remember. After a moment, he said, "He was some kind of sales representative. I think he stayed with us sometimes when he was travelling in our area ... I'm trying to remember ..."

"I think he might be the dark figure in your dream."

"Uncle Henry?"

Barbara sat in silence while Ray wrestled with distant memories. She watched his face, initially puzzled, reveal a series of intense emotions, none of them pleasant. Ray began to huddle in the armchair, his mouth hanging open as the horrors of his childhood began to reveal themselves to him. He put his head in his hands and, with an anguished grimace, he began to moan, at first quietly, "No ... no ... .Oh, God, no .... Not this on top of everything else."

He pressed the heels of his hands into his temples with an intense force as if he were trying to squeeze something agonising from his skull. Then he lurched back in the chair, twisting his head violently right and left as if somehow he could shake loose the horrific memories that were being enacted in his brain. Barbara was sympathetic but knew there was little she could do at this point. She had witnessed this type of remembering before, usually in clients who had been on the cusp of remembering just before they came to her. She wondered what he had meant, however, when he said, " ... on top of everything else." And that resemblance between the parish priest and his uncle, could that have been the catalyst that triggered the repressed memories?

Ray raised his head to the ceiling, his face squeezed tightly in a deep distress. He emitted a terrible "Arrrrghhh" and lashed his body forward again, squashing his elbows, body and head on to his knees. He remained like that for several seconds, every muscle tense, shuddering violently as he fought against the dreadful scenes that were filling his mind.

Barbara glanced at her watch. Fifteen minutes left. She could not allow Ray to leave like this. She was about to rise and instruct her secretary to cancel her next appointment when Ray suddenly straightened and sat up in the chair. His face was still constricted in pain but gradually it settled into an impassive mask until nothing of emotion or distress showed there. Even his eyes were blank. He released a long, shuddering breath and sat silent and unmoving in the chair. After a few moments he turned to the psychotherapist. "Thank you, Barbara," he said quietly. "I have to go. Please send your bill to the Parochial House at Drumkillen."

"Don't worry about that, Ray," Barbara said hurriedly, "the diocesan office is taking care of it. But don't rush off. We need to discuss this."

"No, I'm fine," Ray said, dully. "I need to go."

He took his coat from the hook on the door and left the room. Barbara ran after him. "Ray, wait. Ray. You're going to need follow-up therapy." But he ignored her, letting himself out through the front door and closing it quietly behind him.

Barbara went back into her office. She sat looking at the file she had started on Ray and then began to write. She had never seen anyone change from the distress of traumatic remembering to an icy calm with such speed. She had read something about such calmness. The mind, sometimes under extreme duress, can try to escape the pain it is experiencing by closing down all emotional responses. The condition was occasionally referred to in psychological literature as 'affective impermeability' though it was more commonly known as 'emotional imperturbability'. But it was an inadequate and an illusory condition and it did not last. For a time, how long would depend on the strength of his will, Ray would be able to live his life under strict limitations, a spectator more than a participant in life, but eventually he would be forced to face the awful reality of his past and she wanted to help him deal with it. Right now, however, as long as he resisted therapy, she knew there was nothing she could do.

3

Ray drove home, his expression set, unmoving, his eyes blank. He parked outside the parochial house and let himself in. Father McGennity was in the hall. When he heard Ray he turned and snarled, "Where the hell were you? You've missed three appointments. The phone hasn't stopped ringing."

Ray ignored him and picked up the receiver to make a call.

The parish priest was furious. "Hey you!" he shouted. "I'm talking to you here. Don't you dare turn yer back on me."

Ray stopped dialling and stood still, looking at the wall in front of him. He quietly set the receiver back on its hook and turned to face the parish priest. He moved slowly towards him until his nose was about three inches from the older man's. His expression had not changed. "I want to hear nothing more from you, Father," he said. His voice was quiet but his eyes were filled with a terrible intensity that rendered the older priest intimidated and shaken.

"Do what you like," he blustered as he backed away but his face was ashen and his hands were trembling as he turned to walk up the stairs. Ray turned to the phone again. He dialled a number and waited. A voice answered. It was Tony.

"Hello?"

"Tony, it's Ray."

"Hello, Ray. Good to hear from you. How are you?"

"Fine. Can I see you tomorrow?"

Tony, at the other end of the line, raised his eyebrows. Pretty brusque. This didn't sound like Ray. But he said, "Certainly. Hold on. I'll check my diary." He pulled the appointments book towards him and leafed through its pages. "Yes, I'm free in the afternoon. Would you like to join me for lunch?"

"No, thanks. I'll see you at three o'clock, okay?"

Again Tony's face registered puzzlement and more than a hint of concern. But he said, "That'll be fine, Ray. I look forward to it. See you then."

TWENTY-EIGHT

1

The following afternoon, Tony was sitting in his office working on a paper he was planning to write about the importance of a Faith Awareness policy in Catholic schools. He was in a rare good humour because a letter he had received from Rome that morning had singled out for particular praise a recent essay he had written on priestly celibacy. It had been published in some significant journals and obviously had not gone unnoticed. What were the exact words again? He stretched across his desk and lifted from the top of a plastic tray a sheet of paper bearing the Vatican's logo. He smiled to himself as he read,

' ... The Vatican, which inevitably bears the brunt of criticism and attack, is pleased to note your efforts to join with us in the battle. It is important that voices as strong and as cogent as yours be heard constantly in our Church. Few people understand that when the grace of Holy Orders is received, the recipients are empowered to fulfil God's will in their lives in ways that would not be possible if they were trying to achieve sanctity through their own strength ...'

"You're getting there, Tony," he muttered, pleased. "Slowly, maybe, but you're getting there." Somewhere in the back of his mind there came a faint, almost muted, question. *Getting where, Tony?*

"To where I will be able to do a lot of good," he replied defensively to the imaginary inquisitor. "Isn't that the whole point? The further I progress, the more I will be able to promote a truly solid Catholic agenda."

Of course, Tony. Of course, the soft voice replied.

"Well then, stop bugging me," Tony said aloud, with a shake of his head.

He threw the letter back on the tray and picked up a multi-page document that was sitting on his desk. It was from the office of the Papal Nuncio in Dublin. Every few years priests in the various dioceses are polled by the Nuncio's office. They are asked to complete a complex questionnaire, containing all sorts of elaborate questions, with many addendums in Latin. The purpose of the poll is to permit priests, confidentially, to indicate who they believe is the priest in their diocese most suitable for the role of bishop. The form had arrived this morning and Tony had experienced a small tremor of anticipation when he had opened the envelope and discovered what it was.

During his recent visit to Rome he had been approached by one of the Irish bishops, Colum Powell, who had read his books and most of his essays. The bishop had been impressed by his theology and, hearing that Tony was at the conference, had made a point of meeting him. The two became friends and spent much of the week together. Colum had brought Tony for coffee to the Piazza Navona, one of his favourite places in Rome. In March the weather was becoming balmy and they were able to sit at a pavement table and admire the famous square with its three extraordinary fountains which date back to the sixteenth century. Tony found it breathtaking. The giant figures on each fountain, sculpted with life-like accuracy, were truly amazing works of art and for several minutes he was unable to take his eyes from the majestic Fontana di Nettuno, with its surround of sea nymphs and horses, and the great figure of Neptune with his trident dominating its centre.

He had listened, fascinated, while Colum had explained something of the square's history, how it was commissioned by the art-loving Pope Innocent X and how the rivalry between the two great architects of the time, Bernini and Borromini, world famous exponents of the Baroque style, had resulted in the beauties that now lay before them. Tony commented that that the Piazza Navona did not look really a square in shape and Colum agreed, pointing out that it was a long rectangle that had once been a competition arena for Greek-style games. It was surrounded now by tall, beautiful buildings and it had inevitably become a huge attraction for tourists who could not only admire the square itself but also enjoy the singers, mummers, artists and other street theatre that had become part of its charm.

When Tony had been finally able to take his eyes from the architectural wonders on all sides of him and return again to normal conversation, the issue of the Nuncio's poll came up. Colum had told Tony that a new batch of questionnaires was soon to be issued and he suggested, with a deal of animation, that Tony was in a position to do himself some good. Tony had raised his eyebrows and said simply, "Some good?"

"Yes," had come the reply. "Don't underestimate the psychological factor in these things. Like individuals in most organisations, priests tend to accept a traditional officer class, and they tend to notice guys around them who would seem to reflect their perception of that class.

Typically they image prospective bishops as chaps who stay on at Maynooth and do doctoral studies, who write articles and books, who get jobs as bishop's secretaries or sit on some of the bishop's commissions ...." Colum had sat back and grinned. "Are you getting the picture, Tony?"

"Em ..." Tony wasn't sure how he should reply.

"You're nearly there, Tony. All you have to do is to quietly raise your profile over the next few weeks. A bit of glad-handing here and there, do a few favours that won't go unnoticed, and bingo! Your name will be all over the poll results."

Tony had shaken his head and uttered a dismissive laugh. But he had been keen to hear more. "What exactly happens with these questionnaires?"

"They are stored, but they are perused collectively from time to time by the bishops. They're an important source of information when bishops are asked to make nominations. Ideal candidates obviously must be seen to be a safe pair of hands, to come from a good pastoral base, to have a sound theological stance. You've got all that in spades, Tony, but if your name were to pop up all over the place in these questionnaires ..." Colum had left the rest of the sentence hanging and sat back in his chair, sipping his cappuccino with a knowing expression on his face.

Tony now sat perusing the questionnaire. He had done quite a bit in the diocese's parishes recently to make his presence felt. He had attended various parish meetings, said Masses all over the diocese, made a point of visiting as many parochial houses as possible to show interest and offer support. He knew from the reception he was receiving everywhere that his efforts were appreciated. Now he rather imagined that his was one name that would definitely feature prominently in this particular round of voting. Yes, things were falling nicely into place.

There was a quiet knock on his office door. Tony glanced at his watch. It was exactly three o'clock. He smiled. That was Ray. Punctual to the *n*th degree.

"Come in, Ray," he shouted.

When Ray entered, the first thing Tony noticed was the jeans and the grey sweater. "Hi Ray. Good to see you." And then with an amused glance at Ray's casual apparel, he said, "I never figured you for the jeans type." It was only when Ray made no response that Tony became aware of his set expression and oddly still posture. His own expression sobered and he pointed to a chair. "Sit down, Ray. Tell me what's bothering you."

Ray wasted no time with social niceties. He said expressionlessly, "I visited a Family Planning Clinic in Castlemore, near Belfast, a couple of weeks ago."

The half-quizzical grin reappeared on Tony's face. He had no idea where Ray was going with this. He said, with a short chuckle, "Oh? Are you thinking of starting a family?"

Ray stared at him humourlessly for a few seconds and then said, in the same dead voice, "No, I went there to get rid of one."

Tony's good humour evaporated. He had not yet grasped what Ray was saying but he was experiencing an ominous intuition that Ray had just brought him some serious trouble. Hoping that he had misunderstood, he said, trembling on the edge of shock, "You did what?"

Ray spoke as if he were simply reading a sentence from a book, and reading it badly. "I made a young under-age girl pregnant and I took her to a Northern Ireland clinic to have the baby aborted."

This time Tony understood. He went rigid with shock. But he still clung to disbelief. "I don't understand, Ray. What are you trying to tell me?"

"I'm telling you that I got a young girl pregnant and I helped her procure an abortion." For all the feeling there was in his voice, Ray might well have been reciting arithmetical tables. But Tony was still struggling to process information that made absolutely no sense. Pregnancy? Abortion? Ray Canavan?

"I can't take this in, Ray. You could never do anything like that."

"I'm sorry, Tony. It's true."

Tony put his elbows on the desk and his head in his hands. He couldn't look at Ray. Staring at his desktop, he said, "Just tell me what happened."

"I was going through a very bad patch in my life. I was sick, I think, and deeply depressed. This girl in the choir, she comforted me. One night I made her pregnant. Then I took her to the abortion clinic."

Tony groaned and his head fell even lower as the stark reality of what Ray was telling him sank in. "Oh, dear God, Ray, what have you done to me?"

Ray stared at him, showing reaction for the first time. His tone was almost contemptuous as he said, "What have I done to *you*, Tony?"

Tony realised how his comment must have sounded and felt ashamed. His first concern should have been for the young girl, or for Ray or, perhaps, the Church that he loved. If what Ray was telling him was true, the poor, bruised and battered Church was about to suffer yet another series of vitriolic attacks from those who hated her and who would use this new scandal to pour scorn on her and her priests. Could he allow that to happen yet again? Was there some way he could prevent that from happening? But what of Ray? He looked sadly at the young priest and said, “I can’t understand how you, of all people, could have done this.”

“It was in the best interest of the diocese and of the Church in Ireland.”

“What? Making a young girl pregnant?”

“No. I mean, getting rid of the problem.”

Tony slapped an angry palm on the desk surface and snapped, “That’s a load of balderdash, Ray. You don’t think like that.”

“I accept full responsibility for my actions,” Ray said stonily.

“That old swine McGennity is in there somewhere. I’ll bet my life on it.”

“It was I who made the girl pregnant. I accept full responsibility for my actions,” Ray repeated.

“Did he force you into this? Was it him who set up this abortion? How could he have gained so much control over you?”

“Because it wasn’t really him. It was ...” Ray said instinctively before stopping himself. Then he said woodenly, “I accept full responsibility for my actions.”

“Will you stop saying that, for God’s sake! Don’t you know that this is an excommunicable offence?”

Before Ray could respond there was a knock on the door and it opened immediately. Dan burst into the room without waiting an invitation to enter. "Tony, that McGennity ..." He stopped just inside the door when he saw Ray. "Ray? What are you doing here?"

Ray lips tightened but he showed no further reaction. He continued to stare straight in front of him. He did not look at Dan but said tonelessly, "I thought I was having a private conversation with Tony."

Dan was amazed. "What in the name of goodness is the matter with you, Ray? Why are you talking to me like that?"

"Dan, we're in the middle of something," Tony said. "Could you come and see me later?"

"No, Tony. This concerns Ray. I need to talk to the both of you."

"Please Dan," Tony said.

"Look, Tony. I've just heard from a friend of mine that McGennity is spreading horrific rumours about Ray in Dublin, horrendous things. Fortunately he was in a drunken stupor when he was blathering, so thank God nobody believed him. But he needs to be pulled in and severely sorted before he ruins Ray's reputation...." He was waiting for reaction and was puzzled to find there was none. He looked from one to the other, his face showing his perplexity.

Then Ray said, still not looking at him, "It's all true."

Dan's face showed only bafflement. He stared first at Tony and then at the back of Ray's head. He opted for sarcasm. "Aye, sure! You made an under-age girl pregnant and then procured an abortion for her. Like I could believe something like that?"

Ray closed his eyes and for a moment his face registered pain. Then his expression cleared and he said stoically, “It’s all true, Dan.”

Dan looked at Tony, his face haggard. He was near to tears. He still refused to believe but his voice was anguished as he cried, “Ray, Ray, you could never do something like that. You’re just not capable of it. Please, Ray, please tell me ...” A thought struck him and he said with sudden hope, “You’re covering up for somebody, aren’t you? You’re trying to save somebody’s hide. That’s so like you, you daft clown. Come on, Ray. Come clean. You can’t do this to us.”

Ray turned to look at Dan for the first time. His eyes and face were expressionless. “Look, Dan. I have told you, it is all true. It’s done. There’s nothing anybody can do about it now.”

Dan returned his look, his face ashen. He sagged back against the door. He kept saying, in a stricken voice, “I don’t believe it. I don’t believe it.”

Ray turned away, facing Tony again, who was sitting at the desk with his head in his hands. Dan’s expression began to harden and he said, “You’re telling me that you made a young girl pregnant and then procured an abortion for her?”

Ray looked straight ahead and offered no reply. Dan marched angrily to the chair Ray was sitting in and seized his shoulder, pulling him round to face him. “Look at me when I’m talking to you, dammit! How could you have done this terrible thing?”

Tony raised his head wearily. “Leave it, Dan. I’ll handle this.”

“Handle it?” Dan was livid with anger and a desperate sense of betrayal. “What do you mean, handle it? This is an utter disgrace. Call the bloody police. Let them handle it.

Inform Rome. He has to be excommunicated." Then his anger evaporated and his voice broke. "Ray, Ray," he was almost sobbing, "how could you ...?"

He collapsed once more against the door lintel and in his shattered expression Tony saw again the scared little boy who had sat beside Ray that first day at St. Anselm's. He saw, too, in Dan's big, honest face, a desperate pain, a sudden and awful realisation that all that was good and pure and innocent in this friend of his life had been destroyed. He could see Dan grieve for Ray, and for himself, and for the terrible loss of this beacon, this constant in his life, in whom he had reposed his total trust.

Again Dan moaned, "How could you?" and tears started into his eyes as the extent of Ray's betrayal flooded through him – the betrayal of his priesthood, the betrayal of his Church, the betrayal of his moral code, the betrayal of all that had cemented their friendship. "Oh God," he groaned, overcome with the enormity of Ray's sin. "What have you done?"

Ray sat unmoving, still staring straight ahead. Tony came out from behind his desk and put an arm around Dan. He moved him to one side and began to open the door. "Come on, Dan. Leave now. I'll sort something out. I'll call you later."

Dan swiped the tears from his face, his anger returning. "You can't sort this, Tony. Ray is going to have to suffer the consequences of his actions. Do you hear that, Ray?" he shouted. "You can't expect to get away with this." He stared at Tony and then back at Ray.

Tony had the door open. "Come on, Dan," he said quietly. "Come on. Leave now. There's a good fellow."

Dan shook off Tony's arm, his face white with anger and disapproval again. He walked back into the room and positioned himself in front of Ray. Ray averted his eyes and refused to look at him.

"How could I ever have called you friend?" Dan said, his voice cold. He stared at Ray for some seconds and then he turned and strode out of the room. Tony closed the door quietly behind him and sat behind his desk again.

"Dan's upset. You know what he's like."

"Yes. Black and white."

"He'll come round."

"I don't think so, not Dan."

Tony rested his chin on his joined hands. "Give him time." He sat in silence for a few minutes, still shattered by Ray's confession. Then he said, "There's more to this than meets the eye, Ray. You're no paedophile. Help me to understand."

Ray had been shaken by Dan's parting words. He was fighting to retain his detachment but somewhere in his heart he felt the need to explain what had happened.

His voice remained dispassionate but he told Tony about the pains and the depression and the lethargy, about his meeting with Barbara Whitfield and what had transpired there. Then he said, as if it was a matter of no importance, "I wish now to be relieved of my ministry."

Tony was shocked anew. "Oh God, Ray: dear Jesus. Ray, I need to think about this."

"Tony, you're an expert on Canon Law. You know I have to be excommunicated."

"Ah no, Ray. Holy God, don't think like that," Tony responded weakly, knowing Ray was right but allowing his heart to overrule his mind. "There are so many extenuating circumstances ...." He paused, pain written on his face. "Have you been to confession?"

"I have confessed the sexual transgression but not the involvement in the abortion."

Tony's face filled with anger. "That McGennity. That piece of crap." He bit his lower lip and said, "Ray, let me hear your confession now. Assisting in an abortion demands that you immediately excommunicate yourself. It's a reserved sin, as you know, and only the bishop can absolve you and restore you to the Church. But I am now acting bishop. I'm in a position to ... Please, at least get that much sorted."

"I can't. Not now," Ray said.

"But Ray ..."

"Please, Tony. Not now."

Tony, tense and agitated, had to move. He rose from his chair and paced to the window. He stared unseeing at the rolling lawns outside, at the bare trees that bordered them. His mind was racing. *This had to happen when I was given charge. Underage sex! Abortion!* His face darkened. *It'll rip the diocese apart. And the damage to the Church, at a time when all sorts of stuff is going on already. Good Lord, there'll be all sorts of enquiries, claims for compensation, a media frenzy. They'll want Ray's head on a stick. I suppose the safest thing would be to give it to them.* He was torn between trying to distance himself from what had happened and his affection for Ray. *God help the lad; they'll never understand. I don't understand it myself. Dear Christ, they'll tear him to pieces.*

His mind played back some of Ray's story. *He obviously was in some sort of psychological slough. I'll have to check with that psychotherapist, if she doesn't start with all that patient confidentiality stuff. He can't have known what he was doing. There's got to be some kind of 'invincible ignorance' element here. And that bollocks, McGennity!* Anger filled him again. *I'll bloody sort him later. He's absolutely culpable and he'll suffer the consequences. How would Ray have known where to go for an abortion? He never would even have thought of it. McGennity has obviously brow-beaten him into it. And Ray let him, something about McGennity's appearance and attitude triggering repressed childhood fears? What was that all about? No way are the girl's parents and relatives going to buy that, they'll want his hide.* He sucked in a frustrated breath. *And they'll want mine too. What a mess! But I can't throw him to the wolves. He doesn't deserve that. It'll have to be covered up, for Ray's sake, for the Church's.* And his little inner voice said, 'Yeah, and it'll save your fingers from getting burnt as well.'

He ignored it but he could not avoid the realisation that his cogitations were leading him to repeat the same mistakes other bishops had made before him. Rather than report this ... this what? It was a sexual crime, on the surface, but rather than report it, he was planning to wrap the whole situation in a cloud of secrecy. If that ever got out, the consequences didn't bear thinking about. But this case was singular. He knew Ray, dammit, he even knew his heart. One mistake, a victim of circumstances, he had absolutely no doubt of that. Yet the slightest hint of an investigation, even of an allegation, would see Ray branded as a child molester and a paedophile. Could he in all conscience allow Ray to be subjected to the vicious condemnation that would follow, to be crucified on the cross of public ignominy? He went back to the desk and sat down with a heavy sigh.

"This is a mess, Ray." Ray said nothing. Tony went on. "I can't help but feel that you are something of a victim in all of this." He stared at the silent curate, his face etched with worry. "Okay, you made the girl pregnant; but you weren't yourself." His head was moving slowly from side to side. "You don't deserve to be pilloried for one mistake. I'll have to sort something."

Ray, still resolutely stoic, said, "I'm prepared to accept the full consequences of my actions."

Tony tried to gather his thoughts. "Who knows about this?"

"Just the parish priest, and yourself, uh ... and Dan." Ray's voice was so low that Tony could scarcely hear him.

"What about the girl's parents?"

"No."

"No? How come?"

Ray compressed his lips. He made no response.

"Ray, I need to know the situation if I'm going to deal properly with this. Is she likely to say anything about this?"

"I don't think so."

"How can you be sure?"

"Father McGennity threatened her with the seal of confession, said she was obligated to honour it, said her immortal soul would be damned forever if she breathed a word about any of it."

"In the name of God! What is it with that man?"

Ray simply stared at the desk without comment. Tony, too, sat in silence, searching his mind frantically for options. Eventually he said, “Look, Ray. You probably know that one of my roles is to investigate any problems of clerical misconduct in the diocese. On the face of it, you, a priest, are guilty of statutory rape ...” Ray’s eyes closed and his head went down. “And then, assisting in an abortion?” Tony groaned again. “Suffering saints, Ray, how are we ever going to get around that? But I don’t think you were fully yourself. I can’t say to what extent you are or are not culpable but from what I have been able to drag out of you, I would have to say that you do not remotely fall into the abuse category.” He studied the young priest, his hollow cheeks, the dark-rimmed eyes, a broken shadow of the enthusiastic curate who had gone to Drumkillen only ten months before. Then he came to a decision. “Ray, I want you to go back to the parochial house and pack your things. Don’t say anything to anybody. I’ll pull Gerard Mulvaney from Kilnamoy for the time being and send him to Drumkillen in your place. Ciaran and Dan will have to cope without him for a while.”

Ray looked up at him. “Where do you want me to go? You can’t send me to a different parish. I couldn’t ...”

“It’s okay, Ray. That’s not what I’m thinking about. You’re sick, there’s no doubt about that. I’m going to have to send you somewhere quiet to recuperate. Just come back here tonight. I’ll get the housekeeper to prepare a room for you. I have an idea that might work but I’ll need to make a phone call first.”

“I’m sorry, Tony; you’d need to let me know what you’re planning before I agree to commit to it.”

Tony drummed on his desk for a minute with the fingers of one hand. Then he looked up and said, “Well, I have a friend. He's wealthy and has a villa in the Bahamas and an apartment in a lovely wee town called Torbole in Italy. It's at the northern tip of Lake Garda. He's so busy making money that he has little time to visit either of these places and he's always at me to take time off and go to either residence any time I like. I've been to Torbole once. Beautiful place. It'll be lovely this time of the year. I'm going to phone my friend and ask if I can send you there, away from ministry, away from hassle, away from all that you've had to deal with. My hope is you'll recover there. I'll try to keep the lid on things at this end. Then we'll see where we go from there."

"Tony, that's very kind," Ray said, "but I have done a grave wrong. I can't just walk away from it."

"Nor would I let you," Tony said, "if you had been yourself. But this is a situation full of terrible complexities. You never would have done this thing had you been in full control of your faculties. Look, all I am asking you to do is to take time out, think about things and when your head is clear, we'll deal with it. Okay?"

Ray nodded, still riddled with guilt but grateful for the unexpected opportunity to reflect on his state in a quiet and distant place. He rose to leave. "Thank you, Tony. I'll go and get my stuff." He walked to the door, then stopped and turned with his hand still on the handle. "Why didn't the bishop say anything to you about this?"

"The bishop?"

"Yes. Father McGennity told him about me or, at least, he told me he was going to."

"The bishop is unwell, Ray. Anything like that would have to come through me, and there wasn't a word about it."

Ray looked puzzled. "I wonder why he said he was going to report me?"

Tony made a face. "Sadistic wretch! He was just ... bloody hell, ah, excuse me, Ray, but I would really love to know just how much of the responsibility for all of this can be laid at his door." He pointed a sharp finger at Ray who was about to speak. "Don't. Don't start again with all that accepting full responsibility stuff. Go on now and get your things. I'll see you in a couple of hours."

2

Mrs. Toner was pulling the front door shut behind her as Ray's car came up the drive. She stood on the step waiting for him to get out of the car. "I thought you weren't goin' to be back for dinner?" It was almost an accusation. "I didn't leave anything for you."

"It's all right, Mrs. Toner," Ray said, opening the door. "I'm only here for a minute."

Mrs. Toner made to follow him into the hall. "I can make you a wee bit of something."

"No, no, no, no, it's really all right. I'm leaving again right now. You go on and attend to George."

"Well, if you're sure." Mrs. Toner stared at him. *God help him, he looks desperate.* Aloud she said, "I'm away then. I'll see you tomorrow."

Ray watched her turn away, watched her close the door as she left. He stood in the hall, unmoving. Filling his mind, growing louder with each repetition, was the thought, *She's been very good to me. She's been very good to me.* He ran to the door and pulled it open. Mrs. Toner had reached the gate.

"Mrs. Toner," he shouted. "Hold on a minute, please."

She looked back, surprise on her face. Ray approached her and said, "Mrs. Toner, I won't see you tomorrow. Look, you've been very good to me. Please don't spread this around but, as you have rightly been pointing out, I have been ill. I'm just back from the bishop's house. Canon Mulholland is taking me off my duties and sending me away to get well."

Mrs. Toner stood stock still, her eyes wide, her mouth hanging open. Ray went on, "I couldn't let you go without saying goodbye. I don't know when I'll see you again."

"Oh, dear God, Father," Mrs. Toner cried, already tearful. "It's nothing serious, is it?"

"Ah no, nothing like that; it's kinda stress related."

"I coulda guessed," she said, anger replacing the tears. She scowled darkly and, tossing her head sideways at the house, she hissed, "It was that oul' ..."

Ray reached out a hand and touched her gently on the shoulder. "It's more than that," he smiled wanly. "It's me. Something that needs to heal. But thank you again for all you have done for me." He looked down at her and saw genuine sadness on her face. He held out his arms and she fell into them, crying now. "You've been a mother to me, Mrs. Toner. Thank you. Thank you. I'll come and look you up sometime when I get better."

She pulled away, wiping her cheeks with the back of her hand. "Make you sure you do," she said, attempting to sound ferocious. In that she failed miserably. Then she turned to leave. "The parish will be all the poorer for your goin'. There's goin' to be a lot of unhappy people here in the next few days." She gave him one last look. "It gives me no pleasure to have been proved right about you bein' sick, Father, but I'm glad somethin's bein' done about it. I really hope you get well soon."

Ray gave her a final nod and went back into the house. It took a few journeys back and forth but he managed to squeeze all of his possessions into the car. Each time he returned to the house, he would pause at the hall phone, debating whether or not to phone Maria. Each time he would shake his head and think *'too late'*, and each time he would dismiss the impulse without clarifying in his mind whether he meant too late in the evening or too late because the relationship had now degenerated beyond soft words and apologies. He went back to survey his study one final time before leaving. He'd have to leave the new computer desk he'd purchased, but that was no real hardship. He took one last look around, at the now empty bookshelves, at the table, at the armchairs, at the room where he had begun his priestly ministry with such spiritual intensity and hopes of faithful service. A cloud passed over his eyes. *How could I have allowed it to come to this? Could I have prevented what happened?* Were there really, as Tony suggested, extenuating circumstances?

Anger filled him with a devastating suddenness. *That pervert, Henry! He did this.* Memories, long repressed but now released, again filled his mind. His head ached. He covered his face with his hands and staggered backwards a couple of steps. *No ... no ... no!* He fought to restrain the memories, to blanket the awful pictures threatening to overwhelm him. He inhaled deeply and exhaled a long hissing breath, his face still buried in his hands. He inhaled again, exhaled, and inhaled again, until he regained some measure of control, until he was able to find his way back to that cold, unfeeling place where he was safe.

Lifting his head from his hands, he stared around the room once more. His eyes strayed to the fireplace. His gaze stayed there, becoming unfocused, and a distant but achingly haunting echo began to sound in the recesses of his mind, a far-off song of winter fires, and the flickering colours of orange and gold on lovers' faces. A terrible sadness threatened to overcome him but he shook it off, resolutely turning from the room and pulling the door shut behind him.

TWENTY-NINE

1

Ray had little trouble finding the apartment that was to accommodate him in the small Italian town of Torbole but he had, perhaps, rather more difficulty in coming to terms with its opulence. It occupied the entire top floor of a large three-storey building that was constructed on a high slope not far from the edge of the village. The apartment was large and roomy, appointed with luxurious and elegant furnishings. It had three bedrooms and a lounge with two huge picture windows that allowed panoramic views of the lake and the surrounding landscape. There was also an ornate, Romanesque bathroom, and a fully equipped modern kitchen off which he found a small laundry room. Ray stood at one of the huge windows, almost the width of the entire wall and, dropping his bags, he surveyed the magnificent vista below him.

Torbole lies on the extreme north of Lake Garda's east bank. It sits easily on the slopes of the rocky Castel Penede. Tony had said it was beautiful but that hardly prepared Ray for the cluster of colourful buildings, with their bright red slate roofs, sitting on the edge of the glorious blue lake, for the majestic grey-white mountains that looked down on the village from their enormous heights, for the imposing belfry of the centuries-old St. Andrew's chapel that stood high on the slopes behind the village. In the bright April sunshine, Torbole was utterly charming, a charm enhanced by the luxurious vegetation that had so captured the wonder and the admiration of Goethe who once lived there – palms, oleanders, olives, laurels, and the great cypress trees that towered at frequent intervals but with no discernible pattern over the houses on the hills. For anyone else the views would have been breathtaking. For Ray, whose capacity to feel, whose 'state of soul' was impervious to such outer stimuli, the scene induced merely indifference.

Ray turned from the window, his face impassive, and, after a cursory examination of the apartment, chose for himself the smallest of the three bedrooms. He pondered his indifference to what he could clearly see was nature at her loveliest, to scenes that at another time would have wrung from his lips the accolade 'awe-inspiring'. His reasoning processes seemed also to have deserted him because his mind simply remained blank as he sought the cause of his apathy.

In different circumstances his intelligence might have alerted him to the fact that his behaviour was irrational. There is a profound unity between the seat of reason and the rest of the personality. Feelings and affections cannot be separated from rationality. Reason is bound to feeling; it is inseparable from the unity of the whole person. If either reason or emotions are compromised in any way, if some attempt is made to separate reason from feeling, there would no longer be balance in the way the person would think and behave. The whole person could not function normally.

Nor could Ray. His emotional and mental states were at odds with each other. This imbalance was not for him a transient moment, something ephemeral. Something in him was struggling, subconsciously perhaps but with an intense exercise of will, to remain more or less permanently at a remove from events in his outer reality, events that he was unable to cope with. He sought to remain in a state where his emotional being could be left untouched and unperturbed. Because of the trauma that he was experiencing, past and present, and this response to them, his soul and his heart had become incapable of attributing any value to the things or events of the world around him. These held no significance for him. His energies were focused inwards, into another imbalance, into the frozen wasteland where he was permitting himself no longer to feel, no longer to engage mentally or emotionally with anything that tried to penetrate this preferred state of consciousness. In terms of psychic defence, this choice, paradoxically, was rational; in terms of personality wholeness, in terms of a path to healing, it was wholly irrational. Quite simply, in his bid to escape the pain and horror of his mind and heart, of the external reality of his life, he had cut himself off from his feelings, from his emotions, and from his God.

2

An image, as complete as it was unexpected, filled his mind. He saw, in terrible clarity, a newborn baby lying naked on a sun-dappled rug. The image was banished with ruthless brutality as suddenly as it had come. He shook his head and stared wildly along the horizon for some concrete distraction from this one ideation that from time to time plagued his sleeping hours and was capable of causing him unendurable distress. Ray had left his apartment and now stood at the wall that bordered the lake, his eyes squeezed shut, his fists clenched, as his will clamped down with obdurate intensity on the intruding phantasm.

"That's gone. That's gone. Irredeemably, irreparably, irretrievably," he muttered through clenched teeth. "You must not ... *ever* ... allow that thought to enter your head."

He opened his eyes and tried to lose himself in the glorious burnt-orange sunset that was lying on the far horizon, beginning to fill the evening sky between the mountain peaks, and turning the surface of the lake to molten bronze.

"That is beautiful. That is beautiful," he forced himself to say, feeling nothing of its extraordinary effect. Almost manic, he kept mumbling, filling his mind with thoughts, any thoughts, as he rushed headlong from the soul-suffocating image of the new-born child. "Beauty is truth, truth beauty, that is all ye know on earth and all ye need to know." Vulnerable now, he found tears in his eyes. "Maria is beauty but there was no truth. Oh God ..." He was staring at the lake. "Orange and gold. She'd love it here ...." He closed his eyes again and raised his face to the sky. "Stop! Stop! Stop!" he groaned. "I don't want to do this."

An elderly lady, walking alone and looking distinctly nervous, edged quickly past him, glancing uncertainly over her shoulder at him as she did so. Ray, lost in his struggle, was oblivious to her presence. He stood at the wall for a long time, staring at the sunset, waiting for frozen listlessness to stifle his feelings once more.

He turned to walk towards a little jetty not far from where he was standing. There was a small hotel there, its walls painted a deep red. In front of the hotel, on the jetty, were some tables and chairs, a number of them occupied by visitors or locals enjoying a drink in the balmy evening air. Ray found a place for himself in a small arched alcove that looked out over the lake and ordered a coffee. He sat staring, unseeing, at the scene before him, impervious to his surroundings.

3

A small group of youths, grinning vacuously, jostled each other as they turned, now walking backwards, to stare after two young women who had just passed them. The smaller of the two women, dressed in jeans and denim jacket, might not, had she been alone, have elicited this reaction. Her companion, however, lived with it constantly. Tall, elegant, dressed in tailored black trousers and a cream silk blouse, Armani sunglasses perched on top of blonde, shoulder-length hair that shone in the sun like spun gold, she would escape no-one's eye. The tall girl was beautiful.

Both girls followed the curving footpath that moved away from a roundabout towards the centre of the small town. They ignored a colourful *piazza* that appeared on their left, ignored its shops, its pizza *ristorante* – the Pizza Al Porto. They were headed for their favourite haunt on the jetty, the small Hotel Benaco, the forefront of which, inevitable on the continent, was cluttered with small tables and chairs. From here the view of the lake and its surrounding mountains was magnificent.

As they sat down at their usual place, the blonde girl's eyes swept the nearby tables, passing quickly over two elderly couples, a family of four, and a young couple who had eyes for no one but each other. A part of the jetty passed underneath a covered area, its walls painted a deep and heavy red. Smaller arches, carved into the walls, looked out over the placid lake, shimmering gloriously in the evening sun. The girl's gaze was arrested by a strikingly handsome man who sat alone in one of these side arches. He had not noticed her arrival, a circumstance to which she was unaccustomed. His eyes remained fixed on the lake. She studied him as she sat down, his neat dark hair, even angular chin, straight nose. She could see, too, that the shape of his mouth would have been pleasing were his lips not at that moment compressed. It was as if he were troubled by something dark in his thoughts. He was in his late twenties, maybe thirty, dressed conservatively in a black shirt and trousers.

Her companion had by this point become aware of the tall girl's interest and muttered something that caused them both to laugh. A waiter emerged from the hotel. They ordered two cappuccinos. The blonde girl continued to study the man, a stranger to her. She leaned forward and said something to her companion who laughed nervously and made some negating movements with her hands. The blonde girl smiled confidently and rose from her seat.

The heels of her boots clacked sharply on the small red *porfido* tiles that covered the jetty surface as she walked over to the stranger's table. There was an almost ethereal stillness about him that made her feel uncharacteristically nervous. Summoning a smile, nonetheless, she determined to ask him to join her for coffee. *"Potremmo prendere un caffè o qualcosa insieme?"*

The man turned quietly, raising his eyes to hers, but did not speak. Not comfortable with this silence, she fell back on the safe cliché of asking him if he was here on holiday. *"Sei qui in vacanza?"*

The man's expression registered mild puzzlement. This time, however, he responded. "I'm sorry ...?"

Behind his façade of polite interest the girl could detect a deep sadness but his eyes remained on her as she struggled to maintain a conversation. She wondered if he was waiting for someone. *"Aspetta qualcuno?"*

The stranger's head tilted, turning more directly towards her, and he said, *"Je parle un peu de Français. Vous le parlez?"*

The girl recognised the repeated French verb, almost identical in sound to its Italian equivalent. She shook her head, obliged to reply that she spoke only Italian. *"No. Io parlo Italiano soltanto."*

The man shrugged his shoulders. "*Dommage.*"

A corner of his lips moved, offering her a ghost of a smile. The girl sensed his sadness again. She knew now that if she were to make a conquest that evening, it would not be at this particular table. She returned his wan smile with a wry smile of her own and apologised for disturbing him. *"Mi scusi per il disturbo!"*

"Va benissimo. Non si preoccupi," he responded, the phrases falling easily from his tongue.

The girl's eyebrows arched and her smile widened. This sad young man spoke rather more Italian, perhaps, than he was prepared to admit. She stood looking down at him for a second longer. He raised his coffee cup in a small gesture of farewell and the girl, accepting her defeat with good grace and not a little regret, went back to her companion.

The man's eyes did not follow her. They were turned again towards the lake. Already he had forgotten the girl. Part of his brain was filled with noise; the other part was refusing to acknowledge it. He sat, unmoving and unmoved, in a strange state of feeling and not feeling, of knowing and not knowing. He stared at the tall, flat houses bordering the lake, their colours stark in the evening sunshine – apple green, ochre, cream, tomato red, pink, brown. He stared at the white steamer turning into a small station some yards away. He stared at the high limestone mountains that towered into an extraordinary sky, burnt-orange now in the gathering twilight. And he stared at the blue-green lake growing ever wider at its horizon, its surface gradually being transformed into burnished gold as the huge ball of the sun sank ever lower.

His intellect told him that he was observing a scene of rare beauty. His heart and his spirit told him nothing. These he had forcibly imprisoned in a block of ice. He could not allow them their freedom. To do so would release a torrent of emotions in which he knew he would drown.

4

A small inquisitive moonbeam crawled up along the bed and on to the sleeper's face. Its feeble light showed Ray's expression to be calm, freed in sleep from its customary strain. The moonbeam passed on but not before it revealed a trace of a smile on Ray's lips. He was dreaming. In his dream he saw again the naked child, a boy, lying on its rug, its little arms spread but moving erratically, its little legs kicking. Its tiny mouth was puckered in a little 'O' of pleasure as it relished its instinctive experiments with movement. Then, with terrible suddenness, the baby imploded and became a bloodied mess of entrails and torn flesh lying on the rug.

Ray's eyes shot open and he leapt from the bed on to the floor, gasping in shock and clutching his head with both hands as he tried to squeeze the horrific image from his brain. He lurched to the bathroom and hung over the sink, dry-retching and heaving, tears spurting from his eyes. He clung to the basin for a few minutes and then turned on a tap and splashed cold water on his face. He staggered back into his bedroom and went to the window, still panting fitfully as he stared into the darkness outside.

"Oh God," he groaned, his eyes wide and agitated. "What have I done?"

THIRTY

1

"My understanding of canon law is that the state cannot compel me to hand over any evidence from my investigations. I can handle this internally."

"Rubbish, Tony," Dan snapped with a deal more force than respect. "You know that I defer to your superior knowledge and intelligence but what you're saying is sophistical rubbish. Ray broke the law, unlawful carnal intercourse with a minor. That's it. You have to report him to the police."

Deep down, Dan may have been experiencing some form of pain or grief or distress but his principal emotion was one of righteous anger and it was that anger that had brought him hurtling once more into Tony's office the day after Ray had left for Italy, still vexed and tormented by Ray's revelations. Tony was little pleased by Dan's intrusion and by his uncharacteristic belligerence towards him but he struggled to remain calm.

"Dan, you don't have all the facts. There are things about this case you don't know, so really, you can't form a correct judgement."

"Ray assured me that I had the facts. What else do I need to know?"

"At the moment I have to keep Ray's confidences but there are extenuating circumstances, not least that Ray wasn't himself. He didn't know what he was doing."

"Balderdash!" Dan's anger flared again. "He's bound to have known. She was a schoolgirl."

"Look, Dan, all I can tell you is that certain events in Ray's life have hampered his growth to full emotional maturity. None of us could ever have guessed. But the effects of these experiences emerged as a result of a recent illness, and I have to say, it gives me an understanding of his transgression. I wouldn't try to defend him if I did not truly believe that's Ray's case has nothing to do with abuse or paedophilia."

Dan stared at his old mentor, not convinced. "But you're covering for him. Defend him some other way. Cover-ups have become a world-wide problem, not just here in Ireland. Bishops and cardinals are resigning in countries all over the world, leaving terrible scandals in their wake. And you know as well as I do that there is a terrible sense of bitterness and betrayal in some Irish parishes about the mishandling of clerical sex abuse. Do you want to add to that?"

"What I want, Dan," Tony said wearily, "is to help a friend who is in trouble. One slip, Dan. One slip, for God's sake. He sinned one lousy time. Okay, his act might have been sinful, and the girl might have been underage, barely, but in no way does Ray's behaviour exhibit the extreme compulsion of paedophilia. So why ..."

"Abortion, Tony. Abortion, " Dan almost shouted. "How can you defend that?"

"No, I can't defend that. But I have reason to believe that Ray is being childish about ... maybe punishing himself by accepting blame for another's involvement." He held up a hand as Dan went to speak. "No, I won't talk about that. I have yet to investigate it."

"Tony, you're letting friendship screw with your judgement. If this ever gets out, and it will, the media'll eat you alive."

Tony felt some heat and said sharply, "And on the basis of that possibility, you are prepared to toss Ray, your best friend, to the wolves and to hell with the consequences? Sacrifice without mercy? There's something dangerously immature about your righteousness, Dan, earnest though it may be. There has to be room for compassion and tolerance of human frailties. If you are insisting in perfection in our priests, then you are doomed to failure because nobody is perfect. We sin, for God's sake, but we repent, we get up, we soldier on." He got up from behind his desk and walked to the door. "And furthermore, Dan," he went on, his growing anger forcing him to awaken in Dan some awareness of his own sinfulness, "you might want to read again and reflect on the parable of the Prodigal Son. There is a lot of the older brother in you that you need to take a look at." He stepped aside from the door as Dan approached it. "I'm up to my eyes in this, Dan, and you're not helping. Leave now." Dan's hurt expression softened him. "But come back again in a few days when we've both cooled down and had more time to think about this. Then we'll talk."

2

The white bed sheets were rapidly turning to a terrifying red as the midwife tried to deliver the baby. She knew that blood supply doubles in a pregnant woman but she did not like the look of this at all. She whispered something urgent to the nurse beside her, sending her scurrying from the room. The midwife continued trying to deliver the baby, her hands slipping on the blood that covered the baby's head. There was a fierce panic on the face of the woman who had looked down and had seen the blood. She was panting frantically, unable to form the words to match the question in her wide, frightened eyes. The monitoring machines were beginning to issue warning whistles and crackles that boded no good. The nurse who had been sent out rushed back into the room with a white-coated doctor in tow. He pushed the midwife aside and tried to examine the woman. She was panting loudly, whimpering occasionally in panic, as the contractions grew stronger.

"The placenta has separated from the uterine lining," the doctor muttered, his own efforts to deliver the baby no more successful than the midwife's. "All this blood ... she's losing an awful lot. It may not be able to coagulate." He struggled to drag the baby loose, agitated by the sounds from the foetal monitor that signalled that the baby was in severe distress. "Damn! Retroplacental blood has penetrated the uterine wall. If the myometrium ruptures ... Come on. Come on."

The midwife, at the head of the bed now, trying to soothe the patient, looked at the monitors and hissed, "Doctor, she's going into haemorrhagic shock." She looked at the nurse, her face strained. "Go and get a priest."

The nurse ran to the nurse's station down the corridor and ran her finger down a list of phone numbers encased in a plastic cover on the desk. She found the number she needed.

3

Dan drove away from the bishop's house filled with conflicting emotions. He was still angry. His anger had not been tempered by the effect of Tony's final words to him. He was due to visit the hospital shortly and wondered what sort of comfort he would be able to give the patients in this mood. He stared at the road ahead, his reflections making him oblivious to the fact that he was driving considerably in excess of the speed limit. The Prodigal Son? Was Tony seriously comparing him to the older brother? He drove automatically, his mind flitting erratically between thoughts of Ray and Tony's broadside. A short time later, as he was approaching the gates of the hospital, his mobile beeped. He reached into his pocket and put the phone to his ear.

"Hello, Father Patterson here."

A breathless voice responded, "Father, where are you?"

"I'm just heading into the Mater Hospital. Who's speaking, please?"

"Nurse Tina Maguire at the Mater, Gynaecology. Please, you must come quickly. Mrs. O'Hanlon is in premature labour and she's going into haemorrhagic shock and the baby is ... oh, please, Father, please hurry. They need a priest."

Dan wasted no time seeking further explanations. He sped to the front entrance, parked illegally, and rushed into the hospital. He waited, tense and impatient, for the lift to reach Patricia's floor and raced down the corridor to the nurse's station. Nurse Maguire was waiting for him and led him with equal haste to the private ward. A few feet from the door he saw Terence struggling with two hospital porters who were trying to prevent him from bursting into the ward. Terence suddenly saw Dan running down the corridor and he screamed, his face ugly with worry and anger, "You bastard. You bastard. This is all your fault." He continued to struggle with the porters, each of whom was now holding one of his arms. "If anything happens to either of them, I'll sue you to hell and back. You bastard. D'you hear me?"

Dan stopped for a second, his face radiating shock and uncertainty. "I've got to go in there, Terence. She might need me. I'll talk to you later." He hurried past the distraught husband and went into the ward. He stopped dead just inside the door, stunned into immobility at the horrors before him. The bed and floor were covered in blood, as were the doctor and midwife. Patricia lay on the bed, gasping feebly, staring in fright at the ceiling. The midwife was holding the tiny bloodied body of what was clearly a lifeless baby.

"Oh, my God," Dan breathed, "Oh, my God." Then, gathering himself, he said to Nurse Maguire, "Get some water, quick. I need to baptise the baby."

The nurse rushed out and Dan went to Patricia, smoothing her forehead with his right hand while he searched in his pocket with his left.

"How is she?" he said to the doctor, who was filling a syringe from a little bottle.

The doctor's mouth went down and he shrugged silently.

Patricia's wild eyes turned to Dan when she heard his voice. She struggled to speak between pants, "F ... f ... fa ..."

"It's all right, Patricia. Don't try to talk. I'm going to anoint you with the Holy Oils." He set his little packet on a shelf beside the bed and bent over the terrified woman, slipping a thin stole around his shoulders "Are you sorry for your sins and all the sins of your past life, Patricia?"

The woman nodded frantically, still unable to speak.

Dan smoothed her forehead again. "That's fine, Patricia. Through the ministry of the Church may God give you pardon and peace, and I absolve you from all your sins, in the name of the Father and of the Son and of the Holy Spirit. Your sins are forgiven, Patricia. God is with you now. There's no need to be afraid. I'm just going to anoint you now."

Patricia's eyes never left Dan's during the short rite, not even noticing the injection the doctor gave her or the uncoagulated spurts now beginning to stream down her arms from earlier injection sites. Her breathing became laboured, erratic.

Dan reached into his pocket for a small gold pyx and said, "I'm going to give you Holy Viaticum now," and, as he placed the host on the woman's tongue, he said, "Body of Christ."

It was a struggle for the woman to receive the Eucharist, so erratic was her breathing, but when she managed to swallow the host she seemed suddenly to become calm. She continued to stare at Dan, something akin to gratitude showing in her eyes before they began to close. Dan knelt at the side of the bed, oblivious to the blood that began to stain his clothes. He put his head in his hands and prayed desperately for the happy repose of Patricia's immortal soul.

THIRTY-ONE

1

Maria lay fully clothed on the top of her bed, huddled foetus-like, her knees drawn up to her abdomen. Her red-rimmed eyes held traces of tears and her pale face radiated misery. Her hands were crossed at the wrists under her chin and one of them held her mobile phone. She moved her hand to where she could look at her phone, staring at it as if waiting for it to ring. Her face crumpled and tears began to flow again. She pressed the phone against her forehead and, in a heartbroken voice filled with intensity, she moaned, “Please ... please ...”

But the phone did not ring. Instead, there was a knock on the door and her mother poked her head in. Anxiety was written on her face as she said, “We’re about to have dinner, Maria. Are you coming down?”

Maria’s back was to the door. She did not turn round but simply said, “I don’t feel well, Mum. I’ll just lie here for a wee while.”

“But you have to eat, Maria, you haven’t been eating.”

“Please, Mum,” Maria cut in, almost snapping. “I don’t want any dinner. I just want to lie here.”

Mrs. Rafferty stood looking at the back of her daughter's head. She felt she should try to persuade Maria to eat but she had been through this same scenario several times in the past few weeks and, on the occasions when she had tried to insist, Maria would end up screaming at her to leave her alone. Something was troubling her daughter and she could only hope that Maria would soon realise that mothers were created to listen to their teenage daughters and to comfort them when they were having problems. She fought her worry, said no more, and closed the door quietly as she left.

After the abortion, Maria had experienced a numb relief that had helped her function normally for a few days. But she began to experience sleepless nights during which she was subject to violent mood swings that she found deeply disturbing. The doctor at the clinic had lied. Maria knew that she was falling into depression, fuelled by a terrible guilt and misery at the murder of her baby. And her feelings for Ray, too, had become ambivalent. At times she hated him for what he had done to her and determined she would never speak to him again. At times she ached so much for his presence that she would bite viciously into the knuckles of her hands to try to stem the longing. And all the while she wondered where he was, why he didn't try to contact her. She saw him occasionally at mass and could tell that he, too, was suffering. His face had grown thinner, his eyes rimmed with dark shadows, and on one occasion when their eyes had met, she sensed as much as saw a heartache that matched her own. Her heart had melted then but when he turned his gaze away from hers, she sensed a gulf between them that she was sure could never be bridged and she left the chapel without any attempt to meet him. Yet there were times when, in the depths of loneliness and aching for the sound of his voice, she would start to ring his number but always, before she had pressed even a few of the digits, she would stop herself. What could she say? He wouldn't give up his priesthood. And she couldn't bear to hear him say yet again that there was no future for them, that their relationship had to end.

Her days, as well as her nights, were filled with heartache. Her schoolwork suffered and she had turned her back on her friends, seeking solace in isolation. Tess had tried a few times to break through her shell, to discover the cause of her withdrawal, but Maria had responded with such cold aloofness that even Tess gave up on her. The day came for her follow-up appointment at the clinic and Maria had deliberately ignored it. She would not allow herself to contact Ray to have him drive her there. Any conversation they would have would be too painful.

But last Sunday morning a new priest had said Ray's ten-thirty mass. There had been some speculation about that but no one seemed to know whether the stranger was just a visitor passing through or a new curate for the parish. Today she had overheard a conversation in the classroom during which one of the girls claimed to have heard that Father Canavan had left the parish. A terrible distress had clutched Maria and she realised that while she could refrain from contacting Ray when she knew he was nearby, when there was always a chance they might bump into each other, the thought that he might be gone from the parish devastated her.

Now she lay on her bed, agonising over whether or not she should phone the parochial house and talk to him. Surely they could at least be friends? Surely they could comfort each other whether they had a relationship or not? He owed her that much. Did he not help to ... kill their child? Her head went down into her chest and tears of guilt and self-reproach again filled her eyes. *That poor wee thing. Ah, God help it! How could Ray ... I mean, he's a priest.* And she pressed her head into the pillow and gave herself over to another bout of weeping.After a few moments she stopped and, with a determined look on her face, began to dial the parochial house. She waited in a state of tension when she heard the ringing tone. Her fists were clenched and she began to shake but she managed to refrain from disconnecting.

There was a click and someone said, "Hello. Parochial house."

Maria recognised Mrs. Toner's voice. Taking a deep breath, she said as calmly as she could, "Hello, this is one of the girls from the choir. Could I speak to Father Canavan for a minute, please? It's about ..."

"Oh, I'm sorry, child," Mrs. Toner stopped her. "Father Canavan is not here anymore."

"Not there anymore?" Maria's voice was almost a wail but she was unable to disguise her sudden distress. "What do you mean he's not there?"

"He's gone, child," Mrs. Toner said. "But the new curate, Father Mulvaney is here. Would you would like to speak to him?"

"No. No." Maria was panicking. "It has to be Father Canavan."

Mrs. Toner was puzzled by the girl's insistence and surmised that she was probably someone that Father Ray had been counselling. Instinctively sympathetic, she said, "I'm sorry, dear. Father Canavan has left the parish."

"Do you know where he has gone?"

Again Mrs. Toner could hear that strange anxiety in the girl's voice. She said as much as she felt she could, "No, child, he didn't tell me. He arrived at the door one evening last week just as I was going home and told me he would be away for the foreseeable future. He said goodbye and, I have to say, it sounded like I'd never see him again. Are you sure you don't want to speak to Father Mulvaney?"

"No ... No ...."

And there was a click followed by an electronic silence. Mrs. Toner took the phone from her ear, looked quizzically at it for a moment, and replaced it on its hook.

Maria sat up on the bed, her legs over the side, wide-eyed and hyperventilating. "Oh God! Oh God! Where has he gone? Where has he gone?" She pressed the heels of her hands into her eyes and fought to quell a panic that was slipping out of control. "Oh God! He'll phone. He'll phone. He's bound to let me know. He wouldn't run off just like that." She fell back on the bed again, tucking her knees tight into her stomach and her face into her chest. She began to shiver. "Oh God, Oh God! Ray ... Ray ... please ... please ..." And she lay there, distraught, lost in the depths of a misery that she knew her mother would never understand.

2

It was two weeks later that Mr. and Mrs. Rafferty received a letter from Mrs. McLoughlin, inviting them to an urgent meeting at her office at ten o'clock the following morning. Mr. Rafferty was initially reluctant to take time out of his busy schedule and asked his wife to " ... handle it, whatever it is." But his wife insisted that he accompany her, very aware of the dramatic personality change in her daughter over the previous few weeks. She had no doubt that Maria would be the subject of the meeting.

They arrived at the school exactly on time and were ushered into Mrs. McLoughlin's office. She rose to greet them, shaking hands with them both, and inviting them to sit. When she had settled again in her own chair behind her desk, she said, "Maria will be along in a few minutes but I wanted a short chart with you both before she arrives."

Mr. Rafferty looked disturbed. "Is there something wrong?" he asked, puzzled.

His wife turned to him. "Peter, for God's sake! Of course there's something wrong. If you weren't all the time buried in those drawings of yours, you wouldn't have to ask that question."

Her husband said, somewhat defensively, "Well, I knew that she had been a bit uncommunicative lately but I thought it was just some teenage hormonal thing."

Mrs. McLoughlin shook her head. "No, it isn't that, Mr. Rafferty. I have more than enough experience of that to know it when I see it. No, this is something very different."

Mrs. Rafferty asked in a concerned voice, "Has Maria been behaving oddly in school as well?"

Mrs. McLoughlin nodded. "I'm afraid so, Mrs. Rafferty. But, please, don't assume that you are here for some kind of disciplinary process. Maria is a wonderful girl, one of our best and brightest pupils. I am very fond of her and I am now desperately worried about her. I am not interested in punishment or threats or exclusion, none of those things. I really want the three of us to work together to see if we can help her."

"What's she been doing?" Mr. Rafferty asked, clearly worried now.

Mrs. McLoughlin gestured to a number of handwritten pages on her desk. "Well, I have here some reports from her teachers, they don't make pretty reading." She sighed. "Perhaps if they had referred to some other girls I would have dealt with them as normal disciplinary issues. But these behaviours are not Maria." She shook her head in mystification. "Something's going on in your daughter. I was hoping that you might have had some idea. You don't know if she's been experimenting with drugs or anything like that?"

"Oh God, no. I'm sure I would know if she was," Mrs. Rafferty said, shocked.

"What do those reports say?" Mr. Rafferty said, nodding anxiously at the papers.

Mrs. McLoughlin lifted them and leafed through them making a brief comment from each one. "Late for class, not turning up three times in a row for history, failure to hand in her home assignments, sullen, impertinent, uncooperative, performance in tests poor ..." She looked up at the shocked parents, shaking her head. "And more of the same. That's not Maria at all. And my own observations are no better. She used to be so neat and tidy; now her clothes are wrinkled and she has dull unwashed hair where it used to be shining and glossy. What's more, she never comes to choir practice any more, yet no one loves to sing more than Maria." She set the papers down and spread her hands. "Something's wrong."

There was a knock on the door. Mrs. McLoughlin's lips tightened. "That'll be her now." She raised her voice. "Enter."

Maria came in, looking frightened. "You wanted to see ..." Then she saw her parents and stopped, alarmed. "Dad? Mum? What are you doing here?"

Mrs. McLoughlin pointed to a straight-backed chair in the corner of her office. "Would you bring that chair over, Maria, please, and sit down. We only want to have a chat with you."

Mr. Rafferty studied his daughter, probably for the first time in ages. And he saw an unnaturally pale face, dark-rimmed eyes, lank greasy hair, a wrinkled uniform, and suddenly he didn't recognise her. His heart began to hammer. *What in God's name is happening to my little girl?* Maria brought the chair to the edge of the group and sat down, her knees tight together, her hands clasped, white-knuckled, on her lap. Her head went down and she stared at a spot about halfway up the front of Mrs. McLoughlin's desk.

The principal, too, but with rather less tension, clasped her hands on the desk in front of her and stared at the girl. "Have you any idea why you're here, Maria?"

"No, Miss."

Mrs. McLoughlin waved a hand at the papers on the desk. "Do you know what these are?"

Maria shot a glance at the papers from under her eyebrows and looked away again. "No, Miss."

Despite his anxiety, Mr. Rafferty felt a stirring of anger. "What are you playing at, Maria? Those reports are about you. You know you've been misbehaving. Why pretend?"

Maria continued to stare at the desk and made no reply. Mrs. McLoughlin held up a restraining hand, silencing the parent.

“Maria,” she said gently, “yes, the reports are about you but I don’t care about them. It is obvious to me that you are deeply troubled about something. All I want to do, and your parents, too, is to help you sort out your problem. But we can’t do that unless we know what the problem is.”

Maria remained silent.

“Well?” her father said.

Maria did not look at him. “Well what?” she said.

“Maria!” her father was angry again, and again Mrs. McLoughlin stopped him.

“It’s all right, Mr. Rafferty. Let’s deal with this calmly.” Then she turned to Maria and said softly, “Maria, look at me, please.”

The girl looked up but there was some defiance in her glance. Mrs. McLoughlin elected not to notice it.

“Maria, you are going through a very bad time. We all know it, so there is no point in pretending. We also know that whatever it is, you cannot deal with it alone.” Her voice was almost pleading now, totally unlike the disciplined, dogmatic principal that Maria was familiar with. The defiance left Maria’s eyes as she listened. “Don’t you know you’re loved, child? Do you think that anyone here would see you suffering like this and not want to help? Please, child, tell us what is troubling you. Let us help. I promise you, you won’t get into any trouble.” Mrs. McLoughlin held the girl’s eyes and Maria was unable to look away.

After a moment Maria’s eyes filled with tears and she cried, “I can’t. I can’t.”

“Can’t what, child?”

"I can't tell you anything. I just can't."

"But why not, Maria? We only want to help you."

The parents looked at their daughter who was weeping openly now. Their faces showed their concern but they were totally at a loss. They could only leave the situation to the principal. Maria's head was down again, heavy tears dropping on to her joined hands. "I ... I'm bound by the seal of confession. I'll be ... I'll be eternally damned if I say anything," she sobbed.

Mr. Rafferty rose from his chair. "What?"

Mrs. McLoughlin gestured with both hands this time, urging him to be seated again, while at the same time saying in utter astonishment, "What on earth are you talking about, child? Only priests are bound by the seal of confession. Who or what put that ridiculous idea into your head?"

"Father McGennity says ..." and she stopped, sobbing convulsively.

Mrs. Rafferty had risen from her chair and was standing now with her arm around her daughter's shoulder, her own face taut and tearful. Mrs. McLoughlin stiffened at the mention of the parish priest's name and said sharply, "I don't know what the parish priest said but there is no way on God's sweet earth that a young child like you should have been told that she is under the seal of confession. It is totally wrong, Maria. The seal applies only to priests, believe me, *only ... to ... priests*."

Maria was wailing now, and she turned her face into her mother's breast who had by now put both arms around her.

"Shhhh, Maria! Shhhh! It's all right. It's all right," she said soothingly, fighting her own tears and more concerned than ever about what might be causing her daughter such distress. He husband could only stare helplessly at them, he, too, fearing some awful revelation. Maria raised her eyes to her mother, trying to speak through the sobs that racked her. “Oh, Mum,” she cried. “Oh, Mum. I’m so ashamed. But it wasn’t Father Ray’s fault. It was ...”

Haltingly the story began to unfold, sometimes rushed and garbled, sometimes in such a low voice that her listeners could scarcely hear her. But they gleaned enough to render them shocked, silent, and immobile at the horrors the weeping girl revealed.

THIRTY-TWO

1

The phone on Tony's desk rang. He lifted the receiver and said, "Eleanor, I thought I told you that I can't take any calls his morning."

"I'm sorry, Canon!" the receptionist interrupted. "There are two people here insisting on seeing you and they won't leave until ..." Her voice drifted from the phone as she began to remonstrate with someone at her desk. "Excuse me, hello, excuse me. You can't go in there!"

Tony's office door was opening as his receptionist was speaking. He replaced the phone and stood up behind his desk, waiting to see who was forcing their way into his office. A man of small build, somewhere in his early forties, wearing a light overcoat, strode into the office, followed by a woman who looked distinctly nervous. Under normal circumstances, the man might have been described as nondescript, certainly possessing nothing in his appearance that might be considered threatening. But today his face was clouded by angry determination. Tony had an immediate suspicion about who the pair might be but he decided to pretend ignorance.

"Excuse me, sir. Do you have an appointment?"

"No, we don't have an appointment," the man said sharply. "But we need to talk to you and it won't wait."

Tony remained standing and did not offer seats to his uninvited visitors. "I can't say I'm happy about your approach, Mr. ...?"

"Rafferty. And this is my wife." The man gestured brusquely at the woman who was with him. "Does the name mean anything to you?"

Tony's expression remained blank. "I'm sorry. I'm afraid it means absolutely nothing to me."

The man's eyes narrowed in disbelief. "Does the name Father Raymond Canavan mean anything to you?"

"Of course," Tony replied calmly. "He's one of our diocesan priests."

"What have you done with him?"

"What have I done with him?" Tony echoed, expressing amazement. Then affecting annoyance, he went on, "Look, Mr. Rafferty, what's all this about? Why are you bursting into my office asking pointless questions?"

"Pointless? How's this for pointless?" Mr. Rafferty's ordinary face was suffused with rage as he walked to the edge of Tony's desk. "Father Canavan sexually abused my teenage daughter, made her pregnant and then took her to a clinic in Northern Ireland, without our consent or knowledge, to procure an abortion. Is there enough point in that for you?"

Tony did not have to pretend shock. He sat down, stunned, his mind filling in an instant with visions of diocesan chaos, of Ray in disgrace, and visions, too, of his career in ruins. He gestured limply to a couple of chairs before his desk, inviting the visitors to be seated. He took a deep breath, exhaled loudly and said, “This is a terrible accusation, Mr. Rafferty. There has to be some mistake.”

The couple remained standing.

“No mistake,” Mr. Rafferty snapped. “And Father Canavan has disappeared off the face of the earth. We need to speak to him.”

“I’m sorry, no. Father Canavan has been ill. I had to relieve him from his duties so that he could take time to recuperate.”

“A likely story. That’s far too much of a coincidence.”

Tony held up his hand and said, “I can understand your anger, Mr. and Mrs. Rafferty, if such a terrible thing has happened to your daughter. But why do you think Father Canavan is to blame?”

“Our daughter has told us everything.”

Tony himself began to simulate anger. “And that’s all you have to go on? Did you check her story? How do you know her story is not a delusional fantasy based on a schoolgirl crush or, perhaps, knowing that Father Canavan has now left the parish, she is using his name to protect some young boy she’s with?”

Mrs. Canavan spoke for the first time, scared and tearful. “Maria wouldn’t lie to us about a thing like that. We believe her.”

“Of course you do, Mrs. Rafferty,” Tony said. “Naturally you would want to believe your daughter. But I would need to have far more evidence than that if I am to start a witch-hunt after one of my ... one of the diocese’s priests. There are far too many people falsely accusing priests of all sorts of stuff these days.”

"Excuse me, Canon," Mr. Rafferty exploded. "You weren't there when her school principal forced the admission from her. There can be no doubt that she was speaking the truth. She went out of her way to defend Father Canavan, tried to put all the blame on herself, him a grown man and her only a wee girl ..." His voice broke and he angrily shook his head to prevent emotion overcoming him. "He has to answer for this. And you, too, if you persist in covering ..."

"Be careful, Mr. Rafferty," Tony interrupted him. "Don't start making accusations like that. I have to be very careful here. The least whiff of a scandal can destroy an innocent priest."

"What about my innocent daughter? She'll never get over this."

"I sympathise, I do. But all I'm saying, Mr. Rafferty, is that this has to be investigated. All you have is your daughter's word but I would need far more evidence than that. We had similar accusations in the past that have proved totally unfounded. You can't go running around making serious allegations of child abuse against one of our priests and then it turns out that there wasn't a word of truth in it. "

Mr. Rafferty, who had been leaning on Tony's desk with both hands, stepped back and said, "So, who will carry out this investigation?"

"That'll be my job," Tony replied.

Mr. Rafferty's face expressed something close to contempt. "You? And then that's the last we'll hear of it? No thanks." He turned on his heel and took his wife's elbow. "Come on, Amy. We'll go to the *Gardai*. We'll get some satisfaction there."

Tony knew that the man was adamant. He called to the wife as they were leaving. "Mrs. Rafferty, false accusations are dangerous for everybody. Think of the consequences. I ask you to persuade you husband to wait until I have had time to look into this ..."

He stopped as the man pulled the door shut behind him, cutting off Tony's words. He slumped at his desk. "Oh, shh ... it. There's going to be no stopping this now. It's going to charge all through the diocese, oh God, all over Ireland, like a runaway express train." He put his head in his hands, cursing his impotence. "Oh Jesus, Ray, Ray, Ray. What the hell have you done to me?"

2

For three days, like some desperate sight-seer anxious to miss nothing, Ray had sought to escape his inner landscape by focusing his attention on all that the landscape around Torbole had to offer. On his first afternoon he walked up the hill to the Church of St. Andrew, drawn there by the magnificent belfry, with its four beautiful mullioned windows, that could be seen from all parts of the village. He spent some time in conversation with an elderly lady there who sat behind a desk in the chapel selling little leaflets, cards and candles. She had plenty of time to talk and was happy to spend over an hour, with much pointing and gesticulation, telling him something of the church's history.

With her arms spread she demonstrated the chapel's first modest dimensions circa 1150, and from there she took Ray through details of the frequent additions over the centuries, elaborated with sorrowful mien and much head-shaking on the damage sustained during two world wars and an earthquake in 1975, and finished with proud smiling as she highlighted aspects of its present splendid state. She wanted to spend further time on the ornate statuary - the Madonna del Rosario, St. Anthony of Padova, St. Francesco, St. Teresa of Lisieux, and St. Giuseppe - but when Ray left her alcove, he had eyes only for the magnificent altarpiece that covered most of the back wall.

It was a painting of 'The Torture of St. Andrew', completed sometime in the mid 1700s by Gianbettino Cignaroli. Despite its age, its colours remained vibrant and the contrast between the light on the saint's body and the dark enmity of the armoured horseman behind him was probably still as stark as it had been in the eighteenth century. The old lady explained that the figures had been modelled by various local people of that era and some members, indeed, of the Guiliani family who had commissioned the painting.

But Ray found himself drawn intensely to the main subject of the painting. Something of the acceptance in the apostle's pose as his torturers prepared to carry out the crucifixion, of the utter disregard in the saint's eyes for the gruesome preparations that were going on around him as he stared heavenwards, struck a deep chord in Ray's psyche. But it was a chord that disturbed him, that sent him quickly from the church with a cursory goodbye to the old lady whose offended expression he was in too much of a hurry to notice.

Like Ray, the St. Andrew in the painting had seemed to move out of himself and away from the torture; unlike Ray, St. Andrew was clearly reaching outwards in hope to the light that shone on him. Ray knew that, while he too had moved away from his pain, he had managed only to remove himself to a place that was dark and hopeless. It was the sudden consciousness of the contrast between himself and St. Andrew that had sent him scurrying from the chapel.

He went back down into the village and from there a fifty minute walk took him to the other side of Mount Brione to the nearby town of Riva which reputedly dates back to the tenth century. Riva, he was to discover, was an important tourist destination and he tried to immerse himself in its history, dropping into the 12th century Rocca fortress, which now housed a municipal museum, to examine the many archaeological discoveries that proved early Roman habitation. After wandering for some time in the 'old town' with its tall buildings and narrow cobbled streets, he found a Tourist Office where he spent some time leafing desultorily through colourful brochures. The quality of the photography, particularly the breathtaking aerial shots, amazed him as much as did the awe-inspiring scenes they represented.

Looking for somewhere to eat, he came across the town's elegant promenade along the water's edge and he continued to walk for a while, surveying the glorious views of the deep blue lake as it lapped the base of the nearby Mt. Rocchetta and the grey-white mountains in the distance. His eyes darted here and there, taking mental snapshots for his intellect to analyse and collate for future memory. His emotions and spirit remained neutral and, unlike many times in similar circumstances in his past, there was nothing in him on this occasion that responded with praise and gratitude to the Lord for the wonder and grandeur of his creation.

He found a restaurant near a harbour and, as he ate a scone with his coffee, he observed little white steamers coming in and out of the jetty, heading off to, or arriving from, other towns up and down the lake. After he finished eating he went to the ticket office, procured a timetable for the various sailings, and took a steamer back to Torbole.

The following day, he used the boat service to visit a few towns on the edges of the lake, each more beautiful than the last – Sirmione, with its ancient mediaeval walls, the picturesque little port of Desenzano, Torri del Benaco with its scented olive and citron groves. It was a feast of beauty, all on the same lake, but each with its own distinctive views, its own history, and its own charm. Ray continued to convince himself that his appreciation of these natural wonders remained fixed on the intellectual level, that his aesthetic senses, that his very soul, continued implacably untouched.

What he failed to realise, however, or perhaps could not even conceive, was that the mastery of will he was attempting to achieve takes years of training. Even those who, perhaps because of some physical deformity or other equally compelling reason, spend years relentlessly protecting themselves by living coldly and unaffectedly on the edges of life, can find their self-defence mechanisms disintegrate utterly in the breath of a single emotion, more often than not, love. And Ray did not have years of training in controlling his emotions; he had, in fact, no training at all. He could not have known, therefore, that chinks in his armour of imperturbability could occur in places other than in the forefront of his mind where he applied all of his defensive energies. He did not know that the glories he was absorbing through his eyes each day, delights that were new and therefore to his mind unthreatening, were stealing into his soul and bringing with them light.

It was not until his third day in Italy that Ray found his way to Limone. Nestling alongside lemon groves, beneath the cliffs of the north-western shore of the lake, Limone is a magical place with narrow cobbled streets that wind forever upwards past a myriad of shops, old fishermen's homes, and a historic centre steeped in tradition. From the heights can be seen the magnificent spectacle of the two harbours, classic old arches, and the pillars and walls of the lemon groves dominating the shore as far as Reamol. It is an artist's paradise that offers an immense variety of picturesque and fascinating scenes that never fail to stir the imagination and the soul.

Limone has less than a thousand inhabitants but its fame has spread throughout the world. This is not, however, because of its undeniable colour and charm but because of the discovery in the blood of many of its inhabitants of a beneficial protein, Apolipoprotein A-1, that limits cholesterol and removes fat from the arteries. It was discovered by Cesari Sirtori, a famous Italian professor, and has been found to be efficacious against such problems as arteriosclerosis and heart disease. None of the inhabitants suffer from these health defects and now the medical world continues to try to understand how this genetic mutation has taken place. The people of Limone are proud that the 'elixir of longevity', as they call it, starts from their small village but this particular phenomenon held little interest for Ray who, at that point, had more than once wondered if his life had not already been long enough.

The brochures Ray had gathered advised him not to miss a visit to the parish church at Limone, the Church of St. Benedict, a Romanesque, 9th century chapel in which many artistic masterpieces were preserved. He had seen it from the boat long before he came in to the harbour, an imposing building with a tall baroque belfry topped with an ornate, onion-shaped dome. After his experience in St. Andrew's at Torbole, however, Ray decided to give St.

Benedict's a wide berth. He chose, instead, to stroll around the lower reaches of the town, admiring the district's famed leather goods, the souvenir shops, and eventually he was drawn to explore further.

He wandered slowly, for the day was hot, to the higher reaches at the northern end of the town centre. Tucked away on a ridge, at the top of a flight of stone steps, was a small white-washed building with a slanting roof. Ray climbed the steps and discovered from a plaque on the wall that it was the Church of San Rocco, built in the 16th century by those who had survived the plague. He debated about going in but he was perspiring now and felt the need of shade and rest. He entered the dim, empty interior and was struck immediately by the beauty of the chapel's high altar, with its arched, frescoed ceiling and its huge reredos, a painting of the Madonna and child, surrounded by a number of figures, one of which was the risen, crucified Christ. Soft music was filtered into the chapel from concealed speakers, adding to the atmosphere of tranquillity and peace. Ray's lips tightened as he became aware of the music and he decided immediately to leave without further exploration.

"Don't leave," said a voice, as clear as a bell in his head.

Ray hesitated. He had little doubt that the voice had been his own but in intonation it had sounded so much like his mother's. He wondered what had prompted it. The chapel was cool, however, and he succumbed to the opportunity to sit and rest. He sat on one of the pews at the very back of the church, studying the huge painting. It was obviously old, beautifully executed and carefully maintained, but he could not take his eyes from the figure of Christ, dressed only in the loincloth of his crucifixion.

As he stared at the painting, he listened also to the music and recognised the beautiful Adagio from Brahm's Piano Quintet in F Minor. He fought to remain unaffected but could not ignore the plaintive harmonies of the insistent violins that almost overpowered the piano. And his mind went back to quiet evenings of childhood when he had sat on his mother's lap, listening with her to her much-loved classical recordings, admiring the colourful sleeves that held the collection of large vinyl records she favoured over cassettes. She had rescued them from her father's attic before the old house had been sold and, with her, he had learned to love Tchaikovsky's Swan Lake, Holst's Planets Suite, Beethoven's Pastoral Symphony, concertos and serenades by Grieg, Chopin, Schubert, Bach, Brahms. There were so many. The Piano Quintet in F Minor had been one of her favourites. He remembered her warm, slightly amused smile, as he listened, round-eyed, to her explanation of the intricacies of the composition of the Adagio which she had played, over and over, sometimes resting her cheek on his head murmuring, "Sheer poetry. Beautiful. One long melody from start to finish."

Memories of childhood. He had to close his eyes in pain when horrific images from his nightmares suddenly flooded his mind. Even as the pictures began to take shape he fought against them, moaning, "No ... no ... please, God ... no." He covered his face in his hands and rocked in his seat, eyes tightly shut, his face constricted in the effort of banishing the hideous images of the childhood abuse he had suffered at his uncle's hands. "Dear God ... no ... please." He struggled to hear only the music, to remember his mother's loving embrace, to focus on her touch. Gradually he became conscious again of the familiar airs filling the chapel and he raised his eyes again to the altar, seeking solace in the remembrance of his mother's love. His mother's smile crystallised and set in his mind but even that could give him no pleasure as guilt again filled him. Tears came to his eyes. "Thank God you are not here, Mum, to see me like this."

He leaned forward, despairing, and was about to put his head in his hands when his eyes caught sight of a small holy picture lying on the seat a little to his left. Unthinking, he reached out and lifted it. It was a copy of Rembrandt's famous painting of "The Return of the Prodigal Son". He looked at it briefly and turned the leaflet to see what was on the other side. There he found a sentence, attributed to Henri Nouwen: *'One of the greatest challenges of the spiritual life is to receive God's forgiveness.'*

He put the holy picture down immediately and, burying his head in his hands, he tried to eliminate all thought from his mind. But the music persisted, soft, unobtrusive, yet penetrating his very being. As he sat there, a new and distant sound filled the far reaches of his brain, a sound that travelled ever nearer to his conscious mind. He sensed that it was somehow threatening to his disaffected state and he muttered, pressing his hands into his head, "I don't want to hear this. I do not want to hear this." He put his clenched hands between his knees, squeezing his fingers together with an intensity that hurt. With his eyes squeezed tightly shut and his chin buried in his chest, he said again, "No ... no ... I don't want to hear ..."

His mouth was pulled back in a stiff rictus as the words, despite his efforts, rumbled to the forefront of his mind. *De profundis clamavi ad te, Domine; Domine, exaudi orationem meam. De profundis clamavi ad te, Domine; Domine exaudi orationem meam ...* The Latin words echoed louder and louder in his head, their meaning as clear to him as if they had been English. *Out of the depths I cry to you,*

O Lord; Lord, hear my prayer. Out of the depths I cry ... Out of the depths ...

Ray moaned, clutching his head now, and pressed the tips of his fingers into his skull in an effort to ease a pain that had become physical. His carefully built defences were crumbling around him like the rubble in his dreams and he was tortured anew by realisation of the awful wrong that he had done. He lifted his face to the risen Christ.

"Oh Lord ... that was unforgivable ... that was unforgivable .... Unforgivable. Oh God! Excommunicated ... cut off from my Church ..."

Tears started into his eyes and began to run down his cheeks. Aloud, now, the words of the psalm came unbidden to his lips and he muttered continuously, more and more frantically, "*De profundis clamavi ad te, Domine ... de profundis clamavi ad te, Domine ... de profundis clamavi ad te ...*" until sobs began to shake his body with tremors of such force that he could no longer mouth the words. He cried bitterly for several minutes, no longer able to escape the full horror of his situation as his mind flooded with the stark and awful truth. He bent over on the seat, breathing erratically, trying to achieve a measure of control. When he raised his head again to stare at the painting, his wet face was twisted in pain and despair.

"Oh, God, what am I to do? What am I to do?"

THIRTY-THREE

1

Tony's receptionist showed Father McGennity into his office. The visiting priest was attempting to radiate truculence but his nervousness was visible. Tony did not stand or offer his hand. He simply nodded to a chair in front of his desk and said, "Sit down, Father."

McGennity offered no greeting either but said, "I'll just stand, if you don't mind. I only have a couple of minutes."

"Sit down, Father," Tony said sharply. "You have as long as this is going to take."

The parish priest pulled his mouth down in a 'have-it-your-way' expression, and almost swaggered to the seat.

Tony then said, "You know why you're here?"

"No idea. You called the meeting. You're going to have to tell me."

"Fine, I'll tell you. What was your involvement in the abortion of Maria Rafferty's baby?"

McGennity paled but attempted a puzzled look. "In the what? I've no idea what you're talking about."

Tony stared at him, silent. McGennity began to feel very uncomfortable under the scrutiny and, adjusting his position on the chair, he went on, trying for belligerence, “Has someone been saying things about me?”

“Maria Rafferty has had an abortion,” Tony said, evenly. “What do you know about it?”

The parish priest sat back, a small gleam of triumph in his eyes. “I can’t talk about that under the seal of confession.”

“The doctor in a certain Family Planning Clinic in Castlemore is not under the seal of confession,” Tony responded coldly. “Are you going to force me to interview him about one of the diocese’s parish priests?”

McGennity bristled again. “Who’s been filling your head with this stuff? Has that wee gouger Canavan been ...?”

“That wee gouger Canavan,” Tony echoed, grim faced, “has accepted full responsibility for what has happened. He has not mentioned your name.”

This time McGennity’s puzzlement was genuine. “Well then? Why bring this up with me?”

“Because I know him, and I know you. And I’m telling you this, McGennity, I’m going to follow this up. If you’ve had the slightest involvement in it, you’re out on your ear. Have you got that? Take my advice. Go back to the parochial house and start packing now because I know what I’m going to find.”

“You can’t talk to me like this; you can’t just throw me out,” McGennity blustered, but there was real fear in his eyes now.

"By procuring that abortion, and God knows how many others, you have automatically excommunicated yourself from the Church and in so doing you have removed from yourself the entitlement to stay in any of the Church's houses. I want you out of there immediately."

The parish priest began to remonstrate. "I have rights. You can't ..."

Tony could feel no sympathy for this worldly and unspiritual priest. He ignored the protestations and lifting a page from his desk he began to study it, saying without looking up, "Didn't I hear you say that you had another urgent appointment? Perhaps you should leave now."

The parish priest stood and stared down at Tony for a minute, his lips a thin line of anger. But without further word he turned and stalked out. After the visitor left, Tony put the page back on the desk and rubbed his face and eyes with his open palms. Then, for some minutes, he stared vacantly at the closed door until, heaving a weary sigh, he asked aloud, "What was that, Tony, justice or vengeance?"

THIRTY-FOUR

1

About the time when Ray's humanness was beginning to reassert itself with such intensity in Limone, a tall man in his mid-forties, heavily built and dressed in black, was leading a sad procession to the altar of the parish church at Kilnamoy. Immediately behind him came two young men carrying a tiny white coffin between them, each holding an ornate handle. Behind that came four other men, one of whom was Terence O'Hanlon, carrying a full-sized coffin on their shoulders. Father Ciaran Mussen, dressed in a purple chasuble and carrying a missal, led the rest of the funeral to the reserved seats at the front. The church was packed, with many more standing outside. Patricia O'Hanlon had been popular and highly respected, and Terence's tragic loss of both wife and stillborn child had engaged widespread sympathy. Dan, dressed in white surplice and black soutane, waited on the altar to concelebrate the requiem mass with Ciaran.

The funeral director moved to the foot of the altar where an assistant waited, preparing to open a collapsible steel frame on wheels. They stretched it to its limits so that the two coffins could rest on it during the mass. The young men stood to one side, allowing the larger coffin to be placed first on the frame. They then carefully placed the tiny coffin on a space at the head of the large one. Terence, his face strained with grief, could not take his eyes from the coffins and stood silently grieving until one of the other bearers, his brother Donald, put an arm around his shoulder and began to lead him into the front pew.

Terence looked up, his face twisting as he fought renewed tears, and caught sight of Dan standing at the top of the altar steps. Initially his expression indicated stunned disbelief but this gave way almost immediately to stark fury. Oblivious to his surroundings, and still standing, he pointed at Dan with an outstretched arm and cried, "You? You? What are you doing there? How dare you show yourself at my wife's funeral, you murderer, you murderer."

He tried to make his way out of the seat again.

Donald caught him by the arm and whispered tensely, "Terry, Terry, what are you doing? Do you know where you are? Stop shouting like that."

Terence tried to pull loose, still glaring furiously at Dan who stood transfixed, his expression horrified. The grieving man's voice rose to a crescendo. "You are not welcome here. My wife's dead because of you. Get off that altar. Get off. Why are you here?"

Donald pulled him down on to the seat, pulling his face around to his, his hand cupped around Terence's chin and mouth, "Terry, please, please. Think about where you are. Patricia would never want this."

Ciaran, who had been climbing the steps towards Dan when the shouting started, glanced back and quickly assessed what was happening. He looked at the stunned curate and, tossing his eyes imperceptibly towards the sacristy, said quietly, "Dan ..."

Dan hesitated but Ciaran whispered again, more urgently, “Please, Dan, it’s best you leave.”

Dan’s lips tightened but he hurried down the steps and into the sacristy. A number of people were standing now, especially those near the back, necks craning to see what the commotion was. Others stared around, some seeking enlightenment from neighbouring mourners but receiving equally mystified looks in return. By now Ciaran was behind the altar, facing his congregation, not at all happy with what he was seeing. He pulled the microphone towards him and, anxious to deflect further attention from the unfortunate incident, he somewhat loudly intoned the traditional opening blessing, “In the name of the Father and of the Son and of the Holy Spirit,“ without comment about what had happened, and invited the congregation to sit. In level tones he began the service with a brief reference to the sad reason for the occasion and quickly started the mass. The congregation settled down and Terence, quiet now and in tears again, stared numbly at the two coffins.

Dan stood in the sacristy, the door closed behind him, leaning with both hands against the long divesting bench, his head hung low on his chest.

2

The bishop’s mother lived in a leafy, tree-lined mews in a southern suburb of Dublin. The house, one of a long terrace of identical three-storey Georgian houses, was built high off the street. A stair of stone steps with iron hand-railings on either side led up to the front door. Tony pulled his car to a halt at the edge of the kerb near the steps. It was here that Bishop Flannagan had chosen to recuperate and

Tony had made a point of visiting every couple of weeks, reporting on diocesan activities and seeking the bishop's guidance on various issues that had arisen in the interim. It was a comfortable arrangement. Tony was very successful at what he was doing, requiring little genuine guidance, and the bishop was in no hurry to take up the reins again.

On this occasion, however, Tony felt anything but comfortable. He was here to report the events of the previous week. He sat in the car trying to find some way to broach the report. *Statutory rape by a young priest. Pregnancy. Abortion. My God, the bishop's just going to love this. And the news Ciaran brought about Dan being forced off the altar by a parishioner. Good grief! The bishop sees these two as my protégés. He's bound to see me as partly responsible.* He looked at his watch but did not actually note the time. *Nothing's going to get done sitting here,* he thought. Resolutely he got out of the car, locked it with the remote device as he walked up the steps, and knocked on the door.

It was the bishop who answered, dressed in a sweater and grey trousers. "Ah, Tony. Come in," he invited, leading Tony into a first-floor lounge. Tony nodded his thanks and sat down in his usual chair. The bishop raised his eyebrows. "Tea?"

Tony shook his head. "No thanks, Bishop. I'm fine."

"So," the bishop said affably, seating himself in one of the other armchairs, "what's the latest?"

Tony gazed earnestly at his superior and said, "I don't know how well your heart has recovered, Bishop, but I have to warn you first to prepare yourself for a shock, or a series of shocks."

The bishop pursed his lips. "How bad is it?"

"Just as bad as it gets. Do you think you can handle bad news?"

The bishop waved an impatient hand. "Yes, yes, I'm fine. Just get on with it."

Tony told the story as dispassionately and as factually as he could. The bishop sat wordless but showing evidence of increasing disquiet. When Tony came to a halt, the bishop was clearly agitated. "So the parents know?"

Tony nodded.

"Do they know that you sent Canavan away to cover the whole thing up?"

"No. I told them Ray had been ill and I'd sent him away to recuperate."

The bishop snorted. "And of course they believed you." He sat grim-faced for a moment, thinking. Then he said, "Well, at least you can use that to extricate yourself and the diocese from this."

Tony showed his puzzlement.

"You can go back to the parents," the bishop explained impatiently, "and tell them that you genuinely believed the young priest was ill but that now, in the light of your investigations, etc., etc. Get on their good side."

Tony was alarmed. "You mean, drag Ray back from Italy and dump him right in it?"

"What else can you do?" the bishop said. "And he dumped himself in it, not you."

"But he was ill."

"That'll all come out. But your first priority is to appease the parents, and limit the damage to the diocese. We have to be seen to co-operating in every way possible to try and sort this." Tony leaned back in his chair, his dismay clear. The bishop stared at him. “Tony, your career’s on the line here. You have already made one mistake, don’t compound it. Align yourself with the parents and the girl. They’re the victims here.”

Tony leaned forward again, his head in his hands. “I know, I know.”

There was a moment of silence, each lost in his own thoughts. Then the bishop said, “Has McGennity gone?”

“Yes. I’ve been able to persuade two Redemptorists from Dublin to run the parish until I sort something.”

The bishop sniffed. Then he said, “What was that about Patterson?”

Tony sat up wearily. “He’s fine, a good, solid young priest.”

“Humph! That’s not what I hear. He’s causing more than a few waves with his tight-assed fundamentalism. I’ve had more than one phone call about him.”

“No, no. He might be a bit heavy-handed in his pastoral approach but his ethics are sound.”

The bishop emitted a heavy sigh. “Don’t try to kid a kidder. He’s causing trouble.” He was shaking his head in irritation. “A right pair of geniuses those two turned out to be.” He stared again at Tony. “Look, this is all getting too much for me. You may go away and get it sorted.” His face hardened and he added emphatically, “Sorted in terms of what’s best for the diocese and the Church. I hope you’ve got that.” He raised his hands in the air, almost as if he was fending off the trouble. “Away you go, now. Don’t come back until you have good news for me. And talking about news,” He caught and held Tony’s gaze, “under no circumstances are you to let the media know where I am.”

REDEMPTION

THIRTY-FIVE

1

Ray had sat for a long time at the back of the little Church of San Rocco in Limone, almost in a fugue state. He had been oblivious to the occasional pairs of tourists who came and went, admiring the paintings, the statuary, the stained-glass windows and, from time to time, casting puzzled glances in his direction. He sat with his head in his hands, not praying, not thinking, not feeling. But somehow this time his mood was different. Whereas before he had staved off thoughts and feelings in order to escape the despair that threatened to overwhelm him, this time he was afraid to think or feel because he sensed the approach of an underlying hope. The acceptance of hope in times of distress is every bit as challenging as the acceptance of unconditional forgiveness and he continued to stare at the altar, trying not to think. As he sat there in that little chapel, however, his mind had flooded with thoughts and visions and memories that coursed through his brain with such rapidity that he was both unable and afraid to focus on them.

But as time passed, somewhere in this shifting mêlée, words from Ecclesiasticus, pushing their way up from his subconscious, were trying to make themselves heard. In his tension and uncertainty he shied away from them, fearing where they might lead, but they echoed ever louder in his head, *'Who ever called out to him and was ignored? For the Lord is compassionate and merciful; he forgives sins and saves in the days of distress.'*

"But how can I be saved after what I have done?" he groaned, almost aloud, his fingers pressing his forehead. And the answer from Psalm 33 came quickly: *'The Lord is close to the broken-hearted. Those whose spirit is crushed he will save.'*

"No ... no ... no. Not me. Not me. Not me."

And again he had fought for release in that cold darkness where feelings and thoughts could not hurt him. But the deluge of thoughts and emotions that were then surging through him would brook no denial, and he found himself shivering in agitation as the kaleidoscope of abstractions in his brain fought for substance and purpose and shape. A question, vague, tentative, almost ill-formed, sounded in his head. "Can I truly find my way back to you, Lord?" And there came a voice deep in his being, his own voice yet not his own, a locution perhaps, quoting from Matthew, *'... if you are bringing your offering to the altar and there remember that your brother has something against you, leave your offering there before the altar, go and be reconciled with your brother first and then come back and present your offering.'*

"But how can I fix this, Lord?" he whispered despairingly, tears starting into his eyes again. "How can I fix this? It's done, irrevocable, irreparable."

And the voice answered. *'You must do what you can do, what you know to be right.'*

"But what is right, Lord? What is right?"

There was no answer but there had come in him a growing awareness that hiding in Italy would solve nothing.

"You sweated blood in Gethsemane, Lord, but you still faced your death. You didn't hide." His eyes were fixed on the tabernacle then, and his face began to fill with resolve. "Neither will I hide, Lord. The parish priest was wrong. Tony was wrong. There is no escaping the consequences of what I have done." And he bowed his head again, uncomfortably aware of the rest of the quotation from Matthew: *'... he may hand you over to the judge and the judge to the officer and you will be thrown into prison. I tell you solemnly, you will not get out until you have paid the last penny.'*

2

Sergeant Jack Brannigan, a huge bear of a man in his late fifties, stood behind the reception desk in Harcourt Terrace Garda Síochána station, one of a number of such stations in the South Central area of the Dublin Metropolitan Region. It had been a busy day with its usual run of drunks, drug addicts and car thieves cluttering up the place but was peaceful now in the late afternoon and he was enjoying the quiet moment and the mug of steaming tea that sat on the desk beside him. He was leafing through a newspaper with a vague hope of finding time to check the following day's runners, when a serious-faced young man, dressed in check shirt, grey sweater and jeans, appeared in front of the desk. Sergeant Brannigan drew himself up to his full height and, despite the fact that his too-tight tunic was now hanging casually open on his bulky frame, he was still an imposing figure.

"Yes?" he growled.

The young man flinched imperceptibly but the movement was not lost on the sergeant. His growl was part of an act for the intractable Dublin youth who seemed incapable of understanding any other language. But that flinch told him that here was a young man accustomed to authority, a realisation that allowed Jack Brannigan to be himself. His natural kindness thus manifested itself in an easier, "What can I do to help you?"

The young man was clearly nervous. "I'm not sure if I am in the right place. I ... I need to confess to a crime."

Sergeant Brannigan's heavy eyebrows went down. He was puzzled. This young man showed none of the usual indicators of a criminal nature. Still, it takes all sorts. His eyebrows went back to where they belonged and he said, "Crime?"

"Yes. A sexual crime. I had intercourse with an underage girl."

Sergeant Brannigan was fond of saying that he had seen it all in his years at Harcourt Terrace but this strange confession caught him utterly by surprise. He hardened, however, at the adjective 'underage' and asked immediately, "What age?"

"She was just under seventeen at the time, but I didn't know."

The young man's voice trailed away. The sergeant relaxed. *Not a paedophile then. Seventeen nowadays. Good grief! Who can tell between seventeen and thirty these days?* He pursed his lips. "Ummm! You look like a respectable young fella. You're sure you want to go ahead with this? I mean, she was on the borderline …"

The young man's expression was determined. "Yes."

The sergeant emitted a heavy sigh and went to a series of shelves behind him where there were several stacks of forms, loosely separated from each other. He selected a charge sheet and brought it back to the desk. He picked up a biro and said, “Name?”

Before the young man could reply, however, the sergeant held up a huge forefinger, not much smaller than a cucumber. Someone else had come in to the reception area. “Just a moment.” He went to the end of the desk and lifted a wooden flap. “Come on in here,” he said, pointing to a corridor behind him. “Go on down to the second room on the right and wait for me there. I need to get someone to man the desk.” He went on down the corridor to another door, opened it and shouted, “Bill! Desk!” He then followed the young man into the interview room.

The room was sparsely furnished, a wooden table, three plastic chairs, and a small photocopier in a corner. The sergeant sat on one of the chairs and gestured the young man to sit on another. “Right. Name?”

“Canavan. Raymond Canavan.”

The sergeant wrote on the sheet. “Address?”

“I’m not sure. I suppose Diocesan House, Dublin Road, Castleshaughlin.”

The sergeant’s eyebrows journeyed northwards this time. “Diocesan House?”

Ray nodded. “I’m a priest.”

The sergeant stared, registering extreme disapproval. “Y’er a priest? And y’had sex with an underage girl? Ah, Lord, that’s a bit much now, Father. That’s definitely a bit much.”

Ray, stung despite himself, said defensively, "It was only the one time and I was ill and going through some serious problems at the time and ..." He hesitated. "You're right. It is a bit much. There's no defence."

The sergeant stared speculatively again at the priest, clearly caught between condemnation and an instinctive sympathy for the troubled young man. He put the pen on top of the charge sheet and leaned back in his chair. "Ye'd better tell me the whole story before I fill this thing in. Then I'll have more of an idea what to do."

Ray gave the sergeant a bare-bones summary but it was enough to give the officer a clear picture of his predicament. The garda sucked a hissing breath through his teeth. "Oh man, I think y'er in trouble, all right. If the parents get to hear about this."

"They will now," Ray said. "And the very least they deserve is to see me suffer the consequences of what I have done."

Sergeant Brannigan scratched his head, stared at the charge sheet, stared at the young priest, and scratched his head some more. "I have to tell you, Father, I thought I'd seen it all but this is a new one on me." He pulled the charge sheet towards him. "But I suppose we'd better get this filled in." Tapping his teeth with the butt of the pen, he went on, "I think I'll make it a basic charge. The court can sort it out after that."

He wrote quickly for a couple of minutes and went to the photocopier. The machine whirred briefly and the sergeant came back and handed two pages to Ray. "Sign both of those," he said, not unkindly. "One of them is for you, so you can keep that."

Ray lifted one of the sheets. It showed the station's address, a couple of lines for the date, the accused's name and address, and a reference number. He read the brief charge:

'The above named person presented himself voluntarily at Harcourt Terrace Garda Síochána Station on the above date and confessed to one count of unlawful carnal knowledge of an underage female, aged sixteen years and nine months.

Signed: ____________________ *[Accused]*
Signed: ______________________ *[Arresting Officer]'*

His hand shaking but his face expressionless, Ray signed both forms. He handed the biro back to the sergeant and said, "What now?"

The garda leaned back in his chair. "Well, according to the Criminal Court Criminal Justice Rules, I have the authority to put you on remand until you appear before a judge." Ray nodded quietly but showed no reaction. It was as if this was what he had expected. The sergeant angled his head slightly and eyed Ray sideways as if seeking help with some inner debate. Then he went on in a monotone as if he were quoting something he had learned by rote a long time before. "But the Rules also allow me, if I consider it prudent to do so and no warrant directing your detention is in force, to release you on bail, with or without sureties, and to take from you a recognisance in the form of seventeen point two ... Ah, to pot with that! Wait a minute."

He got up and left the room, leaving the puzzled young priest trying to make sense of what he had just heard. A few minutes later the sergeant returned with another form. "Can you promise me that you'll present yourself for arraignment at the Dublin District Court at ten o'clock next Tuesday morning?"

Ray nodded uncertainly.

"Fair enough," the sergeant said. "Just fill in this form guaranteeing that you'll be there. I'll give you a photocopy of that as well." He looked down at the young priest as he signed the paper. "Take my advice, Father; use the next couple of days to get yourself a solicitor. I know you think the whole business is cut and dried but believe me, these things never are, even if you plead guilty."

3

Dan was reading in his study and was becoming increasingly disturbed by what he was reading. He had found a monograph in the Mind and Spirit section of a local bookshop. The booklet was the work of an Austrian nun who had been a professor of psychology and religion at Turin during the latter part of the twentieth century. She had published a number of works examining the psychological aspects of religion and faith and the one Dan was reading was an examination of the behaviours and attitudes of the three principals in the Parable of the Prodigal son – the Father, the prodigal, and the older brother.

After his violent condemnation of Ray, Dan had spent tortured hours trying to understand why he had been unable to show the same charity towards his lifelong friend that Tony had shown. He began to wonder, too, if that same propensity was the cause of the problems in his ministry. But yet, had he not tried to advise his flock with concern and Christian love? Ciaran had warned him not to neglect his pastoral role but short of permitting members of the parish to bend God's law, what else could he have done? But that dreadful row with Ray. Dan's teeth clenched and he shook his head miserably. *Was I supposed to condone what Ray did? How could Ray have fallen so far?* Dan's heart ached for the loss of a life-long friendship but his rectitude would not allow him to grieve. He was still filled with accusation and condemnation.

He was filled with puzzlement, too. Had he not been a dutiful, obedient and hard-working priest? Was he not admired and respected by his community and peers? Why then did some of the younger parishioners turn their backs on him? Why did Tony get so angry with him that he virtually chased him from his office?

Dan turned to the monograph again. Something in the writer's arguments, in which she denounced the anti-religious nature of legalistic perfectionism, was forcing him to look more deeply at his motivations than he ever had before. And he did not like was he was seeing. Her analysis of the elder brother was scathing and Dan found himself suddenly tense and afraid. His cherished beliefs, his view of himself, his life of struggle against himself and against anything that might sully his soul, were crashing into incomprehension and deep self-doubt. His pursuit of perfection, based on a lifelong passion to '... be perfect as your heavenly Father is perfect' was being rejected by this nun as a path to Pharisaical legalism that makes a person hard and unforgiving of both himself and others, and '... for this reason is the most insidious perversion of religion.'

In reading about the sudden dark force that erupted in the apparently model elder brother, the condemnation, the anger, the bitterness, the jealousy, Dan was confronted with memories of his own irrational anger at Ray, of Tony's cold restraint as he pushed him from his office, of Ciaran's continual efforts to make him focus more on the pastoral aspects of counselling than upon moral rectitude.

As memory tumbled upon memory, dismay and confusion filled him but still he could not understand. *Have I not lived a life of prayer and faith? Have I not fought to be good and virtuous, a worthy example to others? Have I not fought against sin and in my ministry tried to guide others to do the same? What is there in that that is wrong? Oh God, how can this be pernicious? How can it have caused so much hurt and anger and ill-feeling?* He slid from his chair, the book falling on the floor, and he knelt in the middle of the room, hands clasped in front of him and, almost weeping, he prayed, "Oh God, I have got it wrong somewhere and I don't know how or why. Help me, Lord, please help me."

4

Tony stood at the window of his office in the bishop's residence, oblivious to the many indications of a burgeoning spring in the sun-dappled trees and the lawns outside. His mind was focused on the letter he held loosely in the hand by his side. It was a communication from the Rafferty's family solicitor, advising the bishop's office that a civil claim for damages had been made against the diocese on behalf of their daughter, Maria, for the suffering and pain caused to her as a result of an abusive relationship with one of the diocese's priests, Father Raymond Canavan. The letter went on to state that the family also intended to seek justice for their daughter in the criminal courts.

Tony lifted the letter and perused it again, shaking his head like a boxer who had just received a heavy punch. He went back to his desk, threw the letter on it, and slumped into his chair, his head in his hands. "Suffering Jesus, where do I even start with this?" He had not yet made any attempt to follow the course of action advocated by his bishop. Every time he considered it, he saw an image of himself oozing unctuous righteousness alongside the parents like some latter-day Uriah Heep while abandoning Ray, and indeed, the Church in Ireland, to the merciless scrutiny of the media, to the cold letter of the law, to the avid curiosity of the general public. "No, I can't do that. I just can't do that."

He expelled a heavy breath, shaking his head again. "So what are my options?" He raised his head and stared again at the discarded letter. "One, I can do nothing." He thought about that for a minute and sucked in air between his teeth. "Oh shit, that's me definitely out on my ear. The bishop wouldn't countenance that at all. I'd be lucky to get a job as a curate somewhere, never mind a parish." Something clenched in his stomach and his skin crawled. His thoughts went unbidden to a place that his vocalising was trying to avoid. Relegation, disgrace, reputation gone to pot, all hope of advancement gone. *Can I live with that?* His head was shaking even as he formed the thought.

"Option two," he continued to mutter to himself. "Ray is almost certainly going to be brought back to face the consequences of his actions; the parents of the girl will see to that. Whether I do nothing or report him thus becomes irrelevant. The result will be the same. So? So, I might as well do what the bishop says and save my career. Is there any point in me going down in flames along with Ray when I would achieve exactly nothing by doing so? Worse than nothing. I would be giving more ammunition to those who criticise the Church for concealing and protecting abusing priests. Dear Lord, abusing? How could Ray ever be described as an abuser?" And his head went into his hands again. "What do I do? What do I do?" He raised his head towards the ceiling as if seeking inspiration there.

"Option three. I can phone Ray and tell him the girl has talked, advise him to come back and face the music and ..." Something resembling a sneer flickered in his expression. "And you're going to be all sympathetic and supportive while advising him to jump into the lion's den? Nice one, Tony." Irritation suddenly filled him. And he sat angrily back in his chair, folding his arms. "Ray, Ray, how could you have been so flamin' stupid? What do you want me to do for you? Do you want me to abandon my entire career and everything I have been trying to build?"

The phone rang, almost startling Tony. He grabbed the receiver hastily but put it slowly to his ear. "Yes, Eleanor?"

"There's a call for you, Canon. Father Canavan."

Tony sat erect. Ray? "Okay, Eleanor. Put him through."

There was a click and a moment's silence. Then Ray's voice. "Tony?"

"Ray? How are you?"

"I'm fine. I'm phoning from the Garda Station at Harcourt Terrace. I need an address. Is it all right if I come and stay with you for the next couple of days?"

"Garda station? Of course. Of course. But what on earth has happened?"

"I'm sorry, Tony. I couldn't cope with the guilt. I've given myself up to the *gardai*. There's an arraignment on Tuesday morning but the sergeant here is letting me go until then so long as I have an address ..." His voice trailed away.

Tony strove to restrain a guilty sense of relief as he said earnestly, “Yes. Yes. By all means, use this address. Do you want me to come and get you?”

“No, that’s all right. I’ll get a taxi.”

“Well, if you’re sure. I’ll see you in a little while.”

“Thanks, Tony. I appreciate this.”

“Not at all. Get here as quickly as you can. There are things you need to know.”

“I’ll be there shortly.”

Tony replaced the receiver and sat for a moment with his hand still resting on it. His expression was tense. Guilt vied with urgency as he considered the implications of what Ray had just told him. Ray is in it up to his neck now, he thought, but he might have handed me a lifeline. I’ll have to try to salvage something out of this while I still can. He buzzed his secretary again. “Eleanor, could you try to get Mr. or Mrs. Rafferty on the phone for me, please? I think they live just outside Drumkillen. Try Elmwood Grove.”

He hung up and waited on edge for the receptionist to ring back. A minute or two later the phone rang again.

“Which one is it, Eleanor?” he asked immediately, betraying his nervousness.

“I’m sorry, Canon. I can only get their answering machine.”

“Oh? Okay.” Tony felt deflated. “Thank you.”

Tony replaced the receiver, his mind working frantically. If he could get the news to the Rafferty’s before they heard it from elsewhere, he could win from them a level of trust. He would have to try to help Ray as well. The diocesan solicitor would know what to do. He ran both hands through his hair, breathing heavily. *This is going to take some juggling.* He lifted the phone again. "Eleanor, could you get me the Rafferty's number again and let me speak to the answering machine, please?"

"Just a moment, Canon." Tony waited. Eleanor's voice said, "There's the Rafferty's phone ringing now, Canon."

"Thanks, Eleanor. I've only a short message to leave. Could you get me the diocesan solicitor right away, please?"

Tony waited until after the tone and then he said, "Mr. Rafferty, Mrs. Rafferty, this is Canon Mulholland from the bishop's house. I'm sorry I have not been in touch sooner but I have only just finished my investigation into your allegation against Father Canavan. I am deeply saddened to have to inform you that your daughter appears to have been telling the truth. I apologise profusely for my previous scepticism. The bishop has now been informed and I have managed to persuade ... that is, Father Canavan has agreed to hand himself over to the *gardai*. In fact, he has already done so and I understand that he has to appear in court, I presume the District Court, for arraignment next Tuesday morning. This is a sad time for all of us. I'd be happy to discuss the situation with you when you can get back to me and, of course, we'll do everything in our power to ensure that the principles of justice are wholly respected and to try to help bring healing to your daughter."

THIRTY-SIX

There are many courthouses in Ireland that are still deemed to be of historic and architectural significance. Even for edifices involved in the administration of justice, the Heritage Council continues determined, with substantial support from the Courts Service, to conserve such buildings and retain their heritage value. Many of these buildings are elegant examples of a bygone era, with porticoes, Greek columns, and grand entrances at the top of wide stone steps. Wherever possible, efforts are made to restore and maintain the original architecture, efforts that sometimes involve considerable expense.

This determination was not reflected, however, in the District Court of the Dublin Metropolitan District to which Ray was directed on the twenty-third of April in 2004. As was customary, Ray was to be arraigned at a district court close to where he was arrested and, sometime before ten o'clock that morning, he duly turned up at the address near Harcourt Terrace that Sergeant Brannigan had given him. It was true there were indications of some structural refurbishment but the building was decrepit and unprepossessing, and its overall shabbiness offered little to encourage or lighten the mood of anyone unfortunate enough to have business there.

Ray arrived accompanied by Tony and Thomas Donaldson, the diocesan solicitor, a tall gaunt man, with a somewhat cadaverous face and neat grey hair. Ray had fully determined to face the arraignment alone but when he saw the courthouse and experienced an initial instinctive fear, he was glad of their company, particularly since they had a nerve-jangling wait in a corridor for something over half an hour before the clerk called for them.

The courtroom was less dilapidated than the building's exterior, with old polished wooden furnishings, but it was little different from the many courtrooms seen over the years in movies and on television. There was the usual judge's podium, a witness box, benches for the solicitors in the middle of the room and some chairs at one side for members of the public who may have an interest in a particular case. There was, however, no obvious location for a jury due to the fact that the District Court dealt only with certain types of summary offences for which there is no right of trial by judge and jury. Given its role in dealing largely with minor offences and arraignments, it was not a particularly well-appointed court. The only concession to modernity came in the form of new slim microphones judiciously fitted to various key locations.

Ray tried to keep his eyes cast downwards but he could not resist a quick glance at the judge, a middle-aged female of frosty mien in wig and gown. Judge Sheila Carey was flicking through some papers, however, and failed to notice Ray's brief scrutiny. The 'public gallery' was empty except for a couple of bored-looking court reporters. Almost as soon as Ray sat down, however, Mr. and Mrs. Rafferty came in with Maria and sat near the reporters who straightened suddenly, nostrils quivering at the scent of something beyond the mundane. Maria, head down and clinging to her mother, looked stricken but her father's face was filled with angry determination. He was here to ensure that justice was done and that the priest who had defiled his daughter would suffer the full might of the law.

The court clerk stood to read the charge against Ray. “You are charged that on a date in January 2004, you did have unlawful carnal knowledge of a girl aged between fifteen and seventeen years contrary to Section 2 of the Criminal Law Amendment Act, 1935.”

The judge stared at Ray, registering immediate disapproval. “Would the defendant please rise,” she said.

Ray stood up and faced her. Tony stared at the bench in front of him, finding the situation extremely difficult to deal with.

“You have heard the court clerk read the charge against you,” the judge intoned. “Do you understand the nature of the offence and the facts alleged?”

“Yes, your honour,” Ray said quietly.

“How do you plead?”

“Guilty, your honour,” Ray said expressionlessly.

The diocesan solicitor was on his feet immediately but the judge held up a finger, indicating that he should wait a moment. “Have you anything else to say for yourself?”

Ray looked suddenly uncertain. To add to his confusion, he noticed that Dan had just come into the courtroom. Dan sat down as quietly as he could, distancing himself as far as possible from the parents. Ray spoke, almost inaudibly. “I am deeply sorry for what I have done and I have voluntarily presented myself to the court in order to purge my conscience and to offer some satisfaction to the family I have so deeply offended, and to face my punishment so that I may live the rest of my life at peace with my Maker."

The judge eyed him askance, her expression cynical. "Very noble sentiments, I'm sure, Father!" She delivered the last word with a whiplash of sarcasm. Both reporters dived for their notebooks. The sarcasm continued. "You'll forgive me, Father, if I say I have heard too many pretty speeches in this courtroom to be easily swayed by anything a guilty defendant might say. As for the rest of your life, what you want to do with it is of no interest to me except, of course, the amount of it you will spend behind bars. What you have done is a vile, despicable, unconscionable abuse of the trust that this girl and the Catholic people of your parish have reposed in you."

Dan was horrified by the judge's vindictiveness. His friend didn't deserve this. He studied Ray trying to gauge how the withering castigation was affecting him but Ray was staring straight in front now, upright and not defiant, not afraid, not resigned ... what? And then Dan saw it. Acceptance. Calm Christian acceptance. A line from a canticle of St. Peter echoed in his mind: *He trusted to him who judges justly.* Whatever he had done, Ray had made peace with his Maker and was prepared to endure patiently whatever had to follow. And Dan was led to wonder, with equal measures of shame and dismay, what purpose had been served by his own explosive judgementalism in Tony's office. When he focused on the podium again, Judge Carey was in full flow.

"Not only have you caused gross distress to your victim but you have brought shame upon yourself and discredit to the Church you represent. Your behaviour has been disgraceful. It seems to me that nowadays too many Catholic priests ..."

The diocesan solicitor was on his feet again. “Your honour, I must protest. I have affidavits here that clearly indicate mitigating circumstances.”

One of the reporters had leaned backwards and was trying to whisper something to Mr. Rafferty. The judge said sharply, “If you can’t remain silent in my courtroom, please leave.” The reporter raised both hands in apology and sank back on to his chair. The judge turned back to the solicitor who was holding some sheets of paper aloft. “Mitigating circumstances?”

“Yes, your honour. I have here an extensive report from Dr. Barbara Whitfield, psychiatrist and psychotherapist, which shows clearly that Father Canavan was not in full possession of his faculties when the alleged incident occurred ...”

“Alleged? He has just pleaded guilty.”

“My apologies. I should have said, your honour, when the act alleged to constitute an offence occurred.” Mr. Donaldson held the sheets up again. “And I also have testimony as to the uprightness of his character from the bishop’s deputy, Canon Mulholland. Furthermore, there is evidence that the defendant was pursued by the young lady ...”

“You can stop right there,” the judge said sharply. “Whether the girl consented or even instigated the intercourse is not legally germane. The girl was underage. Consent affords no defence.” She nodded to the clerk. “Don’t bother handing me the character reference,” she continued dismissively, “but I will look at Dr. Whitfield’s statement.”

The clerk took the pages from the solicitor and handed them to the judge. Mr. Rafferty peered at them as if trying to read them from his seat. The judge read in silence for a few moments amid heightening tension in the courtroom. The reporters were clearly impatient to dash out to file their stories in time for the evening editions but both were equally afraid that if they were to leave at this point they might miss something significant. The parents looked puzzled and disturbed. Maria now allowed herself to gaze at Ray from time to time, tearful and distressed. Dan's face was an amalgam of confusion, concern and guilt. Tony continued to sit with his head down, feeling the judge's onslaught keenly. It was to this disgrace that only a couple of days ago he had been prepared to sacrifice Ray in order to save his own career. He was shaking his head, wondering how he could have become so spiritually bereft.

The judge looked up at the solicitor. "Very well, Mr. Donaldson; I will hear a brief argument."

"Your honour, Dr. Whitfield's report makes it clear that Father Canavan was not of sound mind when the act occurred and I am not altogether sure that even yet he is of sufficiently sound mind to plead on his own behalf. I am of the opinion that there are substantial grounds for a defence of 'not guilty' and I would submit that you have a duty in this case, your honour, to ensure that there is a basic fairness between the accused, the courts and the public at large."

"Your point?"

"I would suggest, your honour, that the court has an inherent jurisdiction that permits you to give directions to enable it to fulfil its function of administering justice. It seems to me that on the basis of Dr. Whitfield's report, you might, in the interests of truth and justice and a proper regard for the dignity and best interests of the accused, reject the defendant's plea of 'guilty' and direct that a plea of 'not guilty' be entered."

Peter Rafferty jumped to his feet, shouting angrily, “Your Honour!”

The judge glared at him. “Do you have dealings before this court?”

“I am the victim’s father, Your Honour.”

“You have my sympathy but you do not have a role here. Please sit down and remain silent.”

She returned her gaze to the solicitor, rested her chin on her hands, and stared unseeing at him as she digested his argument. Several pairs of eyes watched her intently as they waited for her ruling. Eventually she said, “What if the accused continues to plead guilty and refuses to offer any evidence to a jury? If I read the defendant correctly, that is a strong possibility.”

“I believe, your honour,” responded the solicitor, who had obviously burnt quantities of midnight oil preparing this argument, “that in that case a necessity would arise for the Director of Public Prosecutions to put before a jury all the relevant facts bearing on the issue of guilt and all the available facts bearing on the absence of guilt by reason of unsound mind.”

The judge’s aggressive cynicism was now gone and she betrayed considerable interest in the legal niceties of the solicitor’s reasoning. She was not, however, fully convinced. She flicked once more through the pages of Barbara Whitfield’s affidavit and then said, “I will take your argument under advisement. In the meantime I would require that the defendant submit himself to an additional examination by a court appointed psychiatrist.”

Ray’s head was down again, lips compressed and shaking his head in negation. Mr. Donaldson ignored him. “We are happy to agree to that, Your Honour, and might I request that in the interim, given that the defendant has voluntarily presented himself to the court, he may be released on his own recognisance until the date of his next appearance before you?"

The judge nodded. "Very well. The clerk will notify you and the defendant of the date for psychiatric examination once it had been arranged." She perused the pages of a large diary on the desk in front of her. She wrote something in it and said, "The defendant will present himself for trial or sentencing at the Circuit Court in three weeks, at ten o'clock on the morning of the fifteenth of May."

The clerk called for all in the courtroom to rise as the judge swept out through a door at the end of the wall behind her. Immediately on the judge's exit, the two reporters advanced on the Raffertys, plying them with questions and scribbling furiously. Peter did most of the talking, waving his arms and gesticulating angrily in the direction of the small group at the defendant's bench. Mrs. Rafferty had her arm protectively around Maria, refusing to allow the reporters to question her and was already leading the girl to the exit. On her way out Maria cast a sad glance at Ray who looked up just as she did so. She averted her eyes but not before Ray was able to offer a brief nod of acknowledgement.

Dan left his seat and moved to join Ray and the others. Tony looked up and saw him. He shook his hand and said, "Good to see you here, Dan."

Dan was shamefaced. "Had to come, Tony. But I could have hoped for better circumstances. This is terrible."

The solicitor took hold of Ray's arm and began to chivvy him from the courtroom. He was looking at Tony as he said, “I want to get Ray away from here before the media get hold of this. I have a small house in the country. He’ll be safe there for the next three weeks.” With that he began to lead Ray towards the end of the bench.

Dan watched them, his lips compressed. He was remembering the angry and bitter tirade that was his last words to Ray and felt a sudden spasm of self-loathing. He stood in front of Ray as he emerged from behind the bench and said awkwardly, with his hands spread, “Ray, I’m sorry. I’m sorry for the things I said.”

Ray smiled. “It’s not a problem, Dan. I deserved ...”

“No ... no ... Ray. I shouldn’t have.”

He broke off, staring apprehensively into Ray’s quiet brown eyes but he saw nothing there but understanding and forgiveness. His own eyes began to mist over and when Ray placed a consoling hand on his shoulder, saying, “Dan, It’s all right, honestly. I ...” Dan threw his arms around his friend and held him in a massive bear hug, slapping him on the back with such vigour that Tony experienced a frisson of concern about the possible damage Dan might be doing to Ray’s kidneys.

“We’ll talk, Ray. We’ll talk soon,” Dan was saying, tears in his eyes now, as the solicitor pried him loose and urged Ray towards the exit. One of the reporters noted the movement and disengaged himself from the interview with Peter Rafferty, running along the back of the benches to head Ray off.

“Just a minute, Father. Can you tell the people how long this affair has been going on?”

Mr. Donaldson eyed him with disgust but confined himself to a ‘No comment.’

The reporter persisted. "Did you know the girl was under-age before you had sex with her?"

The solicitor's lips tightened but he continued to push towards the courtroom door, keeping himself between Ray and the reporter. "No comment," he repeated.

The reporter tried to duck around the solicitor in an effort to intercept Ray. "How did you meet the girl? Was it at school? In confession?"

He stopped short when a hand the size of a lion's paw grabbed his shoulder and swung him round. He found himself staring into the angry, blue eyes of the tall, hefty young man who had earlier been sitting a few seats from him.

"Excuse me, pal," Dan growled. "Which part of 'no comment' do you not understand? I'll be happy to explain it to you, if you like."

The reporter held up his hands in surrender and, with one final regretful glance at Ray's retreating back, he returned hurriedly to the girl's father to see what further information he could glean from that source.

Tony had followed the reporter, intending to speak to the family but when Peter Rafferty spotted his approach, he immediately ushered his family to the exit and refused to acknowledge the canon's greeting.

THIRTY-SEVEN

1

After Mr. Donaldson had spirited Ray away, Tony and Dan went into a nearby café for a bite to eat. The waitress finished taking their order and left their table.

"I can't understand what's happened," Dan said, still struggling to come to terms with what he had been hearing. "There was no sign of any of this when we were students together, and we were never out of each other's pockets."

"There wouldn't have been," Tony replied. "Ray had repressed everything. He knew nothing about it. It was only when his body started to disintegrate and he was suffering from that awful depression that the memories started to come back."

"And how is he now?"

"Well, according to Dr. Whitfield, Ray has an open wound there that he has covered over with a kind of scab composed simply of will-power. That will not do, she says. Ray might be strong-minded but the wound won't heal until the underlying infection is cleared out. She believes he is going to need a lot of therapy."

Dan's face was filled with misery and self-reproach. "He was suffering all of that and here was me hammering into him like nobody's business ..." Dan had to wait while the waitress served their soup before he could continue. When she left, he went on, "When McGennity started his rumour-mongering, I called Ray every name under the sun. I disowned him. I ..."

"Don't beat yourself up about it, Dan," Tony said. "You couldn't have known." He stared at his younger colleague. "But a wee bit of trust ..."

Dan grimaced. "I know, I know."

They ate their soup and rolls in relative silence, apart from one or two optimistic comments about Mr. Donaldson's effectiveness as an advocate and the possibility that he might be able to persuade the judge to leniency.

"What do you think, Tony?" Dan asked. "Will Ray go to prison?"

"Hard to say. I asked Thomas about that but he says that sentencing can fluctuate wildly in accordance with the predispositions and attitudes of judges and how they react to the circumstances." He tore a piece off his roll and dipped it in his soup. He took a bite and went on, with a mystified shake of his head. "Thomas told me that in the last week alone, one young man of twenty-four, who was sober at the time, was given four and half years for a date-rape. And two days later, a nineteen year old, out of his mind on drink and drugs was given a suspended sentence by a different judge for raping a seventy-five year old woman. Sentencing is crazy. There's no way to predict what will happen to Ray."

The waitress came back with a coffee pot. "Can I get you anything else? Desert? Perhaps some pastries?"

Tony raised his eyebrows at Dan who shook his head. Tony smiled at the waitress. "No, thanks anyway. We're both on a diet." He nodded his head in Dan's direction. "Can you not tell by looking at yer man?"

The waitress grinned and left them. Tony sipped his coffee and said, "So what exactly happened with that solicitor's wife?"

Tony listened in silence while Dan stumbled through his story, his moral dilemmas, his growing self-doubt.

"That's a hard lesson, Dan. You need to soften your approach."

"You're not saying that I should have condoned the abortion?"

"No, I'm not, but you should never have let it get to that stage. Didn't you say that her doctor warned you that this terrible thing might happen?"

"Yes, but the odds ..."

"You're talking about odds, Dan, when people's lives are at stake? Where was your compassion? Okay, you could not have condoned artificial contraception simply to prevent pregnancy, but what about contraception as a way to save a woman's life? Which is the greater good or the greater evil? Dan, through no fault of their own, good people, good spiritual people, can find themselves stuck between a rock and a hard place. That's when you need pastoral compassion." He stared at his friend, aware of Dan's discomfort. "Look, Dan, there are no absolute certainties here, no definitive answer. Each case is different. It's hugely complex but Christian moral tradition offers a guide. It's the 'double effect', Dan. There were two foreseen possibilities in that case you're talking about, the prevention of conception, yes, but ultimately the issue wasn't one of contraception. It was about saving a life. If the moral intention is entirely good, which doubtless yours would have been, the good consequences must have a, what was it Josef Ratzinger called it, a proportionately greater moral weight."

"But the sin?"

"Sin? You can't know the depths of anybody's heart or of their conscience. That's when you need to focus on God's goodness and mercy. Not the flamin' law. Good grief, Dan, Jesus hammered nine bells out of the Pharisees for that."

Dan's elbows were on the table again and his head was in his hands. "Okay, okay! Enough already." He reached out and lifted his cup to his lips, staring miserably at his friend. Then he said, "I've been reading something about the older brother of the Prodigal Son."

Tony leaned back. "Now, there's a place to start," he said. But seeing Dan's chastened expression, he softened. "But don't be too hard on yourself, Dan. That brother had some dark matter lurking in his depths. You don't have that. You just have a too darned clear picture of right and wrong. But not everybody has that. You just need to start where the people are at. Remember Aristotle's starting point? Where the people are?"

Dan hesitated. "Uh ...?"

"Nichomachean Ethics? Book Seven?"

"N ... not really."

"Gosh, Dan. How did you miss that?"

"Tony, would you quit with the professorial stuff and just tell me."

Tony grinned. "You start where the person you are counselling is, not where *you* are or where you want him or her to be."

"But how do you know? I mean ..."

"Dan, you start with compassion. You try to find out what they think and feel. You try to understand them. Then you gently lead them from there, not from where you are, from where *they* are. And that takes a bit of patience. They're not going to leap to where you are in one bound. They'll have to find their way there in stages. I'm not saying that you don't tell them the Church's truth or that you should not be true to yourself. But you have to let them talk, ease yourself in alongside them. Listen, hear what they say, but don't push or guide or sermonise at the early stages. Am I making sense?"

Dan nodded but did not appear convinced. "I hear what you're saying, Tony. I really do. But at the moment, I just can't see past the sin."

"Love the sinner, Dan. Love the sinner, work with the sinner." He reached forward and patted his friend on the arm. "Dan, your confidence has taken a knock. Don't let it get you down. Even Jesus' words sometimes fell among thorns and on stony ground. Keep the faith. Some people might walk away from you, Dan, but I bet they go away thinking about what you said. Trust me, you'll see. Just go easy on the poor souls. If you do that, some will even come back to you, stronger, more ready to face up to their Christian obligations."

"I'll try that, Tony. What I'm doing now just doesn't seem to be working, that's for sure." He shook his head sadly. "Ask Ray."

Tony looked at his watch. He wiped his lips with a napkin and rose from the table, signalling the waitress for the bill. "I need to get back to the diocesan house, Dan. Lord knows what those reporters have been up to." He shrugged.

"Good luck with that lot, Tony," Dan said, rising too.

They left together but parted at the door. Dan said over his shoulder, "Call on me if you need me."

2

At six o'clock that evening Tony watched the news on Irish Television with more than a little trepidation. There had already been some phone calls from the national dailies but Eleanor had been instructed to inform all media enquiries that neither the bishop nor his representative were available for comment. The television news unfolded in its usual segments, with its inevitable references to the squabbles and in-fighting that constituted the political scene in Northern Ireland. He listened with half an ear to arguments that were worn threadbare from constant repetition over more than thirty years.

"Same old, same old," he muttered. "Only the faces are changing."

The camera switched again to the pretty newscaster who was seen receiving a sheet of paper from an unseen hand. She looked earnestly at the camera and intoned, "Breaking news coming in." She studied the paper for a brief moment and went on, "Today at a Dublin Metropolitan District Court, a Catholic priest," she glanced quickly at the page again, "Father Raymond Canavan from the parish of St. Columba in the diocese of Castleshaughlin, has pleaded guilty to unlawful carnal knowledge of an underage schoolgirl. Father Canavan has been released under his own recognisance and has been instructed to return to the Circuit Court in three weeks' time pending psychiatric review." She looked into the camera again, her expression indicating that here was news of vital importance to the nation. "Father Canavan is yet another in a long line of Catholic priests to face imprisonment for sexual abuse of a minor. We have no further details at the moment but we will keep you informed by special bulletins as we receive new information." She put the sheet on her desk and lifted another. "Some foreign news now ..."

The screen went blank as Tony pressed the OFF button on the remote control. He sat back in his chair running his hands through his hair, his face pinched with concern. The bulletin had been more or less as he had expected but hearing the unvarnished details on national television, deliberately slanted to bring Ray and the diocese into maximum disrepute, left his insides churning. "Where's this going to lead?" he wondered frantically. "And how in the name of all that's wonderful am I going to handle it?"

He got up from his chair and went to the window. It was peaceful outside. *But for how much longer? By tomorrow morning these sedate lawns are going to be trampled into a muddy quagmire by hordes of prurient newspaper reporters and TV crews, salivating at the prospect of yet another juicy sex scandal in the Catholic Church.* He turned away from the window in disgust. "Why do they have to be so vindictive?" he muttered angrily. "Do they ever look at their own lives when they're tearing somebody else's to pieces?" He had a vision of Ray, ensconced in a lonely cottage somewhere, watching that newscast. "God help him. I wonder what it's doing to him?"

He experienced again that same guilty impulse that had afflicted him in court. *You were prepared to hand Ray over to this, just to save your career? Career? Since when did you start seeing your priestly vocation as a career?* He threw himself back into his chair. *Was this what you wanted, a life dealing with the media? Fighting off reporters who want to skin one of your priestly colleagues alive? This is your idea of a vocation?*

He continued to berate himself, becoming more and more acutely aware that during the past few years he had utterly lost sight of his real priestly function. Images of his life since he left St. Anselm's flitted through his mind. There may have been some attempts to serve when he was parish priest of Kilnamoy but his frequent meetings with the bishop, his carefully engineered writings, the alacrity with which he had accepted the bishop's secretarial post, all had a different story to tell.

"But I love the Church. I only wanted to be in a position to ..."

His face furrowed as the truth of his actions crowded his thoughts. Could he truly have been so unaware of the extent to which his need for advancement and ego-satisfaction had numbed his spirituality? A cold hand seized his heart and a feeling of panic began to overcome him. "Lord. Lord." He scarcely knew what to say. "God, what have I been doing? Lord, help me. Help me."

A sudden memory lifted him from the chair again and he went to the bookcase. A couple of weeks before, an article in an issue of The Furrow about an interview with a Vatican Cardinal had caught his eye. He had deliberately ignored it at the time, vaguely assuring himself that he would read it later. Now, almost without thought, he picked it up, feeling another onslaught of guilt as he read the Cardinal's responses to one of the interviewer's questions:

In an era when image is more important than ever before, the priest must be aware of the temptations he faces.

Society's understanding of the concept of image does not reflect the Church's understanding of it. The priest is 'the good shepherd'. His vocation is to image Christ. To see his role as a career, to fall victim to the temptation to acquire a position of authority and public respect, is not a true image of Jesus. Seeking self-acclaim is not the humble service of Jesus. Jesus himself said, 'If I were to seek my own glory, that would be no glory at all'

[John: 8]

Tony put the magazine slowly back on the shelf, devastated by what he had read. He saw this comment as a terrible indictment of what his life had become. He stood at the bookcase, not seeing anything but the ruins of his inner self. "Oh, my God, what can I do to redeem myself?"

Thought seemed to leave his mind. He stood in a state of blankness, remembering vaguely the joyful anticipation of his studies at Maynooth, his keenness for prayer, his early days as a curate and the delight he experienced in that role. When had the darkness begun to appear? Was it when he was appointed President of St. Anselm's? When he gave that television interview about his first book? He leaned with both hands on the bookcase, bending forward, his expression agonised. Thought left him again until, after some moments of total stillness, he began to pray. "Oh, my God, I am heartily sorry for having offended thee. Only your grace can save me now. I leave my life in your will. Help me to fight this accursed ego."

The housekeeper knocked on his door. "Your tea's ready, Canon."

"Thanks, Imelda. I'll be there in a minute."

THIRTY-EIGHT

When Dan arrived back at the parochial house, dusk was settling. Indeed, it was almost dark. For that reason, he did not notice that a car, parked on the other side of the road, contained two occupants who were watching him. As Dan walked up the steps to the front door of the house, one of the other car's occupants jumped out and ran across the road to him.

Dan heard her voice at the bottom of the steps. "Father Dan."

He turned and peered into the murk. He thought he recognised the woman. "Helen?"

"Yes, Father," she said quietly. "Helen Murphy." She pointed to the young man who had also left the car and just joined them. "You remember Eamon Donovan, my fiancé?"

Dan walked down the steps towards them. "Of course. Of course. How can I help you?"

Helen glanced at Eamon who nodded slightly, encouraging her to go on. "Father, Eamon and I have been talking a lot about what you said to us that night you talked to us. We realise now that if we want to bring our children up as Catholics, we'd need to learn the proper practice of the faith ourselves." She looked again at her fiancé. "I'm back living with my mother now and we ... we were wondering if you would hear our confessions."

Dan was stunned but he nodded vigorously. "Certainly. Would you like to come in now?"

"Yes, please, Father."

Dan led the couple into the house. He heard their individual confessions and invited them into the empty kitchen afterwards for a cup of tea. The couple chatted comfortably about their forthcoming wedding and their plans for the future. Dan was his usual amiable self but was uncharacteristically quiet, tending towards responsiveness in the conversation rather than his usual ebullience. He was experiencing a kind of spiritual elation that was making him feel that he should rush to the small oratory at the top of the house and spend time before the Lord reflecting on what had happened. Something significant had just taken place. There was grace here. The Lord had affirmed his truth. Dan could sense that and was filled with the mystery of it.

Some minutes later, as the couple stood to leave, Dan noticed that Eamon seemed to be signalling Helen to say something. He raised a quizzical eyebrow and, with a half-smile, said, "Was there something else?"

"Yes, Father," Helen said. "We were wondering if you'd officiate at our wedding ceremony."

Dan's beam was huge. He spread his arms wide and said, "Of course. I'd be delighted." And he enveloped Helen in a huge bear-hug. Eamon, grinning sheepishly, offered Dan his hand. Dan seized it warmly and Eamon said, "Ooowww! Let go."

THIRTY-NINE

1

Tony's prophecy that the bishop's immaculate lawns would be trampled underfoot was to prove less than accurate. The bishop arrived during the evening, angry, and scarcely able to speak civilly to Tony. His attitude, if not his words, made it clear that he no longer trusted Tony to deal with "this awful mess" and that he was here to see what he could do "... to limit damage already done." He ordered Tony brusquely to carry his luggage to his suite while he made a phone-call. He was finishing the call just as Tony arrived back in his office.

"Okay, Gerry. That's great." He listened for a moment. "Well, it's good of you to say that. I truly appreciate your help with this." He listened again and emitted a sardonic chuckle. "Yes, I suppose you've had your share of them, all right. Thanks again. 'Bye!"

He replaced the phone on its stand and looked at Tony, grim-faced. "That was the Assistant Commissioner of the Dublin Metropolitan Region. He's a friend of mine. He's going to post two *gardai* at the front gates in the morning. I want the gates locked, and I want them kept that way for the next couple of days."

"What about the staff?"

"The *gardai* will let them in but I do not want a single one of those nosy reporters near the place."

"You're going to have to give them something, Bishop, or they'll just make stuff up."

"Hummph! They'll do that anyway." He gave the matter a couple of minutes' thought. "All right, I want you to knock out some sort of a statement tonight, less than an A4 sheet, and make copies for the *gardai* to distribute to the media in the morning."

Tony nodded. "I'll get on to that now." He was about to leave when the bishop called to him.

"Oh, Tony. How are those two Redemptorists getting on at St. Columba's?"

"They're doing very well. Gerard's finding them good to work with."

"Mmmm. Maybe you'd better go there tomorrow and stay for a while, take over, help the parishioners to cope. They must be pretty devastated."

Tony's insides clenched and froze. The bishop had withdrawn his favour and was demoting him. He was numb with shock. Everything he had worked for was ... And then came the realisation, *'Do your hopes for elevation mean so much to you?'* And an echo came with the thought, *'... if I were to seek my own glory, that would be no glory at all.'* Struggling to cope with this bitter blow to his ambitions, he tried to pray. *Is this your will for me, Lord? Must I ...?*

He noticed suddenly that the bishop was staring at him, waiting for his response. He strove for some normalcy in his tone. "I'll be happy to try, Bishop," he said, still fighting the hurt and the disappointment that assailed him. He felt side-lined, even betrayed, but again he tried to find that spark in his heart that was of the spirit. He could accept the role of parish priest and try to use it as an opportunity to reflect an 'image of the good shepherd.' In doing so, he would still earn a chance to turn his life around, to serve the faithful, and to image Christ. This dead feeling in the pit of his stomach would serve as a constant reminder of all that had died in his spirit. He held his bishop's gaze and nodded solemnly. "I agree with you that St. Columba's is going to need some very careful guidance over the next few months. I just hope I'm up to it."

The bishop threw him a suspicious glance but saw nothing untoward in Tony's expression. He nodded. "That's settled then." He turned to his desk but had yet another afterthought. "Oh, I'll pull young Patterson out of Kilnamoy and have him join you at St. Columba's. I'd say that débâcle at the funeral won't have done his cause much good. Gerard Mulvaney can go back and assist Ciaran Mussen. It'll put them under a bit of pressure for a while but they can do a bit of re-jigging of Masses and things. They'll manage."

2

The media scrimmage started early the following morning. Even before Tony had dressed and breakfasted, a crowd of journalists and two television crews were milling around the front gate, buzzing incessantly at the intercom and rattling at the gates seeking entrance. The two promised *gardai* arrived at 8.00 am, just in time to move the frustrated throng back from the huge iron gates which, despite their seeming impenetrability, were in danger of being burst open.

Tony came to the gate and handed copies of the statement he had prepared the evening before through the bars to one of the policemen. The reporters shouted their inevitable questions over each other's heads, none apparently expecting an answer. Judging from the variety of accents, the case had already drawn the attention of some of the big English nationals. Cameras were flashing and TV cameramen were moving around trying to get an angle on Tony through the bars of the gate. Tony, safe where he was, held up his arms for silence. Still the questions came, some deliberately slanted and misleading.

"How many times has Father Canavan been re-posted to escape previous offences?"

"Are you the bishop, sir?"

"Will you be releasing the names of any other protected priests in this diocese?"

"Why are the *gardai* here? Are you hiding the paedophile priest in there?"

Tony lowered his arms and turned to walk away in disgust. Some of those closest to the gates shouted and hissed at their more belligerent fellows and eventually a level of quiet ensued. Tony came back and addressed them briefly, "What I have just now handed to the *gardai* are copies of the bishop's statement on the matter of Father Canavan's arraignment. Each of you will receive one. That is all the bishop intends to say about an issue that is still before the courts. There is therefore little point in your hanging around these gates any longer. No further comment will be made."

The shouting started immediately as hands thrust forward to grab the papers from the policemen. Howls of protest broke out from those who had quickly scanned the statement.

"Ah, come on. There's nothing new here."

"Hey! You can't expect to fob us off with this."

Tony's statement had indeed been bland. It simply read: *Father Raymond Canavan, a priest from the diocese of Castleshaughlin, has submitted himself voluntarily to the Garda Shíochána Station at Harcourt Terrace for alleged unlawful intercourse with a minor. The arraignment was held at a nearby District Court of the Dublin Metropolitan District on 23rd April. Some doubt hangs over the legitimacy of the guilty plea and the Court has not yet accepted it. The priest has been ill for some time and there will be no further movement on the issue until a sitting of the Circuit Court in three weeks.*

Further shouts chased him up the drive.

"Who was the judge? What's causing the doubt?"

"Where's Father Canavan now?"

"What kind of illness, sir? The people have a right to know."

It was as much as Tony could do to keep on walking. He would dearly have loved to turn and berate these reporters for their profession's consistent abuse of what constituted the public's right to know. But he knew that anything he said would be twisted and misquoted, so he walked resolutely back into the house and up to his room to pack.

3

Peter Rafferty was learning quickly how foolish it can be to trust the media. His harangue at the District Court had set in motion a series of harassments of his family that left him deeply regretting his indiscretion. His assumption that the court reporters were on his side was naïve. The reporters were interested only in selling newspapers and fishing out the most salacious details of the story. Some were happy to print details that came from nowhere but the dark recesses of their own corrupt minds. The Rafferty's phone had not stopped ringing for over an hour after they arrived home from court, until, in desperation, they had to leave it off the hook. Despite the fact that the press was prevented from releasing Maria's name for legal reasons, the media had no problem finding out who she was and where she lived. Reporters and TV crews were today crawling all over the house, knocking constantly on the door, peering in through windows, which were now covered by drawn drapes, and calling out, "Come on out, Maria. Just give us a brief statement."

Others were rattling at the back door while one even had his fingers poking through the letter box, shouting what Peter considered to be nothing less than obscenity. "Come out for one wee photograph, Maria, and we'll go away. Wear your school uniform."

Paparazzi kept prowling around the front and back of the house with offensive disregard for the family's privacy, determined to catch a glimpse, or better yet, a photograph, of the schoolgirl at the centre of this scandal. Peter had earlier opened the door, attempting to cow them with his fury, but found himself blinded by flashbulbs, prodded by microphones, and the target of yet more vociferous questioning. He had retreated quickly, managing to push the front door shut. He went back to the lounge where his wife and Maria were sitting, the electric light switched on against the gloom created by the closed drapes.

"No one's to open that door," he gritted. "Those bastards are prepared to push their way into our very home." He glared at the closed door. "Hateful creatures," he hissed again. "Who do they think they are?" He looked around. "Where's Paul?"

"He's upstairs playing with his computer," his wife answered.

Maria was sitting on the sofa, her mother's arm around her, looking strained and tearful. Peter felt a rush of sympathy. No child should have to suffer this. He sat on the armchair opposite them. "I'm sorry, Maria. I should never have let my temper get the better of me in court. Now look at what I have started."

Maria looked at him, tears starting into her eyes. She clung to her mother but she said, "It's all right, Daddy. It's not your fault."

Peter rose again, gave his daughter a comforting pat on the shoulder, and began to roam around the rooms again, muttering angrily under his breath.

FORTY

1

When Mrs. Toner arrived at the parochial house that morning, she was besieged by reporters. She had not seen the news the night before and was utterly mystified by the commotion. She was clearly, however, the centre of attention and for a while smilingly said, “Eh? What’s that? Who?” She was soon to realise, however, that they were talking about Father Ray and that they were accusing him of some terrible deeds. She began to force her way to the front door, shouting, “How dare you come here accusin’ Father Ray of all sorts. There’s no better priest in this diocese.”

One male reporter caught her arm. “Just a second, Ma’am, tell us something about the schoolgirl he raped.”

“You vile-tongued heathen,” she rasped, hitting at him with her handbag. “How dare you?” She started swinging indiscriminately. “Get out of my way, ye lowlife pagans. Get out of my way.” When she managed finally to get into the house, she leaned back against the closed door, breathing heavily, her face a mask of shock. What in God’s name were they saying? *There has to be some terrible mistake. It couldn't be Father Ray they're talkin' about, could it?*

Father Gerard was coming down the stairs, heading out to Mass. "Good morning, Mrs. Toner. What's going on?"

Mrs. Toner put a hand to her fluttering breast. "There's about a hundred reporters at the door saying terrible things about Father Canavan."

"Oh, cripes," Gerard said. "Are they here, too?"

He told the housekeeper to go into the kitchen and make herself a cup of tea. As he left the house, he was immediately besieged with questions.

"What can you tell us about Father Canavan?"

"What was he like to work with?"

"Do you know of any similar incidents in his background?"

"Is Father Canavan in there now?"

Gerard tried to push his way through the throng, hoping that a stony silence would deter them but they pressed around him until he was unable to move. He stopped and said firmly, "Look, I know absolutely nothing about any of this. I have no other comment to make. I have to say Mass now. Please allow me through." With that he managed to elbow his way through them, inwardly disgusted. *What a thoroughly nasty way to earn a living,* he was thinking.

2

Mrs. McLoughlin was distraught. She still had not come to terms with the story Maria had told and, since her affection for Father Ray had become almost motherly, she had difficulty in believing what he was supposed to have done. Nonetheless, she knew the girl was truthful and, despite his offence, she continued to search her heart for ways to excuse the young priest. Maria had said he had been depressed and ill. *He might just have needed comforting. God help him now with all this going on*, she thought, intuiting his anguish and empathising with it. *How's he going to cope?* And her heart ached for the young man she had come so much to admire. And to add to her distress there were reporters lurking around the front gates, stopping her girls and quizzing them about Maria. She had just phoned the *gardai* to inform them that "... there might be all sorts of paedophiles mingling with reporters at my school gates, bothering my girls. I want the whole lot shifted immediately."

She was now roaming the grounds for any stray girl that might not be safe inside the school building and for any reporters who may have trespassed beyond the gates. Assured that her young charges were now safely inside the school, she went to the front gate where members of the media still gathered in small groups, tossing cigarette butts on the ground, muttering vaguely to each other, and eyeing the approaches to the school for any latecomers who might provide them with some titbit of information. There was a bustle of interest when they saw Mrs. McLoughlin striding down the drive.

Even before she had reached them, one had the temerity to shout, "What can you tell us about Maria Rafferty, Missus?"

She silenced him with a glare that would not have disgraced a Gorgon and said, “I want all of you to leave immediately. The *gardai* are on their way and any of you who are found loitering here when they arrive will be arrested as paedophiles. Good morning.”

And with that she turned and strode back up the drive.

The reporters looked at each other and shrugged. Then they simply moved away in small groups to the corners of the various streets nearby, stoically waiting for the pupils to come out again during their lunch break.

FORTY-ONE

Mr. Donaldson stood on the street in front of his office, silent and collected. A small smile played on his lips as he posed for the many paparazzi seeking his picture. He had carefully stage-managed his position so that the morning newspapers and the evening television news would carry clear views of his firm's name printed across his office window. Thousands of euro worth of publicity and it wasn't costing him a penny. So he continued to stand, and smile, and be silent, until the flashing petered to a stop and the TV reporters moved forward with their microphones. His calmness had somehow infected the group and they were relatively quiet, knowing that here was a man experienced in dealing with the media and that they would get nothing from him until he was permitted to speak into total silence.

Mr. Donaldson positioned himself a little closer to the door of the building so that he did not even partially obstruct the gold lettering on his window and smiled broadly. "Good morning, Ladies and Gentlemen. Am I to assume that your collective presence here is indication that you seek information from me about one of my cases?"

"The paedophile priest, Father Canavan," one shouted.

Mr. Donaldson's face expressed puzzlement. "I'm afraid I know of no paedophile priest by that name," he said.

"Do you know any Father Canavan?" another asked.

"Yes, of course I do, but he is not a paedophile."

"Do you have a case pending in which he is the defendant?"

Mr. Donaldson offered the questioner a mirthless smile. "Now, now, sir, you know as well as I do that I cannot possibly comment on any case that is still *sub judice*."

"What can you tell us?" asked a red-haired female reporter, pushing her microphone under his nose. She had a cut-glass English accent. Mr. Donaldson transferred the smile to her but there was more feeling in it this time. He was enjoying himself. "About what, my dear?"

"About Father Raymond Canavan's arrest and arraignment."

"No comment," the solicitor smiled.

"Do you anticipate a custodial sentence?"

Mr. Donaldson smiled courteously at the new speaker, also a female but obviously home-grown. "No comment."

There was some frustrated mumbling and Mr. Donaldson raised his eyebrows questioningly.

"Can you tell us the exact date when the Circuit Court will be sitting?" came a voice from the back of the group.

Mr. Donaldson's smile wavered and he looked puzzled again. "Which Circuit Court?" he asked, expressing interest.

The reporters looked at each other in disgust. Mr. Donaldson smiled again. "Does anyone else have a question?" he asked politely.

Notebooks were closed, biros replaced in pockets or handbags, and the reporters began to shuffle away. No one spoke.

"Thank you all," Mr. Donaldson said pleasantly and went into the building.

FORTY-TWO

1

Dublin's Circuit Court was packed to capacity on the morning of the fifteenth of May. The public gallery was crowded with media personnel who had used their press passes like tickets, leaving virtually no seats for members of the public. Maria and her parents, together with the family solicitor, had been given seats at the prosecutor's bench. This was something of a courtesy since it was unlikely that at this stage of the proceedings they would be asked to offer any evidence. Many of the morbidly curious who were unable to gain seats inside the courtroom chose to wait outside to greet Ray, as he arrived, with loud jeers and angry catcalls. Some thuggish types, shaven headed and tattooed, hurled loud and vociferous insults, waving their fists and trying to break through the cordon of *gardai* to do the young priest physical harm. Among the crowd were some screeching young mothers, impervious to the fright and distress they were causing their children by their screaming vituperation.

Mr. Donaldson and Tony, who were with Ray, walked on either side of him, trying to shield him as much as they could from the ranting mob. Tony kept his head down and, pulling Ray with him, hurried into the building. He had witnessed similar scenes before on television, the violence and the rabid hatred in the eyes of the throng, and this orgy of self-righteousness never failed to mystify him. *Was this the sort of screaming that was going on when Jesus carried his cross to Calvary? How do they justify it to themselves? Do they not realise that there is more than enough for us to do working on our own hearts? Why are they so vindictive? Could it really be something as simple as a psychological need to find someone they can look down on in order to give themselves some sense of superiority? Or was it something more savage, more atavistic, the instincts of the baying mob screaming for blood?*

He stood with Ray in the entrance hall while their solicitor spoke to an official. After a moment's conversation, they were directed to the main courtroom. In the south of Ireland, offenders who engage in acts of a criminal nature which are initially dealt with in a District Court are, more often than not, sent forward for trial and eventual sentencing to a Circuit Court near where the accused person has been arrested. The trial for the case is usually heard by a judge and a jury but if the defendant lodges a guilty plea, the jury and the trial can be dispensed with and the sentencing can be decided at the judge's discretion. Since Ray had initially pleaded guilty, there was no jury empanelled for that morning. Thomas Donaldson had already assured Tony that he could handle the situation for the time being and that there would be no necessity to appoint a barrister to fight the case unless it went to trial. "The judge is going to do most of the talking, anyway," he told him. "We'll just be sitting listening."

There had been a buzz of conversation in the courtroom when they entered but there was a sudden silence as they went to their seats behind the defendant's bench followed by dozens of pairs of curious eyes. Already some of the journalists were writing descriptions of the room and the defendant. At ten o'clock exactly the court clerk entered and shouted, "All rise."

Judge Carey entered briskly, her gown flowing, carrying a large brief case. This she placed on the bench and began to extract several sheets of paper and a spectacles case, all of which she placed to the left of the case. She closed the briefcase and pushed it far to the right side of the bench and straightened the edges of the papers with the tips of her fingers. She put on the spectacles and began quickly to peruse the sheets before her, moving on to subsequent sheets with only the most cursory examination of their predecessors. She looked up and around the silent courtroom a couple of times, and her lips tightened in annoyance at the number of media personnel in attendance. She adjusted her glasses and cleared her throat. "This morning's proceedings are conducted to establish"—she raised a finger—"whether or not the defendant is of sufficiently sound mind to plead guilty"—another finger joined the first—"and on the basis of that finding, whether he is to be sent forward for trial or to receive sentence this morning."

She glanced briefly at Ray, and Tony followed her glance to see how Ray was affected. He was sitting very still, his eyes fastened on the judge's face. Judge Carey looked again at the packed gallery, unable to hide her distaste. "I have a long statement to make here this morning," she said, looking directly at the ladies and gentlemen of the media. "Apart from its obvious interest to those directly involved, it is certain to be dry, even boring." She looked over the rim of her glasses. "You can rest assured that there will be no excitement in this courtroom this morning." She leaned back and took off her spectacles. "If any of you representatives of the press would like to escape, now is your only chance. I will not tolerate people running in and out of my court once I begin to make my judgement. Is that understood?"

No one moved. The judge put her spectacles back on and reached once more for her papers. "Very well," she said, giving the reporters one final judicial glare. She lifted a couple of pages a foot or so into the air with one hand and seemed to study one that was on the pile on the bench. Then she began to address the two parties in the well of the court. "On the matter of the defendant's fitness to plead, I have had, in the interests of justice to all parties, to devote considerable time to examining the reports of the defendant's psychotherapist, the court appointed psychiatrist and, indeed, to the law itself." She glanced down at a sheet before her. "In the People versus O'Mahony, 1985, the trial judge stated clearly that a person who is found not guilty by reason of insanity is deserving of treatment, not punishment, whereas a person who is simply found guilty or pleads guilty, is deserving of punishment. I would have thought such a ruling to be straightforward but when I turned to the psychiatric reports, I found there such a complexity of detail about the defendant's mental state that what should have been simple has become extremely complicated." She looked up as the Raffertys' solicitor had to put a restraining hand on Peter who was about to jump up and protest. She chose to ignore the interruption and went on, "Dr. Whitfield's statement has already been referred to in the District Court. She makes it very clear that the defendant, because of the awakening of long-repressed memories of childhood abuse by a relative," she glanced in irritation at Maria who had sucked in a loud, shocked breath at this revelation and went on, "and because of the trauma attached to such developing awareness, was in a state of acute physical, emotional and mental distress. But does this constitute insanity as legally defined?"

She turned to another page.

"The report from the court's psychiatrist, Dr. David Jennings, offers considerable confirmation of Dr. Whitfield's findings and supports her thesis that, given the circumstances the young priest found himself in at the time of the offence, he would have been emotionally very vulnerable and prone to uncharacteristic behaviours. But again I ask, does that constitute legal insanity?"

She laid the pages down and, with her fingers tented under her chin, went on without reference to any notes. "Where the psychiatrists differ is in the extent to which the defendant is fit to plead. Dr. Whitfield claims that the defendant is suffering such extremity of moral guilt that he is actively seeking and expecting punishment regardless of his legal deserts. On that basis, she argues, he cannot be expected to offer a genuinely just plea on his own behalf. Dr. Jennings, on the other hand, has found the defendant to be cogent and fully aware of the nature of his offence and suggests that his guilty plea comes from the same state of conscience found in ordinary people who commit an offence in the heat of the moment and later come to regret their actions."

The judge looked again at both involved parties and said, "To which of these statements should I give most weight?" She took her spectacles off again and laid them on the desk. She stared down at the solicitors. "I am going to break with court protocol here and offer both sides an opportunity for argument. Mr. Redmond, would you wish to speak?"

Mr. Redmond, portly, balding, dressed in a black pin-striped suit, pushed back his chair and came to his feet. "Thank you, your honour. I would." His voice was thin, almost high-pitched. He cleared his throat and made his points dryly, without drama or elaboration. "There are perhaps three significant points here that are germane, your honour. It has been submitted that the court may reject the defendant's guilty plea if it is based on a misunderstanding of the offence charged. There has been nothing in your statement, your honour, or those of the psychiatrists, to imply that this has been the case. On that basis therefore, I would submit that the defendant is fully entitled to enter a plea." He harrumphed again and said, "Secondly, your court appointed psychiatrist has assessed the defendant as fit to plead. In such case, your honour, surely the defendant is entitled to decide for himself how he will exercise his right to plead? I submit that he should not be obstructed from entering any plea he wishes." He bent down to check his notes. "Thirdly, your honour, without wishing to abrogate your honour's authority, it is my understanding that there are no statutes in Irish law to cover such pleas as 'diminished responsibility' or 'irresistible impulse'. I would respectfully submit, therefore, that in this case you do not have the power to go behind the plea entered by the accused." He sat down somewhat self-importantly, refusing to acknowledge Mr. Donaldson's vaguely cadaverous grin.

The judge wrote some notes before finally looking up. "Mr. Donaldson?"

Mr. Donaldson was on his feet immediately. "Thank you, your honour. Ah ... I could have done with a little time to prepare for this, but ..."

"You've had three weeks," the judge snapped frostily. "Be glad of the opportunity you might otherwise not have had."

"Yes, your honour. Thank you."

Mr. Donaldson might not have been a barrister but he was possessed of considerable histrionic ability and a great deal of confidence. He addressed the court as if there was not only a full jury but a panel of judges as well and, where Mr. Jennings had addressed the judge directly, Mr. Donaldson's gaze encompassed the crowded public gallery. He had some notes in his hand to which he now referred. "Certain blameworthy conduct," he stated, "is defined by the State as criminal. In general, a crime consists of an act, an *actus reus*, and a mental element, *mens rea* ..."

The judge bristled.

Mr. Donaldson added hastily, "Basic law, I agree, your honour, but in this case it is germane. Now, let me emphasise that liability for the crime is dependent, naturally, on the accused committing the act relevant to the crime. But"—he held up an emphatic finger and paused dramatically—"he must also have the mental capacity required appropriate to the crime. And, your honour, as the pages on the bench in front of you attest, there is a substantial doubt as to the defendant's mental state in the crime of which he stands indicted. The mental element, your honour, is a constituent part of the crime and cannot be ignored." He checked his notes again and prepared himself for more theatrics. His eyes ranged the room.

Judge Carey was having none of it. "If you want to talk to the press, take them outside and do it," she said caustically. "Otherwise, address your arguments to me."

"Of course, your honour. I apologise," Mr. Donaldson said, not in the least chastened. He did, however, try for an earnest look. "Your honour," he said, "at the District Court I made the point that in the interests of all, the court should aspire to truth and justice. As part of such aspiration, I am of the belief that people should not be punished if they are not guilty of a crime." He held up his finger again. "That is, if they did not have the mental capacity necessary to commit the crime. Such a person should have the benefit of medical treatment, restorative treatment; not imprisonment." He paused to allow that point to settle. The he went on, this time his eyes focused on the judge. "Your honour will have read in both psychiatrists' reports that Father Canavan has been deemed to need a substantial period of psychotherapy before his psychic wounds can heal." He held out both hands, palms upward, in a plea for understanding. "So, once again, your honour, I would submit that the court should acknowledge the precarious nature of this guilty plea and follow the proper principles and law concerning the whole issue of fitness to plead." He sat down, giving Ray and Tony a reassuring nod.

The judge finished writing a second set of notes, put her pen down, took off her eye-glasses yet again, and stared at the two solicitors. She said, demonstrating some level of uncertainty, "Both solicitors have made cogent and compelling arguments. I would need a little time to digest them and to set them against my own reading of the evidence. I am going to call a short adjournment to give me time to finalise my judgement. Court will reconvene in one hour."

As she rose to leave, the clerk called, "All rise!"

2

The public gallery quickly emptied as thirsty reporters sought coffee and others headed for the rest rooms. One or two of the more brazen tried to approach the parties at the solicitors' benches but the court guards quickly impeded them. None of the people at the solicitors' benches showed any inclination to move.

Tony said to Ray, "How are you holding up?"

Ray shook his head. "I'm totally confused. All I wanted to do is to plead guilty and accept the punishment I deserve. Now I ..." he raised his hands in confusion.

Tony turned to Mr. Donaldson. "You were pretty impressive there, Thomas. What do you think the judge will decide?"

The solicitor shrugged. "Impossible to say, Canon. Redmond's arguments were short but they were legally very sharp. However, one thing I can tell you. Judge Carey is acerbic and very strict but she is as fair as they come. She'll want to do the right thing, whatever she perceives that to be."

He looked up sharply, hearing a commotion at the prosecutor's bench. Tony turned to see Maria struggling with her father who was holding her wrist. She shook her arm from his grasp and came running over to Ray who was, by that time, half out of his seat. Oblivious to Ray's companions, Maria stood in front of him and, her eyes welling with tears, she said, "Oh, Ray, I'm sorry. I'm sorry.

I didn't want this. I'm so sorry. Please forgive me, Ray. I didn't want this."

Ray placed a comforting hand gently on the side of her shoulder. When Peter Rafferty saw this, he rose from his seat but his wife pulled him down again. Shaking his head, filled with his own sadness, Ray said, "Maria, you don't have to be sorry for anything. Honestly, Maria, there is nothing for me to forgive." He stared earnestly into her eyes, amber with flecks of green, eyes that still had the power to break his heart. "You are blameless in this; always remember that. I was the adult. The fault was mine. It is you who has to forgive me."

Maria was openly crying now. "Oh, Ray ..."

By this time, however, her father had had enough. He came over to the group, gave Ray an angry glance, and hurried Maria out of the courtroom. Mrs. Rafferty followed them, glancing neutrally at Ray as she left. Ray sat down again, and put his head in his hands. Tony clapped a sympathetic hand on his shoulder.

"Dear God, Tony," Ray said, "what have I done to those people?"

3

The court began to fill up again some minutes before the adjournment was due to end. Peter Rafferty entered hurriedly, one arm sheltering his wife and the other around Maria, as he fought to avoid the importuning of the persistent reporters who were crowding them. Two court guards came over and hustled the journalists back to their seats with ruthless efficiency.

A few minutes later the clerk came out of the judge's chambers and called, "All rise."

The judge swept to the bench and went through what now was clearly an established routine. She placed the briefcase on the bench, removed some pages and her spectacles from it, set these to one side, closed the case and pushed it, together with the gavel which she never used, far to the edge of the bench. She then tidied the papers in front of her, using the tips of her fingers to order the edges so that the pages sat neatly one on top of the other. Finally, she took the spectacles out of their case but toyed with them in her hands as she began to address the court.

"The judgement I must make presents me with three problems. Firstly, I must try to establish on the basis of evidence provided whether or not the defendant is fit to enter a plea of guilty. Secondly, I must ask myself if I have the power or the duty to decline a plea of guilty, even if I were satisfied that there are substantial grounds for believing that the accused was not in full possession of his mental faculties at the time the offence was committed. Thirdly, I will have to rule on whether the defendant is to be sent forward for trial or whether sentence is to be imposed today."

She put on her spectacles and studied her notes for a few moments. "I have considered carefully the arguments put forward by both counsel. Mr. Redmond's submission has exposed the limitations in Irish statutory law and suggests the need for the introduction of alternative pleas to insanity, such as diminished responsibility and irresistible impulse. Mr. Donaldson, on the other hand, has argued cogently, despite his theatricality, that on the basis of the *mens rea* the defendant should not be stigmatised by a criminal conviction when his requirement is essentially medical rather than penal."

Judge Carey stared for a moment at the Rafferty family and went on, "I am also exercised by two further points. A judge must never lose sight of the fact that she has duties not only to the accused but also to the people of the State and to those who have suffered as a result of the accused's actions." Mr. Rafferty who had been listening intently, nodded vigorously. "On the other hand," the judge continued, at which point Mr. Rafferty's nodding stopped dead, "the dignity of a person is also relevant and there arises the question of whether it is just and proper to treat as a criminal a defendant whose state of mind was such that his act may, in fact, not have been criminal as defined in law."

The judge turned her gaze from Mr. Rafferty's horrified expression to the calmer expressions of the people at the defendant's bench. She studied her notes again, quickly searching through the pages until she found the one she was looking for. She put on her glasses and said, "An additional and unusual factor is the defendant's apparent motivation for entering a guilty plea. My understanding, from both psychiatric reports, is that he is seeking punishment through the court, having tried and judged himself without proper consideration of all of the factors involved."

The judge sat back on the bench, removed her glasses again, set them in front of her, and folded her arms comfortably across her chest, clearly in no hurry to make her judgement until both parties were fully *au fait* with her reasoning and the problems she had encountered. The silence in the room was total apart from the muted but frenzied clicking of the stenographer's keyboard.

"The issue is further complicated by the fact that I can find no precedent for a decision to refuse the guilty plea. There does not appear to be any case law on this point. Were I to accept Mr. Donaldson's arguments, I would be obliged to create a precedent, something any judge would be loath to do unless the arguments were very compelling."

She leaned forward on to the bench again and rubbed her face with her hands. This judgement was one that was causing her a deal of concern. Her arms were folded on the desk now as she continued, "I have decided to base my decision on the two psychiatric reports. The legal issues about the court's entitlement to refuse the plea, the lack of appropriate statutes, or the creation of a precedent, are complex and significant but they do not assist me nor, indeed, do they deter me from arriving at a just and equitable decision."

She lifted one of the pages and held it up. There was a stir of expectancy in the court and the reporters sat, pens poised to attack their notebooks at the first hint of a decision. The judge looked at the defendant and then back at the page she was holding.

"I have studied both reports carefully and I can find no indication in either of them that the defendant was so bereft of awareness that he was acting involuntarily. In fact, if I understand them correctly," she looked out over her eye-glasses, "and I believe I do, it would seem that the defendant's act was prompted more by love and loneliness than by any state of automatism."

There were gasps in the court and a sudden rustle of papers at the press seats.

"It is my judgement, therefore, that the defendant has a right and is fit to enter any plea he wishes."

Mr. Rafferty punched his fist downward with a silent, "Yes." Maria stared aghast at Ray who had been listening intently to the judge. He showed no reaction other than a barely visible tightening of the lips. Tony's head went down, his expression distressed. Mr. Donaldson glanced over at Mr. Redmond and gave him a congratulatory nod.

The judge put down her pages and looked at Ray. "Would the defendant please rise."

Ray stood up and faced her, expressionless.

"Do you understand the nature of the charge laid against you?"

"Yes, your honour."

"Do you understand that Section 2 of the Criminal Law Act of 1935 provides that it is an offence punishable by five years' imprisonment to have unlawful carnal knowledge of a girl aged between fifteen and seventeen years?"

"I have been so informed, your honour."

"Do you still wish to make a plea on your own behalf?"

"I do, your honour."

The judge pursed her lips. "Very well, how do you plead?"

Ray showed only the briefest hesitation. "Guilty, your honour."

There were more gasps and mutterings in the courtroom. The judge frowned at the press corps and said, "If you are not prepared to remain silent, I am happy to have you removed from the court before I proceed to sentencing."

Total silence reigned again. The judge returned her attention to Ray. "Is there anything you wish to say on your own behalf before I pass sentence?"

"No, your honour," Ray said quietly, "other than to reiterate my intense sorrow to the family for the deep distress and pain my actions have caused."

This time the judge did not give vent to any sarcasm. She simply eyed Ray for a moment as if she was still trying to assess his mental competence. "You may sit down again. I have one or two more points to make before I pass sentence."

Ray sat down, vaguely bemused. Tony looked up, suddenly alert, glancing quizzically at Mr. Donaldson who shrugged his shoulders and registered mystification.

The judge tucked the pages she had been using under the pile and glanced at some new ones. She cleared her throat. "The law in Ireland trails significantly behind that in other countries such as England and America in the matter of the criminal responsibility of persons who are mentally ill, or who can make an argument for diminished responsibility, but it is on the basis of the law as it stands in Ireland that I must proceed."

Tony's heart was thumping. The judge was apparently sympathizing with Ray on the one hand but indicating on the other that the law was not allowing her to do anything to help him. Her next remarks were to do little to ease his confusion.

"In the matter of sentencing, the judge has to consider the crime and assess its nature, the damage done, and the effects of that damage. To this end, I earlier asked Dr. Jennings to carry out a victim impact assessment and I have his report before me." She rustled her pages again, studied one briefly and looked up once more. "In essence, Dr. Jennings reports that in terms of the single sexual act, the crime for which the accused now finds himself before this court, the victim experienced, and is experiencing, no negative effects. She fully understands the nature of the act and her own part in it which, while not germane to the issue of the defendant's guilt, nevertheless has allowed the victim to recall and review the act with no detriment to her psychological well-being."

The judge glanced at Maria while she shuffled through her pages yet again. Finding the one she wanted she went on, "Where the victim remains psychologically damaged, however, is in the aftermath of the abortion …" There was another frisson of activity in the ranks of the press to some of whom this was news. The judge glanced impatiently in their direction but went on, "but since this was carried out in another country and since the defendant, although to some degree implicit, did not arrange or procure the abortion, there is nothing there that demands the attention or concern of this court. The sentence must apply solely to the offence of unlawful carnal knowledge."

Peter Rafferty was holding his wife's hand and, if she had not clung tightly to his, he might yet again have stood to protest.

The judge continued, "Furthermore, it is also incumbent upon a judge to assess the accused, the nature of his intent, the circumstances around the act, and anything that might mitigate culpability. It appears in this case that the court has substantial grounds for believing that there was no criminal intent. How does a judge assess a proportionate sentence for such a situation? This court has deemed that the accused is fit to plead but that does not obviate the need to give cognisance to the assessment of the two psychiatrists that the defendant was in considerable physical, mental and emotional distress at the time of the offence and that what was going on in his psyche was extremely injurious to his normal autonomy. Thus I must ask, to what extent would these considerations have impaired his judgement as an adult and as a priest? The defendant allows himself no doubt as to his culpability but the court still bears responsibility for the integrity of the judicial system and to serve the best interests of justice. Is justice to be served by imposing upon this particular defendant a custodial sentence?"

The judge folded her fingers under her chin and leaned forward on her elbows. She adopted a professorial tone. "Bertrand Russell, I suppose he could be described as a twentieth century philosopher, once wrote a short essay on the prison system." She looked up at the massed journalists and said drily, "Some of you may know that he was in a position to write with some authority on imprisonment, having experienced it at first hand." She turned again to the solicitors' benches. "Mr. Russell made the point that the law views imprisonment from three perspectives. It can be seen as a deterrent although there are many who would argue about its effectiveness in this regard. It is seen also as retributive, as representing just punishment against the wrongdoer on the state's and the people's behalf. And it is seen as rehabilitative, that is, it is supposed to give the guilty person an opportunity to reflect on his evil ways and mend his life before he is released. There is much divided opinion on that element. Mr. Russell, in fact, had problems with all three elements as indeed, you may be surprised to learn, do many of the judges who share this bench with me."

She paused and set her page down. Then, pursing her lips, she said, "Nonetheless, it is the only system we have." She leaned forward and folded her arms on the bench. "To what extent is the defendant likely to need a deterrent element in his punishment? I am strongly of the opinion that this young man has already learned a lesson in that regard and the risk of his re-offending is minimal. I also wonder about the extent to which he requires rehabilitation and, indeed, the extent to which prison might be the best place to achieve that. Would the therapy recommended by the psychiatrists serve such purpose more effectively? And, thirdly, I have to say that punishment for crime seen as a matter of the state's vengeance is philosophically questionable, particularly, and I am perhaps trespassing beyond my judicial parameters in saying this, when such vengeance is to be visited upon a defendant whose crime would not be considered such in other civilised legal systems."

Judge Carey looked directly at Ray. "Would the defendant please stand."

Ray stood. Tony was afraid to look up. His hands were clasped tightly between his knees. Mr. Donaldson looked fascinated by the length and complexity of the judge's comments. Maria had the forefingers and middle fingers of both hands crossed and her eyes were closed as she waited for the sentence to be pronounced.

"Father Canavan, you have pleaded guilty to unlawful carnal knowledge of a girl below the age of seventeen and above the age of fifteen." There was utter silence in the court. "Taking into consideration all of the circumstances that emerged during this enquiry, you are hereby sentenced to twelve months in prison, suspended for three years. You will also make yourself available for non-custodial supervision for a period of not less than twelve months and attend a full course of psychotherapy until your therapist declares you healed. This court is adjourned."

There was much noise and discussion in the courtroom, much of it from reporters barking text into their cell phones, but Ray scarcely heard it. He looked over at Maria. She was standing now, looking back at him with tears running down her face. But she was smiling and gave him a delighted nod before turning to leave with her parents.

EPILOGUE

October

A silver Ford Mondeo, with two male occupants, drove along a narrow road that bordered a magnificent lake. On their left they were passing a succession of private estates, largely concealed by tall trees that grew along the side of the road. On their right was the lake itself. There were some low-lying shrubs and bushes between the road and the shore, but not enough to obscure the majestic view of green and purple mountains etched against the clear blue of the sky in the far distance. Sunlight sparkled on the waters and the man in the passenger seat, who had been admiring the scene, said, “Beautiful here, isn’t it?”

The driver nodded but made no reply. He had been driving for over two hours and they were now nearing their destination. He was suffering a degree of tension although he had already, more than once, chided himself for such unnecessary concern. The road began to lead upwards and away from the lake into a country area. Wide fields, some hedged, others defined by stone walls or wire fencing, spread out in all directions. They drove on through a little village with a few houses, some shops, and a picturesque church with a tall spire sitting atop a nearby hill. The road meandered downwards again through seemingly uninhabited countryside until, in the distance, the travellers could see a collection of grey buildings with heavily slanted slate roofs, sitting in solitary splendour on a few acres of land and surrounded by a low fence.

"That's it," the driver said quietly.

They drove through the gate and parked near the main entrance. They knocked on the door and while they waited the younger man turned full circle on the doorstep, surveying what the area offered. "Looks awful quiet," he remarked.

"That, I think, is the idea," his companion replied.

They heard a rattle at the lock on the other side of the door and an elderly Benedictine friar slowly pulled the door open. He peered at the two men through the heavily magnifying lenses of his spectacles. "Good day," he said, in the weak breathless tones of the elderly. "Welcome to our Benedictine Community."

"Thank you, Father," the older of the two visitors replied. "We've come to see Dom Francis. I believe we're expected."

"Come in, come in," the old friar smiled. "I'll go and find him." He led them to a room a few yards down the hall. "This is our visitors' room. You can wait in here."

He left his visitors to find themselves seats. The room was large with a high ceiling. There were several armchairs scattered about and a small occasional table near the window with some copies of The National Geographic on it. A massive, polished oak table with ornately carved legs occupied the centre of the room. The younger man went back to the door and stared up and down the corridor.

"Gosh, it's like the grave in here." He smiled at his companion. "Do you think you could handle living like this?"

The other man grinned. "I'm not sure."

The younger man went to the window and looked out. All was still. He sucked in a breath. "No thanks," he said. "This would drive me up the walls."

Footsteps could be heard in the corridor outside. A young man, dark-haired and handsome, wearing a long cream Benedictine habit, came into the room. The younger visitor put his hands on his hips and studied the newcomer.

"Dom flaming Francis," he said, with a wide grin. Then he ran over and encased the young friar in a huge bear hug. "How are you, Ray?" he asked.

"Great, Dan. Really great," Ray replied. He extracted himself from Dan's grip and went over to embrace Tony. "Great to see you, Tony. No problems getting here?"

"Straight through," Tony replied. "No bother at all." He returned Ray's embrace. "Well, how're things here?"

"Good. Good. I'm happy. It's a life I need and a life I want."

"Rather you than me," Dan said. "Do you not find it desperate quiet?"

Ray laughed. "That never bothered me, Dan. It was your incessant chattering I couldn't handle."

Dan raised a huge fist. Then he laughed. "No, but seriously, how do you cope with all this silence?"

"It's not a bother, Dan," Ray said earnestly. "You get to love the contemplative peace. I'm here nearly six months and I feel as if I have hardly set foot in the place."

The old friar knocked on the door and pushed in a small wheeled trolley with coffee and biscuits on it. He smiled at them and turned to Ray. "Do you want to do mother, Brother Francis?"

Ray smiled back. "Yes, Father Sebastian. I'll serve my friends. Thank you for bringing it."

While Ray was pouring the coffee, Dan said, puzzled, "Brother? Have you been demoted?"

Ray smiled again. "No. We're all priests here although the Order does have brothers as well. But here in the monastery, according to conventual order, juniors call senior friars 'Father' and senior friars address juniors as 'Brother'." Dan's expression prompted Ray to continue, "But it's not a very important consideration in terms of the essence of monastic life. It's just that St. Benedict tended to emphasise mutual respect among the brethren and we always use some form of address when speaking to each other."

"Why 'Francis'?" Dan asked.

"Well, I thought about that for a long time. Francis for a Benedictine? It's maybe a wee bit odd. But for a time, Francis of Assisi suffered the world's disapprobation. Francis the Fool, he was called. It seemed appropriate."

Tony grinned. "You're really into this life now, aren't you?"

"I am, Tony," Ray replied earnestly, "and I can't thank you enough for going to bat with the Apostolic Penitentiary for me."

"Not a bother," Tony replied, remembering his two-day visit to Rome earlier in the year. The Apostolic Penitentiary is the visible manifestation of the ever-present forgiveness upon which the Church was built and, under special circumstances, an appeal can be made to him on behalf of excommunicated priests. The normal procedure would be a letter to Rome from the bishop but the wheels of Rome's appeal machinery, at least when conducted on paper, tend only to have two speeds – dead slow and stop. Tony had experience of this and had made a point of spending much of his two days meeting with the Penitentiary, arguing, explaining, pleading, until the return of Ray's priestly status was agreed. The fact that it was Ray's avowed intention to enter monastic life rather than return to the parish work of a secular priest made it easier to convince the Vatican prelate to agree to lift the excommunication. Secretly, however, Tony had some concerns when Ray told him that he felt drawn to a monastic life. Was his calling to the contemplative existence genuine or a way of hiding from the world?

Now he said, "So, Ray, your decision to enter the monastic life, you're still happy with it?"

Ray smiled and nodded. "I know exactly where you're coming from, Tony. You think I'm just hiding out here. Have no worries about that. I have had dozens of soul-searching talks with the Abbot and he assures me that he believes my vocation to be genuine."

"Good. Still seeing Barbara?"

"Yes, that's going well, too. She's got me down to one visit every three months. She says she's surprised at my progress. Puts it down to the contemplative nature of my life."

Dan waved his empty cup. "Any coffee left in the pot?"

Ray laughed and poured Dan another cup. "I see you're starting to get your priorities right. How are you two getting on together at St. Columba's?"

There was a brief silence. Then Tony said, “Pretty good. Dan and I still have some issues to contend with ...”

Even as he was speaking, he was reminded again of the suffering he occasionally experienced in turning his back on his cherished ambitions. When the Spirit is involved in such change, the experience can be positive, even cathartic, but it doesn’t happen overnight and it is not without its psychological difficulties. When he had first sought advancement during his early days in St. Columba’s, he had convinced himself that all he wanted was to be in a position to do good for the Church. But something darker had taken possession of him. And he was learning that, even when the light has shone on the dark places, old yearnings can haunt the psyche when the guard is down, bringing with them a sudden clenching of the stomach, a bitter regret, an almost disabling sense of opportunity wasted. It was not easy but he was trying daily to use this pain as a reminder of how deeply wounded his spirit had been. He smiled at Ray. “It’s a work in progress. But we’re getting there. Right, Dan?”

Dan’s grin had faded and his expression was serious. “Ye ... sss.” He sounded hesitant but he shrugged self-deprecatingly and went on, “I can’t be sure about anything anymore, but yes, Tony. I think we’re getting there.” He turned to Ray. “Tony’s keeping me right and I think I’m learning, slowly.”

“Of course you are. I’ve complete faith in you,” Ray said. He turned his eyes to Tony. “Tony, how did that civil claim from Maria’s parents pan out?”

“Oh, that didn’t materialise.”

“It didn’t? That surprises me. Peter Rafferty was very determined.”

"Yes, but apparently not as determined as his daughter. I learned a little while back that she threatened to leave home if he didn't drop the suit."

Ray nodded slowly. "She's a good girl." He fished around inside his habit and took out an envelope. His face was serious. "As you probably know, Tony, new entrants to the religious life give all their possessions to the Order they're entering. I was quite wealthy, you know, my father's estate, but I kept back fifty thousand euro and set up a trust fund to take care of Maria's university education. I think she's going to study medicine at University College Dublin next year. She needn't know the funds come from me. But I need someone to administer the trust. Maybe the Raffertys could be allowed to think it is a form of compensation from the diocese?"

Tony took the envelope and put it in his pocket. "I'll talk to the bishop. And have no fear. I can guarantee right now that this is one responsibility he'll be happy to shoulder. It'll make him look good."

"Thanks, Tony." Ray turned to Dan. "Keep a discreet eye on her anyway, will you, Dan? I still feel very guilty about her and don't want to be the cause of messing up her life."

"Don't worry about that, Ray. We'll both watch over her. She'll be fine. And don't be worrying about her. Seventeen? She'll get over this. You may have been the first to break her heart, but I seriously doubt you'll be the last."

"Thanks, Dan." He hesitated.

"Something else?" Dan asked.

"Yes, could you leave her space for a few wee shades of grey when you're dealing with her? None of that black and white stuff."

Dan's head came up. He started to rise from his chair. His expression was fierce as he said, "Tony, you're the expert in Canon Law. Is there a canon in there anywhere that prohibits a visitor from hammering the heck out of a friar in his own monastery?"

Tony grinned. "Well, now that you mention it, I don't believe there is. I think they missed out on that one."

"Right, that's good enough for me."

And, fists raised menacingly, he advanced towards Ray who was already retreating, laughing, behind the heavy table.

The End

Thank you for taking the time to read Fallen Men. If you enjoyed it, please consider telling your friends or posting a short review. Word of mouth is an author's best friend and much appreciated.

Brian O'Hare

Because of a debilitating illness, Dr.Brian O'Hare [B.A., ADCE(Hons.), M.A., Ph.D] took early retirement in 1998 from his post as Assistant Director of a large Regional College in Newry in Northern Ireland. It transpired that he had an irreversible liver disease (a childhood affliction) that required a liver transplant. Married with three children and ten grandchildren, he now enjoys full health, plays golf, and writes from time to time.

Books by Brian O'Hare:

Non-fiction

A Spiritual Odyssey

(Columba press, Co. Dublin, Ireland, 2005)

The Miracle Ship (Crimson Cloak Publishing, Missouri, 2015)

Fiction

The Doom Murders (Murder Mystery, Crimson Cloak Publishing, Missouri, 2015)

Coming Soon: *The 11:05 Murders* (Sequel to *The Doom Murders*).

THE DOOM MURDERS:

Prominent figures in Belfast are being murdered. The bodies are left naked and posed in grotesquely distorted shapes. No clues are left at the forensically immaculate crime scenes except odd theatrical props and some random numbers and letters concealed at each scene by the killer. How are the victims linked? What is the connection between these killings, the bible, and a famous mediaeval painting of The Last Judgement?

The Doom Murders **has been the recipient of three literary awards - *The IDB Award* in 2014; *The New Apple Award*, 2014, for Excellence in Independent Publishing; and the *2015 Readers' Favourite International Book Awards* (Bronze Medal Winner).**

The Chief Inspector, Jim Sheehan, is drawn so deftly and with such genuineness, you can feel him breathing. (Eugene Fournier, novelist and screenwriter, film and TV)

The most subtle of clues are intricately interwoven into the storyline, and even the most astute mystery buff is apt to miss them. (Donna Cummins, Author of the Blacklick Valley Mystery Series)

Incredibly addictive page turner. (Meghan, Amazon Top 1000 Reviewer)

O'Hare leans toward the human side of his characters, imbuing them with a real world presence that is in turn witty and passionate. (Roy.T James, for Readers' Favourite)

THE MIRACLE SHIP:

YOU WON'T BELIEVE WHAT YOU'RE READING BUT EVERY WORD IS TRUE!!

Do you believe in miracles? Do you believe in demonic possession? Do you believe in exorcism?

A little girl with irreparable brain damage was pronounced dead by two hospital specialists. Today she is a healthy teenager. A teenage boy whose spine was crushed by a lorry was diagnosed as permanently paralysed. He now plays football with his friends. A curse that brought death over five generations has been lifted. People tormented by demons have been set free.

How were such miracles wrought? What do they have in common? They have John Gillespie in common. Who is he? How has he been gifted with such extraordinary power? This true account of his life, of the miracles and deliverances that follow his prayers, will amaze you. Millions of people love to hear and read about miracles. Sr. Briege McKenna's book *Miracles Do Happen* has sold all over the world in its millions. If you read and liked *Miracles Do Happen*, you'll love *The Miracle Ship.(69 reviews x 5* to date on Amazon.co.uk)*

The Miracle Ship was awarded Top Medallist Honours in the 2015 New Apple Awards for Religious Non-fiction.

Fascinating story of an incredible man (Luana Ehrlich, author of One Night in Tehran)

This is a beautifully crafted book of faith and acceptance of god's will (Ronesa, author of the Mystical Emona series)

Forced me to reassess myself, my beliefs, my spirituality, and just about everything I thought I knew (Joy Nwosu Lo-Bamijoko, author of The Saga of a Nigerian Female Ethnomusicologist)

A SPIRITUAL ODYSSEY:

A Spiritual Odyssey is the compelling story of a six-year journey on two converging paths - a burgeoning spirituality, and a dramatic physical degeneration that took the author to the doors of death. While the book is essentially a witness to the miraculous grace of God, and how it reaches into both soul and body, the author also describes his medical journey from death's door to new life. Add in some little vignettes of vacation time spent in France and elsewhere, laced occasionally with wry humour, and the whole becomes an interesting mix. The author describes his hospital experiences in gory detail while, at the same time, struggling with questions of a theological nature. The questions, however, are not academic. They emerge from the practical, often confusing circumstances in which the author found himself as he coped with dying and tried to understand his growing spirituality.

Significant commentators had this to say about A Spiritual Odyssey:

1. *"Some of the medical descriptions chill the blood but the religious explorations are heart-warming, ranging from reading theologians as different as Sean Fagan and Basil Hume, to a meeting with the sensible and down-to-earth Sister Briege McKenna, and to a pilgrimage through the holy places of France, all of which makes this a fine exposition of the riches of the Catholic tradition.* [David McLaurin, The Tablet]

2. *Well written and should appeal to readers who draw inspiration from accounts of others' experiences. Of interest to public libraries* [Denise J. Stankovics, Connecticut Library Association Review, USA]

3. *Intelligent and sensitive...very moving...gives a graphic account of suffering and anguish...gives us wonderful vignettes of people he met on his journey. His description of Lourdes is truly evocative and marvellous.* [Anthony Redmond, The Irish Catholic]

52391491R00210

Made in the USA
Charleston, SC
17 February 2016